FOCUS

For Jane and Sid
Wonderful friends

Steve

ALSO BY STEPHEN PEARSALL

Yesterday, A Memoir

Counterpoint

FOCUS

A NOVEL

STEPHEN PEARSALL

Order this book online at www.trafford.com
or email orders@trafford.com

Most Trafford titles are also available at major online book retailers.

Printed in the United States of America.

ISBN: 978-1-4907-1250-5 (sc)
ISBN: 978-1-4907-1249-9 (e)

Trafford rev. 01/07/2014

 www.trafford.com

North America & international
toll-free: 1 888 232 4444 (USA & Canada)
fax: 812 355 4082

For my brother

Henry

This story takes place during the years

1960-1961

SAMANTHA

Book III

Cast of Characters

Samantha Norquist, twenty-six year old American photojournalist.

Meredith Nicholas, *Echo Magazine* editor.

Katheryn Brighton, London socialite.

Nicholas Andropolis, London-Greek ship owner.

Saeed, Iranian journalist.

Thomas Kimbamba, American educated, Katanga school teacher and aide to Tshombe.

Alex McLean, Thomas's college chum, deputy chargé d` affaires, US Embassy, London.

Larry Madison, CIA junior officer.

Karel van Riebeek, South African wine merchant.

General Leclercq, Belgian Congo military expatriate.

Colonel Lefebvre, Belgian Congo military expatriate.

Adraan Batuta, van Riebeek's foreman.

Joseph Sanimbi, Katanga Police Superintendent.

Benjamin Kigali, Senior officer, Katanga militia.

Colonel Willame, Remaining senior Belgian army officer, Katanga.

*Moise Tshombe, President, Republic of Katanga.

*Godefroid Munongo, Minister of Interior, Rep. of Katanga.

Henri Bordeaux, Manager, *Union Minière du Haut* copper mine.

Jay Carleton, Asst. Dir., Office of Central African Affairs (AF/C).

Jonathan "Kitch" Kitchell, Director of AF/C, Dept. of State.

Bryce Donaldson, Officer, AF/C, Dept. of State.

Dieter Reinhardt, van Riebeek's nephew in Holland.

Brian Wellesley, United Nations deputy for African affairs, South African attorney.

Arne Norquist, Samantha's uncle, CIA.

*Allen Dulles, CIA, Director.

*Richard Bissell, CIA, Deputy Director of Plans.

Jasper Fox, CIA, assistant to Bissell.

*Bronson Tweedy, CIA, Chief of Africa Division.

*Patrice Lumumba, DRC first Prime-Minister.

*Mobutu Sese Seko, DRC Army Chief of Staff.

Morgan Palmer, Professional Hunter and Safari Guide.

Lynch, Morgan's assistant.

Keane, Morgan's assistant.

*Joseph Kasavubu, President of the DRC.

Branca Abreu Mello, Morgan's attractive friend from Mozambique.

*Rajeshwar Dayal, Indian diplomat, head of UN peacekeeping mission in the DRC.

Bhagat Singh, Mozambique importer.

Colin Waite, Morgan's bush pilot.

Anibal Senna da Silva, Customs Officer, Chinde, Mozambique.

Robin and Ronne Thistle, Owners of Rapid End Resort.

Robert Smith-Stevens, Lt. Col., Rhodesian Army.

Kaila, Thomas's sister.

*Dag Hammarskjöld, Secretary-General, United Nations.

Jillian Pienar, Director, Interpol, South Africa.

Ian McQueen, National Police Commissioner, South African.

Osvaldo Rodrigues da Cunha, Officer, Dept. Colonial Affairs, Portugal.

Alfredo Gavarnie, Portuguese businessman, Angola.

Rory McCray, Mercenary.

* indicates authentic historical people.

SOUTHERN AFRICA
1960

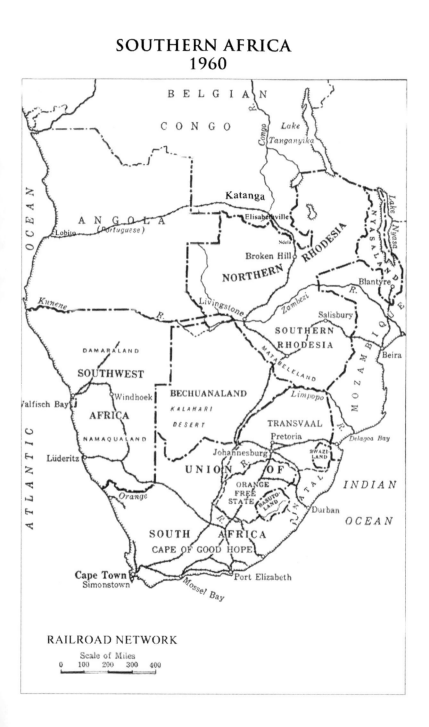

RAILROAD NETWORK

Scale of Miles
0   100   200   300   400

PROLOGUE

June 1960

Kasai Province, Belgian Congo

The village was nothing more than a cluster of wattle houses along the railroad track. A morning breeze rustled the palm fronds in the thatched roofs and swirled the dirt off the road into every cranny of the huts. A noise startled Okebo and he arose quickly from where he had been sleeping on his mat and padded across the dirt floor to the open door to investigate. His wife and two children slept on. He looked at the sky to assess the day before him. It would be just another day, no different than the ones before. He watched the equatorial sun pop over the eastern horizon exposing the savanna, the solitary dirt road, and the rows of huts in the village. He heard again the noise that had snatched him from his dreams and realized it came from steel tools scraping together on the shoulders of his neighbors as they trudged toward the fields. He had overslept. He slipped back into his hut to gather his implements, a wax paper package containing some spiced rice his wife had prepared the night before, and his prized possession, a broad brimmed cotton hat. He smelled the smoke from the morning fires and he watched the men of the village heading for their meager farmland that stretched to the west of the railroad track.

Okebo scampered across the tracks and down the embankment to the beginning of the farming land. Each family worked a portion of the field, prisoners to a small plot of tilled ground. The crops varied, but always a section of each family's land was devoted to cotton, a mandate proscribed by the Belgian authorities. The cotton crop was tithed to the exploiters and shipped, without compensation, to mills in Belgium. Okebo felt good about the cotton bounty because he had already supplied this year's quota. Now he could concentrate on his vegetables, which together with chicken and goat meat, would provide a meager income. Some of his produce would be sold to passengers, if the train paused briefly, otherwise it would be shipped to street vendors in Luluabourg, a large city to the north.

He walked rapidly through the field, his bare feet gripping the parched ground. The soil looked tired and impoverished from centuries of farming. The men marched through the field sometimes acknowledging each other with a wave or a smile. They were friends; all members of the Mongo tribe, a people not admired by the Belgians and looked down upon by neighboring tribes, especially those with conquest in mind.

Okebo worried about the Balubas, a more populous, war-like tribe that occupied the land to the north. He knew they would be a problem when the Belgians left. He had heard talk in the village that the *occupiers* would begin to leave today; that this was the first day of Congo's freedom. He arrived at his patch of land and surveyed the health of his crop. It needed water; there had been no rain for a month. No, he thought as he leaned on his hoe, his life would not change; it was naked of embellishment. The future was immediate.

The tropical mid-summer heat enveloped the farmers as they began to cultivate their gardens. Okebo grunted in disgust when he realized he had forgotten his water bottle. He could not work through the day without water. Now he would have to trudge back. He hoped his wife had noticed the bottle and was, even now, carrying it into the field. As he walked, he saw dust rising from the single-lane road as three trucks raced toward his village. The sun was in his eyes, sweat had already drenched his cotton shirt and the simple but demanding task before him smothered any thought of danger. Puzzled, he watch as the trucks halted in front of the row of huts, spewing men and boys armed with AK-47s and with grenades strapped to their backs. Some, their faces painted, carried poison-tipped spears, in deference to their ancestors. Others swung broad machetes, honed to a razor's edge. Someone blew a horn and the rag-tag army began to scream and systematically and dissolutely kill the unarmed villagers.

Okebo stopped and stood still listening and then tilted his hat to shield his eyes from the sun still low in the sky. He saw the smoke and fire and watched in horror as mud huts exploded from grenades. He could see women and children running wild-eyed seeking safety. They were viciously cut down with machetes. Some had their throats sliced open with long knives. His eyes blinked, attempting to erase the scene before him, but he could move no further. Paralysis enveloped him. His stomach erupted. Everything that was important in his world was destroyed. His wife, his children, his friends— still he did not move. The other village farmers were running in the direction of their village. Some carried a tool but most were empty handed. Okebo wiped his mouth and then raced back to the furrow he had been tilling to find his knife.

Men with AK47s headed for the fields to intercept the farmers who now had stopped and stood in stunned horror, unable to comprehend the slaughter occurring before their eyes. The men with the AKs shot the farmers indiscriminately, and followed by desecrating their bodies: hacking off arms, splitting open chests and severing heads with mouths still open in silent screams.

It took the Balubas less than one hour to destroy the village. They slaughtered everyone—men, women and children. They gathered the chickens and goats, took some of the farming tools, looted the food pantries and left as quickly as they had arrived.

In the mayhem, Okebo escaped into the far fields where he watched his village burn. His children were dead, his wife butchered. He knew he had no chance to save them. It was the Bulubas and they were too well armed. He felt powerless, impotent—consumed with shock and grief. His knees collapsed beneath him and he stumbled to the ground and buried his face in the earth that now meant nothing to him and wept. After a while, when all was quiet, he lay still and began to dream of reprisal.

On this day the Congo descended into chaos and turned blood red.

JANUARY 1960

New York City

Meredith Nicholas studied the cover of *Echo Magazine's* December issue. A black and white photograph of a cigar smoking Ché Guevara wearing a beret stared out at the world. His face was serious and his dark brooding eyes looked directly into the camera. On the inside of the cover was the photographer's credit: Samantha Norquist.

For the first time in its thirteen years of publishing, *Echo* had sold out. The whole world was watching Fidel Castro march on Havana as Fulgencio Batista prepared to flee to the Dominican Republic. The article, written by an Italian journalist, was smooth and interesting, but let's face it, it was the stunning in-your-face photos of Castro, Ché and their camp that were causing people to buy.

Meredith was the editor of *Echo*; in fact, she owned controlling interest in the magazine. Her studious, erudite father had launched *Echo* in 1947, more as an expensive hobby than as a challenge to established periodicals. His entire adult life had been devoted to writing, both newspapers and magazines, in addition to teaching journalism at Columbia University. *Echo* was his attempt to focus his readers on situations he felt they should know about, and perhaps even become active in changing. He painted with a broad palette, sometimes running a piece in French or Spanish, but always challenging his readers, which included local politicians and foreign government officials. The "Letters to the Editor" section was what most readers perused first, and with great relish. Until the time of his death in 1955, the magazine had avoided lawsuits, while it developed a small but addicted audience throughout the world. Financially the magazine barely managed to stay solvent. There were five permanent employees, paid irregularly, with the articles and photographs coming from independent journalists and photographers. The free-lance journalists, who covered stories too sensitive or too removed from mainstream attention to be picked up by the major publications, always knew they had an outlet in *Echo*.

Meredith took over the management of the magazine when her fifty-eight year old father died suddenly of a brain aneurism and she settled in quickly and comfortably, changing nothing. When she became editor, she had just turned thirty and had worked on every aspect of the magazine for five years with her proud father looking over her shoulder, hopeful that she would be as committed to *Echo* as he was. Before that there had been brief stints as a reporter for rural newspapers. Now she had no other life but *Echo* and she harbored a nagging and recurring thought that she ought to back off a little and balance her life. At this moment however, her thoughts were on Samantha Norquist and the astonishing photographs she had taken.

She looked up from the magazine and gazed at the Manhattan skyline. "Lisa," she called to her assistant, "See if you can reach Sam Norquist for me."

The following afternoon, Samantha was sitting across from Meredith in a white blouse, jeans and high healed boots. Her well-worn leather jacket had been tossed on the spare chair. She seemed relaxed as her cool blue eyes briefly appraised the office, then settled on Meredith. Lisa brought coffee and closed the door.

"Great to see you again, Samantha. Thanks for coming. Your photographs from Cuba are incredible. Absolutely dynamite. We sold every issue." Meredith picked up a copy and slapped the cover with the back of her hand and turned it to face Samantha. "You're famous."

Samantha laughed as she swept her heavy blonde hair back from her forehead. "Yeah, I'm now acknowledged in some publishing circles but hardly famous. I've received some interesting overtures from a couple of well-known American magazines."

Meredith studied Samantha. The two had worked together several times over the past three years. Their relationship was good, she thought. They trusted each other. They had the same goal—excellence in their work—and Meredith liked that. Samantha's steely strength amazed Meredith; she seemed to operate with a maturity beyond her years. Opening the world's eyes to injustice with photographs energized Samantha; she possessed an uncanny instinct for finding unfairness and exposing it. Meredith wanted to know more about her, and asked, "How did you become so adept with the camera."

"My father gave me a box camera when I was a child—I must have been around ten. We spent summers at our lake house in Southern Wisconsin where my father and I would spend hours together shooting pictures of everything in the neighborhood: the dairy farm and its animals, birds (there were lots), plants, boats in the marina and, most important, people. He was supportive and by the time I reached high school we had built a small developing room in the garage."

"What propelled you to become a photojournalist?" Meredith poured fresh coffee from a thermos Lisa had left on the desk.

"I studied photography in college under a professor who inspired me. He said I had the talent to peruse a career and introduced me to some magazine contacts. After graduation, I worked for one, but soon left to freelance."

"Would you consider working again exclusively for one magazine?" Meredith asked tentatively.

Meredith watched Samantha's gaze shift to the view of the city. Her response was not a surprise. "I prefer not to be at an editor's beck and call or assigned to stories that are not challenging," Samantha said in a strong voice, looking back at Meredith. "As a freelance photographer I can direct my focus to subjects that not only interest me but cry out for attention."

"Would you consider working for *Echo* if you were allowed greater latitude?"

"Well, that's an interesting thought. *Echo* chases the type of stories I'd like to photograph, but there are some important questions. How do we decide on my assignments? Who would editorialize? And, can you afford me?" The last question Sam posed brought a smile to both of their faces.

Meredith held up the copy of *Echo* with Ché on the cover. "This photo and the ones inside sold out this issue and my subscriptions are up 20%. I can afford you if you're not too greedy in the beginning. There are any number of freelance journalists who would jump at the chance to write for this magazine, and to investigate earth-shaking subjects. As for the selection of assignments, we can do this together, as a team. I would expect you to cover some prosaic areas to help keep us afloat but I would not impede your desire to confront and reveal. Let's leave Southeast Asia alone for awhile. There is a lot going on in Europe, not to mention Africa, which is about to explode. I know you speak Spanish and I am as intrigued as you are with what is happening south of our border."

"It's a flattering offer. Let me think on it. What do you have in mind as a beginning assignment?"

"Iran." Meredith let the name linger a moment before continuing. "It sounds romantic or maybe exotic but the Shah's regime is repressive. The people are unhappy and the prisons are full."

"Iran would be interesting," Samantha said as she stood and walked to the window. "I wonder if I would be allowed the freedom to wander the country photographing people and how they live their lives."

Meredith joined Sam at the window and gazed at the city below. "I can offer you the independence and challenges you crave. Iran would just be the beginning."

"I'm intrigued. Can I have some time to think on this? I'm looking for an apartment, but once I'm settled I will organize my schedule and my thoughts on your proposal."

Meredith turned toward Sam. "If you work for me you wouldn't need the apartment. You would live in London. I have a flat that you can use for as long as you wish. London is sophisticated, international, fun and it's where the action is. I'd like you to start working for *Echo* soon, spend a few months in this office and then move to London in April. You could do the Iran assignment almost immediately, before the country bakes in the summer heat."

Sam headed for the door and paused as she opened it. "I'll call you within a week." She didn't wait for a reply.

The restaurant was narrow. All old Italian restaurants in New York City seemed the same, Samantha thought: noisy, cramped and with delicious food. She sat along the wall near the front and watched the maître d' greet each customer as if they were special. Her thoughts drifted back to a damp autumn day four months earlier.

On that September day, the drizzle had failed to discourage visitors to the small well-known art gallery on East 52d Street. It was the opening day of an exhibit of 1959's acclaimed photographs, with one room devoted to Andy Warhol. The gallery opened at 11 a.m. for patrons with invitations. A caterer provided white wine and hors d'oeures. By 11:30 the gallery was packed.

Samantha's acclaimed photograph of Ché Guevara, dramatically enlarged, hung in the gallery entrance where Che's brooding eyes greeted visitors. Samantha entered and snapped her umbrella closed while looking up to study her photograph. She remembered clearly that humid day in the Cuban jungle and Guevara's reluctance to be photographed. Visitors moved quickly past the Guevara photo, most were heading for the Warhol room. She noticed two men who were not rushing with the crowd and stood close to her photograph peering up at Ché. One was gesticulating vigorously. Their conversation sounded intense.

"It's good, but it's not Guevara," said the red-headed man.

"Of course it is. The photographer has caught his intensity. This is the picture that appeared on the cover of some magazine." He had stepped back as he said this to allow Samantha to move closer to the photograph.

"What I've read of Ché, he wouldn't have allowed this picture to be taken, especially by some American woman in the Cuban bush," the red head retorted.

The taller man then turned to Samantha who obviously had been listening to their debate. "Pardon me. Please settle our argument. What do you think? Is that Ché or is it not?"

Samantha remembered Brian's face vividly when she had turned toward him and looked into his soft brown eyes. They were so incongruous with the physical energy of his body, and she experienced a peculiar wish to touch him, or be touched by him. "It's Ché. I'm certain," she said with a faint smile, still looking into Brian's eyes.

"How can you be so certain?" said the red headed fellow.

"I took the picture. My name is Samantha Norquist."

"Hello, Samantha Norquist. You are a wonderful surprise. My name is Brian Wellesley." His smile was contagious and she found herself grinning back at him. Brian's handshake was firm and she felt his strength through his touch.

Returning from her musings, she realized that Brian was late, unusual for him, as he would habitually arrive early and have her glass of wine already on the table. He had telephoned her shortly after their brief encounter at the gallery. Sam smiled as she remembered his long-winded explanation of how they had met. She recognized his voice immediately; the accent was not quite British. She accepted a dinner invitation without hesitation; they had dined in this very restaurant. Since then, they had been seeing each other regularly.

Samantha had not been looking for romance – not even companionship. Her work absorbed her days. She was away a great deal, traveling on assignment, which prevented attachments. Brian became a gust of fresh air in her life. He seemed unaware that he was very good looking. She found his self-effacing attention to her attractive, his acquaintances from the United Nations, where he worked, stimulating and his carefree selection of weekend activities, refreshing. He would surprise her with prized theater tickets. When the weather was fine, they would walk the length of Central Park or find a boat trip up the Hudson. By December, they were taking weekend trips and had become intimate. He had become the only man in her life.

She watched him hold the front door open for a group heading into the restaurant; the two women turned to bask in his smile. His gray suit looked good on his 6'3" frame. When he saw her he grinned, ignoring greetings from diners and waiters. He bent, kissed her on the lips and then slid into the chair facing her. He smelled of soap and clean, fresh skin. His sandy colored hair, in deference to the American style, was trimmed around the ears but still long and thick on top. "I apologize," he said, taking a deep breath. "Today has been extraordinary. I have news."

Samantha listened quietly as Brian related the events of his afternoon culminating in a conference with Secretary General Dag Hammarskjöld. "He asked me to become his deputy for African affairs and to manage the section from our Swiss office. He asked if I could wind up my affairs in New York and move to Geneva by the end of the month." He sniffed and swallowed some of his red wine, nodded to the waiter, and looked back at Samantha. Silence ensued.

"Am I an affair to be wound up?" Sam said abruptly, in a soft voice. She regretted what she had said almost immediately. Her question had not been in disappointment or envy but more of a reflection. She had always been candid. Samantha was unsure of her feelings for Brian. She had been struggling with her growing attraction to him; it was an unfamiliar emotion. It was new because it was enduring. He had never attempted to encroach on her life; he understood clearly that it was her photography that possessed her heart and soul. "I didn't mean to sound flippant. I'm happy for you. This is a promotion you deserve and Africa is where the action is."

"Come with me. Live in Europe. You can run your freelance business from any large city."

"That's a nice thought. Switzerland is so far away. I would miss you," Sam said, flashing her seductive smile and added, "and the thought of covering Africa is compelling." She decided not to detract from Brian's excitement and reveal her *Echo* offer. "When is all of this happening?"

"Next month. The first part of February, if possible. The secretary-general wants me to accompany him to Africa in March. I will need to prepare myself with a visit there first."

"Where in Africa will you visit?"

"Cape Town for sure. Maybe Leopoldville as well. The Congo is preparing for independence."

Samantha's mind became muddled. Brian had become a significant ingredient in her life and only now did she acknowledge it. She did not want to be an ocean away from him. And the very mention of Africa made her heart pump faster. She would call Meredith tomorrow and accept her offer.

"I have more exciting news," Brain said, interrupting her thoughts. We have been invited by the secretary-general to a reception and dinner. He wants to meet you. I accepted."

The reception line stretched from the ballroom entrance around the circular lobby and into a long hallway. It seemed as if everyone in New York wanted to shake Dag Hammarskjöld's hand. Brian knew a few people in the line, chatted with them to pass the time and took pleasure in introducing Samantha. He thought she looked smashing in a long silver dress accented by a single-stringed necklace with five immaculate blue sapphire gems. They were the color of the sky and matched the clear blue of her eyes.

Dag saw them approach. "Hello Brian. I have been watching for you. I'm so glad Samantha is with you." His eyes sparkled as he stepped out of place to greet Brian.

"You're Excellency," Brian said, somewhat stiffly. "May I introduce Samantha Norquist? You may be familiar with her photographs in *Echo Magazine*."

Dag turned to Samantha, "Norquist . . . are you Swedish, Miss Norquist?" His gaze on her, with those remarkable eyes, was so intense, she felt as if they were the only people in the room. She started to answer when he stopped her with his index finger in the air. "No, no, no, I'm wrong." He smiled. "You're a *Norsk pike*. In fact, you are the better of two worlds. My final guess is that you are an American-Norse." Others in line were leaning forward attempting to determine why the secretary-general was spending so much time with this young couple. "Now, if you will say something, I will establish your home ground."

By this time, Sam was laughing out loud. "Brian has undoubtedly prompted this exchange. Your Excellency, you already know the answer."

"You're a Midwesterner." Dag snapped his fingers, "raised somewhere between the Dakotas and Wisconsin. I am very pleased to make your acquaintance Samantha. I look forward to talking with you at greater length. Brian will arrange it." The reception line began to move again.

APRIL 1960

London

Samantha's luggage passed through Heathrow Airport's inspection without scrutiny and she moved quickly across the crowded terminal toward the exit leading to the taxi rank. The taxi queue moved with discipline and soon she was ensconced in the spacious back seat of a London taxicab. A spring drizzle freshened the air.

"Where to, young lady?" the taxi driver said with a Cockney accent.

"Notting Hill, please. 21 Dunworth Lane—it's a Mews, I believe."

"That it is, Mum. Lucky you. They are very nice mews, too, I might add. It's hard to believe they were stables in the old days."

Forty minutes later she was standing in Dunworth Mews, a narrow cobblestone alley with mews houses on both sides; each slightly different in construction and size. They may have been stables in a prior century but now were elegant pied-à-terries for the London elite. A large box rested by the door. She opened it tentatively on the spot and gazed at a lavish bouquet. The note said, simply: I can sense your closeness. Can't wait to see you. Love, Brian.

Samantha hurried up the stairs to survey what would be her home for the next year. What she found caused her to squeal with delight. She stood motionless surveying her new home. The room was long, with windows at one end only. The furniture was Barcelona-Scandinavian modern—leather and steel. There were a few abstract paintings, all subdued colors and no form. Black and white photographs and etchings filled the living room walls. Sam studied the photos closely and decided that she would place a few of her own alongside this select collection. The hardwood floor radiated permanence and strength to the soles of her feet, and she yearned for a little yoga before a nap. It was perfect in every way. Meredith will have to dynamite me out of this beautiful apartment, she thought. A phone rang, startling her as it shook the silence. She thought about ignoring it, then, hoping it might be Brian, impulsively picked up the receiver.

"How do you like it?" Meredith purred from across the Atlantic.

"Your timing is impeccable. I just arrived, and I've already decided to stay here forever. It's wonderful in every way."

"I want you to be a happy girl," Meredith said, "and comfortable so that you can get right to work. And along that thought, I've heard from Saeed, my stringer in Tehran. The Shah has never heard of *Echo* nor does he wish to be interviewed. He has, however, offered an invitation—to you, Samantha—to visit Iran and photograph the work he has accomplished for his people. I guess that would mean schools and public works."

"Meredith, I don't photograph buildings."

"Well, you could quietly deviate from their agenda. Plus, Saeed will be with you to assure an interesting itinerary."

"How soon do you want this story?"

"Settle in as quickly as you can and book a ticket to Tehran. I'll cable Saeed's contact information to you. We're holding the July issue for you."

Samantha's mind began to calculate the time line. "I'll need the rest of April for preparation. Tell Mr. Saeed I will join him the first week in May."

"Good. That's settled. Also," Meredith added, "I have an old girl friend who will pop in to meet you tomorrow. She has stocked your fridge and turned on the water heater. Katheryn just turned thirty and lives in Mayfair. She's impoverished aristocracy, knows London in and out, loves to party and sometimes behaves badly—you'll love her. Talk with you soon."

Katheryn telephoned the following morning to say she couldn't make it. "I'm so sorry but I'm really hung out to dry today. I was hoping you would like to meet me for supper though and we could chat about this crazy London town then."

Samantha replied quickly. "Supper would be wonderful. When and where?"

"Abigail's. The cabbie will know it. A friend will join us, Nicholas Andropolis—you will enjoy him. Say, 7:30?"

"Perfect. I'll be there."

Samantha arrived on time. She was hungry, and with her appetite still in another time zone, she was thinking about lunch. Abigail's packed bar and clatter announced its status as an "in" watering hole. She stood in the entrance, waiting for Katheryn to show herself. Within minutes, a well-dressed man emerged from the crowd, his eyes fastened on Samantha.

"I know who you are, Samantha Norquist, by your striking beauty." His upper-class British accent was music to Samantha's ears. "Katheryn told me all about you and asked me to entertain you until she could find a cab." He introduced himself—"I'm Nicholas Andropolis, an old friend of Katheryn's. Come, I have a table in the back dining room where there is less noise. Let's wait for Katheryn there. May I offer an aperitif; what would be your pleasure?"

Samantha had developed a posture of reserve when she was with a man for the first time. She had grown up with men, three aggressive brothers, and she had learned to stifle her alpha instincts, remain reserved, and not give up too much of herself. "Thank you for rescuing me, Nicholas. A dry white, please. You select."

He was attractive, with a thick head of dark wavy hair with gray streaks beginning to impinge on the temples. A large nose dominated what otherwise was a well-proportioned face. Samantha's wine arrived.

"May I call you Sam? Samantha is such a mouth full."

"Yes, of course. I prefer Sam." Samantha was surprised to find herself opening the conversation. "Your name sounds Greek. Were you born there?"

"Yes, I'm Greek and, yes again, I spent my youth on an island in the Adriatic. My father owned a few ships, both small tankers and freighters; however, we moved to London when I was twelve because he could run the business more efficiently from here. I'm now what's called a London Greek." He smirked.

"What other kind of Greeks are there?" Sam met his gaze. She observed that he smiled easily but his eyes remained evasive.

"Well, I'm talking about ship owners and we Greeks are divided into the London Greeks and the Piraeus Greeks. Of course, Onassis doesn't fit into either group. He runs his shipping empire from Monte Carlo."

"So, you work with your father managing the shipping business?"

"I did for about ten years. I went to the states for two years to Harvard for an MBA and to learn how you Americans do business. After graduation, my father put me to work onboard tankers that generally ran from Rotterdam to the Persian Gulf. For a year I worked in our small Piraeus office, and when my father thought I was ready to manage, he brought me to London to work closely with him. Then, quite suddenly, he died." Nicholas swirled his drink, his eyes appearing sad and pensive.

They both sat quietly, lost in their own thoughts. Sam broke the silence. "Ships have always fascinated me – carrying exotic items and plying foreign ports. What cargo do your freighters carry and where do they go?"

After a reflective moment, Nicholas shifted defensively in his chair and did not answer her question. "I thought you were a photographer. You ask questions like a journalist."

At that moment Katheryn appeared at the table, dressed more formally than Samantha, and asked, "Am I interrupting?"

"She was just finishing her interrogation," Nicholas laughed, as he stood and adjusted the chairs so that Katheryn could sit next to Samantha.

Samantha stood as well. When Nicholas stood next to Katheryn, Samantha realized Nicholas was short in stature— less than six feet.

"How has London treated you so far?" Katheryn's dark, friendly eyes examined Samantha. "Meredith told me that you were a beauty and warned me that you were cautious, so I won't ask too many questions tonight."

Katheryn appeared more Irish than British. Her curly brown hair wasn't quite shoulder length. She had enormous brown eyes and the inevitable peaches and cream skin. Her age was difficult to decipher; she looked older than thirty, and in twenty years, she would probably appear younger than fifty. Samantha guessed from the ensuing conversation that there had been more than a few men in her life.

Perhaps Nicholas was one of them, she thought.

The evening sailed past swiftly. Samantha found it refreshing to meet two people who were self-confident, interesting, and very funny. They allowed her into their world without asking for anything in return. Katheryn was a Londoner who came from a prosperous banking family. Well-educated, she now worked for a wine distributor. Her position allowed for travel throughout Europe to visit the wineries represented by her employer.

"There is another advantage," Nicholas added. "Katheryn is on the invitation list to every worthwhile social event in Southern England." Nicholas pondered the wine list, then consulted Katheryn on his choice, and finally ordered a Monticello de Brunello from Tuscany.

Samantha admired Katheryn's manipulation of their conversation. She moved it back into Nicholas's court. "Let's persuade Nicholas to describe the estate he purchased near Gilford."

Nicholas described what he called "his farm," in Surrey. It sounded like a movie set, with a subterranean wine cellar, stable, a barn housing two milk cows, land for hunting rabbits for dinner and a house that slept sixteen. In fact, he was planning a party in the autumn. He leaned forward and said earnestly to Samantha, "I want you to join us. Will you be in England this September?"

"I've no idea where I'll be this fall. Everything in my life seems immediate. For example," Samantha gushed, "Next month I'm going to Iran on assignment. An Iranian journalist will accompany me; we plan to travel throughout the country for several weeks. But, yes, I would readily accept an invitation for a weekend in the Surrey countryside. May I bring a friend?"

Nicholas hesitated momentarily. "Of course. Will one of your brothers be in England in September?"

"I have a good friend, Brian Wellesley, a South African, who is attached to the United Nations in Geneva. I know he would come in a flash. He was educated at Oxford, so this is home ground for him."

Katheryn's eyebrows had arched. "I have a better idea. Ask him to join us for the Henley Regatta in July. My employer will have a spacious tent to display his wines. Nicholas will be there—won't you dear?"

"I wouldn't miss it and I'd like to meet Mr. Wellesley."

Attention swung back to Samantha. "Meredith told me you grew up near a lake in Wisconsin and come from a family full of amazing men. Will I ever meet any of them?" Katheryn asked.

Sam speared a tomato and didn't rush into the subject of her family. "Actually,"—she took a sip of wine—"I will see all of my family in June. My brother Quinn's wedding is to be in Oslo. A Norwegian girl he met while skiing in Austria."

"Tell me about your family, especially your brothers." Katheryn gave Samantha a minx's smile over the rim of her glass.

Sam continually attempted to sort out her complicated and ever changing feelings about her family. She took a sip of wine before tentatively launching into a murky subject. "My family is paradoxical. We are a tightly-knit family, supportive of each other, enjoy each others company, while, at the same time, find ourselves exceedingly independent. It would be best if you meet them sometime. For starters, I'll bring photos back from the wedding."

The three lingered over coffee; the evening disappearing in conversation. "I can't remember an evening I have enjoyed more," Samantha said as she rose from the table. "Now I need some sleep."

Both Katheryn and Nicholas kissed Samantha's cheeks before putting her in a cab. Then arm in arm, they headed into the night.

Samantha had remained in New York for several months after Brian moved to Switzerland. Phone calls from Geneva were frequent and flowers arrived with perfunctory notes. *His mind is on Africa* she admitted to herself. In March, she told Brian that she had taken his advice and planned to move to London. He was ecstatic and apologized that he could not be there to greet her as he would be in Africa. They had settled on late April. She would be immersed in her preparation for the Iranian assignment. He would take a week and come to London.

The library was noisy. Students clomped up the isle and with little regard for those reading, slapping their books on the table. The librarian made no pretense at maintaining silence, her shrill voice greeting acquaintances as they arrive. Samantha had selected a remote corner table, one with a lamp, as the gloom of the day had encroached on the crowded room. Before her was a pile of British and American magazines, each containing articles on the Shah of Iran. The world was presented with a picture of orderly opulence. The banquets, with everyone in formal dress, were in the palace. Many of the photographs were of the Shah, along with western diplomats, reviewing military activities. Rarely did the articles touch on the life of the everyman. The message implied that all was well.

Someone sat down next to her, rather close, she thought, but she didn't look up from her reading. Suddenly a hand covered her outstretched hand. Samantha whirled and jerked her hand back. Brian leaned closer, took her head between his hands and kissed her lips. She felt her body melt; ice cream left too long on the counter. "You rat. You didn't call," she murmured, close to tears, and rapped her arms around this neck.

"I've called many times—you are never home. I thought, to hell with it, I'll fly over to London and surprise her. Let's go back to your apartment," his voice was a little husky.

For a week, Brian illuminated her life. They lunched out and dined in. One evening Katheryn and Nicholas joined them at a boutique restaurant in Chelsea for a late supper. Katheryn gushed and talked nonstop; Nicholas was surprisingly taciturn, his thoughts were elsewhere. Brian picked up the gauntlet and regaled them with stories of his visit to Africa.

That weekend, they rented a Morris and drove to Oxford to visit Brian's college. The weather held warm and dry. Samantha would never forget the day. With Brian driving, the air from the open windows gusted havoc with her hair and as she tried to keep it out of her eyes, Brian reached over and gathered it in his hand. He had left his hand on her neck. They hadn't spoken, each lost in their thoughts, enjoying their closeness. It was on this day that Samantha admitted to herself that she had fallen for this tall South African with the wonderful accent and lovely demeanor.

They arrived in Oxford midmorning and immediately headed out to walk Brian's turf. After lunch, they found an inn facing Christ Church Meadow that offered walking distance to the colleges and the River Thames. Time stood still. Samantha did not snap one photograph. "How about some punting?" Brian urged as he grabbed Samantha and headed across the meadow. They easily found a punt, a flat bottomed boat used on small rivers, and Samantha settled in a canvas chair in the bow while Brian poled. Sheer bliss.

A bleak drizzle arrived Sunday afternoon in time for their return trip to London. The gloom of the day inhibited their thoughts and propinquity. Brian returned to Geneva on Wednesday; the month of May and Iran loomed.

MAY 1960

Iran

The BOAC flight from London touched down on the Mehrabad airport runway at precisely 2:45 on an unseasonably hot May afternoon. Iran's capital, Tehran, lay 50 km to the east, easily distinguishable by the cloud of polluted haze hovering in the distance. The prop-engine disgorged its passengers into the °30 C heat where two open-air buses waited to ferry them to the terminal building.

Saeed stood slightly back of the crowd and held a sign announcing his name, not Sam's. He was the perfect picture of a stringer: middle-aged, slender, a refined man with curious, blinking eyes looking through small, round spectacles. There were shots of gray piercing his dense, dark hair, and he wore a conservative suit, which made him look like a professor.

Within minutes they were on the highway to Tehran in Saeed's slightly dented two-door Aria. Saeed explained his sedan was really a small Rambler, assembled in Iran. "Let's go directly to your hotel," he said, "and then we can drive around for a bit before dinner." His accent was British and his diction refined.

The open deck of the restaurant where Sam and Saeed sat facing each other offered a slight breeze as the heat of the day departed. Inside, a huge open heath glowed with spits of lamp and beef. A din of voices speaking Farsi came from the diners, most of whom sat away from the deck to escape the sounds and smells from the street below. Over a glass of wine, Sam and Saeed explored each other's background and quickly reached a comfort zone where they could exchange ideas on the job before them. Saeed extracted an envelope from his jacket. "Here's the Shah's invitation to you—with an official stamp and seal—to travel throughout the country as his guest. He apologized for not being able to meet with you. The good news is that it offers us safe passage. The bad news is the list of places he wants you to photograph. Mostly buildings of his creation."

"We'll shoot a few of his monuments," Samantha said grinning, "to protect you, because you live here." She moved the table candle in order to see Saeed's face clearly. "I have read about the Iran that the world already knows. I want to meet the real Iran, the common man, the Iran that most of the world does not acknowledge. Would you be comfortable with that?"

"Yes." Saeed paused, looked off into the darkness of the night and he smiled. I've wanted to write this story for a long time, to reveal, through the peasants, a picture of the reality lurking just below the horizon. We must do this subtly so as not to irritate the government. We will find our story in the country."

For two weeks Samantha and Saeed drove almost the length of the country, stopping in Qom, Esfahan and Persepolis, as well as every little, dusty village in-between. By the second week, Samantha had learned basic Farsi, taken six hundred photographs and gained a respect for Saeed, not only as a journalist, but as a deep-thinking, reflective person. He knew Persia's 5000 year history, and related its glories, along with the many conquests it had endured. His insatiable curiosity exposed opportunities for Sam's camera that she would have missed if on her own. She did not see the Iran that the Shah wanted her to photograph. Her lens penetrated the superficial veil and found anger, anguish and immense fear. The peasants lived the same desolate existence Samantha had seen and photographed in other impoverished areas of the world. The young educated men and women were emasculated by the harsh restrictions of the government. The clerics were equally unhappy, brooding and plotting for a change. I want my photographs to show this dark side, to expose the guts of Iran, she thought.

Late one afternoon, in a small, unmemorable town in central Iran, when the sun was mellowing in the west and offered the perfect light for photography, Samantha left Saeed in his car and walked toward a mosque. She had heard the exotic call to prayer, a sound both peaceful yet demanding. In front of the mosque, a group of women talked among themselves. All wore burqas, the full body cloak worn by Muslim women. Children were running about on the lawn nearby. Perhaps their fathers were praying inside. Sam approached them confidently with her camera hanging from her shoulder and fully visible. The women stopped talking to watch her approach.

"Hello," Samantha said in Farsi, "I'm a magazine photographer. May I take your picture?" She had pronounced this request in Farsi so many times over the past few days that it had become, according to Saeed, understandable.

The women stepped back, pulling their head covers down to their eye brows, all shaking their heads—except for one. Samantha noticed her eyes immediately; they were an exquisite green, flecked with gold. The woman, who appeared younger than the others, stepped forward slightly. Her eyes showed no fear and locked on Samantha's. Her eyes were smiling.

In hesitant English, she asked, "Are you an American?"

"Yes, I am. You speak English, how wonderful. I work for a magazine named *Echo,*" Sam replied, hoping the magazine name would help.

"You may take my picture but you must hurry. Our husbands would be angry." She turned to the other women and apparently explained to what she had agreed, amidst much mumbling and head shaking.

Samantha moved quickly, focusing on the young woman's expressive eyes. Wow, she thought, I have my cover photo!

At that moment a burly Mullah swept around the corner of the mosque, shouting at the woman as he headed for Samantha. His tirade turned toward her, his outstretched arms reaching for her camera. The women, meanwhile, had quickly moved away.

The Mullah's contorted face leaned close to Samantha. He was actually slightly shorter than she and she found herself looked down into his dark eyes. He had his hand on her camera while he pushed her shoulder with his other hand. His breath was foul.

Samantha glanced over her shoulder, looking for Saeed. Two men in dark suits were running toward her. Now what, she thought. Oddly, the men ignored her and wrestled the Mullah toward the mosque's front door. Sam raised her camera to record this just as Saeed came to her side, whispering, "We should leave now!"

Samantha zoomed in on the Mullah's black eyes, black robe, black beard, framed by the white of the mosque. He was outraged, glaring at her camera. She took the picture and knew it would be as good as her Ché cover. Saeed grasped her arm and pulled her toward the car, as the two government men in suits watched.

As they sped out of the village, Samantha asked, "Who were those men?"

"Probably SAVAK," Saeed replied, keeping his eyes on the road. They have been watching us from the moment you arrived. Not unusual. I just didn't want to worry you."

Saeed and Samantha parted in Shiraz. He headed back to Tehran. She flew to Dubai, then on to London. Saeed had given Samantha his journal with the comment, "Meredith will know how to tune this up. I'll finalize my article and mail it in a few days—but one never knows about the SAVAK and their curiosity in a journalist's package headed for New York."

Just before Samantha boarded her flight to Dubai, Saeed had held her hand in both of his and said, "I have watched you work, how you choose your subject, your use of angle and light. You are a young woman with exceptional talent and this will soon be recognized." He looked into her eyes for a long moment and then said something she would never forget, "Your eye, your mind's eye, is old and wise."

Saint-Cloud, France

Known for elegant homes, tennis tournaments and bucolic normality, in 1960 the Paris suburb of Saint-Cloud concealed the nerve center of a police operation with connections throughout the world. On a quiet side street, a rectangular red brick building, assumed by the locals to house unimportant government business, actually contained the headquarters of the International Criminal Police Organization (ICPO), more commonly known by its telegraphic address, Interpol. Supported by most nations of the world, its job was to provide liaison, communication and cooperation between police forces focusing on international crime. Gun smuggling and money laundering were two examples of its purview.

A Saint-Cloud two-day seminar on weapon trafficking caught Jillian Pienar's attention. As head of South Africa's Interpol operation, it was her responsibility to coordinate police information on gun smuggling with other southern African countries. So far her efforts had produced negligible results. Jillian signed-up and booked a flight to Paris.

Jillian knew all of the other ten attendees, most by first name. She was young for the responsibility, thirty-two, yet respected by her colleagues because of her competence and determination. She was a large woman, tall, but not plump, and had that square jaw common to Afrikaners. She had attended police school, and then worked her way through the ranks of the Cape Town police department before transferring to the national police force. Jillian became the senior officer in the South African Interpol organization in 1958, appointed more as a token gesture by established police entities suspicious of an agency with foreign connections. By the spring of 1960, she had become the leading Cape Town authority on international crime. African politics were in transition. Colonialists were reluctantly departing, leaving their colonies without law and order. Guns were the equalizer. Smuggling was rampant.

Interpol's weapon expert, Monsieur Lemont, plump and middle aged, bounced into the room and shook hands with each of the ten police officers sitting at the circular table. "The common language for us today is English, so you will have to cope with my poor pronunciation."

Jillian wondered if her long and bumpy flight from Cape Town would be worth it. She turned to Bill Bartlett, her counter-part in Rhodesia, for a reaction and received a shoulder shrug in return.

"You are all familiar with the AK-47. Have any of you fired one?" Lemont asked as he turned toward the screen.

The Portuguese man from Lisbon raised his hand. "I have. I was with our army when they confiscated about fifty rifles in Angola. The rebels had abandoned them in their haste to escape. We were in a remote part of the country so we were allowed to fire them."

"Tell us about the gun," Lemont asked.

"It has a short stock, slight recoil and is not very accurate."

"Was it you or the weapon?" Lemont questioned and everyone snickered.

"Probably both," the Lisbon policeman replied. "What I remember clearly about the gun was its light weight."

"That is the subject of our discussion," Lemont said, interrupting. "Let me show you a few facts." He dimmed the lights and turned on the slide projector. A photograph of an AK-47 appeared on the screen and Lemont began his lecture.

"While the rest of the world, the Americans in particular, obsessed as they are with powerful cartridges, was diligently perfecting highly engineered automatic rifles, an unknown, unskilled Russian sergeant by the name of Kalashnikov, submitted his automatic rifle design to the Soviet weapons community. He did this shortly after the conclusion of the Second World War. His rifle design languished for several years. The Soviet army finally investigated Kalashnikov's design, but scoffed when they tested it, complaining that the parts did not fit snuggly." Lemont chuckled as he warmed to the subject. "This, as we all know now, was the rifle's ingratiating feature. The very fact that the parts were loose fitting meant that the rifle would be less likely to jam when dirty, inadequately lubricated or clogged with carbon. It is the most reliable gun on the market. It works even when rain soaked or coated with sand. It weighs ten pounds and is less than three feet long. The best part is that it provides blistering fire for a distance of 200 to 300 yards. Any dimwit can operate it without training."

"What does the "A" stand for if his name is Mikhail?" someone asked.

"The 'A' is for *automat* or automatic and 1947 was the year it was invented. We will soon be looking for a newer model, the AKILOMETERS, with the 'M' standing for modernized."

"Who is making the AK-47?" someone else asked.

Before responding, Lemont clicked through a series of slides showing assembly plants in Russia and East Germany, following with several photos of the weapon being used in harsh conditions. He switched the lights back on before walking to the space between the half circles of desks. "Of course, Russia. There is a large facility in Wiese, Federal Republic of German and we understand Finland will soon begin production. The AK-47 is in use in every location where there is armed conflict. It is the gun of choice by terrorists and guerrillas. The Chinese have a factory and are distributing to the North Vietnamese. We estimate most Eastern Block countries will ultimately manufacture or assemble the rifle."

Lemont gazed at his class. "Five of you here today represent our organization in Southern Africa. All of the countries in this area offer an enormous market for illegal weapons. For the next two days we will discuss methods to anticipate and identify gun smuggling operations and how to work with various police forces to interdict shipments. For us to be totally successful, however, we must ultimately find the brain center, that elite group who remain anonymous, who work in secret to finance the operation, arrange the transportation and negotiate with the manufacturers. They are businessmen concealed behind legitimate companies and live artificial lives. Any questions before we begin?"

"Yes," a man with a French accent said. "Wouldn't it be quicker to investigate the source? There are fewer factories than smugglers."

"Good question. We are doing that and the subject will be a part of our study. The amount of money involved is enormous and everyone, especially the Soviet controlled countries, are reluctant to cooperate. Interpol needs to work both ends of the supply chain."

Jillian raised her hand. "How do we find these people?"

Lemont did not smile. "Follow the money."

JUNE 1960

Elizabethville, Katanga Province, Belgian Congo

After the Belgians leave, everything will change. Moise Tshombe sat on his front porch brooding. Yes, he muttered to himself, the Congo would be independent, but old wounds would open and there would be bloodshed. Katanga must protect itself.

Tshombe's modest home was located on the western fringe of Elizabethville, the capital of the Province of Katanga. His neglected garden had breached all boundaries; poking through the porch railing and concealing the pathway leading to the road. The afternoon would soon spend itself; shadows had stretched to the fence that separated his land from the street. He was waiting for the son of an old friend to arrive. His mind stroked good memories of this friend and the years when they were young men—full of hopes and ambitions. They had spent their youth in the western part of the Province, south of the great copper mine and close to the Rhodesian border. Both were educated in Christian schools run by Methodist missionaries. When Tshombe's father passed away, he inherited enough money to move to Elizabethville, where he established a furniture business. His friend traveled a different path, heading north to the mountains to become a park ranger. Tshombe married the daughter of an influential Lunoa Tribe chief. This marriage, his flourishing business and his harmonious relationship with the Belgian colonial authorities, granted him a respected position in the community. He became a leader before he thought of becoming one. It was thrust on him and he grew into the mold.

Moise Tshombe was not an imposing man if not for his eyes, which were large and could be penetrating. He was clean-cut, average height, and usually conservatively dressed. His stomach had rounded and edged over his belt line and, perhaps, that's why he usually wore a jacket. It was not his appearance but his position, socially and politically, that set him apart. Tshombe wore a jacket regardless of the occasion. Even on this humid June afternoon, he wore a suit, white shirt and tie.

The sound of a car door slamming snapped him from his reverie. Thomas Kimbamba appeared at the street gate and waved at Tshombe. The young man, his friends son, couldn't be more than thirty, he mused. As Thomas walked the path to the deck, Tshombe scrutinized him. He was tall, over 1,90 meters, broad shouldered and possessed a face that women would find attractive. His black, close-cropped hair set off a high forehead and a narrow nose that might belong in North Africa. The tall young man's skin was mahogany-colored, touched with burnt umber that radiated health. Tshombe marveled at Thomas's graceful and confident stride. He was even more handsome than his father. Tshombe rose from his chair to greet his old friend's son and they embraced warmly.

"I'm enjoying a beer. Will you join me?" As Tshombe shuffled into his house, he looked over his shoulder and added, "Take off your coat, Thomas, the humidity has become intense. I will too." Once the two bottles of beer rested on the table, the two men sat facing each other in silence, weighing the moment.

Finally, Tshombe spoke. "I have been sitting here enjoying memories of your father and our friendship. He was more focused on his future then most men, and I'm including myself. He wanted to live in the mountains, close to nature, and that's exactly what he did. You were the benefactor, growing up in the Upemba National Park. I miss your father."

"I too think of him a lot. He often talked of you, Moise, with fondness and respect. He told me once—the future of Katanga would someday rest in your hands. It seems he was right."

"One of your father's greatest attributes was his remarkable accuracy with a rifle, and even more amazing, his discretion when it came to using it. He rarely fired his rifle and I wish he was here to instill such good judgment in our young men. I fear there will be too much killing."

Both men knew the despised Belgian colonialists would leave and independence would come to the Congo in weeks, if not days. Ambitious men would scramble for power in Leopoldville and their greed would concentrate on the great mineral wealth in Katanga and the gold just across its northern border. Both men knew Katanga would have to secede from the new nation. They cradled their beer and considered the future. The sun pushed further toward the western hills.

"Moise, what will happen when we declare our independence? Will we have to fight the rest of the country? Why can't we become a peaceful nation, directing our resources toward the betterment of our people?"

"Because it won't be allowed. Everyone covets our resources, so we must protect ourselves. I know you were raised a Christian—so was I. How deeply one believes in the Bible varies from missionary to convert, from man to woman. Killing is abhorrent, so we were taught, but Christian history is full of blood. Our brothers are first and foremost members of a tribe. The honor of the tribe is everything; it is our cultural legacy, not just from our fathers and grandfathers, but inherited from tribal society over hundreds of years. It is embedded into the African psyche. The Belgians clamped a lid on the tribal hates, jealousies and revenges, but now, the lid is off and the killing will begin. It will be terrible."

"How can I help you?" Thomas asked, holding his still-full bottle of beer.

"There is a part you can play that is essential for our success," he smiled as a grandfather would, "and you are best qualified to do what I am going to ask. Your appearance, your linguistic ability, your pleasing nature and your bearing—all these qualities make you presentable and believable to our European and American friends. I have three tasks for you." Tshombe extracted some papers from a worn valise. "I would like you to visit Luxembourg immediately. Here is the name of a bank and an officer there who knows me. Open an account with the small amount of money in this envelope. As you will read in these documents, I am the only person allowed to withdraw funds. However, in the event of my demise, you and Godefroid Munongo will become the joint authorized signatories. The money that will soon pour into this account belongs to Katanga and is to be used for its preservation. Tell no one about this. Pack your bags and slip across the Rhodesian border to Ndola to catch a flight."

"Moise, I am a school teacher. I know nothing about banks, guns and politics, but I will help you the best I am able, as my father would. You mentioned there were three assignments."

"Yes. In this second envelope are five-thousand US dollars in small bills to cover your travel expenses. You once told me you had a school friend working in the US embassy in London. Go to London and contact him. Make it casual . . . touching base with an old friend. My guess is he will jump at the chance to discuss Katanga."

"What's my objective?"

"We want the United States to support our independence. Casually suggest that we would be good friends in a hostile environment. Remind your friend that we possess the uranium the US covets. Suggest that you would bet Katanga would reject any overtures from the Soviets. He will send all of your comments to Washington immediately and you will suddenly become important."

"What response are we seeking?"

"I want the US to support us or, at least, remain neutral. The UN will be a problem for us. Having the US on our side will help. They, of course, being Americans, will be indecisive."

"In between Luxembourg and London," Tshombe passed a paper to Thomas, "contact these two men in Belgium. They are retired Belgian military officers who once commanded here in Katanga. I believe they can lead us to sources of the weapons we need. Be careful, both are venal. Ask them to arrange for the weapons and ammunition delivery along with the promised mercenaries. Four men should be enough. Make sure that the mercenaries can speak French. We need small arms, AK-47s, grenades and rocket-propelled grenades, as well as uniforms, helmets and medical supplies. When they provide you with a list of merchandise, a delivery date, and an acceptable cost, we will transfer half of the amount due to their source's bank account, the remainder when the weapons arrive. They must be extremely cautious when selecting the delivery route. Our enemies will be watching."

Thomas did not take notes. His father had honed his phenomenal memory by calling out the names of birds and plants as they hiked the wetlands, subsequently asking for recall at dinner time. "Will you be able to issue instructions to the bank from here?"

"Yes. If we have disruptions here, I can use the *UMHK* (Union Minière du Haut Copper Mine) communication equipment or cross over into Northern Rhodesia. The bank should receive a handsome deposit within a fortnight." Tshombe held his bottle up and touched Thomas's. "Be careful Thomas, trust no one and move swiftly."

It was now dark, and the sounds of the jungle enveloped Thomas as he walked the path back to his aging Renault. He heard nothing; his mind was focused on the task before him.

Belgium

The town of Brasschaat sits in the center of farmland fifteen kilometers north of Antwerp. Europe's oldest air base resided here, now rarely in use; the hangers looked as if they were a movie set from the early forties. Grim, gray buildings bordered the runway, projecting a somber face to the base. In contrast, the farm fields to the east were so rich and fertile that the crops appeared lush and ready for harvest, even in midsummer. Along the edge of the town, facing the fields, was the Élégant Oie, a restaurant favored by the farmers, townspeople and especially the military personnel stationed in Brasschaat. When the weather was pleasant, diners would enjoy their drinks in the garden before heading indoors for long lunches or late dinners. This mid-afternoon, under dark clouds hanging low to the west, two men were the sole occupants of the garden. One, a colonel in the Belgian army, wore his uniform; the other man appeared to be a civilian. They were both drinking beer, talked little, and looked as if they were waiting for someone.

Thomas peered apprehensively out from the barroom door, spied the two at the far end of the garden and walked toward them. He knew the colonel slightly from the soldier's days in Elisabethville. Thomas remembered him as callous. The short man in a suit, he knew better.

The uniformed officer rose, extended his hand and greeted Thomas in French. "Good to see you, my friend. You're lucky to be here rather than back in the Congo, no? Come, sit down. Would you like a beer?"

Thomas accepted and sank into a chair. As he waited for his beer, he recounted the details of his journey from Leopoldville. He sighed as he described the difficulties. "I crossed the river with hundreds of your countrymen fleeing the chaos in Leopoldville. Some were getting out with just the shirts on their backs. Brazzaville was a madhouse. I had to wait three days to get a seat on a plane to Europe. As you must understand, I am glad that you are leaving the Congo, but we will miss the security that you provided. It will take a long time before law and order returns. And, regrettably, I must return to Katanga soon."

The civilian, a stocky man in his late fifties, smiled cryptically. His French had a hint of a Walloon dialect. "Your time is valuable, Mr. Kimbamba, and a thunderstorm is threatening. May I begin by asking why you contact us?"

"For a number of reasons. Both of you were stationed in Elizabethville for many years and are familiar with my people and our aspirations. It would be a misfortune if our land fell under the control of Lumumba and the Kasavubu government in the north. We intend to quickly establish our own independence before troops are sent to occupy Katanga. Tshombe has already begun to consolidate his authority. We have some of our own military elements, but they lack training. We have almost no guns, in fact, few weapons of any type." Continuing his conversation, directed mainly to the man in the suit, he ventured further. "Our hope is that now that you have retired, General Leclercq, you could put us in touch with munitions suppliers."

Apprehensively, Leclercq looked down at his hands now folded in his lap and shifted slightly in his chair. "Even if we could, how would the supplies enter Katanga? You are cut off from the port, and the countries to your south have their own problems. In all likelihood, your borders have already been sealed."

"True," said Thomas wearing a smile that masked his anxiety. "But, no doubt you can connect us with someone resourceful, someone who is familiar with our part of the world and able to arrange supply,"—he let his request linger a moment,—"and delivery. We are able to pay cash and would be generous with you. There is another requirement." Thunder adumbrated in the distance and all three men turned to the sound. Thomas Kimbamba's eyes searched the heavens looking for inspiration.

The retired general looked at his colleague, Colonel Lefebvre. Lefebvre spoke rapidly, his eyes darting from Leclercq to Thomas. "What you are asking of us is, obviously, dangerous and fraught with difficulties. The United Nations will soon be all over the Congo and any Belgian activity will be scrutinized thoroughly. We will have to think about this, but if we have a little time, I promise to research the possibilities carefully. If we are successful and comply with your requirements, we would want to be paid a flat fee in advance, deposited into a Luxembourg bank. Is there anything else?"

Thomas smiled again. "As a matter of fact, we will need a few good men to teach us how to use the weaponry."

"How do we reach you?"

"Our phones rarely work. Here is my telex address. Merely say you are ready and I will return within one week. I've your phone number and we can meet here." Thomas Kimbamba rose quickly and extended his hand. He was lithe for such a large man and his grip was a vise. The storm arrived and the three men scattered.

Thomas drove directly to his hotel in Brussels in the rain storm. His thoughts dwelled on his meeting with the two Belgian officers. Would they cooperate? Could they be trusted to provide a reliable source for firearms and mercenaries? If they failed, what was his backup plan? He took a deep breath and tried to switch his focus to the increased traffic. The steady rain added gloom to his already somber mood, yet his anxiety was somewhat assuaged by a gut feeling that the General would come to the party. Leclercq's brokerage fee would likely be steep.

The downpour had snarled the traffic. Thomas decided to return the rented car and walk the short distance to his hotel. His bones were chilled by the northern weather. In his room, he showered, changed to dry clothes and then wrote a brief message to Tshombe.

MISSION COMPLETED STOP OUR FRIENDS REQUIRE TWO WEEKS STOP RETURNING IMMEDIATELY VIA LONDON STOP TK

He asked the front desk to send the telex immediately and tally his charges so that he could check out quickly in the morning. He would make one long distance phone call to London from his room and, finally, he asked for the name of a good travel agent.

London

The rain followed Thomas to England but did not dampen his spirits. He was home again; at least it seemed so, as he watched the familiar landscape fly past his taxi window. As a boy, he had attended a public boy's school in the village of Oxshott. Perhaps he would rent a car tomorrow and visit the school before his late afternoon flight home. The cabbie waxed away about the football match of the night before, a familiar subject for Thomas, but his thoughts were on the task before him. The taxi dove into the center of London, skillfully maneuvering through the traffic, and finally depositing him at the Connaught Hotel, ironically, a favorite watering hole for colonialists home on leave. Thomas was comfortable in the British environment; his English was as fluent as his French. He marched into the elegant lobby, his stride reflecting self-confidence.

The Connaught was also a favorite of American diplomats. The giant US Embassy faced Grosvenor Square, a convenient half block walk from the hotel. Thomas did not unpack. He sat down at a large desk facing the window, thumbed through his date book and found the phone number for Alex McLean, his friend from college days in the United States. Alex had become a career officer in the State Department, currently assigned to the Court of St. James as deputy Chargé d'affaires. Thomas drummed his fingers on the desk as his call flowed through a series of secretaries.

"Thomas, is it really you?" a familiar squeaky voice came on the line.

"Hello, Alex. How are you, old friend?"

"Overworked and under paid. I got your message from Brussels. Where are you? Let's have lunch."

"I'm checked into the Connaught. I see the rain has stopped so why don't I walk over. Should be under your roof in fifteen minutes." Thomas rang off, stood and stretched. He unpacked and found a striped tie to wear for the Americans.

The US Embassy was enormous by any standard and Thomas had to navigate several reception desks before his presence was announced. Alex soon appeared accompanied by another gentleman. His old school chum was now almost bald, but otherwise looked the same, beaming and jolly, obviously delighted to see Thomas again.

"Thomas, you're even taller than I remember." Alex would have hugged Thomas except for their difference in height, which made it awkward.

"And you," Thomas said spreading his arms, "have shrunk a little, and I think you have been eating well."

"It's my job. All I do is attend official dinners." Alex turned to his companion and said, "Larry, meet my old college friend, Thomas Kimbamba, maybe the best midfielder Johns Hopkins has ever known."

"Hello, Thomas. I'm Larry Madison. Alex invited me to join you for lunch. Hope you don't mind. I'm visiting from D.C.

The sun, high in the sky, was intent on drying-out soggy London. The three decided to walk back to the Connaught for lunch. Thomas was glad he had worn his one suit as both Americans wore three-piece suits, but it was he who commanded attention when they entered the Connaught dining room. It was his good-looks and bearing that set him apart and he was used to this attention. Thomas asked for a table away from the other patrons, and after quickly ordering their lunch, the three began to talk about the situation in the Congo.

"What will Katanga do when the Congo becomes independent?" Alex asked casually.

"We will form our own country." Thomas didn't wish to show all of his cards too quickly.

Madison joined the conversation. "In the long term, would that be wise? The Congo would be stronger, healthier and perhaps an important world player if Katanga remained as a province of the country."

"What is Tshombe's position?" Alex questioned intently, before abruptly changing the tone of his questioning. "Instead of us peppering you with questions, why don't you bring Larry up to date on what is happening in the Congo and why Katanga wishes to become independent."

Thomas juggled a small coffee cup while looking over the rim into the two pairs of eyes intently watching him. He placed the dainty cup in the saucer and began to speak.

He knew that the Congo was off the US government's radar screen, a minor player on the world stage. Colonialism had existed for more than a century; the world was inured to its vileness. The fact that Thomas's people had been exploited, humiliated and diminished appeared merely as a blip among many conflicts. But in just one week, the Belgians would finally depart, in a hurry he imagined, and the Congo would be an independent country.

"We will finally have freedom and that's what we all cherish, isn't it?" He continued without waiting for confirmation. "What we will not have is a judicial system in place, schools and teachers, infrastructure and, most importantly, law and order." Thomas explained clearly and in great detail the complex problems facing the Congo. The country was politically underdeveloped. Although the population is literate and healthy by African standards, Congo was short of doctors, dentists, engineers and lawyers. The highest rank of a Congolese in the Belgian occupying army was sergeant. Thomas knew that as the days counted down to independence, there would be civil disorder. The army would mutiny. The remaining European community would panic and call for military protection. There would be none as the bulk of the Belgian army would have left.

"Who will run the government in Leopoldville?"

Thomas returned to his coffee. He was addicted to the beverage. "There is no one, really. My country is enormous, almost as large as Western Europe If you look at a map of the Congo as it is today, not next week, it is neatly divided into provinces, all ostensibly with provisional governments reporting to a federal government, which in turn reports to Brussels. The reality is that we are a land of tribes—each with its own language, customs and leaders. In fact, my strongest allegiance is to my tribe and then to Katanga.

"Look, try to understand the situation from our point of view. We have no officer corps to lead and discipline our soldiers. They haven't been paid. They will be on the loose with their firearms and machetes. There are, perhaps, twenty men who have a university education. Women have been subjugated. There is no one to take control. This is why we must take care of Katanga."

Alex interrupted. "You will still have the same problems in Katanga as you have just described in the rest of the country."

"Some, yes, but we have a strong leader in Moise Tshombe. We can operate our copper and cobalt mines and earn foreign exchange. And finally, we have persuaded a few Belgians to remain and help us organize and rebuild."

Madison had remained quiet but seemed to absorb everything. Thomas suspected that he knew more about the African scene than he had let on. Finally, revealing his familiarity with Thomas's narrative, Madison asked. "How will you ship the copper ore? You have no port. The eventual government in Leopoldville, when it does get its act together, will object to your succession and will send its army south. And, have you thought about what the United Nation's reaction will be?"

"I am a teacher, not a diplomat. I'm in London on other business and took the opportunity to say hello to an old friend. So, my opinion means nothing. I can only assume that the Katanga leaders would wish for the US to remain, at least, neutral and to influence the UN to do the same."

No one spoke immediately. Larry and Alex did not look at each other and seemed almost at a loss for an answer. Finally Madison asked, "Have you ever met Tshombe?"

Thomas's eyes scrutinized Madison's face. The question was sincere. "Why yes, I had a beer with him only the other day. He and my father were best friends."

Thomas now had the information he wanted. The US was more concerned about the Soviet Union than internal Congo politics. He bet Mr. Madison would contact him again.

Alex settled the lunch check. The three men walked together for several blocks and then went their separate ways. Madison is certainly CIA, Thomas concluded. Thomas returned to the Connaught, picked up his room key and headed for the elevator. I might as well have one luxurious night before returning to the war zone, he rationalized to himself.

Oslo

Samantha peered out the airplane window. Her eyes were searching for land, but found only the North Sea stretching to the horizon. Her SAS flight had left Heathrow at noon, with a promise to put her in Oslo before three o'clock. She tilted the seat back, stretched her long legs and let her mind drift. Her family would be waiting in Oslo. She had lost touch with her parents and brothers and hoped the wedding's events would allow time for her to catch up with them. And now she was to finally meet Quinn's love, Mette. How would the two families blend, she wondered? Why hadn't Quinn sent her a photo? Well, that was about to change because she had brought her camera.

The stewardess's announcement snapped Samantha out of her reverie. "We will be landing in Oslo shortly and now would be an excellent time to fasten your lap strap. Also," she purred, "it would be a good idea to cross your fingers since our pilot today is a Swede," she giggled, alluding to the long time rivalry between the Norwegians and their Swedish neighbor.

Abruptly the airplane banked and the stewardess was thrown against the bulkhead. The pilot's deep voice came over the speaker system. "This is Sixten Karlson, your Swedish pilot speaking. I am wondering if anyone back there has a map of Norway. We can't seem to find an airport near Oslo. They may not have one and we would have to divert to Stockholm."

The passengers loved the exchange and the laughter relaxed everyone.

The jet was much lower now and streaking up the Oslofjord. Samantha could clearly see the granite cliffs jutting up from the shore and a scattering of homes perched on giant rock formations. Sailboats wrestled for position at the starting line of a race and, as the plane dropped even lower, she could make out sunbathers splayed on the rocks along the shore. It appeared all of Oslo was on vacation.

The Swedish pilot somehow found the Oslo airport. Samantha soon moved through passport control and followed the passengers to the luggage conveyer. She surveyed the faces of the crowd waiting in the arrival lounge. She immediately spied Quinn, his reddish-blond hair blending well with the Nordics. A Scandinavian ice princess stood next to him: golden-haired, long-legged, tan and wholesome, dressed in a pale-blue blouse, shorts and sneakers. She was laughing at something Quinn had said and then turned to the gate to scan the passengers pouring forth. Sam collected her luggage and walked through the gate to the waiting room. Her eyes and Mette's locked. In that instant, Sam experienced that odd sensation of having met someone before. This discovery remained unsettling but was muted when Quinn hugged her and then introduced his bride.

Years later, when she was living on the other side of the world, Samantha's mind would sometimes drift back to that day and to the joyous week she spent with her family in Oslo. Her long repressed feelings for her family had gushed; she had felt like the unsophisticated little girl she had been while growing up in her hometown of Elmwood and during the summers spent at the Wisconsin lake lodge.

Mette's family, the Solbergs, had gathered in their summer home on the Oslofjord to become acquainted with their new American in-laws, the Norquists. Sam smiled when she remember her father speaking broken Norwegian to Mette's father, Lorenz. Lars was ebullient and greeted the Solberg's friends as if they were his. All were invited to visit the Wisconsin lake lodge. Samantha's mother, Elizabeth, on the other hand, appeared ill at ease with a crowd of unfamiliar faces, the drinking and trivial chatter. It had been Mette who had moved to her rescue, introducing her to friends and asking for her help in the kitchen. This sensitivity did not escape Samantha.

The food came from the sea, always accompanied by strong beer or French wine. Guests would linger for drinks or dinner, and then slip away. Endless toasts punctuated the night and provided an unpretentious gaiety, which Sam found charmingly nostalgic—it reminded her of her college days.

From the very first day, Mette and Sam had a special affinity for each other and developed a closeness that surprised Samantha then, as it did in later years. They would make eye contact, one would tilt her head toward an unoccupied corner of the room and the two would slip away to chat. The two women, both in their twenties, communicated easily, with an openness that was refreshing. There was an innate kinship, which Samantha couldn't put her finger on.

"Tell me about Iran. Were you able to talk with people in all walks of life?"

Sam thought for a moment. "Yes, but it was more challenging than I anticipated. The country's roots reach deep into earlier centuries, yet with all of that time-span, the people are still searching for their identity. There is a dark energy below the surface; it will explode some day soon."

"Will your photographs reflect this—how should I say— agitation?" Mette questioned with acuity, not just to make conversation.

On another occasion, when they were sitting together on the steps leading from the deck down the granite slope to the water, Mette revealed the story of her meeting Quinn during a ski vacation to Lech. "When did you know it was not a casual dalliance?" Samantha ventured.

Mette smiled as she looked off toward the fjord. Then, turning back to Samantha, she reached out to touch her hand. "I knew this man was special when we were in Austria, but it wasn't until I returned home that I acknowledged to myself that I was in love. Thoughts of him consumed and disrupted my days. I began to write Quinn in San Francisco, then I invented an excuse to meet him in Victoria, Canada and it was there that I convinced him that he should love me too." She squealed with laughter, "It was *easy*."

"And you, Samantha, what about you?"

Samantha remembered Mette's question and how she struggled with a fitting response. Unknowingly, she was on the eve of her own great love affair and unaware of the converging events that would alter her life—forever. "I think I've met my "special" man," she said hesitantly, looking past Mette to the vivid blue sky. "He's a South African and works at the UN. When I'm sure, I'll follow your technique to ensnare him."

Relationships evolve, generally. This one with Mette was different. They were soul-mates, bound to eventually find each other again. They sailed together, hiked, drank beer while basking in the mid-summer sun and finally, at the end of the week, Samantha stood at the alter watching her brother and her new friend become wedded.

Reality is in the moment. Then it moves to the past and becomes a pawn for one's memory: to twist, enhance, even obliterate. Writing captures the moment and, if true, preserves it unadulterated. But a photograph is pure; a face looking out into the camera, captured forever as it was in that precise moment. Samantha preserved on film her precious week in Oslo. With the photographs, she could transcend time and relive those moments. Sometimes she would reach for the phone and call Mette and say, "I'm looking at you, we are on your sailboat and I can feel the wind on my face." They would laugh together as they had, years before, in Oslo.

Cape Town, South Africa

Karel van Riebeek's financial empire began in a small and obscure fashion. In 1945, when the world gave a sigh of relief and began the arduous process of healing and repairing, van Riebeek had rented a nondescript two-room, second-floor office on Jordaan Street in the Schotschekioof district of Cape Town. At the government offices nearby, he registered his company and with no name in mind, called it Jordaan Trading Ltd. For two years the company imported exactly nothing.

During these two years, van Riebeek was busy organizing and planning. He seemed to have ample funds and his banker was deferential. Although van Riebeek professed to be an Afrikaan with roots in the farmland north of Cape Town, he possessed the ability to alter his accent or switch languages smoothly. He called on the wine trade, which was predominately English. He spoke English, a little guttural perhaps, asked a lot of questions without being obtrusive, and was polite and always vague about his background and purpose. When asked about it he would answer with—"I grew up on a farm, loved wine, and when my father died, he left me a small purse so that I could pursue my interests."

Van Riebeek frequented the Cape Town port area where the oceangoing ships were unloaded and the government custom offices were located. The dock laborers were black, with a few of their own color as supervisors. The wharf was controlled, de facto, by Afrikaners. Englishmen dominated the government offices. All were South Africans, but with very different ideas of how the country should be run. For two years he ingratiated himself with the important players, never asked for a favor, took gifts to the black *baases* and entertained the Africans and English—never together.

If someone asked the wine merchants or the dock superintendents about Mr. van Riebeek, they would have to pause to think a moment. Then they would typically exclaim, "Yes, I know who you mean. Van Riebeek. Nice fellow. Soft spoken and polite. Why I had dinner with him just the other night. I really don't know much about him except that he grew up on a farm."

When commercial flights to Europe began to operate with greater frequency, van Riebeek would disappear for several weeks. No one knew where he went. No one cared. The only telltale sign of his absence was the small pile of mail on the office doorstep.

In the autumn of 1947, van Riebeek hired three people. They were a strange lot and seemed incompatible. Stella, a stout woman in her forties who spoke Afrikaan and English, became the office manager. Her Afrikaan husband worked on the docks as a gang *baas*, and provided van Riebeek with a respected contact in the port. At the same time, he hired Edgar because of his background in the liquor trade. Edgar had served in the South African army in Europe, where he had collected shrapnel in his right foot, causing a slight limp.

The wine and liquor merchants throughout Cape Town and the surrounding towns liked and trusted him. He assured van Riebeek that he could sell the wine van Riebeek promised to import.

The third employee was more interesting because of his appearance and background, and because no one could quite put their finger on exactly what services this man provided for van Riebeek. He had a single name, Adraan; the lack of a family name increased his mystique. His hair was closely cropped. His skin had a fish-like look, pasty and devoid of hair. But an observer would first notice his unrevealing green eyes and small, tight mouth, both rendering Adraan's face a menacing quality. His clothes were always dark and the long sleeves and turtleneck acted as both a shield against intrusion as well as a cover for his numerous tattoos. He rarely spoke and went about his duties quietly without involving those around him.

By Christmas of 1947, Jordaan Trading's first shipment of Spanish and Portuguese wine arrived. The wine was not spectacular but priced right. Edgar sold the entire consignment within a fortnight. The French and Italian wine industry had been decimated by the war but there was promise for the 1948 harvest. Van Riebeek also offered Riesling from the Rhine. The South Africans were so eager to receive it that no one thought to ask how van Riebeek was able to import German wine. The business flourished with Stella running the office, Edgar handling sales, while Adraan remained in the shadows, periodically appearing on the wharf.

In 1954, van Riebeek purchased a small vineyard on the outskirts of Stellenbosch. Situated back in the hills, the house, cellar, and several other buildings were surrounded by vineyards. The vineyard had a poor reputation and bottled very little of its own growth. Van Riebeek immediately changed the name to "Riebeek Vineyard," and brought a Dutch vintner, of obvious German ancestry, to improve the quality of his wine. Van Riebeek decided to spend most of his time in Stellenbosch. He remodeled the old home and built an annex in the back, which he called the "office." Van Riebeek did not have a family. He eventually hired a cook plus a general servant to manage his home. They were black and native to the Stellenbosch area. Adraan spent some of his time at the vineyard, where he had his own small quarters in the annex.

One oddity stood out in the transformation of the Riebeek Vineyard. A dirt road was constructed running several kilometers from the back of the vineyard, angling up into the hills. No one knew its purpose and the local employees were prohibited from using it. Adraan was seen periodically using the track, either hiking with a pack or bumping over the ruts in a small truck. The sound of distant gunfire was heard periodically but no one paid attention. Guns were commonplace in South Africa.

During the following six years, van Riebeek's life remained unremarkable. His wine importation business grew steadily, especially the Rieslings. The Dutch vintner proved to be a shrewd investment, and by his third year he produced white wine worthy of export to Europe. Van Riebeek's UK importer offered to commit to the entire production, if van Riebeek was willing. Van Riebeek's banker took notice of the growing value of the Riebeek Vineyard account, smiled, shrugged, and asked no questions. Periodically small trucks would visit the vineyard, usually with up-country, Transvaal license plates. The villagers near the vineyard did not know von Riebeek, in fact, many had never seen him. He and his vineyard were not a mystery, but simply not of interest to them.

On a chilly day in late June of 1960, van Riebeek sat in his Cape Town office sorting through his mail. A Western Union delivery interrupted the serenity that prevailed and Stella brought the unopened telegram immediately to van Riebeek. He read it twice and smiled.

> GREETINGS MIJNHEER VAN RIEBEEK STOP HAVE CLIENT URGENT NEED YOUR PRODUCTS AND INSTRUCTORS STOP CONFIRM ABILITY SUPPLY STOP YOUR PRESENCE MEETING EUROPE MID-JULY ESSENTIAL STOP REGARDS LECLERCQ

Van Riebeek knew with certainty who the client was and why they had contacted him. General Leclercq had spent years in the Congo and that enormous country in central Africa was about to become independent. The country was fundamentally tribal and most observers expected what was known as the Belgian Congo, to fragment into a civil war. Since the Belgian army took their weapons with them when they left the country, there would be a significant need for replacements. They had contacted him knowing that he had the experience and knowledge of contraband firearms, and could also provide mercenaries to train on their use.

Van Riebeek stared at the message, his mind racing. Leclercq had been the Belgian commanding officer in Katanga during his last years in the colony. Surely it was this mineral-rich province that required help. He rose from his desk and walked into the outer office where Edgar was chatting with Stella. "I am going to be tied up on some business for the next week and I do not want to be diverted from this. Stella, you must manage the office as you always have, and Ed, it is time for you to take responsibility of our wine imports." Without waiting for an answer, he returned to his office, closed the door and began to carefully compose a telegram.

RECEIVED RETIRED BELGIAN OFFICER INQUIRY SUBSTANTIAL 47 PLUS OTHER AND INSTRUCTORS FOR KATANGA STOP ADVISE INTEREST AND MEANS FOR SUPPLY AND DELIVERY AND BANKING

Van Riebeek unlocked his desk drawer and withdrew a thin black notebook. His code book. He carefully translated his message into an innocuous translation, which would not raise eyebrows at the telegraph office. The cipher referred to the wine business. He then placed the two unencoded messages in the small notebook, returned it to the drawer and locked it. The telegraph office was a fifteen minute walk. He put on his coat and headed out into the chilly weather. The walk and fresh air would do him good, he thought.

The following morning, the Western Union deliveryman arrived with another telegram. Van Riebeek used telegrams to communicate with his clients in Europe so there was nothing suspicious or unusual about the delivery. Stella put it on his desk and closed the door. Van Riebeek arrived at his office mid morning, chatted with Stella briefly and moved on quickly to his office. He sipped his coffee and tapped the edge of the telegram on his desktop thinking about what the contents would reveal. He would not be surprised.

> ACCEPT ORDER STOP WILL PROVIDE SOURCES TO NIJMEGEN STOP TRANS-PORTATION BALTIC TO INDIAN OCEAN AVAILABLE STOP SUGGEST EMPLOY MORGAN FOR OVERLAND AND TRAINING STOP OFFER ATTACTIVE FEE PLUS EXONERATION OBLIGATION STOP USE BANK ALPINUM AG 7492391 LICHTENSTEIN REGARDS

Van Riebeek would not sign on to a large weapons order for delivery outside of South Africa. For seven years he had successfully supplied weapons to customers in the northern extremity of South Africa. He knew, with certainty, that in many cases the weapons moved across the northern border. He had escaped detection for several reasons: the shipments were small and infrequent, they arrived concealed in crates of wine, his customers were appreciative and discrete and van Riebeek resisted a flamboyant lifestyle. His profits were transferred as payments for wine and rested untraceable in a Lisbon bank.

He had, on occasion, ventured further afield: Mozambique, Southwest Africa and once to Tanganyika. For ventures abroad, he deferred to a munitions czar, of whom there were a half dozen, all European. The risks were enormous, both from the many police authorities investigating smuggling and the smuggling syndicates. The latter did not tolerate free-lance competitors, and if he worked with them, mistakes were unpardonable. They, naturally, retained the lion's share of the profits. Van Riebeek became a middleman. He would have less responsibility and, of course, receive a smaller share of the profits.

Van Riebeek set about organizing the scheme. He divided it into four sections: communication, supply, delivery and finance.

His first telegram went to Nijmegen, an old city in Holland on the German border. He addressed it to his nephew, saying simply that he would soon need a large consignment of Riesling and to prepare for his arrival in early July.

The second message was addressed to his Portuguese banker. He asked him to reactivate his dormant company, S. A. Vine Ltd. and to open a new numbered bank account, with no connection to his Lisbon commercial bank account, the location to be at his banker's discretion. Once he received the account number, he would wire funds.

Van Riebeek sat quietly for a long time, almost as if in a trance, thinking about Morgan Palmer and the part he would play. No, he said to himself, I will wait before contacting Palmer. It would be more effective to present our proposal in person. I need to finalize supply and delivery to an African port first. Then I'll fly to Lusaka and meet with Palmer. Not an attractive prospect, he thought, and grumbled audibly. Palmer's company, Big Five Safari Ltd., maintained a small office there. When Morgan was on safari in the bush he would infrequently check his office for messages and mail. Van Riebeek decided to wait until the last moment to spring the plot on Palmer and give him no time to reflect and reject it. Palmer owed the smuggling syndicate a great deal of money and this would be an opportunity to retire the debt.

Palmer was extraordinarily adept with small arms, and arguably the best big game hunter on the savanna north of the Zambezi River. He had the dubious reputation of being a sure shot, an unscrupulous businessman and a Lothario. His parents had immigrated to Rhodesia from Northern Wales, raising him and his sister on a tobacco farm midway between the Zambezi River and Salisbury. His two safari colleagues were also Rhodesian and were equally at home with the prolific animal population along the Luangwa River. Yes, he mused, Palmer would be perfect for this mission.

His final dispatch was a reply to General Leclercq, confirming his interest, his ability to provide the product and his willingness to meet in July. Although he planned to visit Holland, he suggested England as a neutral ground and, besides, he had other business to transact in London.

JULY 1960

Elizabethville, DRC

Elizabethville straddled a sluggish green river that meandered from the plateau in the north through the city, as it headed south into Northern Rhodesia. The sprawling, overgrown town bestowed on its habitants the same dust, odors, and misery experienced by all the villages along the railroad track. The streets were mostly unpaved with the exception of a few tree-lined boulevards that met at roundabouts. They had French street names, and the few large municipal government buildings in the center of the city reflected a French architectural influence. The newly vacated Belgian villas appeared forlorn. On this first day of July and the first day of independence, the city was desolate. As the Belgians fled, the bulk of the 750,000 natives who lived in shacks and small homes, peered out of their shanties wide-eyed and frightened, like prisoners, whose jailers had suddenly decamped, leaving all doors open. No one knew who was in charge now or how independence would affect their lives, nor did they know what it meant to have no one in charge. They were just as frightened as the departing Belgians.

Two men, who thought they knew the answers to this terrifying time, sat at a plain wooden table in a second-story room in the former Belgian courthouse near the center of the city. Documents from flung-open metal file cabinets sat in piles on the floor like lilies on a pond. A large woman wearing a colorful, towering, head scarf placed a pot of tea on the table and quickly left, closing the door. The smoke from their sweet smelling Corporal cigarettes hovered near the ceiling. The electricity was off, rendering the ceiling fans motionless. Through the large gaping windows, the air was still, and the build-up of the morning heat was already stifling. The shorter of the two, Joseph Sanimbi, sat hunched over the table studying a map of the Katanga province while the other man, Benjamin Kigali, talked loudly in an alarmed voice.

"Where is Tshombe?"

Without looking up, Sanimbi replied in a steady voice. "He should be at the radio station by now. He'll explain our new situation, asking the people to remain calm and to return to their normal activities. He will also mention," a smile creased his face, "that he is now in charge."

"Does Tshombe think that the entire province will follow his leadership?" Kigali asked, still very animated. Kigali's lanky body was sinewy. His light clothes concealed well-exercised muscles without hiding his black skin color. He had been in the sun a great deal all of his life. Although his six foot frame stood out in a crowd, people mostly noted his singular face. It was flat, as if cleaved with a machete from the tip of his forehead to a drooping chin. A long bulbous nose clung to his face, dragging his features downward, and overpowered the small closely-set, hooded eyes. The nose signaled alcohol; the eyes menace. Everything else associated with his head was large—the ears, jaw and teeth, as well as the size of the head itself. His skull was hairless, giving the drops of perspiration free rein to trickle onto his flat face. He mopped both vigorously with a red handkerchief.

The two men communicated in French because they didn't understand each other's tribal language, a problem common throughout the Congo. Sanimbi's pronunciation was cultivated, Kigali's rough. Both men were dedicated but time would reveal that their aspirations were not congruent.

Sanimbi leaned back in his armchair and studied his compatriot. His 168 cm tall body had become fleshy. The skin on his arms hung loose when he rested his short arms on the table. His skin was very dark – almost black—and appeared shiny, as if it had been waxed. His hair had been cut tight to his scalp. A round face and large eyes looked at Kigali, revealing nothing, neither threatening nor friendly.

"Do you think you could persuade your ex commander, Colonel Willame, to remain here with a regiment of his best soldiers?" Sanimbi's voice was smooth and controlled.

"*Merd,*" Kigali snarled, "we have waited seventy-five years for them to leave. Now you want them to stay!"

Sanimbi turned his map toward Kigali and pointed at a spot just north of the Katanga—Kasai border. His finger touched the line of the railroad that ran from a bend in the Kasai River at Llebo, then south through the gold fields, traversing through the center of Katanga to Elizabethville, before entering Northern Rhodesia. "This railroad is the life-line for our mineral wealth. It must operate or our aspirations to become a separate nation are futile. Do you know what happened here this morning?" His finger drummed on the map. "Let me tell you. A tribe—doesn't matter which one—attacked a small village belonging to another tribe and killed everyone. The Belgian police and army were no where around. They have abdicated their authority. If we are not careful, the same thing could happen here."

The stillness in the street just below the windows was suddenly disturbed by the sound of cars. Kigali strode quickly to the open windows, peered down at the line of cars now parked in front of the building and turned toward Sanimbi, "*Ils sont ici.*"

Minutes later, the door flew open and Tshombe marched into the room, followed by Godefroid Munongo, his longtime friend and now political advisor. Tshombe greeted Sanimbi and Kigali with a quick smile, dumped his briefcase on the table and turned to the armed guards standing around the doorway. "Everyone wait outside. We will be working here for an hour and do not wish to be disturbed." The door closed; Munongo sat down opposite Tshombe. The three men looked at Tshombe, the newly acknowledged leader of Katanga, the man who controlled the Provincial Council. Within the week he would become President of Katanga, and the province would secede from the DRC.

When he spoke, he spoke quickly and made eye contact with each man at the table. "The four of us have an enormous responsibility, much to accomplish and very little time to do so. The government in Leopoldville is weak and vacillating and the country is slipping into chaos. Tribal vendettas are already occurring and without the Belgians, we have no law and order. So let's prioritize and divide the tasks among us."

He looked at Kigali and said, "We must convince the Belgian army, at least a regiment or two, to remain. Benjamin, you were in the Belgian army and served under Colonel Willame. I understand he's still at the airport. Go there, now, and invite him to stay in Katanga to work with us. I am confident that his government will support this."

Kigali shook his large head and looked skeptical. "I was a corporal. Willame does not know me and will not listen."

"He knows me very well," Tshombe responded. "You will carry a letter from me asking for help. At the appropriate time, I will ask him to move you up in rank so that you will learn how to manage our own army when the Belgians leave for good."

He turned to Sanimbi. "As head of the police, you need to organize your men, assure them that they will be paid, and return order and stability to our city. When our people see shops opening and are able to buy food, we will have their support to combat the problems ahead. You are the perfect person for this job; I know I can count on you." Tshombe reached across the table and shook Sanimbi's hand.

He continued. "Godefroid and I will concentrate on our infrastructure. I see that power has returned,"—he lifted his gaze toward the ceiling fan that had begun to twirl. "Now we need the phones. Most of the Belgian management and engineers have remained at the Union Minière Mines, so our copper is safe. Godefroid, you will be our Minister of Interior. Work with the mines and the utility companies. You will be "Mr. Inside," while I will handle the problems beyond our borders."

"How? Who? Where?" the three men asked almost in unison.

Tshombe began writing furiously and continued the conversation. "The central government in Leopoldville will resist our departure; we have too many assets. Lumumba is already in Stanleyville courting the Soviets. Later this month he will likely fly to Washington to seek the United States' support for his leadership. None of these players will support us either. I am banking on Belgium. They will want a piece of the action here; the copper, the gold, the cobalt. The Americans will sit on their hands, something they do so well. They will shift the responsibility to the United Nations, who will move with deliberation. I have a friend, a young teacher, who has connections in the US. He was educated there and speaks perfect English. I have asked him to visit Belgium and develop a back-up plan, which I will outline to you at our next meeting. Now, let's get on with our tasks."

The following day, within hours of Colonel Willame's agreement to remain with two regiments, Munongo headed for the copper mine. He turned his battered, gray '53 Peugeot off the paved highway onto a dirt road that headed northwest into the hills. The road faithfully shadowed the railway, a spur track servicing the Union Minière du Haut Katanga copper mine some forty-seven kilometers ahead. Kigali sat silently in the front seat, his head turned toward the hot air pouring through the open window. The terrain was not attractive; it was rocky, fallow, with sparse vegetation. The mining office was just beyond the ridge of the hill, which dictated that they drive along the periphery of the giant mine cavity.

Munongo exclaimed, "They are working. I see white faces so the Belgians have remained. *Merci, merci.* Now we need to cut a deal with these shrewd bastards."

The Union Minière was the crown jewel of the DRC. Munongo mentally calculated that if the mine operated normally, without interference, sales this year would exceed 200 million US Dollars. No wonder the Belgians remained, he thought smiling, and they probably think all of this is still theirs. As he parked in a cloud of dust, he made out the faces of the two men standing on the porch that lead to the offices. One was in a military uniform, the other in bush clothes.

Munongo knew both men well. He crossed his fingers hoping his discussion would be with Bordeaux, a friendly but taciturn man. Henri Bordeaux had managed the Union Minière for close to twenty years. He had arrived from Belgium as a young man, worked his way through the company ranks, ultimately taking over at age fifty. He could truthfully say he knew every facet of the mining business. Munongo liked him particularly because of his just and friendly relationship with his native laborers. Colonel Willame was just the opposite: arrogant, intolerant and oppressive.

Munongo chuckled when he heard Willame shout, "Sergeant Kigali, we meet again so soon. Should you not be in uniform?" He took charge and led the three others into an air-conditioned office, sat down first, and waved his swagger stick at three chairs.

"I can't tell you how pleased President Tshombe and I are that you have remained to help us," Munongo said slowly, using the title prematurely. "In a few days we will declare our independence, which will attract the wrath of the Leopoldville government and the world."

"Brussels will not be unhappy," Henri replied. "What will be our relationship?"

"We will be more just with you than you were with us when you were in charge," Munongo said, without batting an eyelash.

"Why don't we retain the same arrangement?" Willame said. "We will manage the mining activities in Katanga and our troops will protect the operation. We will sell the minerals and ore and pay you an attractive royalty." It wasn't expressed as a question, but as fait accompli.

Kigali squirmed but said nothing. He already knew what Tshombe wanted and was sure Munongo would get it.

"Monsieur Bordeaux," Munongo said deferentially, "we want you to stay as general manager of Union Minière. Everything will remain the same as before with the exception that we will jointly manage the sale and distribution of all minerals exported from Katanga. The proceeds will flow into a European bank of our choice and we will split it with you right down the middle."

"You're not serious?" Willame murmured.

"We are dead serious and furthermore, you will pay for all of your operating expenses, both civilian and military, out of your half of the proceeds. Before you say anything, stop and think. You will be the envy of the world. We have giant deposits of uranium, cobalt, tin, and zinc along with this copper. We will share 50/50. Your problem will not be with the Katanga government, it will be with the Leopoldville regime and the United Nations. Lumumba will become hysterical."

Colonel Willame stood, walked to the door and then turned pointing his swagger sick at Munongo. "We will consult with Brussels and advise you of our decision."

"Not advise. Confirm, *naturellement*. If not," he paused for effect, "we will quickly make alternative arrangements," Munongo replied, as he pushed back his chair and got to his feet. "One more item requires your immediate action," he said irritably, handing Bordeaux an envelope. "This contains clear confirmation of our proposition, signed by Tshombe. He also instructs you to transfer 35 million US Dollars to a bank account in Luxembourg. This will partially compensate us for your theft of money belonging to Union Minière and this country. Before we became independent, you cleaned out this mine's bank account. We expect to hear of the transfer within a week. *Au revoir messieurs*."

Washington D.C.

As a boy, Jay Carleton used to fish from the banks of the Mississippi River, on the Missouri side, about 70 miles south of St. Louis. A good student with an affinity for languages, he headed east to George Mason University to study political science. His summers, always spent somewhere in France, provided him with an accent almost acceptable to the French. Jay's name sounded Eastern seaboard, the khaki pants and white bucks helped his ivy image slightly, but to the observant eye, he was a Midwesterner from a small rural farm town. Following two years in the army, where he somehow avoided the Korean conflict, Jay joined the State Department as a junior Foreign Service Officer. After two years in the Bureau of European Affairs, Jay transferred to the Brussels Embassy, with the title of Third Secretary of Embassy. He discovered his true self in Belgium where he encountered wines unknown in Missouri and gastronomy beyond his mid-western imagination. His sole ambition was to remain in French-speaking Europe. His disappointment was enormous when, after three years in the embassy's political office, a marriage to a local girl and a life in which he felt fulfilled, he was transferred back to Washington to be assigned to the newly formed Bureau of African Affairs. His title was Assistant Director of the Office of Central African Affairs. Jay guessed that his selection for this post was based on his fluency in French, the principal language spoken in the Congo and numerous countries and colonies in North Africa.

In Belgium, Jay had been asleep. He had coasted through his duties and certainly had not paid attention to his host countries growing problems in central Africa. He had cultivated few valuable contacts in the Benelux countries, or for that matter, anywhere along the diplomatic channels where he roamed. Jay arrived back in Washington unfilled and, essentially, still inexperienced.

His new responsibility, Africa, was exploding. Something snapped in Jay's mind and he awoke to a new world with challenging responsibilities. Gradually, after years of dormancy, his energy and curiosity began to flow. He spent long hours in his office studying briefs on the changing politics in Africa. Wisely, he cultivated associations with people in Washington who could add to his knowledge bank. By the time the Belgian Congo was on the brink of independence, Jay's competence on its history and politics was good enough to be sought by others in the Department of State.

On July 5, 1960, fishing was on Jay's mind as he jostled his way through the maze of corridors at the State

Department. He absentmindedly greeted colleagues, all eager to talk about their Fourth of July weekend, but Jay's focus was on the events taking place in the middle of Africa. He nodded and waved without stopping and ducked quickly into the African Bureau, walking directly to his office. It was a small area, barely accommodating two straight backed visitors' chairs, but it did have a window and privacy. While he had been fishing the Chesapeake and drinking Black Label on the stern of a 52-foot Grand Banks, the Belgian Congo ceased to exist and overnight became the Democratic Republic of the Congo. He kicked himself. He ought to have remained in his office. Events taking place in the Congo came as no surprise; he was prepared. He was not sure about his superiors, running all the way up the line of command to the President. They were all distracted with Cuba and Vietnam.

He pulled the window blinds to cut the sunlight and temper his anxiety, then stood at his desk, hands resting on the edge, staring at the towering pile of dispatches before him. Most were from the Embassy in Leopoldville, but many dispatches were arriving from embassies and consulates in European capitals, especially Brussels. Jay's head throbbed, a blend of a hangover, sunburn and fatigue. Before he could sit down and digest the memos, the phone rang.

"Good morning, Jay," Jonathan Kitchell purred. Kitch was Jay's boss. "Secretary Herter would like to be briefed on the unfolding Congo situation this morning. I'll see you in the conference room at 10 and," he paused as if debating what he would say next. "Bring along anyone from your section who you feel might add to our discussion. I have asked both AID and the Agency to send someone.

Jay had formed a valuable relationship with a young man in the Bureau who had just returned from Africa. After graduation from Amherst, Bryce Donaldson had spent two years traveling around Africa. He had lived in the Congo for six months. Jay grabbed his phone and dialed. "Bryce, good morning, Jay here. I'll pick you up in an hour. We are having a high command meeting on the Congo. I need you to stay close to me."

"You got it, Jay. I'll be ready."

The conference room was windowless and stark, the incandescent lights transforming everyone's somber countenance to placidness. Nine people sat around the dark rectangular table, coffee cups and papers already littering the surface. Jay recognized five faces, all from his section. He wondered which one was from the Agency. Secretary Herter arrived, accompanied by two aids. He muttered a greeting, grabbed a chair at the end of the table, sank his tall frame on to it and opened the meeting without formality.

"The President called me at dawn asking about the Congo. I'm to brief him tomorrow," he paused and looked around the room, "and as you know, he does not like surprises. We have our hands full at the moment. Both Cuba and Southeast Asia are demanding attention and now the U2 incident. So tell me what you know, without embellishment, noting sources and veracity."

Kitch spoke first; his Ivy accent softened his words. He began with an identification of the major players: our ambassador and consular officers on station, Prime Minister Patrice Lumumba and background on the President elect, Sanimbi Kasavubu. His basic message was that the United States did not want to become directly involved in any stabilization activities. Peacekeeping, if and when required, should be the United Nations' responsibility. Kitch then introduced Jay to the secretary, commenting, "Jay is our eye on the Congo."

Jay's stomach lurched as he rose; his mind went totally blank for what seemed an eternity. Herter eyed him and waited. Jay looked at Donaldson, who winked, and finally Jay began his report.

"Good morning. Let me summarize the mountain of dispatches received over the past twenty-four hours from Ambassador Timberlake. Apparently the phone system is down. He and his staff are safe for the moment; they have water, electricity and some food. The CIA Chief of Station is due to arrive in Leopoldville in five days. Ambassador Timberlake has not been able to contact President Kasavubu or anyone with responsibility. Businesses are closed, the streets are empty and segments of the army are pillaging shops throughout the city. Our embassy had not been able to communicate with our consulates in Stanleyville or Elizabethville."

"Describe the major political figures emerging," Herter asked. "Who is really running the country?"

"The President elect is Sanimbi Kasavubu, a politician familiar to the Department and considered pliant. It is the Prime Minister, Patrice Lumumba, who is our concern." Jay knew a great deal about Lumumba and was about to launch into a description of his background when Herder interrupted.

"What does Timberlake suggest we do immediately?"

Jay hesitated a moment before answering. "He asked for instructions."

Herter looked at Kitchell. "Prepare a letter to President Kasavubu for The President's signature expressing our elation over their independence. Say we support him and the Democratic Republic of Congo as they move forward, etc. etc. However, until our operation is up and running, you might consider contacting our friends in Brussels." Herder thanked everyone and headed for the door.

As the door clicked shut, Jay turned to Kitchell. "There is one other point I failed to mention. Patrice Lumumba has indirectly aired his desire to visit Washington and President Eisenhower." With that, a discussion of Lumumba's background and irrationality ensued. The general opinion of most at the conference table was that Lumumba was in the Soviet camp and should not be trusted.

Kitchell held up his hand to quiet the room. "Before we summarize, I would like to introduce you to a new member of our team, Bryce Donaldson. Bryce spent a good deal of time in Africa while a student and lived in the Congo after his graduation. I thought he could paint a more intimate picture of what we are dealing with in the Congo."

Jay watched Donaldson move quickly to a huge map of Africa hanging from the ceiling. He was impeccably dressed, almost overdone for a hot July day—including cufflinks and a double vent in his jacket. His six foot height, clean-cut looks and deep-resonant voice immediately commanded attention. Quite incidentally, he was a Black American.

Donaldson flashed an enigmatic smile, stabbed his pointer into the middle of the map and began. "The country I am touching with this pointer is no longer *the Congo*. Its new name is the Democratic Republic of the Congo, and its capital is Leopoldville. The Congo is here," he moved the pointer to Brazzaville across the river.

Everyone in the room had missed that minor detail.

"To give you a brief perspective of this new country, picture a land mass the size of our country east of the Mississippi River. The name Congo comes from the ancient Kingdom of Kongo that inhabited the lands at the mouth of the river. But, it's the river itself that shapes the image we all have of the country. The sources of the Congo River are in the highlands and mountains of the East African Rift. The source is fed from Lake Tanganyika and the Luapula River. This deepest of all rivers flows north, and by the time it gradually loops westward, it is broad and fast flowing, making its way through one of the greatest and last rainforests on earth, until finally it reaches the Atlantic Ocean. The DRC is 60% rainforest, 40% savanna. It contains an enormous and vibrant variety of wildlife and exotic hardwoods, and the ground is brimming with mineral wealth: gold, copper, cobalt, diamonds, manganese and uranium. Furthermore, the river presents an enormous potential for hydroelectric power."

Donaldson reached for a glass of water and drank slowly, a gesture speakers often do when in control of themselves and those around them. Jay was impressed, thinking to himself that he needed to get close to this man.

His pointer was now following the river. "Belgians plundered the country with a cynical brutality rarely matched in colonial history. This river was their conduit for discovery, conquest and trade. They bilked the country mercilessly. They will not give any of this up easily."

Someone raised a hand and asked, "Who will run the country now?"

"Ah, that is a great question, and one I cannot answer. I can tell you this; there are fewer than 20 college educated men in the country. Women are relegated to subservience. There are no lawyers, doctors, engineers or university professors. Here is an area where the United States could become involved and make a difference. The army is large but all of the officers were Belgian. We should be concerned about two critical issues: the DRC is strategically placed in the middle of Africa, and its European friends will influence other African countries located all the way to the Mediterranean. According to my contacts in Stanleyville, the Soviets have already inserted military advisors."

He broke off and his eyes took on a sudden weariness. "The potential for chaos—deadly chaos—is what I fear most. When I lived in the Congo, I traveled throughout the country and made many friends there. I am convinced that without law and a strong police force, there will be inter-tribal violence based on historical hatreds. The country will quickly slip into unimaginable poverty and chaos. My bet is that the army is mutinying as we talk. The Congo," he continued with a crooked smile, "is *The Heart of Darkness*, and right now, the heart is weak and the pulse is fast. Thank you."

Nijmegen, Holland

Van Riebeek flew first from Cape Town to Lisbon, where he finalized his banking arrangements. He instructed his Portuguese banker to establish a bank account in Maputo, the capital of Mozambique. He planed to use this account to fund the supply line to Katanga. He felt certain Palmer would agree with his judgment that the Zambezi River would be the safest route.

He spent the night in Lisbon, breakfasted leisurely on the hotel deck overlooking the ocean, and at noon caught a direct flight to Amsterdam. The small Schiphol terminal building teemed with summer tourists, mostly Americans just off their transatlantic flights. Van Riebeek, not wishing to face city traffic or the chore of securing an accommodation, booked a first-class seat on the late afternoon train to Arnhem. Before boarding, he called his nephew, Dieter, with the arrival time.

The bucolic scenery provided pleasant memories for van Riebeek and rendered the rail trip restful and uneventful. When the train came to a halt, Van Riebeek with his one bag in hand, leaped to the platform and walked briskly through the small station to the curb where Dieter was waiting beside his car. The early evening summer light allowed them to navigate the narrow back roads leading to Nijmegen. They drove in silence, Dieter waiting patiently for his crusty uncle to open the conversation. Not until they had stopped at a rural inn for dinner did van Riebeek speak.

"Have you heard from our friends?"

"Yes, someone telephoned yesterday. The person spoke in German but with a foreign accent." Dieter replied.

"What were the instructions?"

"The voice with an accent told me very little. I was given the names of suppliers; some were manufacturers, some simply merchants, and all are in Germany. Apparently you will need a lot of AK-47s. The supplier is in East German and they are expecting my visit in two days."

Van Riebeek let his eyes prowl the small dining room. No one appeared interested in them. "Were you given sources for helmets, uniforms, web belts, and the same type of first aid and medical products we have supplied before?" he said quietly in Dutch.

Dieter knew better than to probe for details. His narrow face remained expressionless. "I have everything I need. I'll be gone four days."

Dieter sat back in his chair to contemplate his trip. For a thirty-five year old Dutchman, he knew a great deal about weapons and the munitions industry. Though he was born in Holland, his German mother retained her citizenship enabling them to move back to Germany in 1935 when he was ten years old. During World War II he worked in a Mauser factory and quickly developed a passion for guns. He studied large and small bore rifle manufacturing in Europe and realized that Germany was behind in both design and production. Mauser recognized his knowledge and moved him to their secluded research and development facility near Berlin. At the end of the war he'd eluded allied investigators by moving back to East Holland and burying himself and his identity in a bicycle factory. His uncle had escaped notice by the allies as well, leaving Germany through Holland, ultimately immigrating to South Africa. It was van Riebeek's insatiable appetite for munitions that lured Dieter back to his passion.

"Let's talk in the car," Dieter suggested and he rose and headed for the cashier. He paid in guilders, chatted briefly with the proprietor, laughing as they shook hands, and headed for the door.

Near midnight, they crossed the West German border with no difficulty. They drove swiftly on the excellent

German roads to Wesel, where Dieter had booked lodging on the outskirts of town. In the hotel parking lot, Dieter turned to his uncle, "Sleep in, Uncle. I must leave for Wiesa early as I will enter East German through the back door."

"One last point," van Riebeek said to his nephew. "Our supplier must be discrete. The crates are to be marked as airplane parts and shipped to a port on the Baltic where we will take possession. They need not know the destination. Our friends will pay them in US Dollars from a European bank. That should be attractive. Can you arrange this?"

"Yes, uncle. Sleep well."

Henley on the Thames

The shell darted cleanly through the rippled water. Eight ores lifted in unison made it look like a caterpillar trying to fly, reaching, catching, stroking, and lifting, all to the cadence of the coxswain in the stern. The oarsmen's arm muscles flexed with each command as their thin, sleek boat shot forward and then held as they reached for another stroke. Henley on the Thames, in July, blossomed like a Renaissance pageant with tents, flags, outdoor kitchens, souvenir peddlers and hundreds of spectators dressed to kill. Colorful hats flapped in the soft breeze. The weather provided an exceptional day, warm, with a sky of blue mixed with high wispy cirrus clouds. Picnics, bleachers and enormous tents, sponsored by London merchants, stippled both banks of the river. Some tents displayed the insignia of a crew, its country or school. The weather, the water and the sport provided a festive atmosphere.

Brian had flown in from Geneva the day before, had rented a car and now stood next to Samantha wearing a charcoal gray English tailored suit. Samantha had complied with the dress code as well, and wore a white frock with a royal blue jacket. Her wide-brim cloche hat's color matched her jacket. A gross grain ribbon in darker blue tied in the back accentuated her sun-streaked ash blond hair, which fell smoothly to her shoulders. She really didn't care about the clothes so long as she had her camera, a professional habit developed early in her career, when she had been caught-up in a developing drama without her equipment. Having her camera close was so ingrained that she almost felt naked without it. A 35mm Nikon with a zoom lens swung on a strap from one shoulder, her other hand held on to Brian's arm.

"Hey, you two," Katheryn shouted from a spot up the hill from where they were standing. "Come on up. We have been waiting for you. Lunch is in the offering." Katheryn stood in front of a large dark-purple tent with white stripes. It belonged to her employer, Brighton Co. Ltd., Fine Wines, and housed an extensive display of wines plus a bar with several wine stewards. The party mood had begun inside the tent.

In one corner Nicholas held forth before a cluster of well dressed women. He spied Samantha, excused himself and walk toward her, arms spread, never looking at Brian. After embracing Samantha, he turned slowly to Brian, and extended his hand. "Nice to see you again. Have you witnessed the pageantry of Henley before?"

"Hello, Nicholas," Brian replied smoothly. "Actually, yes, I have been here before. When I was a student at Magdalen College, I rowed for the Oxford University Boat Club. And after I finished school, when I was living in Cape Town, I had another go at rowing at Henley. We South Africans were beaten badly that year but won the lager drinking contest."

Samantha ignored the men's sparring and took a seat next to Katheryn. The table perched under a canopy, which bordered the front of the tent—sort of a proscenium— offering a sweeping view of the Thames. The scene before her resembled a Brueghel.

"This is spectacular," Samantha gushed turning to Katheryn. "Do you come here every year?"

"Henley has become an important occasion for our company. Our customers and wineries have come to expect us to provide this elaborate tent with a catered lunch and ample wine."

Brian and Nicholas joined them. Nicholas, who enjoyed controlling a conversation, picked up where Katheryn left off. "Henley on the Thames is all about boat racing: different sizes, different distances and different boat designs. But through the years, the occasion has become a fashion feast and one would never know there was a race." "Nicholas carried forth as Brian listened.

Samantha found the shipping business fascinating, for some unknown reason. "Do you travel a lot, Nicholas? Do you ever visit your ships while they are in port?"

"Rarely. I have a couple of engineers working for me who do that. I do travel abroad a bit," Nicholas said looking off toward the river, as if he wished this topic of conversation would end.

Samantha persisted. "Where do you go? You must do business everywhere in the world," she offered, more as a statement than a question.

Katheryn saved him. "He'll never marry. No woman would stand for the life Nicholas leads. He's away all the time."

"I must go. See you back here around four," Nicholas muttered. He moved into the tent, greeted several men at the bar and disappeared through the rear exit.

Sam whispered to Brian, "Take me to the river. I'd like to photograph the action that everyone else is ignoring. "She chucked her cloche, slipped on a blue head-band, clasped her camera in one hand and Brian's arm in the other and they headed down the hill.

Brian pointed toward a jetty where a long sweep-oar boat was being lifted from the water. "That's the University of Cape Town boat and I know the crew. I used to be one of their coaches. Most boats represent clubs or schools yet country competition inevitably presents itself. That boat is South Africa's great hope. They're a strong team. Come, let's go down and meet them and I can explain the sport better by showing you each type of boat."

The team members all knew Brian and greeted him exuberantly. The coxswain was diminutive and appeared older than his oarsmen who were, to a man, young, sun tanned and extremely fit. There were several types of boats racked on the dock. Brian stood in front of one with his arm around the bow and said, "I rowed on this type of boat when I was at Oxford. It's an eight man sweep-oar boat. Each man holds one oar. If his ore is on the port side, he is on the stroke side and if the oar is on the starboard side, it's called the bow side. That small man that you just met is the coxswain. He sits in the stern and steers the boat, encourages the crew and controls the rate of their strokes.

The combinations are endless; four-man or "quads" and eight-man, with or without a 'cox', and then you have the sculls where the crew rows with two oars, one on either side. Sculls are especially challenging because the oar handles overlap at the mid point forcing the oarsman to keep one handle above the other.

As she listened, Sam scrutinized this man from Africa who was slowly and systematically captivating her. He fit in with the rowing team. The same fitness, the same energy. His face reflected no guile. It was the broad chin that gave it strength. She loved looking at him. She swung the camera to her eye and snapped this beguiling face with the soft brown eyes looking into the lens.

"You're not listening to me," Brian admonished, shaking his head.

"Stay where you are. I want all of you lined up along the boat—maybe for a magazine cover."

The sun was warm, the air wonderful. Brian put his arm around her and they strolled along the racks of boats until they reached the end of the dock. The river bulged here and the current appeared to diminish as it parted around Temple Island where the races start. Meadows stretched up from the river and eventually blended into wooded hills. Samantha didn't covet photographing landscapes, yet the mélange of colors was too compelling and the racing fine boats added zest. Her camera clicked. She swung the camera angle to the right, along the river bank, attempting to catch the British in full dress. She zoomed, looking for the wildest hat. Suddenly she held the camera still, working the focus. It was Nicholas talking with another man. Always curious, Sam zoomed to the maximum and centered on their heads and shoulders. The conversation appeared serious. Both men stood stone still. Their faces were inexpressive. Nicholas kept looking around while the other man talked. He was older, thin hair and bent forward slightly as older men do. His suit was dated. He did not belong here, Samantha thought as she snapped two photos. At that moment, Nicholas looked in her direction. She jumped back behind one of the shells. Why am I hiding and sneaking shots of Nicholas, she frowned at her own silliness. Did he see me?

Brian decided to visit the Oxford Club jetty located a good hike along the river bank. Samantha headed back up the hill to the Brighten tent. It was now three o'clock; she preferred to sit on the deck to watch the passing parade of people.

There were two more tables under the canopy, both to Sam's right. At the far table two men were speaking earnestly in French. She noticed them because of the language they were using and because one of them was a black man, and from his profile, handsome. The other table on the deck was unoccupied. She settled in at the far end table and spread out her photographic equipment. She remained aware of the French being spoken; like background music. Her fluency in French was excellent but rusty from lack of use. Gradually, words and phrases from their conversation began to intrude upon her thoughts and then, quite suddenly, she was listening attentively. They were not talking loudly but seemed secure in the French language knowing the British were rarely able to cope with foreign languages. The stocky man had a raspy voice and was doing most of the talking. He wasn't French; perhaps Belgian and the conversation soon confirmed that. He was ex-military, she guessed.

The man that Nicholas had been talking with when she found them in her zoom lens appeared on the deck and strode past her table. Sam looked up and their eyes locked briefly. He took no notice and walked to the far table where 'raspy voice' introduced him to the black man. Sam never looked their way again but she heard a great deal of what they had to say. What they were discussing took her breath away. They were talking about weapons, gun-running and the Congo. How extraordinary, she thought, plotting death in this bucolic ambiance. Sam could hear the black man clearly. His voice was deep and resonant. He was the buyer and he came from the Congo.

Brian, Katheryn and Nicholas all arrived simultaneously from different directions. Their arrival disturbed the discussion going on in French. The stocky fellow stood, gathered some papers, quickly shook hands and departed. Katheryn noticed them and waved at the older man. "Karel, come over and meet my friends and join us for a drink."

The black man stood and observed. Samantha looked at him more closely. His stature was distinctive; tall and broad shouldered and his dress was impeccable. The older man arrived at her table and shook Katheryn's hand. Then, before she could introduce him, he turned to Samantha and asked her in French, "I couldn't help noticing you working with your camera equipment. I'm planning to buy a camera and I wonder if you could offer some advice on which models I should consider."

Brian stifled his surprise as he stood, but it was Samantha who replied courteously in English, "I'm afraid I don't speak French. I'm an American and we're terrible linguists. You speak English, perhaps?" She smiled up at him.

"Please excuse my impertinence. We have been talking at our table in French and I sort of lost myself." His English was good but with a guttural tone that Samantha couldn't place.

Katheryn introduced him to Brian and Nicholas. "Karel van Riebeek is one of our most important suppliers." Van Riebeek shook hands with Nicholas as if they were meeting for the first time.

This is extraordinary, Sam thought. What's going on?

"I own a wine import business in Cape Town and a small vineyard in Stellenbosch, South Africa's main wine growing district," van Riebeek offered. "Part of the fun of my business is to visit Henley every year and showcase my products. Samuel Brighten and I exchange wine and we have become good friends. And of course, it's winter in Cape Town—June can be a most unpleasant month."

The African man had now joined them and van Riebeek introduced him as his friend from Katanga, Thomas Kimbamba, who greeted everyone in English. "Please use my Christian name, Thomas."

What is going on here, Samantha asked herself again? This is becoming very interesting.

Samantha studied van Riebeek while he remained standing. He had a narrow angular face, featuring a small pointed nose with two lines deeply etched in his cheeks from the edge of his thin lips downward toward a long thin jaw. His skin was pale, almost pasty—unhealthy looking. He combed his sparse hair straight back giving wide berth to large ears. His countenance was malevolent and appeared weary of life. His penetrating, peregrine eyes peered at Samantha, holding her gaze for several seconds. Sam struggled to control her breathing. Was he on to her? Then, casually, Van Riebeek turned back to Brian and said, "I am very proud of my Riesling and Mr. Brighten has a case here. I would be honored if you would try a glass." Without waiting for a reply, Van Riebeek disappeared into the tent.

Brian moved a chair so that Thomas could sit between him and Samantha. He readily accepted and dropped his large, athletic frame smoothly into the chair. "Katanga is the southern province of the Congo, is it not?" Brian asked.

"That's correct," Thomas replied in an American accent. He was obviously very comfortable in English. His full lips parted into a broad smile and he continued, "Today, Katanga is still a province but tomorrow, who knows? Maybe it will be an independent country."

Brian restrained his excitement. "The Congo became independent two weeks ago. The Belgians have finally left. In fact, I think the Belgian king is attending the ceremonies in Leopoldville right now. You are missing all the excitement, Mr. Kimbamba?"

Thomas leaned forward and folded his giant hands on the table. "If I had been there today I would have remained in Katanga. The Belgians are leaving us with a decrepit infrastructure with very few who are trained to teach in our schools, operate the few hospitals that exist or manage our country. There will be chaos, especially in Leopoldville. Many will die. It is not a good place to be right now."

Van Riebeek reappeared followed by a waiter carrying a bottle of white wine, a cooler and six glasses. "Riesling," he announced, "must be served very cold." He took the bottle from the waiter and held it so that Brian and Sam could read the label.

Riebeek Cellars
Stellenbosch
South Africa
Riesling
1958

He poured the wine into each glass and then held his up, grasping it by the stem. "The long stem has a purpose. If you hold it instead of cupping the glass with your hand, the wine will remain chilled."

Samantha watched Brian and then Nicholas. Both were very quiet. She watched Thomas grasp the stem of his glass and say, "To the Congo and its rebirth."

"I will drink to that," Samantha said, noting the ambiguity of his toast.

Van Riebeek looked first at Brian and then back to Samantha, ignoring Nicholas. "Are you in the wine business?"

"No, we're both here as guest of Katheryn"

Brian offered no information, to Sam's relief. It was she who continued. "Actually I am living in London for a year or so. I am a professional photographer and I work for *Echo*, a small American magazine."

"I read *Echo* periodically," Thomas said. "Don't tell me you are the photographer who took the famous Guevara photo? I remember that issue; the photographs were sensational.

"Yes, that was my work, but only the pictures. I'm not a journalist."

"What is your preferred canvas?" Thomas asked with keen interested.

"I like to photograph people in all walks of life. There is so much inequality in our world today; misery, unhappiness, pain and brutality. I want to record it. My market, by and large, is the United States, an insular nation. The vast majority of Americans are ignorant of world injustices and are reluctant to become involved. I hope my photographs jolt them into reality, but I rather think, regrettably, that most sink back into lethargy."

Nicholas stood, apologized to Katheryn that he had another commitment, shook hand with everyone at the table and marched off.

Thomas continued to probe. "Tell me, do you ever shoot a prosaic subject or must it always be intense drama?"

Samantha laughed. "I have just returned from a week in Norway where I photographed my brother's wedding. A few of the shots will be buried in the back of the next issue."

"Well," Thomas said, smiling broadly, "you must visit Katanga sometime. Maybe in a few months after the dust of independence settles. I would be pleased to show you around. I might even be able to introduce you to our leader, Moise Tshombe."

Samantha extracted a card from her pocket. "Here's my contact information. I would accept you invitation, whenever you felt my visit would be convenient for you."

Van Riebeek had remained stony silent throughout this exchange. He waved his hand as if to dismiss Thomas and offered, "Katanga is much too dangerous, Miss Norquist. Come to South Africa. We have so many possibilities for your magazine." He handed Samantha his business card and gave another to Brian. "I am serious. Please come and call on me. I will show you the most beautiful wine terrain in the world. And now, Mr. Kimbamba and I must be off. How very kind it was of you to ask us to join you."

Thomas leaned toward Samantha. His deep voice hushed. "There will be a time, perhaps soon, when it would be appropriate for you to visit Katanga. It might be mutually beneficial. And selfishly, I would enjoy showing you a magnificent country with unimaginable trees and flowers and birds and animals that will awaken your countrymen to a new world. Your camera would have much work to do in my country." When he stood, he then turned to Brian and extended his hand. "You have been very quiet, Mr. Wellesley. You are English? Do you live in London as well?"

Brian took his hand and smiled. "I'm South African, actually, but I live in Switzerland."

Thomas's eyebrows arched. "Very interesting. You are an African. When Miss Norquist decides to visit my country, you should come with her." He turned and vanished through the tent flap.

Later, back at the mews, Samantha cradled the phone to her ear. "Hi Meredith, it's Sam. Is it too early to talk?"

"I was going to call you. Our July issue is on the stands. Have you seen it? No—you haven't seen it yet—well, wait until it hits Europe. You, my dear, will be famous. We have the frowning Mullah on the cover and the issue focuses on Iran. Your photographs are marvelous and insightful. I'm sure you will receive calls from every direction. Just remember, you are an *Echo* girl. How is swinging London treating you? I hear you were at the Henley Regatta."

"That's what I want to talk about. I met some interesting people at the Regatta. I think I'm on to a story which, if it develops, will knock your socks off. I can't give you any specifics now. But I do need your permission to spend some time on this story and a little money for research and travel."

"Give me something to chew on, Sam. Travel where?"

"Africa."

"Well . . . hmm . . . Africa is a big place. Where in Africa?"

"Belgian Congo, or I should say the Democratic Republic of Congo. Give me a few days to develop solid information. I need the promised invitation or I'll never get into that country."

"I'll give you three months, but I want you to check in at least once a fortnight. Funds will be wired to your London bank. Also, I just received your photographs from the Oslo wedding. It's not a lead article unless your brother will allow us to put Mette on the cover." As she chuckled, Sam could picture her with her feet on the window sill looking out at Manhattan.

"You can do what you want with the Norway photos and next week you will have my shots of the Regatta. Why not introduce Middle America to Henley on the Thames? Take care. I'll be in touch."

Samantha stared at the phone while pondering the events of the day. She wanted to go to Katanga. There was a huge story there and pictures could tell it. Should she contact Thomas Kimbamba or chance that he would invite her right away? The discussion on gun smuggling made her blood rush. She had not shared this with Brian nor had she told him about Nicholas and van Riebeek. She needed to do that, but there was one person she wanted to talk with first. She found her uncle's home number and asked the international operator to put the call through.

His voice sounded just like her father's. "Samantha, what a delightful surprise. Your call makes this old man very happy. Why am I so honored?"

Samantha explained everything to her Uncle Arne. He was a senior officer at the CIA and had spent his life involved in the Agency's activities in Southeast Asia. "I want this story, Uncle Arne. And the story includes the smuggling aspect. How can we cooperate on this?"

Arne laughed. "You're messing with dangerous stuff, Sam. What's the man's name who might invite you?"

"Kimbamba. He's an aide to, or at least a friend of, Tshombe."

"Let me chat with the people here who would know about the situation. In the meantime, you should not go to Central Africa until it returns to status quo. May I also suggest that you talk to your boyfriend at the UN. He should provide the smuggling information to Interpol."

Sam and her uncle exchanged news of their family, promised to contact each other, and rang off.

AUGUST 1960

Washington D.C.

The drama emerging in the Democratic Republic of the Congo shifted by the hour. Kitchell realized that the country was slipping into anarchy and he found the US's inattention alarming. The State Department's preoccupation with the Cold War along with events in Vietnam left him with the responsibility to monitor and respond to events in the DRC. As Deputy Assistant Secretary for AF/C (African Affairs, Central), it was his task to understand the events transpiring. On Thursday, August 3, he called Jay Carleton, instructing him to set up a meeting with all "players" for Friday morning. There had been random discussions held during the past month, yet no one at State appeared to grasp the significance of the events occurring in the DRC. President Eisenhower demanded both evaluations and solutions.

Meanwhile, across the Potomac, the Central Intelligence Agency was exhibiting intense interest in Central Africa. The Agency had rushed one of its best men, Larry Devlin, to Leopoldville in early July. His terse reports caused anxiety. On this same Thursday, Director Allen Dulles made a rare call to his counter-part at State, Christian Herter. "Good morning, Christian." Both men usually observed formality, but Dulles sensed he should use Herter's first name. "Do you have anyone with knowledge of what is happening in the DRC?"

"Ah yes, the Congo, or rather the old Congo," Secretary Herter almost whispered, after a long moment. "The President asked the same question just yesterday. The answer is yes and no. We seem to have been caught with our drawers around our knees. Tomorrow we're assembling our knowledge in one room. I will call you with a summary of our discussion."

"I have a suggestion," Allen said quickly. "Send four or five of your most involved people over here tomorrow. I will ask Dick Bissell to set up a meeting with our Central African Bureau. How about 10 a.m.? The front desk will direct your people."

Jay Carleton had been on pins and needles from the moment he stood in the shower at 6 a.m. He had never been on the Agency grounds, and was both excited and intimidated. His anxiety mounted when he considered the paucity of hard data coming out of the DRC. He knew Kitchell would call on him first. Jay had asked Donaldson to accompany him.

The first thing Jay noticed upon entering the conference room at Langley was the total absence of papers on the table. The four men on one side of the empty table rose to greet their visitors from the Department of State. Jasper Fox, a small man, almost dainty, with hawk-like facial features and a tuft of red hair, introduced his colleagues. Jay knew he was an assistant to Bissell and not the senior man in the room. A non-descript fellow, with gray hair and rimless glasses, stood next to Fox, peering quizzically at the three rather low echelon men from State. Bronson Tweedy ran CIA's activities in Africa, his hands periodically immersed in murky activities. His hint of a British accent tempered his dominating presence. Sitting next to Tweedy was the young, well-dressed Larry Madison, who smiled affably when introduced. The fourth attendee, tall and Nordic, sat somewhat removed at the end of the table. He introduced himself as Arne, without explaining his presence as an observer. The redheaded man began the discussion.

"Good to see you again, Kitch. I know time is precious for you, so let's get started. We are most anxious to improve our intelligence bank on the DCR. The Director indicated that you had fresh information," he hedged, while moving the control of the conversation to the other side of the room.

Kitchell picked up the gauntlet. "Our reports from Ambassador Timberlake are sketchy. Apparently most Belgian military officers simply boarded outbound planes, leaving the Congo army directionless. Some elements of the DRC army have run amok, terrorizing foreigners attempting to leave the country. They are fighting among themselves as well. The violence and anarchy have prevented our people from meeting with President Kasavubu. Our best information is coming from Brussels. We just learned that the United Nations has ordered the remaining Belgian military units to withdraw immediately."

Before he could continue, Tweedy interrupted brusquely. "It would be best if we not depend on the Belgians for our information. They may not provide disinformation, but they don't tell us everything. For example, they are inserting paratroopers into Katanga as we speak. Pardon my interruption."

Kitchell picked up a piece of paper and slid it across the table to Tweedy before picking up where he left off. "Secretary Herter wrote this letter to President Kasavubu offering both congratulations and recognition. Our sense is that we should remain somewhat removed until the country stabilizes, and then offer aid and assistance to hospitals, schools, farmers, etc."

Fox, looking like a rooster, his head jerking forward, asked, "Where is Lumumba?"

Jay jumped in to the fray. "As you no doubt know, he was here last week. President Eisenhower would not see him. However he did meet briefly with our Secretary, before heading to the United Nations. Lumumba is deeply concerned about Katanga's secession. He and the secretary-general discussed this core issue during their meeting in New York. Later, Hammarskjöld told the press he would declare that Katanga's secession posed a threat to international peace. He planned to ask the Security Council to pass a resolution calling for the complete withdrawal of Belgian troops from all areas of the DRC, with the United Nation's peace keeping forces replacing them."

Tweedy bumped in again. "I suspect Lumumba is back in the DRC, probably not in Leopoldville, but more likely heading for Kisangani where he has strong support."

Jay continued, "He is the Prime Minister, which is the most powerful and influential office in the DRC right now.

He is bright, charismatic and pulls strong support from the tribes in the east. We need to deal with him."

"What do you mean, *deal with him*?" Fox's squeaky voice emerged, sounding an octave higher.

"I would like our ambassador to meet with him soon and establish a dialogue," Kitchell replied.

Tweedy leaned forward in his chair, folding his hands in front of him, his eyes sweeping the faces before him. "He is not our friend. He is a bloody commie and he's already working with the Soviets. We have reports of a number of twin-engine Russian Il-14 cargo/passenger planes landing at Ndjili carrying at least 200 Russian advisors, plus many boxes marked with a Red Cross symbol. The boxes seem remarkably similar to small arms and ammunition crates. I'm not sure your strategy is the right one but something must be done quickly; the Soviets covet the Congo and they are moving swiftly."

"We have it from the top. Do not get involved. Let the UN handle the security and politics in the DRC." Kitchell leveled this pronouncement almost defensively.

Fox turned to Madison. "Larry, you should share the information you developed in London."

"Yes. I had the good fortune of meeting with a close confidant of Tshombe. His name is Thomas Kimbamba. I believe he is an unofficial emissary of the secessionist province of Katanga. He informed me that President Tshombe wants him to visit Washington in order to lobby Katanga's desire to establish a close relationship with us. I gathered from our talk that Tshombe dislikes Lumumba and prevented him from visiting Katanga. If you like, I could arrange for him to meet with you when he comes here."

"We would like that very much. Thanks. Do you have any information on the DRC military?" Jay questioned.

Larry answered quickly. "There is one man who is quietly emerging as a force in the army. His name is Mobutu. We know only that he was a sergeant in the Belgian Congo army and has emerged as a confidant of both Kasavubu and Lumumba. Our station manager in Leopoldville is arranging to meet with him. We think he is a man to watch."

Jasper Fox stood and dismissed further discussion. "Thanks for trooping over here, gentleman. I understand my contact at State is Jay," he said with a tight smile and stuck out his small hand.

After the three State Department officers departed, the four men remaining sat in silence. Finally Bronson stood and paced the floor before stopping to turn to the others. "I have solid orders to eliminate Lumumba, one way or another. There is a Security Council meeting on the 18th and I understand this subject is on the agenda. We will wait for their decision." He turned to Arne Norquist and smiled. "Arne, you have been very quiet. What do make of all of this?"

Arne shrugged and unwound his tall frame from his chair. "I'm a Southeast Asia guy, so this is new territory. This young fellow," pointing to Larry Madison, "suggested I sit in. I found Larry when I search our files for Kimbamba. Where did I get his name? Well, strange as it seems, my niece who lives in London, met Kimbamba recently. She is a photojournalist and believes he will invite her to visit Katanga."

"Can we contact her?" Fox asked.

"I'd rather you didn't. She will call me and I'll keep you in the picture. As to our meeting this morning, what strikes me as peculiar is State's paucity of information on Katanga. Tshombe declared the province independent and my understanding is that there are one thousand five hundred Belgian paratroopers and army personnel in a staging area near Kamina. This will be a big problem for you. They will fight for their independence and the UN will attempt to intervene. My suggestion is that you cultivate Kimbamba."

London

Les Ambassadeurs was not incognito. The elite club occupied an elaborate building nestled on Hamilton Place in Mayfair. The building professed opulence and its purpose was for gambling and dining. It was a club suited for the upper end of society and offered a legitimate and secure environment for the wealthy after public London closed down at 11 p.m. Henry VIII allegedly had placed his hunting lodge on the land now occupied by Les 'A', as it was fondly known by its members.

Samantha and Brian sat at a table near a window in the far corner of the lavish dining room. A sudden summer rain squall pelted the window, obscuring a view of pedestrians cowering under their umbrellas or scurrying for cover. A lamp on the table flooded the starched table cloth and silverware with light but left their faces largely in shadows. Samantha furtively studied his hands. They were tanned and sinewy; the dark hair on the back looked sun bleached and was offset by perfectly manicured nails. Sam smiled to herself and thought how much Brian was like his hand: strong, athletic, and always casually well-groomed.

"May I select a glass of Chablis for you?" he asked signaling for the waiter.

Sam looked up and nodded. She reached out to cover his hand with hers. "Oh Brian, I'm so relaxed being with you. I really like that we have so much to talk about. Right now I have something really important to tell you but first, tell me, who belongs to this fancy club besides an impoverished UN officer?"

"Well, let's see . . . ," he said with a wry smile. "Don't turn around, but Zsa Zsa Gabor is just behind you."

Sam was about to peek when she saw a party led by a beaming maître d' navigating toward an empty table. As they moved past, Roger Moore turned and slapped Brian on the shoulder. "Brian, my dear fellow, how are you? Are you living in London these days?"

"Hello Roger," Brian said standing to shake hands. "May I introduce Samantha Norquist?"

"Now I know why you're here," Moore said arching his famous eyebrows while engulfing Sam's hand in his enormous paw. "Let's get together," he offered while still looking at Sam before he sauntered off toward his table.

"My father handled some legal work for Roger in South Africa. Something about a movie that never happened. I met him in Cape Town when he stopped on his way to India. Amazing that he would remember me. Anyway, now you have met a member of this club."

Sam's eyes roamed the dining room, settling subtly and briefly on each table. The combination of lavish décor, an international set, both young and mature, everyone dressed to kill and the cacophony of conversation exuded unadulterated pleasure. The world's economic playing field is so tilted, she thought. War in Southeast Asia, tribal slaughter in the old Belgian Congo and inexplicable poverty and bigotry in Brian's country were egregious examples of a long list of human lunacies. And here we sit, poised to relish Dover sole. But the world has always been composed of inequities, she rationalized. It will never change; I will therefore enjoy this fish and being with this man, she decided firmly.

They were silent for awhile, enjoying this discovered moment. It had been just thirty days since they were together in Henley. Brian's month long absence had carved a void in her existence, which for her was a new sensitivity. Samantha's romances had always been confined to the moment, which she admitted, cast them as shallow. Discussing the future was forbidden and inquiring into the past occurred rarely, for she and her men never delved deeply. It was her preference—she liked her freedom. Sam never acknowledged her selfishness. But with Brian, she hungered for knowledge of his life—his family, friends and youth, his aspirations, his values and direction and . . . how he felt about her. Can there be karmic connections between souls, she wondered? Am I destined to love only one man or are there random possibilities? She looked up into Brian's face and searched for an answer. The tight, unblemished skin of his lean face was tanned to the color of polished amber. His long, fine nose stretched from under the shelter of thick, wide eyebrows to a guileless mouth that squeezed her heart when he smiled.

"Have you been traveling?" She broke the spell.

"DRC again. We have inserted peace keeping troops—Swedish. South Africa and Belgium, naturally, are objecting. The French are no help."

"What about Katanga's session?"

"Lumumba is having a fit. The Leopoldville government is in disarray and threatening to send troops into Katanga. The secretary-general wants us to do the same." Brian sat back as his plate was removed. "What have you decided to do about the gun smuggling conversation you overheard in Henley? I can't sit on this information much longer."

"My uncle called me back. He's worried that African gunrunning would be no more than a pot hole in the CIA's current agenda. The information was vague and not verified. He suggested that you turn what little we know over to Interpol. And, I must tell you," Sam paused and took a deep breath, "I've written to Mr. Kimbamba. The note probably will never make it to Katanga, but . . . I want this story, Brian. It could be huge."

Brian leaned forward, resting his elbows on the table and Samantha felt the burning intensity of his eyes, but he said unemotionally, "I know what you do for a living. It is an inherently dangerous profession. And visiting Katanga right now would not be prudent." He touched her hand and his eyes softened. "Our affair is no long an infatuation. I feel deeply that you should not go." Brain smiled gamely. "Let's go to Cape Town. I know the head of Interpol. She and I attended school together."

Samantha held onto his hand. "Why don't we talk about this tomorrow before you leave for Geneva? It's getting late and we're supposed to meet up with Katheryn and a group of her friends. Let's find a taxi."

They simultaneously noticed the huge, owl-shaped headlights of a Bentley swing out from a parking space on the street, maneuvering silently to where they were standing under their umbrellas. The back door opened and a voice from within barked, "Get in. I've come to save you from the rain. We are all waiting for you at Jennebell's. And Samantha, I get the first dance." It was Nicholas.

Katanga

Tshombe's command center was on the ground floor of the Belgian officer's club, a relic of early colonial days. The golf course had returned to nature; it was now thick brush, home to small animals, snakes and colorful birds. A large, murky, green pond in front of a veranda provided a landing strip for migratory birds. Ten Wattled Cranes consumed Tshombe's attention as he stood leaning on the deck railing. Munongo stood next to him with his back to the pond. He was watching the frantic activity transpiring inside, visible through the large windows now open to capture a breeze. The two men talked without looking at each other.

"We have reports that Lumumba is in Kasai." Munongo's voice was conspiratorial.

"Look, here comes another formation of these beautiful birds. They are probably on their way to the delta." Tshombe gazed at the birds before responding. "Lumumba could be anywhere. He is a ghost; yesterday in New York, today on our border and tomorrow—who knows—probably Stanleyville? We've been independent for one month and already our enemies are knocking at our door. Kasavubu has moved several regiments of DRC troops into the Kasai province, threatening us, but more probably searching for gold."

Munongo turned toward Tshombe, who continued to gaze at the activity on the pond. "What should be our response?"

"Instruct Colonel Willame to station a third of his men on our northern border. Our brothers from the north will not fight when faced with trained and well-armed foreign troops. Where are his men located now?"

"Most are camped along the river on the far side of the mines."

"Good," Tshombe growled. "Leave half there and move the rest to the perimeter of the airport. I have just learned that the UN is planning to airlift their Ghanaian and Tunisian soldiers and have asked for clearance to land here next week. Have Kigali take control of the airport and do not allow any planes to land."

Munongo motioned to Kigali, who was standing just inside the French doors. His posture was menacing, arms folded on his chest and a frown creasing his forehead. He wore a Belgian officer's uniform with his lapel boasting glistening Captain Bars.

"Ah, Kigali," Tshombe said with a smile, turning toward Kigali as he walked toward them. "I see you have made rapid advancement. The last time we were together, you were a sergeant. Colonel Willame recognizes talent."

"I commissioned myself," Kigali said perfunctorily. "I don't trust the Belgians. They will be leaving soon anyway."

"Have you moved ahead with your plan to form a Katanga army?" Tshombe asked.

"I have some men, but we have no equipment. We need uniforms and weapons."

"I'm working on that. Have you seen Thomas Kimbamba this morning?"

Kigali glared at Tshombe. "He is here somewhere—asking to see you. I told him to come back later. I don't trust him. He's from the Lingala tribe. They are not dependable and this man is too foreign. He is not one of us. Be careful of him."

"I will do that. Find Kimbamba and ask him to join me on the deck. Munongo is heading for the airport now. You should join him and have your men train there."

Soon Thomas appeared wearing a sport jacket and dark trousers. He smiled and shook Tshombe's hand. "I have many things to report."

"Good. Let's talk in the corner, away from the commotion. How did your trip go?"

Thomas handed Tshombe a large envelope. "Here are the documents covering the Luxemburg bank and our arrangement with them. I telephoned them from London. Our account has received a large deposit."

"Excellent, excellent," Tshombe murmured. "How did your meeting go with the gun people?"

"Leclercq accepted our proposal and can deliver. His source is South African. No surprise there. We are to transfer US$200,000 to a Liechtenstein bank immediately. They will arrange for the supply of all our requirements, including three mercenaries. The first delivery will be in October."

"When can you leave for the United States? We need America's support or at least a commitment to not interfere." Tshombe placed his hand on Thomas's arm. "Your mission is critical for our survival."

"I have a request, or maybe I should call it a suggestion, which could benefit Katanga. I met an American photographer in London who expressed a keen interest in visiting Katanga in order to portray our country in a respected American magazine. It would enhance our image and persuade influential people to stand with us. She is an extraordinary photographer, not a journalist, and would not ask questions."

"She!" Tshombe exclaimed. "Not a good idea for a western woman to be trooping around at this time. We can expect our brothers from the North and the UN to be knocking on our door at any moment." He waved his hand to dismiss the suggestion.

Thomas persisted. "I would stay with her the entire time to make sure that she was photographing what we want. And," he paused and smiled, "she would put your face on the cover of her magazine."

Tshombe's expression slowly transformed from a scowl to comprehension; a smile of satisfaction appeared. "On reflection, it might be a good ploy." He nodded to himself. "Let me know in advance when she will be here."

SEPTEMBER 1960

Northern Rhodesia

Leopards are nocturnal hunters, elusive and cunning. They kill by clamping their jaw on the throat of their prey, thereby choking them. They are able to drag a victim weighing twice their own weight up a tree for safe keeping. Leopards are cautious and vigilant, evaporating at the first hint of danger. The plateau and savanna of Northern Rhodesia offers the perfect habitat for leopards with its ample game and thick tree cover near the rivers. The other trophy animals are larger and seem fiercer, but it was the Square Rosette Leopard that became the prize for big game hunters because it is tricky to isolate and requires a long true shot. It was always that shot that worried Morgan Palmer most when hunting with amateurs.

The male-puku carcass dangled from a thick branch of the acacia tree. Several ropes were attached to its hind legs, which were strung so that the carcass remained out of the reach of hyenas. Palmer admired his work.

The puku's position was perfect. A cat would need to climb the trunk and move along the main branch to reach it. The leopard's torso would be broadside to a hunter positioned 100 meters downwind. The acacia grew in front of a sparse grove of river bush willow, which gave a perfect backdrop to the lure.

Winter had arrived late this year on the Luangwa plateau. It was now early September and it had not rained for three months, leaving the grassland parched and dusty. The grazing animals were on the move, searching for lower grasslands and water. Palmer had placed his camp site in a sheltered ravine near the river shore, about three kilometers from where he was standing. His top hunter had shot the puku in a dombo north of their camp along the Luangwa River. He and the two natives hired by Palmer had hoisted it up the tree. Palmer was now carefully tightening the connection screw on the Weaver adjustable scope to the 30-06 Winchester and then he positioned the rifle for a clean shot to where he suspected the animal would crouch in the tree. He set the tripod securely on the ground close to a rock formation, allowing a clear view of the tree, the bait and the surrounding area. The scope was aimed at a spot three feet to the right of the carcass. Palmer slipped a cartridge into the chamber, set the lock, and lay down again on the blanket to correct the rifle's elevation fractionally. The afternoon temperature was a perfect 18°C with a soft breeze coming off of the plain. The wind would die down once the sun slipped over the hills.

Palmer looked back at his client from Oklahoma, Roscoe Lambert, who lounged in the comfort of a canvas chair. He didn't belong here, Palmer reflected. The out-of-doors was not his arena; he belonged in a library or an expensive restaurant. Lambert's short, plump frame reflected this life-style. Like most of his clients, Palmer guessed that the only thing Lambert—or maybe his wife—wanted was a trophy for his den wall. The tall boots, multi-pocketed jacket and wide-brimmed hat misrepresented him. Morgan knew that deep down Lambert didn't want to kill anything.

Two white men worked along with Palmer to prepare the shoot site. Both were a sun-baked brown and moved with a litheness acquired from a life on the savanna. One of the men, Lynch, the one who had shot the bait, worked with the two natives securing the puku and removing evidence of their presence. The second hunter, a young man named Keane, hung back with the gun bearers, squatting next to the Range Rover as he cleaned his large hunting knife.

Morgan Palmer was everything his clients were not: confident, commanding, attractive and eminently personable. He had just turned forty-one, still muscular and sinuous, and spoke with a mellifluous voice that carried both strength and certainty. His voice was like a magnet; it captured your attention and held it. In the evenings after dinner, he sometimes played his guitar and sang, his eyes closed, as he seemed to drift into a different world. In the firelight, his dark features, long black hair and bushy dark eyebrows would invariably attract the gaze of the women on safari.

Although Morgan appeared insouciant to his safari clients, his true nature was as dark as his Welsh countenance. His moods sometime revealed an unexplained anger with people, a shadowy mood that startled those around him with its intensity. His affinity was for animals; he understood them and respected them. He took no joy in killing them. It was a business and he was selective and compassionate when game was found. He held no such admiration for people, black or white; his relationship with humans was as a puppeteer. Once, on safari, after an explosive outburst, Morgan tried to explain his moods to a very good client.

"My mind and body are in tune with nature, with the life on this grassy plateau. I am at peace in the silence that reigns here. Humans disturb the tranquility of this place, and in turn, my mind. It's then that I erupt and for this display of poor manners, I apologize to you."

The Palmer family name went back generations; the clan had spread throughout Wales and in the twentieth century some had restlessly migrated to lands offering hope and prosperity. His father, mother and sister immigrated to the British colony of Rhodesia in 1914 and began farming tobacco. Morgan was born in 1919, his younger brother arriving two years later. Tobacco, as a cash crop, provided a tenuous income, always in flux, dictating that the Morgan family live close to the ground. Their laborers were black, transient and undependable. His sister was raped and brutally beaten by a gang of farm hands. This heinous act not only institutionalized his sister, it altered Morgan's attitude toward black Africa. He lost respect for both the black natives and the ruling white government. He knew he could not continue farming and decided he needed to leave Africa for a while. His love of books compelled him to seek further education, so he applied to Aberystwyth University in Wales. He left home in 1938, a week after his acceptance arrived. His discipline would be English and Welsh literature, which allowed him time to pursue his passion for music. He divided his time between the library and the choir. Then, his studies were interrupted. War arrived in Europe and Africa.

Morgan returned to Rhodesia to join the Rhodesian African Rifles. He quickly learned how to survive in the African bush and mastered the use of weapons. In 1945, he was discharged with the rank of Captain and he immediately returned to Wales.

After completing his education, Morgan returned to Rhodesia to help his father. The market for tobacco was thin, hampered by the growing animosity between blacks and whites. He endured five futile years on the farm and as an officer in the fledgling counterinsurgency police force. Finally, his life reached a point of hopelessness and he chucked everything and headed north, across the Zambezi River in search of a new way to live. He found it as a hunting guide He became a professional hunter which allowed him to follow his zeal for guns, hunting, animals and living in the wild.

Financing his new life soon became a problem. Morgan needed money for supplies, camping equipment and for sustenance during the off season. His father had died requiring that he support his mother and sister. One of his first clients was a school chum who lived in London. He recognized Morgan's plight.

Over a camp fire after a day of hunting, Morgan's friend began to expound on the subject. "You need some seed capital, Morgan. May I suggest that you borrow enough to finance your company. You have an exceptional talent for hunting, this plateau provides the animals and ambience and if you had some help and provided first-class accommodation, your business would thrive beyond your wildest dreams."

"Good thought," Morgan muttered, "but I can barely muster enough to support my family. My banker in Lusaka would howl."

Both men studied the fire and listened to the sounds of animals prowling for food. "I have a thought," the London man mused. "I'm in the shipping business. I've gotten to know a young man who owns some ships and has become successful and wealthy. He's a risk taker. He might loan the funds you require."

"In return for what?" Morgan asked.

"Not sure. He would want collateral or something in return. I'll find out."

The seed money arrived and Morgan's business soon flourished. Lynch joined him and together they outfitted the hunting operation to attract the well-heeled from Europe and the US. The source of the funds remained anonymous. A London bank collected a nominal interest on the loan. Several years lapsed and the business expanded. Keane came on board.

About the time he began exploring the possibility of running a safari operation, Morgan received the first of what became regular requests from his unknown London money source to perform borderline services. His creditor's interest was ivory. Morgan wasn't asked to kill elephants for their tusks, but to search for elephant burial grounds, recover the tusk from a carcass and transport the ivory to a port on the Indian Ocean. To do this was illegal. Morgan complied because he was not able to pay off his debt and it seemed a harmless request. He did this dirty business during the rainy season. The "source" compensated Morgan with reductions to the debt amount.

One day, when Morgan returned from safari to his one-room Lusaka office, he found an elderly South African man sitting at his desk. He introduced himself as Karel van Riebeek, a wine merchant. Morgan didn't like him from the moment they met. Van Riebeek claimed to work for Morgan's money source. He needed assistance and had been assured of cooperation. This time, the caper was serious. They wanted Morgan to transport small shipments of weapons. Morgan's life became a deception. The illicit activity accentuated his antipathy for humanity. Van Riebeek never returned to Lusaka but did communicate instructions concerning the shipments. Morgan wondered when it would end. When would he be able to pay off this debt hanging from his neck? He lived a double life.

Morgan had gravitated to the vast plateau north of the Zambezi River in search of excitement and found it again in the world of wild animals. The land was covered by deciduous savannah, small trees, grassy plains or marshland and inhabited by a plethora of animals. He moved in with them— he camped in remote areas, tracked, stalked and hunted and become an exceptional marksman. His father had given him an old Jeffrey 404 magnum, which never left his side when he was in the bush. By the time he was thirty-five, he had tired of killing; there was no money in it anyway, so he began to organize a safari company that would utilize his talents amid the beauty of the plateau and its inhabitants.

The tsetse fly presented a problem, a deterrent to attracting European hunters. At first he ran his fledgling company with the help of only local tribesmen. When on safari the local tribesmen would cover their exposed skin with an exotic translucent solution and were rarely bothered by the tsetse fly. Eventually he insisted that his clients use what became known as the "Palmer Balm," and the aggressive fly left them in peace. His business flourished.

Hunters from Europe and the Americas wanted him to lead their expeditions because he could deliver trophy animals from the big five: the elephant, lion, leopard, rhinoceros and Cape buffalo. During safari season, he maintained permanent camps, always secure and always situated to exploit the beauty of the landscape. To sit in a camp chair with a whiskey in hand, watching the outline of thirty elephants moving across the river, silhouetted in the gold of a setting sun, could become a moment in a client's life that was relived again and again. Life with Morgan Palmer on the savanna was basic, pure, exhilarating and offered an eccentricity and uniqueness not available back home.

Now, suddenly, he stood up and nodded to the other two men who were watching and turned to his client. "What do you say we return to camp for supper while we wait for the night to envelop our trap?"

After they had eaten, the two men and Lambert's wife, Eloise, retired to the fire pit and brandy. Palmer paid scant attention to the woman. It was heresy, he thought, for a woman so shallow to have access to so much money. "Roscoe," he said draining the last of his brandy, "tonight you will shoot your leopard. Keane has been tracking a beautiful male for two days and believes the cat will be close enough to catch the scent of our puku. It's a waiting game. You'll need to be relaxed and patient. I'll be close if there is trouble—but there won't be. I'll touch you when our cat is near the tree. You won't be able to see it."

"How can I shoot it if I can't see it?"

"When it climbs the tree and grabs the carcass, the motion will trigger a spot light. He'll be startled and gaze at the light without moving. It's at that moment that you must squeeze the trigger and place your shot well back of his shoulders and down a foot from the spine. You want to hit the heart or lung."

Later, both men lay near to each other, using old army blankets to cut the coldness of the earth at midnight. They were alone with their thoughts; the others were well back of them in the ravine. Roscoe did not want to kill this leopard; he really didn't like guns. The thought of extinguishing a life, human or otherwise, was repellent. He did not want a stuffed animal in his office; if anything, he would like the stuffed heads of a couple of his friends on the wall. The thought made him smile. He moved his forefinger to the rifle to caress the safety catch. He was farsighted so he had to keep his glasses in one of the many pockets in his jacket.

Morgan did not relish this kill either. He had shot his fair share of leopards, and each kill was followed by anguish and remorse. They were magnificent specimens of life and this plateau was their home. Morgan respected this animal, in fact, he admired it. He was the intruder. He assuaged his discomfort with the knowledge that this specie was not threatened and that the old fellow they were hunting did not have many years left. If Roscoe could shoot straight, the cat had no time left.

The two men, so dissimilar, waited in silence, hesitant to even scratch their ears. Then Morgan's antenna flared. His extrasensory perception developed from years of tracking and living near wild animals, told him that the cat was near, perhaps at the base of the tree. He gently poked Roscoe as he grasped his own rifle.

Time stopped. Nothing was happening; no light, no cat—nothing. Morgan smelled Roscoe's sweat and heard him brush away the perspiration on his forehead. The sound seemed to shriek in the silence of the night. Morgan worried that Roscoe wouldn't pull the trigger. The flood light came on, revealing a male leopard with both forelegs encircling the puku. It seemed that his large eyes glared directly at the two hunters.

"Shoot," Morgan growled.

Roscoe leaned to his rifle, focused as he had been instructed and squeezed the trigger. He later thought back to this moment reflecting that some invisible force had pulled the trigger. The small caliber bullet caught the leopard's heart, destroying his life instantly. His inert body remained stretched on the tree branch as if he were taking an afternoon snooze. Roscoe didn't get up; he had no strength.

"Nice shot," Morgan shouted as he lurched down the ravine toward the lone acacia tree and the trophy lying amid its leaves.

At the end of the week, after two more kills, a kudu and a roan antelope, Roscoe's and Eloise's extensive luggage was loaded into the Range Rover, and with Morgan driving, the three headed for Lusaka. The road was no more than an animal path, bumpy and dusty. At times the road petered out entirely giving their journey a surreal feeling, as if they were driving on the moon. Roscoe and Eloise were both quiet. Morgan was grateful, basking in the absence of chatter. They kept the Muchinga Mountains always to their right and generally followed the right bank of the Luangwa south toward the Zambezi. Before the two rivers joined, Morgan turned west on the only road to Lusaka. It took them another three dusty, sun-baked, monotonous hours before they reached the provincial capital of Northern Rhodesia. Lusaka was a day's journey north of Lake Kariba and the extensive east-west waterway connecting Mozambique and Livingstone. It was a frontier town: clubs and a golf course for the white settlers, schools and a hospital for the blacks, and an airport. After two days of driving, Morgan deposited the Lamberts at the airport hotel, collected the remainder of his fee and bid them a safe journey. Something compelled him to turn to Roscoe and ask, "Was it worthwhile?"

Roscoe set his pack down and turned back to Morgan, laughing. "You know, I have been asking myself that question for the past two days." He looked off toward the distant hills basking in the African sun. "Now that you've asked me the question, the answer is suddenly very clear. The ten days I've spent with you in this magnificent country have opened my mind to the importance of nature being in balance and also the need for me to rebalance my nature. I know this sounds stuffy. What I'm saying is—I can do more with my life as you have done with yours. Can you understand?"

Morgan replied, "Read Spinoza," as he climbed into the Range Rover.

Morgan drove straight to his bungalow. It belonged more in the cabin class; one story with a corrugated metal roof, desperate for paint, elevated two feet above ground on a platform that extended beyond the walls to provide a deck. On the other hand, the interior was neat, thanks to a devoted caretaker. Morgan was looking forward to four things in specific order—a whiskey, a shower, a steak and a real bed.

The following morning, when he sauntered into his office, Morgan once again saw van Riebeek sitting at his desk. The man looked older and even more disagreeable. Morgan's heart skipped a beat. Now what devious request did they have for him? It was time to end these terrible activities. He had reached middle age and needed to change his life. But how? Before he said a word, Morgan slid open the window, switched on the ceiling fan and placed his dusty boots on his desk. Only then did he acknowledge van Riebeek who watched him through his shifty eyes. "What now? Why are you here?"

"Our mutual friend has an important request of you and asked me to deliver it in person. It is a large operation with substantial risk. We expect you to take this job and perform with your usual adroitness."

Morgan exhaled deeply. "Let's have the details."

"We want you to bring a large shipment of guns and equipment up the Zambezi River."

"Wait a minute," Palmer almost shouted. "Who's getting the guns?"

Van Riebeek continued patiently. "The shipment is now on the high seas destined for a Mozambique port. It is to be delivered to Katanga and we want you to organize the delivery so that it is not observed in transit. You would be paid sufficiently well to cover all expenses plus a profit. In addition, if you complete the mission satisfactorily, your benefactor will forgive the rest of your debt."

There was complete silence. Morgan could hear his heart thump. He dropped his feet to the floor and began to pace the room. Finally, he returned to his desk chair, leaned forward so that he gaze fixed on van Riebeek. "I'll do it, this one last time. I want the loan part of this bargain in writing from the bank. Give me all of the details and I will do this next month, before the rains come. I'll need money soon as this will require significant equipment."

They did not shake hands. Van Riebeek departed with a tight smile creasing his wrinkled face.

Guildford, Surrey

Nicholas saw the hawk circle slowly over the meadow. It had seen something. Its eyes were riveted on the river bank. Perhaps it had seen a movement, a flash of gray. The hawk was waiting, circling; Nicholas wished he could be so patient. An average hunter at best, and now he was watching a professional at work. He saw the rabbit leave the seclusion of the thick brush along the river and hop toward the open field. His eyes returned to the hawk as it banked slightly, its feathers shining in the hazy sun, and for a moment he identified with the rabbit. Sensing something, the rabbit stopped eating and looked unseeing toward the sun. Suddenly a shadow obstructed the sunlight. Then, nothing.

Nicholas stood, stretched, and turned toward the path leading to his home. He had hunted early, just at dawn, when the morning light exposed the loveliness of the landscape. The farm, Nicholas never used the term "estate," encompassed ten hectares, and bordered the River Wey about an hour south of London. He strode quickly up the hill toward the elegant house, which sat partially secluded in a grove of oak trees. His gait reflected confidence. His thoughts dwelled on the weekend festivities and his guests who were coming from as far away as Greece and Italy. But first, he had business to attend to.

As he drew closer to the house, he stopped to admire its symmetry. It embodied his life-style: imposing, proud, and egocentric. The original farmhouse had been leveled and replaced by this two-story angular home. The elegance was in stark contrast to the simplicity of the barn and stable, the home to two Jersey cows and three horses. The surrounding land had returned to its natural state, with high-grass meadows punctuated by groves of great oaks and the river meandering along its edge. Nicholas smiled with delight as he continued up the path. Hunting was a pleasure, yet he savored three things even more: French claret, French cooking and women—not necessarily French and not necessarily in that order.

Farming held no interest for Nicholas, nor did the solitude of the location. Comfort for this Greek was found in activity: people, action, discourse. Nicholas's greatest comfort came from surrounding himself with people, preferably in an environment which he could control. He relished the prospect of becoming the puppet master. He could accomplish this pandering, ever so subtly, here, this weekend, on his farm.

The weekend was to be Nicholas's first extravagant party on the farm for his friends. To be included was the height of acceptance in his social circle. Most of his guests would stay in his home; the overflow would find accommodations in the nearby town of Guildford. The evening dinner party promised to be the high point of the celebration. Nicholas's French chef would serve the rabbit and most of the revelers would think it was chicken. This always amused him and he smiled now as he thought of it.

He hurried to his bedroom to shower and change. His guests would begin arriving late morning, which allowed him time for several business calls. Feeling invigorated from hunting and a shower, Nicholas descended the stairs which dropped steeply from his bedroom to a large office. A gun display cabinet occupied one entire wall. He paused to admire his collection. Many of the weapons were illegal in England, but for him they were collector items and laws were an inconvenience. His hand caressed the smooth wood of the old Winchester.

He rang his London office first. "Good morning. I have only a few minutes. Update me on the important issues." He listened intently and did not take notes. "Has the *Trireme* left Wismar?" He listened for a moment. "Good. Send a message to the Captain. Advise him that the Mozambique port has not been determined. Have you heard from Africa?" Nicholas nodded, now looking back at his gun collection. "Reluctant, you say. That's an agreement. Wire the funds to Lichtenstein. And," he smiled to himself, "I'll be out of touch until Monday."

A few of his London guests had already arrived and were wandering the grounds sipping Veuve Clicquot Champagne. Their calculated casual dress was the kind of clothes city dwellers wore in the country. His friends were young, carefree and attractive. Most were single. Nicholas preferred the opportunities this presented.

It was early afternoon, when off in the distance Nicholas spotted a car moving unhurriedly along Pottery Lane. When it stopped, a telephoto lens would momentarily protrude from the back window—like a sniper's rifle. Then it was withdrawn, and the car moved forward slowly before pausing again. Nicholas recognized Katheryn's Vauxhall and knew that the person holding the camera was the blond American girl, Samantha Norquist. His pulse quickened slightly as he pictured her. She was bright, stunning and interesting, as well as frosty. Nicholas had suggested to Katheryn that she bring Samantha along for the weekend and was thrilled when she'd agreed to do it. He was somewhat less thrilled when Katheryn invited Samantha's South African friend, as well.

"Hello, Nicholas," Katheryn purred as she kissed him on both cheeks. Samantha emerged from the back seat of the car, her camera in hand. She flashed her radiant smile in Nicholas's direction and began to exclaim rapidly about the countryside and the marvelous potential for photography. Nicholas's gaze shifted from Samantha to the tall man who stood leaning up against the car on the far side. He seemed absorbed in the scene before him. The man's eyes then shifted to Nicholas, and wearing a smile, he walked with long, lithe strides around the car to shake Nicholas's hand.

"Hello, Nicholas. Good to see you again. I can't apologize enough for crashing your party. I'm really happy to be here and to have a chance to see this magnificent part of England. You know that Katheryn invited both Samantha and me. I do hope it's all right."

"I was forewarned, and, of course, you are very welcome to join us. As you can see, it's a cast of thousands." Nicholas swept his hand across the landscape.

Samantha bounced into their conversation, exclaiming, "When you mentioned your farm, I pictured a barn and some animals." She wore an African safari hat, a suede sleeveless jacket, denims, and hiking boots. "I can't wait to walk the path along the river. We saw some Jack Snipes, and we think a Firecrest." She beamed at Nicholas. "Do you like birds?" She didn't wait for him to answer. "I really like hiking and bird watching. Sometimes I can get a fantastic photo while just out for a stroll."

"Tomorrow is for hiking," Nicholas announced, with a wry smile. Turning to Katheryn, he continued, "I have set aside the two best bedrooms for you and Samantha; one overlooks the river and the other has a bay window that catches the morning light. Let's get your luggage to your rooms, and then I'd like to show you around the farm. Come along, Brian, we'll find a room for you at the house as well."

By late afternoon, clouds were intruding on a golden sun that hung prominently in the western sky. There was a hint of rain in the air. A gaggle of Nicholas's guests now surrounded him, all pointing in different directions as they peppered him with questions about his life on the farm. They descended haphazardly down a knoll to the stable, where two chestnut colored horses stood munching hay. Nicholas explained that the breed was Arab and that they were not twins although they looked similar with white blazes on their foreheads. Along the fence, a large black horse arched its neck, demanding attention from her owner. "She's a Swedish Warm-blood," he said smiling as he caressed the giant horse along its glistening flank. She and I wander the trails early in the morning, especially along the river. She's not a jumper, not terribly fast, but she's sure-footed and steady so that I can shoot from the saddle."

The hardy, pungent aroma of the barnyard enveloped the on-lookers, driving a few back up the hill to seek a breeze. Samantha smiled to herself as she pictured Gunnar, her beloved childhood friend and mentor and the farmer who had sold her father the land which now held the Norquist lake house; her mind rummaged through her youthful days on his Wisconsin farm. Thank you, Gunnar, for my barnyard education—be well wherever you are.

"What's her name?" a dark eyed woman asked in a European accent, not Italian, but definitely Mediterranean. "Surely she has a Greek name even though she's Swedish," she giggled."

"I named her Thalassic, the Greek goddess of the Mediterranean. And speaking of Greeks," Nicholas replied with a smile, "I have a couple more residing in that shed over there," he said, pointing toward a small barn that was painted the rich red color of so many Swedish barns. "We shall meet them next. In fact, someone will be tested when we do."

Samantha listened and watched quietly on the edge of the Champagne-drinking crowd. Her eyes returned to the two Arabians, and she wondered if she would be allowed to take one out on the trails she saw stretching from the meadow into the woods. What about Brian, she thought to herself, can he ride?

As the group closed in on the barn, a great lowing sound pierced the tranquility of the afternoon. Nicholas's farm superintendent, a small man bent by a lifetime of farm work, slid open the barn door. "I would like you all to meet Erato and Aphrodite," Nicholas said with a flourish. "As you can see, and hear as well, they are demanding to be milked. Anyone wish to volunteer?"

While the rest all stood like stones, clutching their Champagne glasses, Samantha moved smoothly to the side of Aphrodite, placed her hand on the cow's shoulder and turned to the farm manager. "If you would be so kind as to bring a clean damp cloth, I will gladly milk the lady of love." Then she settled on the stool and splayed her knees outward to make room for a pail. With the cloth, she cleaned the tumescent udder and teats, placed her forehead on Aphrodite's shank and began to draw the milk. Her fingers grasped the teats knowingly, squeezing, in sequence, drawing downward. While she worked, her hat fell onto her back and dangled from the draw-string, exposing her blond hair and the nape of her neck. To everyone's astonishment, Samantha began to softly sing a lullaby from her childhood.

Nicholas watched Samantha with admiration and arousal. There was an earthiness about her that exuded sexuality. How naturally she had become a milkmaid and how very desirable that made her. He caught hold of his thoughts and moved to the stool next to Erato. With each caress of the udder, he thought of Samantha. She was rapidly becoming an obsession.

As the sky had promised, a storm drew in shortly after midnight. It carried with it a hard rain that pelted the roof and the bay window of Samantha's bedroom. She undressed slowly, listening to the clatter of the rain drops while her mind sifted through the events of the evening: the rabbit dinner, the excessive drinking. A blur of faces washed across her memory. Nicholas had been like a shadow, constantly at her side, his amorous intentions obvious and undeterred by her disinterest. At dinner, Brian was seated at the other end of the long, baronial table, where a raucous group of both French and British guests were intent on consuming all of Nicholas's Bordeaux. Like most large dinner parties, at the beginning, the mix of people and conversation was challenging, interesting and provocative. As the claret softened pretension and resistance, cabals emerged as the talk became boisterous and banal. Connections were made and bedroom locations noted.

As Samantha sat on the edge of the bed rolling down her stockings, she felt an unfamiliar anxiety, a longing. Her thoughts kept drifting to Brian, as they had throughout the day. He had become so much a part of her life. She shook her hair out; her mind scarcely noticing the tapping sound of the rain on the window pane. She prided herself on her *savoir-faire*, her nonchalance toward male attention, and her self-confidence in quickly sorting out relationships. She was not inexperienced, and at age twenty-six, she could look back on a few infatuations, but, she admitted, never an enduring love.

This month, September, marked the one-year anniversary of their meeting in the New York art gallery. It had also rained that day so this storm was fitting. How the year had flown by, full of challenges, adventure and now this love that consumed her thoughts. A strong current had caught hold of them and they were in the flood waters. They floated on a sea of activity that masked their compelling attraction for each other.

Each morning, Samantha's first thoughts were of Brian. This distraction from her work disturbed her. She began her usual diagnostic drill and looked for flaws in him and in their relationship. But Brian stood close inspection. A consummate listener, he would offer a concise observation to Samantha's ramblings, subtly influencing, without dogma. They were, in some ways, very different. Brian accepted reality and looked for accommodation. Samantha was hell-bent on changing all that was unfair in the world.

She tossed her stockings on the bed, stood, undressed and slipped on a robe. Her reverie became more immediate. Earlier, when the raucous guests finally staggered from the dinner table and spread to the great room and out onto the deck, Samantha found herself standing alone. She watched Brian as he was guided by two giggling women toward the deck. Her pulse quickened. Nicholas suddenly glided up out of nowhere and handed her a glass of port.

"Come with me, Samantha. Let's sit in the garden and watch the party from a distance. My home, with every room lit, is magnificent."

At that moment, Brian reached the double door leading to the deck. He extracted himself from the two tugging ladies, turned and let his eyes search the enormous room. When his gaze captured Samantha, his face radiated pleasure.

Their eyes locked. For Samantha, it seemed the existence of all others in the room evaporated. She watched as Brian crossed the room to where she stood. Nicholas scowled and moved away.

Brian slipped his arm through Samantha's. "Come with me fair maiden. Let's sit in the garden and observe this frivolity from afar." Samantha followed willingly.

The sound of a door closing awoke Samantha from her trance and she guessed that the game of musical bedrooms had commenced. Suddenly she felt incredibly aroused and wanted desperately to be with Brian, to touch him and to admit her feelings. Without thinking about it any more and clothed only in her silk robe, she tiptoed across her room, quietly opened the door, and peaked around it to find the hallway quiet and empty. The long hallway was lit at the far end by a solitary lamp that barely illuminated the antique chest and the two chairs on either side of it. Samantha headed in the direction of Brian's room, but when she heard the faint rustling of clothing, she ducked behind a large armoire just in time to see Nicholas appear from the staircase. He marched directly to her door, and paused only briefly before entering quietly without knocking. Then, just as Nicholas shut the door, Katheryn emerged from her own room and slipped down the staircase headed, Samantha guessed, for Nicholas's bedroom. Before Samantha could move, Nicholas came storming out of her bedroom, crossed the hallway, and opened the door to Katheryn's room. It was all she could do not to giggle out loud.

When all grew quiet again, she turned to the door behind her and placed her open palm against it, wondering if Brian could sense her presence there. As she pressed her hand against the wood, hesitating at the audacity of what she was doing, the door opened slightly, a shaft of light spilled into the dark hallway, and Brian pulled her into the room. He smiled briefly and whispered, "You are a cheeky girl to wander around the hallway in the middle of the night." He looked down at the soft curve of her breast, revealed now as the robe had slid open slightly. With a groan, he pulled her close until their bodies melted together. Samantha felt his kiss devour her as he deepened it. This, then, was what it was like to want someone with such desperation.

"Bed," he murmured.

The heat from their naked bodies was searing. Sam rested on one elbow, peering down on the face of the man with whom she had fallen in love. She kissed his nose, then an ear and soon her tongue slid across his lips. She marveled at the graceful shape of his eyes. With her hand tracing his breastbone down the middle of his chest, she blew softly along the line her fingers drew on his skin. He had a swimmers' body, no bulging muscles, but long and lean like Michelangelo's statue of David, she thought. She kissed him slowly, letting her hand caress his chest and then moved to the hollow of his stomach. Her exploring hand drifted further.

This time they made love with exquisite care: knowingly, unselfishly and thoroughly. It was as if they had known and cherished each other for a very long time, in another lifetime, perhaps for an eternity. Samantha would always remember this night, not only for the abandonment and fulfillment, but for its ineffable exquisiteness. Their lovemaking was profound and complete. It completed her—she felt that with certainty.

Dawn broke with a clear sky. The rain had cleansed the earth and in the air a septic odor of spruce and bitter cottonwood, witch hazel and the smell of willows all blended together, and wafted through the open window to greet Samantha as she stirred from her slumber. The birds presented a cacophony of sound, all wanting to be heard first. Samantha smiled as she listened to Brian's steady breathing and watched his chest move quietly.

Brian woke smiling. "I don't think I've ever awakened in a happier circumstance, my love," he said. "What's on our schedule for this glorious Sunday morning?" He reached for Sam and pulled her close. "Oh, I have a splendid idea . . . let's stay here, in this very bed and have your friend Nicholas arrange to have breakfast brought to us along with some delicious white wine. Yes, you agree of course," he smirked

"Not such a bad idea really," purred Samantha, "but there are other possibilities," she whispered. Last night Nicholas had agreed to have the two Arabians saddled for them. "Let's postpone breakfast, take advantage of this perfect day and go horseback riding. Yes, you agree of course," she mimicked him. "Come on lover, get your britches on."

Brian and Samantha rode abreast, their legs almost touching, their bodies moving in sync with the gait of the horses, whose heads bobbed like moored ships on a wavy sea. For a long time they didn't speak, but when the trail turned away from the river and plunged into a dense grove of trees, Brian turned to her, "I'm going home in December."

"To Cape Town?" Samantha asked with surprise, looking at him. "Will you be there for Christmas?"

"December is mine to squander. The secretary-general has plans to return to Sweden for the holidays. Taking some time off was his suggestion. It's a long overdue opportunity for me to close down my law business. I can't run it from Geneva; my few remaining clients require regular attention. I also want to spend some time with my father."

"What a good idea, Brian. I've been thinking of returning home for Christmas, as well. My schedule is so full; I keep putting future plans on hold."

"Here is an idea I'd like you to consider," his voice sounded abraded, as if he had talked through the night.

Samantha turned in her saddle and studied Brian's face for a long moment, her mind racing through a jumble of thoughts. "I'm all ears."

"My idea," his voice faltered, caught in his throat. He paused, and then began again, a little too rapidly. "I'd like you to come to South Africa with me to see my roots, to meet my family and even help me repair my garden. I have a house, you know, a stones throw south of Cape Town. The garden will be exploding in color and crying for attention. If my old car will cooperate, we could drive up the coast, or even better, visit the wine country around Stellenbosch."

Samantha turned away and looked at the trail ahead. For a moment her mind went blank, but then, sounding nervous, Brian continued. "We could even visit one of the game parks. My brother, Jason, who is a park ranger, would want to join us.

Sam's heart tugged as she pictured hippos and lions and traveling with Brian to this new world. She reined in her horse and turned in the saddle. She could see Brian was apprehensive. "Yes," she said firmly and laughed.

"Yes, what?"

"Yes to everything! I want to see Southern Africa, I want to meet your dad, I want to see and photograph every animal in the park and I want to be with you." She leaned toward Brian, and they kissed.

"I'm so pleased," Brian almost shouted. His face radiated joy. "We should make plans soon. You could visit Geneva and we could fly to Cape Town together."

Samantha did not answer immediately. The ensuing silence became awkward. Finally, almost impulsively, she said in a quiet voice, "Brian, I have been invited by Thomas Kimbamba to visit Katanga." She thought she would explain, but the words caught in her throat. Neither one spoke.

"Katanga is one of the most dangerous places on earth, Samantha, especially right now. How will you get there? Who will guarantee your safety? How long will you be there?" His eyes searched her face for doubt or apprehension, or even hesitancy.

"The story is too good to miss, Brian. Thomas has promised to show me not only Elizabethville, but the giant copper mine as well. I'm to meet the new president, Moise Tshombe." Samantha offered this reasoning with conviction.

Brian scowled, looked off for a moment before returning his gaze to Samantha. He voice had reclaimed confidence. "When will this happen?"

"Do you remember the sequence of events when we were at Henley? The conversation I overheard? I want to follow this trail and Kimbamba is the key. There are two stories here: the turmoil in Katanga and gun smuggling."

"Both are dangerous stories. Is *Echo* interested?"

"Yes, very much so. To answer your question—my trip has been tentatively set for the end of October. I hope to stay two weeks."

"I would go with you, but UN officials are blocked from entry to Katanga. Their airport is closed."

"I'll fly to Northern Rhodesia. Thomas will meet me there. He assured me the border is open. We will spend a few days in Elizabethville, meet Tshombe, and then drive to the mine. Thomas's sister lives in the hills and has offered to take me in for a few days. Thomas wants to write the report."

Then Brian said something that Samantha would always remember. "It sounds like an opportunity you should not pass up. Let me help you with the flight arrangements. Also, there may be a South African government chap I know still stationed in Katanga. He would be a useful backup. And when you finish this crazy adventure, have Thomas take you straight back to the Northern Rhodesian airport to catch a plane to Cape Town. I'll be waiting for you there."

"I'm famished," Samantha shouted as she wheeled her mount and cantered back through the woods to the trail that paralleled the river.

The River Wey shimmered in the early morning light. Standing in the river was a lone figure, a fisherman waving his flyrod in a four-stroke count, looking for a fish to rise. Nicholas looked up from his casting and watched two horsemen, caught in the sun light, riding along a dirt corniche. The riders were unaware of his presence, lost in the motion of the horses and their thoughts. This unusual American woman was a trophy that had escaped his net. He wondered if the fish would surface again.

Washington D.C.

Jay Carleton stared at the giant map of central Africa hanging on the wall directly in front of his desk. The DRC, or the "Congo," as every old timer at State still preferred to call it, intimidated its neighbors in size, population and wealth. Although unrest existed throughout Africa, the DRC probably led in chaos as well. Jay was the United States' "eye" on the DRC, an enormous responsibility, considering what was transpiring there. Jay pondered this thought while he dialed Bryce Donaldson's extension.

"Good morning, Donaldson here."

"Hi Bryce, its Jay. Got some time for me this morning? I need to tap your brain."

"Well, tapping my brain will be a quick exercise, Bryce replied warmly. I'll be in your office in ten minutes."

The two Department of State junior officers stood before the map of Africa as if proximity would provide inspiration. Jay began the conversation. "Our Leopoldville embassy is talking directly with Colonel Mobutu. Yesterday, September fifteenth, he neutralized—that's Mobutu's word—the DRC government and tossed President Kasavubu and our friend Lumumba out of office."

"Yeah," Bruce muttered, with a soft exhale. "My sources tell me that Lumumba has left Leopoldville. He probably is running for Stanleyville where his tribe and the Soviets can protect him."

Jay walked around his desk to extract a one page dispatch from a mound of papers. "This, from our Embassy in Leopoldville, arrived this morning," he said handing it to Bryce. "They think Mobutu will bring law and order to the country. He has made himself Chief of Staff, and along with a group of young educated men from different tribes, intends to govern the country. He wants us to recognize his government."

"What's your opinion?" Bryce retorted.

"It's a coup. We are slow to accept coups. Anyway, he has his work cut out since one DRC army regiment has already mutinied. As I see it, Bryce, we are caught in a triangle. The US prefers to not recognize the DRC government and certainly not the breakaway provinces of Kasai and Katanga. The UN wants to run the show. They have inserted several thousand international troops plus an Indian politician, Rajeshwar Dayal, to assume control of the Congo operation. He has been on station one week and has succeeded in antagonizing all sides. He's vehemently anti-American." Jay sat down and placed his elbows on his desk while looking at Bryce beseechingly. "You know the DRC well. What do you think we should do next?"

Bryce pulled up a chair, took off his perfectly-tailored suit coat and proceeded to vigorously rub the tight black curls on his head. "I think we should absolutely require the Leopoldville government to handle the Katanga secession issue directly, with no UN involvement."

Jay looked up from his yellow pad. "Lumumba is a loose cannon rolling toward the Soviet bloc. He should be captured and returned to Leopoldville for detention. We should insist that Mobuto put Joseph Kasavubu back in the president's chair, as a first step in securing the United States' recognition. The UN should not reinstall Lumumba as prime minister."

"That's a heavy order," Bryce said, chuckling. What else?"

"Well, my gut tells me that our friends across the river are hatching a plot to take out Lumumba. They think he is in the communist camp. They, and the FBI, see a commie behind every bush. This would not sit well with other African countries. Why don't I set up a lunch with Larry Madison? Maybe we can ferret out some solid information."

"Let's do it soon. The situation is deteriorating as we speak." Bryce grabbed his coat and headed for the door.

Rivers are the arteries of the world. All living things must have water and rivers are the lifeline. The Zambezi River provides many essentials to man and animals living near its shores, from its source in western Northern Rhodesia (now Zambia) to its shark infested mouth on the Indian Ocean.

The Zambezi begins in the Katanga Plateau just below the DRC border, passes briefly through a protrusion of the eastern Angola border, then flows straight south to touch the Caprivi Strip (Namibia) and ultimately joins the Chobe River at Livingston. The Victoria Falls is about midway in the river's journey to the sea. From the spectacular falls through the man-made Lake Kariba, the Zambezi makes its way eastward, passing through woodlands, narrow gorges, class-five rapids and finally the flood plains surrounding the broad reach of the river as it nears its journey's end. In the dense jungle and woodlands bordering the river lives one of the greatest concentrations of wild animals in the world. The exquisite bird population provides amazing colors and shapes, while the river itself is the home to a plethora of fish. The people of this vast region depend on the river for transportation, laundry, crop irrigation, and, unfortunately, sanitation. Traveling the Zambezi often provides wild excitement.

Morgan Palmer's Gunrunning Route on the Zambezi River and across the Northern Rhodesian Savanna to Katanga
- 1960 -

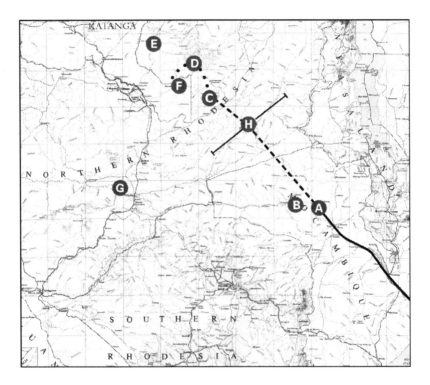

A. Lower Zambezi River route, ending at the Rapid End Camp
B. Cahora Bassa Rapids
C. DC-3 route to Morgan's bush camp and airfield
D. Wetlands, called the "Sponge"
E. Fort Rosebery
F. Delivery of weapons at Mwenda on the Luapula River
G. Lusaka. Morgan's home
H. Africa Under Canvas safari area

OCTOBER 1960

Mozambique

Morgan, Lynch and Keane, each wearing a freshly pressed khaki bush jacket and carrying a weather-beaten satchel, stepped from the Fokker F27 Friendship to the tarmac on a steaming mid-afternoon. They all walked quickly to the unpretentious Beira airport terminal building and passed quickly through customs. Soon they were in a cab heading for the Grand Hotel.

After checking in, they all met on the hotel veranda to sample the local beer. It was not as strong as Morgan would have liked and overly chilled as well. The street fronting the hotel led to the docks, providing a kaleidoscope of colors and activities. Keane had never been out of Rhodesia, and, in fact, had spent most of his young life in the bush, so he was mesmerized by the passing parade. The natives were darker than the blacks he knew in Northern Rhodesia and there were many Indians, most of whom were dressed in white and all appeared to be selling something. Keane also saw his first Chinese: a short fellow, distinguished by a broad-rimmed hat, standing on a lorry bed. The street hawkers, honking vehicles and horses clopping on the brick street created a cacophony. "I like the beer and the sea breeze, but this noise and commotion would soon drive me back to the bush," Keane observed as he continued gaping at the street activity.

"Later I'll take you to a bar where you can meet some Portuguese women," Lynch said, with a sly smile. "Then you won't be so anxious to leave."

"The women are a mix of Portuguese and African and, who knows, maybe Indian," Morgan added. "It's the mix that makes them so beautiful—so desirable."

"You will join us, won't you Morgan? Most of the gals know you and will be asking after you." Lynch said this casually, but actually hoped for Morgan's companionship because he attracted women like flies to honey.

"Thanks, but no thanks. I'm going to relax in the bathtub for a long time and think about our plan. Branca is joining me for dinner and we'll taste every delight from the sea. I'll meet you here at eight for breakfast. Be on time, please!"

Several hours later, Morgan sat in the high ceilinged dining room, tasting the rum and sensing its mellowing effect as it was absorbed into his blood stream. The room was nearly empty as it was still too early for the European crowd, who generally dined after nine. Branca breezed into the dining room as if it were her personal fiefdom, flashing her brilliant smile to those she knew as they turned to enjoy her entrance. Morgan stood and watched her as well. She was beautiful, he admitted to himself and as he felt a long absence stirring in his loins.

"Morgan," her voice was softer and lower than one might expect. "I have been thinking about you and apparently I have conjured you up, for here you are." She wrapped one golden arm around his neck and pulled it down to kiss him briefly on the mouth. Morgan led her to the table he had selected near the windows. Branca sat next to him, allowing both of them to watch the street activity while they talked.

Morgan had known Branca Abreu Mello for many years. They had first met at a party in Cape Town; he had been there for a conference on wild animal conservation, she to meet clients for her jewelry business. Their attraction to each other had been instantaneous. Over the years they had met many times, sometimes in Maputo, where she lived and ran her business, but just as often somewhere in South Africa, as well as once in Madagascar. Morgan felt more comfortable with Branca than any other woman he had ever known. She always smelled natural, as fresh as wild flowers, and her love making was exuberant. But best of all, she never asked more of Morgan than just the moment they shared. She valued her freedom knowing that he would never settle for her preference for city life.

Branca's father had been a business man in Goa, where he had met and married a much younger Indian girl. They soon left Goa for a better opportunity in Mozambique, settling in Maputo where Branca was born. Branca was genetically gifted with the best of both parents: her father's golden skin color, her mother's expressive eyes, her father's energy to succeed and her mother's curiosity about all things.

"Are you in between safaris?" she asked, as she tasted the white wine Morgan had ordered. "I detected in your message that you were off on a new adventure." She held the wine glass in the candle light. "This wine is very good; must be French." She rattled on, "I am still waiting for you to let me tag along on a safari."

Morgan laughed before saying, "You wouldn't last three days. Insects, animals growling in the night, simple food and no bathtub, and that's just for starters," he teased. "What we should do is go to Lisbon for a month. After I finish this job, I will be able to take you. Now," he said looking at his menu, "what will you have this evening?"

"Think I'll start with an arugula and orange salad, then the lobster tail with butter, wine, coffee and—after that," her eyes narrowing—"you."

"All of this in the dining room?" he questioned, looking into her dark eyes with a half-smile creasing his mouth. Morgan returned to the menu and said to the waiter, "I'll have the grouper with garlic and butter and begin with the same salad as the Senhora."

The sun was long up when Morgan joined his two ragged-looking partners for breakfast. Without asking about their evening on the town, he presented them with a single sheet of paper outlining their tasks in Mozambique. They ate quietly, and after their breakfast dishes were cleared away, they were left alone on the veranda.

The street sounds were already distracting, prompting the three plotters to bend their heads over the table in order to hear each other. "We have a lot to accomplish in one week," Morgan began, turning his attention to the fair-haired Lynch. "You need to visit Chinde immediately. The arms we are to deliver to Katanga are already on the high seas and are scheduled to arrive in Mozambique in ten days.

You can get there by coastal steamer, but I suggest you rent a car that is capable of handling the rutted road along the coast. Here is the name of a small ship's chandler in Chinde. We will need two twelve-meter river boats with powerful engines. Remember, we will be traveling with a heavy cargo, upriver, against the current. When the river narrows, the flow becomes fierce. Find four natives to crew for us; not just to help handle the cargo, but competent enough to bring the boats back down river. If the boats look like fishing cruisers—all the better. Once you have the boats and crew, begin to organize supplies. The boats will not need to leave Mozambique territory. My plan is to off-load the cargo below the Cabora Bassa rapids at a camp run by a friend. We'll be on the river seven days, maybe eight."

"I'm off," Lynch replied as he stuffed the envelope Morgan had given him into his shirt pocket. "But, what about the docks and customs?"

"I hope to have an answer on that today. The freighter is 30,000 DWT and should be able to safely dock at the Chinde port. It will pass through the Suez, so Chinde is on its course. I'm meeting with our South African friend's importer today. He should be able to arrange for the ship to pick up copra and sugar in Chinde for delivery to India."

"And customs?" Lynch asked.

"Ahhh, here is our first risk. The documents will say 'aircraft parts.' They are for delivery to Rhodesia, which is an important customer for this country. Our ace in the hole is Branca, who claims to know the customs officials. We will work on this situation when I join you at the end of the week."

Morgan and Keane walked the seven blocks along the coastal road to India Circle. The importer's office building was freestanding, yellow in color and had a screened deck circling it like a belt on a fat tummy. They waited briefly on the deck until a smiling Mr. Bhagat Singh emerged and ushered them into a large room with a ceiling fan struggling to temper the heat. He was a stout man who wore antique wire-rimmed glasses perched on his large, straight nose, with a thick, white-streaked beard shrouding his chin. Because he was a Punjabi, his long hair was concealed under a neatly tied white turban. Tea was served, and the three chatted amicably about the Grand Hotel, the weather and other mundane subjects before settling into the business at hand. Singh admitted that he did not know Van Riebeek even though he had handled several shipments for him, all successful, and always paid for in advance.

"Several weeks ago," ventured Singh, as his thick eye brows arched, "a Mr. Adraan visited me on behalf of Van Riebeek. Since I had already agreed to import the airplane parts I began to wonder why Adraan had traveled all the way from Cape Town."

"What did he have to say?" Morgan asked.

"A strange fellow, I must say. Difficult to place his origin. He's African, but not native. North African perhaps? His message was that you would soon visit me and that I was to cooperate with you in every way. My compensation was satisfactorily negotiated. So, I am at your service, Mr. Morgan."

"Tell me about the freighter."

Singh opened a thin file and shuffled through its contents. "The *HS Trireme* is a tramp, 30,000 DWT, with Liberian registry. The owners are Greek with offices in both Piraeus and London. Nothing special about the ship except its age; it was built in the early 1920s. The ship officers are Greek and the crew is Basque. Its run is usually Europe to India and back."

"Is there anything on its manifest that would prevent it from off-loading our cargo in Chinde? We plan to take it up the Zambezi." Morgan was now doing all of the talking while Keane kept notes of the conversation.

Singh hummed as he pored through the documents. "No, no problem. The Chinde port can handle cargo ships of this size. But let me ask you: we have a railroad running straight to Salisbury. Wouldn't it be easier to offload in Beira and use the railroad?"

"It would seem so," Morgan said quickly, "but these parts are destined for a remote air field in Northern Rhodesia."

"Say no more. I understand. I will contact the ship owners and arrange for berthing in Chinde. Customs will be your challenge."

"Is there anything we need to do for you, Mr. Singh?" Morgan asked as he pushed back his chair and extended his hand.

Singh clasped Morgan's hand with both of his small hands and gleamed. "I have been compensated. May your trip to the interior be successful. I wish you peace." He pressed his palms together in front of his chest.

Next, Morgan and Keane walked uptown to the bank. The morning had become sultry; no wind and no cloud cover blanketed the sun's intensity. They hailed two cycle-taxis and soon arrived at the Banco de Sofala. Ostensibly it was a Mozambique bank, but *de facto*, it was a branch of a large, merchant, financial institution headquartered in Lisbon.

It took less than 30 minutes to transact the withdrawal of Van Riebeek's first payment. Morgan had always been parsimoniously cautious with his money. Over the past few years, he had conscientiously provided funds to his mother and sister, with the balance going to a broker in London for investment. Today he wired half of the Riebeek payment to his bank in Lusaka, pocketing the rest to cover expedition expenses.

"I think we deserve a cold beer," Morgan pronounced, with gusto. "I know an excellent spot for lunch around the corner."

During lunch they finalized their plan. "Keane, I know you're new to this kind of adventure. If you have concerns, you're welcome to back out now. Yet be assured that you can still work the safari season with me next year. What we're about to do is illegal and dangerous." Morgan tipped his bottle of beer, sat back and let the statement sink in.

Keane had completed several years of service in the Rhodesian army. He had been with Morgan for two seasons, and had become an astute game tracker and a sure shot. He knew that Morgan felt comfortable with him on his flank.

"I like working with you, Morgan," Keane finally replied, looking straight into Morgan's eyes. "Although I know it's wrong, I have no compunction about smuggling arms into an African country. Everyone seems to have a rifle and the killing is pervasive. I've no idea who will receive the guns we're transporting, and I really don't care. It's the old feeble excuse—if we don't supply, someone else will."

"I detect some hesitation."

"I have trouble rationalizing the killing of a human being. My time in the Rhodesian army frequently exposed me to my dilemma when we were deep in the jungle chasing rebels. I was never sure that I could, in that ultimate moment, actually pull the trigger." His eyes averted Morgan's as his voice became husky. "The opportunity never presented itself, thank God! The adventure and the money, plus my respect for you, compel me to accept. Ultimately we're to train someone on how to use these guns. That I can do as well, but I'll not join them in battle. This is a very fine line and I hope you can both understand and accept it."

Morgan remained silent for a long time, as his breathing slowed. Finally he shrugged and looked off toward the bar. "Strangely, your morality teeters on hypocrisy. Yet I hear my inner-self shouting exactly what you profess. Deep down, unacknowledged, I feel the same way. Let's do our job and not pull a trigger. I'm pleased you'll join me." Morgan stuck out his giant paw and Keane grasped it. "Now let's go over our plans one more time."

Morgan placed a note pad in front of Keane on which was a penciled list of items. "As soon as you arrive in Lusaka, call our old friend Colin Waite. He'll either be flying or in his air charter office at the airport. Ask him to charter a DC-3 for three days. About 80 kilometers up-river from Tete is a well-known lodge where rafters spend a night or two after shooting the Cabora Bassa rapids. It's called Rapid End, and Colin knows the landing strip near the camp grounds. Hire Colin to pick up our cargo there and fly it to a camp on the west side of the Muchinga Mountains. Here are the coordinates. It's an untamed area, but I'll be in the cockpit with him to help navigate the landing. The landing strip there will be solid this time of year and it's certainly long enough. Lusaka is loose on checking flight plans. He should log our usual base camp site as the destination, listing general safari supplies as cargo."

Keane interrupted. "I know Colin's girlfriend—she'll know how to find him. But he will need funds to charter a cargo plane. How do I pay him?"

"I'll get to the money part later," Morgan replied, as he drained the last of the beer in his glass. "After you arrange for the plane, contact the company where I buy and lease our lorries. I want to lease three relatively new Mercedes Unimogs—the 405 series. They may have to bring them up from Salisbury. Ask for new canvas tops and have surplus gas tanks installed. I want them in perfect running order. They have only two weeks to do all of this, so don't let them lollygag. While they are working on our lorry requirement, start assembling supplies in our warehouse. Provisions for a month, medical supplies, our usual assortment of rifles and ammunition—don't forget my Jeffrey. Here's a list of miscellaneous items to include such as binoculars, a radio and rope. Put some of the supplies on the plane so that it appears to be on a legitimate trip. The rest can come with the lorries."

Keane wrote furiously, never looking up from his note pad. "Where do I find your Morgan Balm?"

"There is a village just west of town called Mapin. The village elder knows me and it is his people that make my balm. You will be traveling through the Mopane woodlands where the tsetse is fierce. You'll need a lot of balm. The tsetse fly will be around, the Rhodesian military, probably not."

Keane looked up from his notes and asked, "Where will we meet and when?"

Morgan spread out his detailed map of the lower Zambezi and poked his finger on the Cabora Bassa Rapids.

"We'll off-load at the Rapid End jetty just below the rapids. If things go smoothly and the ship arrives soon with our cargo, we'll head up river in two weeks. It's over 400 kilometers and the going will be slow because of the current and sandbars. Let's allow for seven to eight days on the river, so, all in all, you have about three weeks to gather the equipment. I plan to have the two trawlers arrive at Rapid End by Sunday, October sixteenth. You should schedule the plane to arrive on the following Tuesday. I figure it will take Colin two trips since the crates are heavy. Can you do all of this?"

"Shit, Morgan, are you kidding? What about the authorities? Won't three large lorries heading into the bush arouse suspicion?"

"Yeah, good question, and one I have been thinking about. Hire three local natives who have worked with us before. Have them leave at different times—early morning would be a good time. No one will notice. Be prepared for some rough travel as we'll be in some remote parts of the country where there are no roads. Bring trinkets for the villagers, but absolutely no booze."

Morgan folded the map and stuffed it in his satchel along with the plan notes. He withdrew an envelope containing Rhodesian currency. "Here is enough money to get you started. I will wire my bank to grant you credit up to £30,000, enough to make down payments on the lorries, cargo plane and supplies. We will talk by phone at six p.m. each evening and once I'm on the river, we'll use a radio. Drink up and get to it"

The Chinde port offered two berths for ocean-going vessels. The Chinde estuary to the Zambezi was the best of the four entrances, primarily because it was deeper than the others. Still, the silt accumulation demanded constant dredging and the chugging noise from the dredge was an accepted intrusion in the daily life of the town. Ships unloaded here were usually coastal vessels, feeding even smaller boats that could ply the river. On this warm Wednesday in October, 1960, two events attracted the attention of the villagers who were either working in the port or just hanging around the docks enjoying a perfect spring day. The *HS Trireme* appeared in the roadstead and to everyone's surprise, with the help of two ancient tugs, eased into one of the berths. Soon a crane was swinging rectangular, wooden crates on to the wharf, where a tractor quickly moved them into a nearby warehouse. The more laborious loading of sugar and copra followed. The European officers watched the activity impassively from the ship's bridge.

The other curious sight was two women walking determinedly toward the warehouse. The ship officers' interest suddenly quickened when they caught sight of Branca striding at the side of the well-known chief customs officer, Anibal Senna da Silva. Da Silva was shorter than Branca. Her official inspector's coat did not conceal her ample girth. The two were deep in a conversation and unaware of the many eyes following them on the wharf.

"I am happy for your visit, Branca," da Silva said as she touched Branca's arm. "I remember well when we met each other at the jewelry show in Maputo. Now the Good Lord has sent you to Chinde, where I can buy a bracelet or two directly from you. If you would arrange that, I would be in your debt."

The two women entered the warehouse where Morgan's shipment was stacked. The crates were all identical in size, each with a numerical code, a part name and the label, "Product of the GDR." Da Silva inspected some of the crates, peering closely at the markings, crosschecking with the documentation on her clipboard. "This is a lot of airplane parts. What are the Rhodesians building, an Air Force?"

Branca replied quickly. "They want to service and update their planes because the political developments on their borders have become alarming. They prefer to be inconspicuous about this and have asked a friend of mine, Morgan Palmer, to bring the parts shipment up the Zambezi."

Da Silva turned to Branca and asked, "Why your involvement?"

"Well, for several reasons. Morgan is tied up finding river boats and asked me to meet with you since we already knew each other. But the real reason I'm here, and Morgan doesn't know this yet," as the two women exchanged knowing smiles, "is that I am going up the river with him. I've always wanted to travel the Zambezi. I'm really excited. Have you been up the river, Anibal? May I call you Anibal?"

Anibal appeared to relax; her attention drifted away from the stack of crates as she responded enthusiastically. "Of course, Branca, we are friends. Call me Anibal. Anyway, and I know you will think I'm crazy, but I love sport fishing and the Tiger fish is something else; a courageous fighter and a delectable dinner. And, I've seen this guy Palmer around— *bonito!*" She said all of this with a straight face while signing off on the consignment.

"If the Rhodesians have miscalculated, they may have to reorder, and the additional shipment would not arrive here until the end of the rainy season next year." Branca added perfunctorily.

"No problem," Anibal almost purred. She slipped her arm through Branca's and headed toward the open warehouse door. "Now why don't we have coffee and talk jewelry?"

That night, Branca brought her duffel bag and slipped it on board. Afterwards she had returned to the village, where she found Morgan and Lynch having dinner in a seaman's bar along the wharf. She slid into a chair between them, flashed her brilliant smile and calmly informed Morgan that she was coming with them up the river. "By cracky, Branca, you can go right back and get your duffel; you are not going along with us!" he exploded. "This is crazy! It's too dangerous and, anyway, there's no room for you." All of this from Morgan, as he sat stupefied in his chair.

Lynch stared in amazement at this brazen woman and his boss's lack of fortitude. He knew with certainty that Branca would end up coming with them and he liked the idea. She was fun, good-looking and maybe, just maybe, she could cook.

Branca sat down and ordered fried fish on rice and a beer. "If you remember, Morgan, I delivered my part of the bargain. Senhora Senna da Silva is working with us, thanks to some expensive jewelry, for which you need to reimburse me. I will carry my weight by cooking Portuguese food like you've never tasted before. I looked at your pathetic food supply. Let's go to the food market when we finish dinner." Morgan capitulated grumpily and Lynch smirked while Branca dove into her fish dinner.

"When we reach the Rapid End lodge, everything changes. The trawlers return down river and we head into wild country carting contraband goods. You would—"

Branca cut Morgan off. "I'm only along for the boat ride. A friend will fly in to pick me up. There is a small airstrip near Rapid End."

"You seem to have thought of everything," Morgan growled. "Who is this guy with the plane?"

"You don't know her. I have flown all over Mozambique with Andrea. She's a great pilot and a good friend." Morgan shook his head while Lynch chuckled as the three headed for the night street market.

As dawn broke, two trawlers, both wallowing in water up to the gunwales, headed up the Chinde estuary. The lead boat looked newer, had a fly bridge and towed a barge with a canopy covering the cargo. A lone helmsman in the stern worked the rudder. The other boat followed a thousand meters behind. It had a low-slung cockpit, but its 12-meter length offered greater storage space both above and below deck. Both boats had Volvo Penta 150 HP diesel engines and, most important, their draft barely reached a little more than two meters. The two boats had been carefully outfitted to navigate the Zambezi River; they had large fuel tanks, powerful engines, broad 2-3/4 meter beams and maximum space for cargo. Amenities were minimal.

It was first light and Morgan glowered at the chart before him and then at Branca. "This will not be a cakewalk, my pet. Are you seaworthy?" Gesturing toward the small galley, Morgan suggested, "Now would be a good time to display your professed culinary skills."

Branca's beaming face balanced Palmer's dour mood. Her excitement radiated from just being with Morgan and the long dreamed of trip up the Zambezi accentuated her happiness.

The two trawlers soon left the estuary, swinging west on the Zambezi River. The early morning sun promised good weather and caressed the river water causing it to shimmer. In order to appear as if they were not traveling together, the second boat, with Lynch and two native crewmen, hung back and allowed Morgan's boat to disappear behind at least one bend before coming into view. The thick jungle along the river's shore had been cut back in most places to allow for human encroachment. Many small villages, with houses built on stilted legs to withstand the spring flooding, dotted the shoreline. Small fishing boats clustered in areas closer to the shore, their owners flinging great nets with athletic skill before slowly hauling in the catch.

When the river widened, Morgan steered closer to the center, following the deepest channel indicated on his chart. He noticed a larger boat upriver that seemed to be having trouble with the current. Branca grabbed the binoculars to study the boat and its predicament. "It's a ferry boat. There are animals onboard," she yelled into the wind—"my God, it looks like something is in the water."

Morgan yelled down to his two crewmen standing on the prow watching the commotion. "What's happening up there? The ferry seems to be floundering."

"They crossing river with cattle. One fall in, *Chefe*," they called back, using their word for "boss" when addressing Morgan. "Big fish—big problem!"

Morgan and Branca saw the dark dorsal fins simultaneously. "Bull sharks," Morgan muttered. "A cow has fallen into the river and is being torn apart. It looks like there are five or six sharks." Now visible amidst the blood on the water's surface were huge thrashing sharks fighting for the flesh.

Branca was mesmerized. She couldn't tear her eyes away from the brutal scene before her. The cattle onboard were terrorized and threatened to capsize the boat. "What can we do?"

"Here, hold the wheel and maintain our course." Morgan grabbed his rifle and jumped down the steps to the main deck. As the trawler passed one of the sharks, Morgan steadied himself, aimed and put six bullets into a six-foot Zambezi shark, causing it to roll over and spew blood. The other sharks immediately attacked it in a frenzy of fins and frothing water, colored red from the blood. As the trawler swept past the ancient ferry, Morgan watched as they gradually brought the boat under control and continued their crossing of the river—minus one cow.

When Morgan climbed back to the wheelhouse, Branca, looking a little pale, asked, "I thought sharks lived in the ocean. What are they doing up this river? They're huge!"

"Yeah, everyone along the river thinks the Bull shark lives only here, but actually, they are all over the world; Australia, the East Coast of the US, and other waters off Africa. They're very unpredictable and often aggressive. The so-called Zambezi shark is unique among shark species because it can tolerate warm fresh water and travel far upstream." He looked behind them at the churning water before continuing. "When they're in the sea, they hunt just below the surface, rarely going below 40 meters. You don't see anyone swimming in these parts, do you?" Morgan took the wheel with one hand and wrapped his other arm around Branca's waist, pulling her close to him. "I'm glad you're along, actually. I find your company stimulating." He leaned over and kissed her cheek and when she turned her face to look at him, he captured her lush mouth with his. For a moment, his other hand left the wheel as they embraced eagerly.

They were making good progress. Morgan estimated they would cover 100 kilometers this first day, putting them ahead of schedule, a saving they would likely need, since he knew the river could be full of surprises. One day at a time, he muttered to himself, as he began to search for a mooring spot away from the main thrust of the current. October was the end of the dry season, offering both advantages and problems. The river was at its low point with the flow of water less swift than in the fall when they would make another trip up the river with the second shipment. The shallowness would present problems further up the river. They were now working closer to the northern bank, in quest of a mooring. The uninspiring landscape along the river sloped gradually through high reeds to muddy banks. The occasional small villages were set back from the river, always on the highest land around. Enormous crocodiles lazed in the sun, motionless, watching and hungry. Morgan found an inlet with a thin stratum of gray and yellow sandstone, an outcrop from the river bed that would provide a dependable anchorage.

Thirty minutes later, Lynch's trawler swung into the cove and joined them. The native crew, who had their own supply of food and water, remained on Lynch's boat. The breeze had waned, and with the light diminishing rapidly, insects swarmed. Fortunately the windows in the wheelhouse and main cabin were screened, allowing Branca to cook comfortably while the two Rhodesians, beer bottles in hand, watched her prepare their dinner.

Their second day on the Zambezi offered no changes. The river was still wide which allowed them to pass river traffic at a safe distance. There seemed to be more crocodiles, and something new appeared on the scene, large pods of hippopotamuses. They were usually submerged with only their bulging eyes and half of their enormous mouths above the water surface. Only once did Branca see one on land, a calf moving surprisingly fast down a path leading to the water. Morgan and Branca stifled the monotony by relating stories of their lives, sometimes delving into their childhoods, interspersed with Morgan relating hilarious incidents of hunting on the savanna. They discovered that they enjoyed similar things: food, new places to explore, books, music and long periods of silence. They became increasingly caught up in each other, joking, touching, looking at each other longingly and enjoying the precursors to lovemaking.

After dinner and coffee on Morgan's boat, Lynch returned to his trawler where the four crewmen were camped out. Morgan and Branca watched him cross to his boat before they turned and entered their cabin. Without hesitation or inhibition, Branca unhurriedly stripped off her clothes and then methodically undressed Morgan. He loved the sensuality of this foreplay. As Branca removed each article of clothing, she massaged his body with uncanny wisdom, rolling the aches away. Even the soles of his feet received her attention. She marveled at his physical strength, the large muscles through the shoulders and down his arms, the mat of black hair on his chest. He was big in every way. She grasped his erection, massaging insistently until he could stand it no longer. He grabbed her wondrous body, and as she shrieked with delight, he swung her onto the bunk, where he took control of their now slightly-out-of-control lovemaking.

The morning of day three on the river broke with a promise of a clear sky. Branca sat on a hatch on the stern sipping black coffee while watching the sun rise quickly out of the Indian Ocean. Today will be a hot one, she thought, as she pondered the prospects of the day ahead. The river was very wide, perhaps four kilometers, and the far shore was merely a vague outline on the horizon. She loved the journey, insects and all, because she was with Morgan and away from her usual routine in the city. She sensed him behind her, and without turning, said, "Good morning, Captain. What's our heading today?"

Morgan kissed the crown of her head before moving to the rail to watch the assembling river traffic. "Today, my pet, I am taking you to lunch in the city."

"City, lunch? The nearest city is Salisbury."

Morgan turned back to Branca smiling. "If we start soon, we should arrive in Tete by late morning. The docking area is on the south shore, which will add an hour to just crossing the river. We need to arrive ahead of Lynch, who will loiter down river. Big eyes will see the barge and tongues will wag. You and I can head into town for lunch and shop for provisions, while Limbua takes our boat back to claim the barge. That will allow Lynch to dock and refuel."

"You should have been a general, Morgan. You seem to have thought of every detail. After lunch I really want to see some wild animals. So far, I've seen sharks, crocs and hippos. Where are the big five?"

The town of Tete straddled the river, which was no small task as the distance across was several kilometers. A narrow, rutted road came in from the south to a dock area that serviced two ferry boats equipped to accommodate anything and everything from cattle to trucks. On the north side, the humble road headed into the wilderness. Tete was a frontier town, unattractive and banal. Morgan made good his promise of lunch. The café hugged the river bank and served fish that must have been caught an hour before.

By mid-afternoon the two trawlers, now low in the water with full fuel tanks, headed northwest and cut diagonally back to the north side. As they churned around the first bend and the town disappeared from view, the Zambezi perceptibly narrowed, causing the current to increase. The sky had turned the color of buttermilk and birds—land birds too—skimmed the water, searching for insects before darting back to shore. The land along the shore rose more sharply here, as reeds gave way to thicker undergrowth and trees. They had left the flood plain and were entering the middle section of the giant river.

A storm blew in suddenly; the rain fell hard, causing a clatter when it slapped the foliage along the bank. It slipped away just as quickly, adding a delicious freshness to the air. Morgan searched for an inlet where they could lay up for the night. After the two boats and the barge were secure in their moorings, Morgan lowered a yellow canoe into the placid shoreline water, got in and helped Branca settle into the bow. With a basket in the center full of cheese, crackers and a flask of Rum and Coke, they paddled toward the islands that hugged the shore. Morgan had never been here, yet he instinctively knew where to go. The sun had by now dipped below the cloud cover, its rays splashing a scarlet hue on the underbelly of the clouds.

They came to an escarpment facing west over the narrow river. Morgan beached their canoe and pulled Branca up the embankment, where they settled on the trunk of a fallen tree. Branca thrilled at the scene before her. This is so perfect, so beautiful, she thought, almost ethereal. I will never forget this moment. She placed every nuance in her memory bank. As she reached for Morgan's hand, she heard them. It sounded like an off-key trumpet and then, again, another one, this time the tone of a trombone. A herd of elephants appeared in a line across the river forcing Morgan and Branca to look into the sinking sun that bathed them in a subdued light. The elephants' broad ears flapped; they were linked tail to trunk. They turned to cross the river just above where Morgan and Branca were sitting, breathless and transfixed.

"There must be twenty-five or thirty," Morgan whispered. "Look, see how the leader is a female! No mature bulls are allowed in the herd. They are only admitted back when it's time to select a female for breeding. They are magnificent animals aren't they? After all these years in the bush, my flesh still ripples with awe at the sight of them."

The sun had now become a half circle, rich in gold, and silhouetted against its declining moments, a line of Egyptian geese streaked north, heading for the Nile.

On the sixth morning, under a heavy sky, the two boats and a barge lumbered slowly to the center of the river and headed into the surging current. The river had narrowed, squeezing the water flow. They progressed slowly and Morgan struggled to keep his boat on point. This would be their last day on the river. Morgan's thoughts centered on the task of transferring his cargo to the land portion of the journey. Branca, standing close to him, felt a sense of melancholy as her adventure would soon end. Morgan had become important to her life.

After dinner, Limbua joined Morgan and Lynch to review their strategy for landing and transferring their cargo early the next morning. Morgan expected his friend, Robin Thistle, to meet them on the river's long reach before it came to a sharp bend. Robin's camp, called "Rapid End," occupied that bend and the land beyond. He and his Rhodesian wife, Ronne, ran a well-known destination camp for rafters coming down the Zambezi. The final class-five rapids were five kilometers north of the camp. Guests would usually elect to stay on for several days after rafting, to fish for the famed tiger fish and photograph the animal kingdom that surrounded the camp. Ronne ran a very good kitchen and the individual bungalows provided elegant living for this remote part of the world.

"Tomorrow we need an early start so that we arrive at Rapid End by mid-day," Morgan announced, while checking his river navigation charts. "Most of their guests will not have arrived or will be on safari. The dock is past the camp and large enough to handle our trawlers, one at a time. There is only one truck, so we will park our cargo away from the docking area. What is special about this location is the landing strip a short distance in from the river. This is how Mr. Thistle's clients leave after rafting. Any questions so far?"

Lynch said, "The barge will be difficult. How will we land it?"

"We'll use both boats to slowly usher the barge to the dock. Once empty, we'll anchor it up river while the two boats are unloaded. Limbua, you and your friends will unload. Mr. Thistle has a small forklift so he and his people will load his truck or move the crates to a staging area. When everything has been off-loaded, you four will leave immediately for home. Are you ready for that?"

"Yes, *Chefe*, I know river well. We ready."

"Listen to me carefully, Limbua. There will be no time to talk tomorrow. You will have enough fuel and provisions to stay you over to Chinde. Have the boat works mail to me the certificate indicating the boats were returned in good shape. When I receive it, I'll send your bonus. All of you will receive your agreed stipend tomorrow. The first day you will need to maintain a faster speed than normal, otherwise the barge will swing and you will lose control. When you reach the flood plain, keep your speed under fifteen knots. Never leave your boats, never run the river at night and carefully moor away from traffic and people. Got it?"

"Si, *Chefe*. We will be careful." Limbua said, as he rose and left the trio to their own plans.

Lynch reached for the beer, opened three bottles and tapped his bottle against Branca's and Morgan's. "It was a pleasant trip on the river; now to the tough part of our journey."

The Zambezi River turned gradually north, deviating from its steadfast northwest passage toward the belly of Africa. Livingston, in his bid to sail into Africa, abandoned the river near this point. Both shores were now covered with vegetation, at times lush, while in the distance low slung mountains framed the milky sky. Pods of hippos demanded total concentration when steering the trawlers. At one point they encountered elephants on one side and Cape buffalo on the other. Further up river, four zebras standing on the shore eyed a crocodile snoozing in the mud below them before moving further down river to quench their thirst. The radio hissed, and after delicate adjusting, Keane's voice came through. "The plane is ready. We should be on your airstrip by 0900, Tuesday, the day after tomorrow."

"And our trucks, have they left for the camp yet?"

"Yes, they should arrive at our camp on Tuesday as well."

"Well done," Morgan said, preferring to not use a name. "Don't forget Jeffrey," referring to his rifle. "Godspeed," he offered as he clicked the radio switch off. Morgan turned to Branca, "You had better radio your pilot and suggest that she drop in on us on Tuesday."

Well up the reach of the river a small motor boat raced toward the two trawlers. When it drew closer, Morgan trained his binoculars on it and exclaimed, "Blimey, Robin got himself a new fishing boat. Business must be good."

Robin was standing on the fly bridge smiling broadly. He swung the fishing boat in an arch and came abreast of Morgan's trawler. Through a small megaphone he yelled, "Morgan, you scoundrel, if you don't have my merchandise, you'll have to turn around."

"Hey, Robin, would I forget your passion?" He reached down to a box on the floor, withdrew a bottle of Johnny Walker Black Label and waved it at Robin. "Two cases, mate, one for you and the other for Ronne."

They trailed Robin for several kilometers before the camp buildings on the point came into view. On the far side, past a row of bungalows and the large main building, the docking area appeared. A small forklift sat at the end of the pier, and Morgan could see a flatbed truck near a warehouse. He swung his boat around to catch the back of the barge. Lynch performed a similar loop to the other end of the barge and the two trawlers, like tug boats, slowly maneuvered the barge to the end of the pier. It was secured to the piling, where unloading began immediately. By mid-afternoon they were finished, with the luggage coming ashore last. Ronne had come down to the landing to greet everyone. She was a short, well proportioned woman with dark blond hair, cut short like a man's, and a smile that exuded contentment and joviality. After introducing Branca, Morgan returned to the pier for last instructions to Limbua, handed him a brown envelope and watched him climb to the trawler fly-deck. The two boats slipped back into the main rush of the river, heading with the flow toward home. The sun had moved west and fast moving clouds cast fleeting shadows on the river, like an old black and white movie blinking on the screen.

As Morgan walked back to the huddle of people standing in the shade of the warehouse, he noticed a tall, thin man standing near the trees at the end of the landing area. He wore bush clothes, shorts, a multi-pocketed shirt and high boots. "Good Lord!" Morgan muttered in a whisper out loud. "It's Roger Smith-Stevens. What the hell is he doing here and why is he nosing around our landing?"

The tall man waved a walking stick, which he used more as a swagger stick, as he marched toward Morgan. "Good to see you again, Palmer. It's been awhile, what say—three years, or more?"

Smith-Steven sported a brush mustache which overlapped his upper lip, partially concealing a tight smile. His eyes did not share the smile; they were cold and menacing. "Hello, Roger. What a surprise finding you in Mozambique. Are you still in the Rhodesian army chasing rebels?"

"I'm here with my two sons, who dragged me down the Cahora Bassa rapids in a raft. It's safer fighting rebels, by Jove, and, yes, I'm still in the army; recently made Lieutenant Colonel, I'm pleased to say." He paused while looking over Morgan's shoulder and pointing his walking stick at the disappearing trawlers. "I say, saw those two boats coming around the point. They belong around the mouth of the Zambezi, I should think, not in this section of the river. Too big, I'd say. What in the world is in all these crates?" He pointed at the cargo with his swagger stick. "Are you still running big game safaris on the Luangwa plateau, Palmer?"

Morgan's mind was moving fast. This man was all questions and had a nose for trouble. The army ranks knew Smith-Stevens as "SS," which some said meant swagger stick. What a bad piece of luck to run into him, Morgan thought.

"Yes," Morgan replied, answering the second question and avoiding the first. "We are preparing and stocking our safari camps early this year. We're heavily booked next autumn."

Branca and Ronne walked toward them causing Roger's mind to lose focus. The two women changed the conversation, and soon Ronne was escorting the group to the main camp area. Morgan had not answered Roger's questions but he knew they would be asked again in the evening.

The main building was perched on a low hill and located well back from the river. It featured a great room, which was open to the elements, including flying insects. Once darkness took hold, the air became chilly, and caused the insects to disappear. A throng of excited rafters crowded a long bar, and by the time Morgan and Branca arrived for dinner, the stories of the perils of the Cahora Bassa had expanded with each rendition.

After dinner Morgan and Branca escaped to the porch of their bungalow. They sat in silence, sipping good whisky as they listened to the sounds of the jungle. Branca moved closer to Morgan on the bench, and reached over to touch her mouth to his ear, letting her tongue caress the intricate folds. "Thank you for letting me come with you on the river," she whispered. "I have never enjoyed anything so much. You are wonderful to travel with, to be with," she giggled, "both in and out of bed. I want to go on a safari with you. When will you take me?"

"We'll go tomorrow morning early." His voice was husky, "Robin will take the two of us on a drive through the national game park. You'll see a lot of animals: elephants, zebras, giraffes, hyenas, and maybe a wild dog or even a pride of lions. The birds are beautiful. You will see flowers you have never heard of. The park is a special place. If you like the experience, I'll take you to the Luangwa savanna on a hunting safari next spring." Without missing a beat, he continued, "And in return for that offer, I would like to begin by removing your clothes."

"You may, but do it ever so slowly, please," she said softly. "Will our revelry disturb the rest of the camp you think?"

Morgan only grunted in response. His hands had already slipped under her blouse, deftly unsnapping the bra and with one swift movement he lifted her onto his lap facing him. She could feel his arousal and felt the responding heat in her loins. Her slacks were already on the floor when his tongue began to slowly lick her now stiffened nipples, pulling gently, before moving to the soft curve of her breasts. Their tongues met and worked eagerly in an erotic dance all their own.

"Are you going to have me here in front of the hippos or should we go inside?" Her voice was hoarse. Without collecting their discarded clothes, they retreated to their bedroom.

The night was wondrous; the moaning and laughing resplendent, while the hippos remained unaware of the celebration taking place in the bungalow on the rise above their pod.

Tuesday brought low, gray clouds and a guarantee of rain. Morgan's thoughts were gray as well. He joined Robin and Lynch near the stacked crates along the runway where they stood in silence, their eyes searching the sky to the west. Morgan had accompanied Branca on yesterday's safari to avoid Smith-Stevens. The man was a pest and would certainly inquire about Morgan's activities when he returned to Salisbury. Would he check on flights out of Lusaka, he wondered? Morgan turned to Robin, "Did Roger press you for details of my activities here?"

"Seriously mate, he was all questions. He even inspected these crates, no doubt noting the shipping label. His kids were running all over the place, which did distract him somewhat. Thankfully his flight arrived on time and they flew off to Salisbury around 9 a.m. He asked me what the crates contained. I said I thought mechanical parts. I don't think he bought that."

"Thanks, Robin. I hope this doesn't kick back on you. If they contact you, just say that I'm an old friend with a lot of supplies, heading off on safari."

Branca and Ronne pulled up in the open safari wagon. "I thought you two would be half way to Luangwa by now," Branca said, her eyes resting only on Morgan. She held his gaze when he didn't reply. Their relationship had now become complicated and deeper, as they became intimate friends as well as lovers. She felt inordinate joy being with him, even in silence. Saying goodbye would be swift. Morgan liked it that way. "Maybe my little plane will beat yours to the tarmac," Branca purred to no one in particular.

Morgan searched her face for something, though he wasn't sure just what. Sadness, a smile or some sign of sentiment. There was nothing except exquisite beauty. He felt the urge to take her in his arms. For the first time, he wished a woman, this woman, would stay with him. His trance was snapped by Lynch's shout that a small plane was approaching from the east. It dove toward the runway, dropped its retractable wheels and settled without a bounce.

Andrea swung the Beachcraft 35 Bonanza skillfully so that the door opened near the huddle of bystanders. The plane had a rakishly streamlined shape, giving it the appearance of a fighter. Andrea climbed out from the cockpit, stepped on the wing and jumped to the tarmac with a fluid motion before skipping to Branca to give her a hug. "Are you ready, girl, we need to head? There's bad weather brewing." Andrea was short, stocky without being plump, and wore an outfit that would be suitable for snow skiing, causing Morgan to wonder if the plane interior had heating.

After introductions, and all too soon for her, Branca turned to Morgan, wrapped her arms around his neck and kissed him briefly on the lips. "I miss you already, my darling. Come back to me soon. Be safe." Then she turned to join Andrea in the cockpit. There was a puff of smoke as the engine responded and purred. Soon they were taxing, turning, and then racing down the airstrip. The little plane banked sharply and descended steeply toward the group standing on the tarmac, before zooming overhead and pointing southeast, away from the approaching storm. Branca smiled and waved as they dusted the airstrip.

The DC-3 came in so low that it sneaked up on them. When the engines were cut, both Keane and Colin jumped to the ground and greeted everyone. Colin had the same message as Andrea. "Let's load this puppy quickly. I'd like to get well away from the storm heading our way. This old bucket has flown a lot of miles and is not anxious to fight head winds."

Morgan had calculated perfectly. The DC-3 accommodated half of the crates. He shook hands with Robin and hugged Ronne as they all walked to the plane. "Colin will return tomorrow, about the same time, and collect the rest of our boxes." As he closed the hatch, Morgan yelled to Robin, "I owe you a big one!"

Katanga

The storm that threatened the band of smugglers on the remote airstrip along the Zambezi blew into Northern Rhodesia during the evening. The wind heralded the rain, and then slipped away. The rain drops were large, heavy nuggets that raised a din when striking the runway. Ndola's terminal building was a long shack which hugged the only runway. The air was heavy inside the building, causing the small group of people waiting for the flight from Salisbury to take shelter. The racket of the rain hitting the metal roof and the darkness provided solitude for each man in the all male group. A few white men clustered together in the terminal building chatting quietly and smoking. The rest were black who stood in an open shelter on the outside of the perimeter fence. Only whites were allowed in the compound. Thomas stood at one end of the shelter, oblivious to both the storm and other people. He was dressed nicely in long dark trousers and a white shirt. The briefcase and umbrella set him off from the others. He looked out to the runway and listened for the sound of the plane he was meeting.

Another Katangese hung back from the others, remaining in the shadows. He too was waiting for the Salisbury flight, but his attention was focused on Thomas. Kigali usually wore a khaki Katanga army uniform, but he had thought better of wearing it in Northern Rhodesia. He watched Thomas with a loathing, reflected in the menacing whiteness of his eyes, even in the darkness that shrouded him. He resented Thomas's stature, dress, intellect and tribe. He did not trust him. His dislike was intense and it consumed him. He knew with certainty that one day he would need to acknowledge his enmity and perhaps eliminate the cause.

As if a ghost appearing from heaven, the DC-6 dropped out of the angry clouds, hit the runway, bounced, and then settled amid the roar of the four engines. Thomas considered it a miracle for a pilot to orchestrate a safe return to earth in weather as threatening as Ndola was enduring on this evening. The prop plane pulled close to the fence, allowing the open canopy to cover the disembarking passengers. Samantha was easy to spot: tall, lissome, blonde and toting a large canvas camera bag. Thomas guessed she must be close to 175 cm tall. The khaki bush jacket did not camouflage her svelte figure. She saw Thomas, smiled broadly and waved. As Kigali watched them shake hands his anger turned to disgust.

One of the last passengers to emerge from the plane was a thin man dressed in black, including a black stocking cap. No one noticed him except Kigali. They had never met, but each had a description of the other. They nodded without shaking hands and walked quickly to the car parking lot.

Kigali and Adraan drove in silence, each waiting for the other to bridge the gap between them. They passed through immigration easily and entered Katanga. Finally Adraan removed his stocking cap, turned to Kigali and asked in a falsetto voice, "Have you heard from the white hunters?"

"Not directly, but their office has communicated twice. They are in three trucks somewhere west of the Muchinga Mountain range. They flew there from an airstrip in Mozambique. The second message indicated that there was a spotter plane circling the area delaying their progress." Kigali related all of this while dodging in and out of traffic.

"Whose plane?"

"We don't know. Its Rhodesian airspace so we are assuming it's their military. But why is another question."

Adraan's physical frame was slight. He seemed lost in the large bush wagon. "When and where do you think they will cross into Katanga?"

Kigali suddenly changed the subject. "Are you African? You're not white nor are you black."

"Does it matter?"

"Here in Katanga it's important to know someone's origin—his tribe."

Adraan did not speak for several minutes. He seemed to be mulling over the impertinent and unnecessary question.

Finally he muttered in a quiet voice, "I come from nowhere specifically. It is not important where I was born and raised nor is it any of your business. I am African in blood and disposition. I'm here on business and you are my customer. I will stay only as long as it takes to assure delivery of our merchandise. I do not wish to meet with your superiors and finally, I would like to be at the border when the three trucks cross. Do you have a problem with any of this?"

Kigali broke into a grin. Maybe he could get along with this stranger from South Africa. "Elizabethville has been occupied by UN troops from Ghana. The Belgian military remains at our copper mine. There are others too and, happily, all gather in town to drink beer as if they were friends. You will stay with me in a barracks outside of Elizabethville. In two days we will move with some of my men to the border location where I believe the trucks carrying our weapons will enter Katanga."

Adraan asked, "How far is the border and where will you train the men to use the AK-47s?"

They were speaking French and Kigali was beginning to enjoy their conversation. "Let me give you a geography lesson, if I may. All of Africa belongs to us—us Africans. The Belgian dogs have finally departed and soon Rhodesia will crumble. The French, the English, the Germans and the Portuguese will soon all be gone from Africa. What they will leave behind, besides chaos and hatred, are artificial boundaries, established by the white man to suit his benefit. No consideration was given to dialects, tribal history or physical features of the land. Take a look at the arbitrary borders of Katanga sometime. Note the projection of

Katanga territory jutting: it's just like a prick peeing on the white man, 200 kilometers into the Federation of Rhodesia."

Adraan now had a flashlight and was peering at the map in his lap. "I see what you are describing. Tell me more."

Kigali was driving dangerously fast in the rain storm. Adraan's flashlight beam made it difficult to see through the rain pelting the windshield. He spoke slowly, concentrating on his driving. "We don't know this white hunter, Palmer, but he is well known in Northern Rhodesia. I understand he guides safaris in the Luangwa River valley, east of the great mountains. He must know the area well and my guess is that's where he's heading. We have no idea how he plans to get from there to our border. To the southeast, there are a few roads and villages, but also the Rhodesian military. In the north, they would be confronted by the Muchinga Mountains that rise over six thousand feet from the valley floor. If he is resourceful, this Palmer will somehow skirt the Katanga protrusion, cross a lot of waterways to the north, keep south of Fort Rosebery and enter Katanga somewhere around the Luapula River. The roads are nothing more than ranger tracks or elephant paths. It is remote and too far from Elizabethville to arouse suspicion. We will train right there."

"Fine, then let's go to this place immediately and set up camp." Adraan folded the map, doused his flashlight and settled back in his seat. He didn't say another word until they reached the barracks. It was only when Kigali parked the car that he realized that Adraan was fast asleep.

In another car not far behind Kigali's, Samantha and Thomas watched the windshield wipers struggle to cope with the torrential deluge, each waiting for the other to open the conversation. Thomas's deep voice broke the silence. "Thank you for coming to Katanga, Miss Norquist, he said in English. I'm sure you were advised to not make this trip. You will soon find that your decision was a good one. I will do everything possible to avoid dangerous situations and still show you our country. Your visit will be worthwhile, for you and for Katanga. How long will you stay with us?"

Samantha turned her head and looked intently at the man who had just promised to protect her from danger. She didn't know him at all. They had met briefly at Henley and after that, only one letter and a phone call. "My time schedule is rather loose, Thomas. Let's use our given names—I'm Samantha. I would guess we would be working together for a week."

The rain diminished as they approached the Katanga border. The line of cars passed through the Rhodesian perfunctory inspection with little delay. The Katanga side surprised Samantha for there was no inspection booth or gate across the road. Just one soldier, smoking a cigarette, standing next to several sawhorses, waving them through.

"Our security is lax," Thomas said, with a tight grin. The poor condition of the road required the line of cars to slow. "You came from London, I gather. How was your flight?"

Samantha chatted about her uncomfortable flight to Salisbury and the long delay there. The darkness and rain prevented her from seeing the land she had come to photograph so she settled back in her seat and explored with Thomas the week before her. "What's our schedule tomorrow, Thomas? I'm bushed now but I'll be ready to start at the crack of dawn, if you wish."

She listened to Thomas's intricate plans wondering if seven days would be sufficient. There were few lights as they drove through the outskirts of Elizabethville, Katanga's capital, revealing a sleeping, desolate city. They reached a broad boulevard, navigated several traffic circles, and parked in front of Samantha's hotel.

"This old colonial hotel is our best. I hope you will find it adequate," Thomas offered as they entered the deserted lobby. Thomas pointed to the cafe. "You will find a French breakfast over there beginning at seven. I'll pick you up at 7:30. We'll have plenty of time to see the city come alive. You are to meet President Tshombe at eleven. Again, Samantha, thank you for coming." Thomas extended his hand.

The following morning, at seven sharp, Samantha nursed a cup of coffee and watched the sullen waitress head her way with breakfast. She was one of three in the café. She had slept fitfully. Her room was fine—clean and specious, but it was the heavy, humid air that had disrupted her rest. The open windows and a ceiling fan provided no relief. Still, awaking in the middle of Africa gave Sam a jolt of excitement and all thoughts of fatigue evaporated. *Echo Magazine* had condoned and funded this assignment. She was to photograph the life of the people the colonialists had left behind and the developing military action. All of this Thomas had promised to deliver. But there was another story; one she wanted most of all. She knew Thomas was involved in gun smuggling. She would be patient, Sam promised herself. Thomas had the information she wanted. The challenge would be to extract it.

She saw him enter the lobby, walking rapidly in long strides toward her table. He is a handsome man, she admitted to herself. Black men had never captured her attention before but Thomas Kimbamba was attractive; his stature was enhanced by a physicalness that exuded energy.

"Good morning, Miss, ah, Samantha," he pronounced his stumbling greeting with a broad smile. Thomas signaled the waitress for coffee and turned back to Samantha. "Are you rested and ready for an interesting day?"

Samantha discovered that Thomas was a teacher of science. Botany and zoology were his compelling interests and he explained that he had no interest in politics. Over a second cup of coffee, he explained his relationship with Moise Tshombe, the self-proclaimed president of the Province of Katanga, which had seceded from the DRC only a few months before and declared itself a country. "My father and Tshombe were great friends when they were young." He told Samantha about their upbringing and his childhood in the mountains to the north. "My father taught me to ride a horse and to shoot a rifle. But more important, he exposed me to the abundant plant and animal life in the park where he was a ranger."

Samantha listened in rapt attention. She marveled at Thomas's diction and accent. It was as if she were talking with a young American man. Reluctantly, she moved the conversation to the present. "Tell me about Tshombe. How should I address him?"

"Call him Mr. President. He'll like that. He speaks English but prefers French. I've noticed you understand some French. Can you speak it?"

"My spoken French is rusty, Thomas. "I haven't used it since school. Let's stay with English, if possible." Samantha said this with caution. *Does he remember the South African man asking me if I spoke French when we met in Henley,* she pondered? I have to be careful. Then she plunged in to the dark undercurrent of their task. "Why are you doing this? Thomas. What's your connection?"

"Come. Let's get out of here. I'll answer your questions in the car."

Samantha settled in the front seat of Thomas's battered Renault. The engine purred but the right front fender rattled as they bumped down the street in the direction of the river. They found the bridge that lead out of the city center to what appeared to be a cramped residential area. It teemed with people, bicycles but, strangely, Sam thought, no animals. As they slowly navigated the crowd, Samantha could see the river bank from the car; every foot appeared to be occupied by women washing clothes. Children played in and about the water. There were no men. Samantha asked about their absence.

"Working somewhere," Thomas said, shrugging. "Some were probably conscripted into our new army. Others work in mines or plantations too far away for them to return home at night."

"Can we stop, Thomas? I'd like to get closer. Maybe peek in their homes." Sam got out and walked across the street to where a group of children were watching her intently. Thomas joined them and asked if they could take pictures. This request caused great commotion and many smiles. The children surrounded Sam and lead her down a dusty, narrow street, all pointing to small clay hovels, which were their homes. Sam photographed everything: the children, the street and their homes. Her Nikon caught the food stalls, the drinking water well and one policeman. This is great stuff, she thought as Thomas hurried her back to their car, reminding Samantha that she had an appointment with the president.

Tshombe, dressed in a white shirt and blue suit, sat pensively on his front porch. When he saw Samantha and Thomas walking toward him on the garden path, he rose to greet them at the top of the steps. Standing before him as Thomas introduced her, Sam realized Tshombe's height matched hers. It was Tshombe's head that captured Samantha's attention for the singular features were all large. The round face circled enormous and expressive eyes, which at this moment, were sparkling. Tshombe's prominent lips stretched from one side of his face to the other and he had not yet smiled. He surveyed Samantha briefly; his broad smile together with his shining eyes radiated pleasure. Tshombe began talking in English, with trivial banter about last night's storm, which quickly put Samantha at ease. After green tea was served, Tshombe settled back into his cushioned chair and expound on Katanga's tenuous political position and his aspirations for the future of the renegade province. Samantha sat quietly, fingering the Nikon camera in her lap.

"I've asked Thomas to show you around our country. We have many enemies and it is a dangerous place, so there are some areas you probably should not visit. Interview the people—Thomas will translate—and report to America how happy they are and how much this government is doing for them. I do not trust the Soviets or the ever-changing régime in Leopoldville. It is America's friendship that we seek. We will be a great partner in this part of Africa. I hope you can express this wish for us."

Samantha turned to Thomas, who did not return her glance. She turned back to the president and held up her camera. "This is my notebook, Mr. President. I'm sure Thomas reported that I'm a photographer, not a journalist.

My magazine, *Echo*, rarely takes political positions. It gathers and reports facts allowing its readership to make decisions and take sides."

Tshombe interrupted. "Then tell me how you will report on our country?"

"With photographs, sir. If you are willing, I would like to take a portrait of you. It will be considered for our cover, which will afford you broad exposure. The photo piece I will submit to the magazine will consist entirely of black and white photographs depicting life in the city and the countryside as it really is. The camera does not lie."

"I'm glad for your visit, Miss Norquist. You will enjoy traveling around our country. Katanga is a land rich in resources and beautiful, with mountains and cloud forests. But it is the people who live here who are important. We want to live our lives in peace." Tshombe paused to sip his tea and gather his thoughts. Samantha leaped into the pause.

"Does everyone here in Katanga support secession?"

Before Thomas could assuage the question, Tshombe said, "A reasonable question and one the world is asking. We, who are taking the lead, believe our actions are in the best interest of our people. Most know little about politics. They want food, water, employment and safety. Given time, we can provide that."

"I should take your portrait soon while the light is right." Samantha said, standing and moving her chair. Tshombe was still talking as she assembled her tripod and camera.

"Should I be standing or sitting?" Tshombe asked, while dusting his suit coat and smoothing the hair on the side of his bald head.

"Let's do both." She snapped rapidly but never seemed to achieve a happy, smiling face. Tshombe peered into the camera with an inquisitive look, as if searching for answers to the problems confronting him.

When the picture-taking session had finished, they sat again, briefly, chatting in generalities. Samantha instinctively knew this man could be ruthless and did not have the best interest of the Katangese in his heart. She recognized the great story she was following. The key to understanding the underlying currents resided with Thomas.

For two long, dusty days, Samantha toured the width and breadth of Elizabethville. She had little interest in the establishment: the government buildings, clubs and manicured suburbs. Her subjects were people in everyday activities, much of which involved water. The city people, women mostly, seemed to spend the day searching for and toting water to their homes. It was drinking water that was precious. The wells were crowded with women and children. The river offered no relief—a shallow flow of mud and debris. Sam and Thomas walked many of the roads that were too narrow for his car. The conditions were desperate, yet the women smiled at Samantha when she showed interest in their children. Sam took photos of everyone who would allow it, and often of some who were unaware.

At one point, Sam exclaimed, "These people are living in some of the worst conditions I have ever seen! I thought this province was rich in copper money. Where does it go?"

Thomas shrugged—a frequent gesture of his when he didn't have a good answer. "They seem poor by your standards but not by African standards. These people are better off than many in rural villages. At least there is a doctor, and soon we will have the schools functioning again."

"Let's go to the business district. I'd like to see your hospital with this one doctor." As they drove back across the bridge, Sam commented, "One thing I have noticed is the lack of passenger cars. I see lots of military vehicles, a few trucks but almost no cars."

"It's paradoxical," Thomas replied. "The city is full of cars just sitting and rusting. The Belgians, in their haste to leave, left their cars with the key in the ignition. But most people here, the women for sure, don't know how to drive. Those that do can't afford the petrol, which is in short supply. Look," he said pointing, "there's five sitting in a parking lot."

Sam noticed the quietness of the city. Like a lull before the storm. She noticed lots of rifles in the hands of uniformed men. A few were white men not in uniform. "Who are the Europeans?" she asked, watching Thomas's eyes.

"They are retired army officers from several countries, who have come to train our troops. They won't stay long." He evaded Sam's gaze.

"Mercenaries," Sam said, with emphasis. "I'd like to photograph them. Would they be willing?"

"Not likely, but we can try." Thomas was beginning to rethink his invitation to this inquisitive American woman.

Early on the third day, Samantha checked out of her hotel. She stood near the door of the empty lobby watching for Thomas's car. No breakfast this morning, she mused, as she scanned the street. Thomas arrived, loaded Sam's luggage and soon they were out of the city, driving west into the bush country. Samantha sat quietly watching the false dawn. The early morning had promised something it could not deliver—the sun, as the old saying goes. It did deliver an intense heat that the open windows of the car merely redistributed. The cloud cover eventually dispersed allowing the sun to intensify the temperature. By mid-morning, they had left the main highway, and began to ascend. The narrow dirt road angled toward the hills and the Union Minière copper mine. Thomas drove without talking. The heat had drained all energy. Samantha pulled at her water bottle and watched the hills and the desolate bush country as they slowly gained altitude. Eventually vegetation appeared and a lethargic stream here and there.

And then the mine loomed in front of them, a great mound of brown earth with trucks moving high up the ridge on a circular road. When Thomas's car puffed to the top and Sam could look into the vast pit, like a wound in the earth, she could see hundreds of nearly naked men working in the giant pit. She grabbed her camera and began firing.

Henri Bordeaux, the mine superintendent, emerged from the office building and stood waiting for them, his hands clasping his hips. A frown creased his forehead. Thomas jumped from the car and yelled through the dust. "Bonjour, Messr. Bordeaux. I'm Thomas Kimbamba—I called you about our visit—and I have the American photographer with me."

Samantha emerged from the car and walked to where Bordeaux was standing. "Good morning," she said in English.

Bordeaux continued, speaking in French. Samantha understood perfectly what he was saying. "This is inconvenient. Perhaps you could observe the mines operation from here and then be on your way."

As Samantha listened to Thomas politely reminding Bordeaux that she was a guest of President Tshombe, she edged away from the where the two men were standing. She had noticed uniformed European soldiers milling around and quietly, surreptitiously photographed them. Her 135mm lens bridged the distance and measured their faces. They were not young, innocent faces but the countenances of men who had experienced war and would not draw back from killing.

"I cannot allow you in the tunnel or the pit. They are too dangerous and you might interfere with the work," Bordeaux yelled while walking rapidly to where she was taking pictures. He had become somewhat desperate. "You are welcome to take pictures of the train, our equipment and of the mine from the top. The train is almost loaded and will move off by midday. The engine with smoke would be a good shot," Bordeaux offered, hoping to divert Sam's attention.

The mine had provided poignant photo opportunities. I think I captured the mood, Sam pondered. She had felt like a spy, listening to Bordeaux remonstrating in French and pretending she did not understand. By the time Thomas had translated, she had moved on to another picture. Those faces, she thought, the faces of the men working in the pit, were pictures of desperation.

Thomas drove fast leaving a trail of dust in the air. Both were hungry. Bordeaux had not offered lunch and the land they were driving through now offered nothing; not a town, not even a building. Thomas seemed to know where he was headed and had promised an early supper. "As soon as we reach the hills, we will find villages and markets where we can buy food.

They came to a bend in the road where a group of men were standing. Some were soldiers in uniform and a few were white men dressed in bush clothes. All carried weapons. The sun had disappeared in a cloud bank to the west leaving the road shrouded in darkness. Thomas stopped the car but did not get out. Sam watched apprehensively as two white men sauntered toward them. One moved to Samantha's side of the car.

"Let me see your papers," the bearded one said in French, leaning in Thomas's window.

"What papers?" Thomas replied. "I live up ahead in the hills not far from here. Who are you, anyway?"

The man on Samantha's side just stood there peering at her, with a leering expression

"I ask the questions," the other man said as he wrenched open Thomas's door. "Get out."

Thomas slowly emerged and stood looking down at the white man, who had moved back, surprised at Thomas's height. Thomas said, "I am a friend of the president and we are traveling on official business. I ask you, politely, to step back, and we will be on our way."

"I can't allow that." There are DRC military forces between here and the national park. You must turn around." Several black soldiers had wandered over to listen to the exchange. At that moment, two things happened that changed the scenario.

The moon faced mercenary—for that's what they were— reached for Samantha's camera case. He had to lean in the window to do so. Sam uncoiled, jamming her elbow in his face. For her, it was a conditioned response from growing up with three brothers, plus aikido classes in college. "No one touches my camera without my permission," she said rapidly in French. The man fell backwards, his face bloody. His rifle had fallen to the ground and he reached down for it while screaming obscenities. Thomas had turned toward her, panic on his face.

At that moment an explosion pierced the darkness. Automatic weapon fire ensued. The soldiers were scampering in different directions, obviously not sure of the gun fire source. A burst of fire caught the men standing near Thomas. One bullet hit the bearded mercenary in the shoulder, throwing him backward against the car. He sank to the ground, his shirt bloody. One soldier lay dead on the ground, his back shattered with holes. Sam leaped from the car holding her Nikon. She shot the moon faced man kneeling on the ground and then raced around the rear of the car to photograph the dead and wounded. She zoomed in on the skirmish. The Katanga soldiers were returning fire and moving forward into the bush.

"For God sake, Samantha, get in the car. Let's get out of here!" Thomas wheeled the Renault in a half circle and retreated down the road. He was breathing heavily.

"Do you have a gun?" Sam asked.

"Why would I have a gun? I have never carried one, I don't even like them." Thomas was incredulous and looked over at Sam in astonishment. "And your French suddenly has become fluent."

"How will we get to your sister's house?" Sam said in English. "The road is blocked. There's a war going on back there."

They drove without talking; gathering their thoughts. Thomas turned abruptly onto a dirt road. "I grew up around here. Only the locals use this road. In my youth, it was just a path."

Samantha studied Thomas's silhouette as he concentrated on driving. Finally she said in a soft voice. "Are you involved somehow in illegal gun trafficking?"

Thomas didn't answer immediately. Not looking at Sam, he replied in French. "We should be honest with each other. Why do you ask that question?'

"My French is good enough that I was able to understand some of your conversation in Henley. I couldn't help myself, I eavesdropped."

Gun fire in the distance broke the silence. "Yes, if you must know. It's not your concern and I would rather not discuss it."

I want to know about this gun business, Samantha said to herself. She persisted. "We're both a little rattled from that close call back there. I'm a realist. There are guns everywhere in the country. It seems all of Africa is at war with itself. Bringing weapons to Katanga isn't going to help, is it, Thomas?"

"We need to protect ourselves. Katanga is a small country with many enemies. My involvement is too complicated to explain. Let's leave it, at least for now. We should reach my sister's home in an hour." They were going up a small mountain and a fine mist had enveloped them, offering security.

Northern Rhodesia

Morgan Palmer sniffed the air searching for the scent that precedes the rain. No, he thought, not a hint. The rains are late this year and a good thing for where we are going it would be impassable in the rain. Morgan stood on a rocky outcrop searching the southern sky with his binoculars. It was mid-morning and the early spring sun moved quickly over the mountain range to the east. This is the best time of year up here on the plateau, he thought to himself as he peered up at a cerulean sky. The usual humid air was now dry, with a breeze ever present. The rains would come soon, he knew, but until then, the animal herds would stay close to the rivers and pools. Of course, the predators were there too.

The DC-3 finally approached from the east, directly in the sun's path, so that Morgan was unaware of its arrival until he heard the drone of the twin engines. It used the entire runway for its landing, then turned and bounced its way to the grove where Morgan's trucks were parked. When its cargo was loaded and secured in the trucks, the pilot, Colin, joined Morgan in his tent. Morgan was listening to a shortwave radio but flipped the switch off angrily when Colin entered. "That imbecile Colonel Smith-Stevens has been on the radio for the past twenty-four hours asking for my location. He saw the crates at Rapid End and is suspicious."

"Yeah, he was on my wave length too," Colin replied. "I told him I was heading north to Fort Hill. Is he a problem?"

"He is a problem. If he finds us in Rhodesia with all of these weapons, we will be in a pot of lava. However, his job is to find and destroy rebels in Rhodesia and I don't think he gives a toss about Katanga. All we need to do is get across the border. Then Colonel SS should become less of a nuisance. I'm hoping he'll look around the Luangwa Valley." Morgan stood up, stretched and stepped outside with Colin behind him. "Thank you, Colin, for doing this. I'll be back in Lusaka in a week to settle up with you."

"Come in, Palmer, come in. Smith-Stevens here. Can you read me?"

"Yes, Roger, I can hear you now. What can I do for you?"

"What is your location? Give me your coordinates."

"Difficult to do at the moment, Roger. We are in the Luangwa Valley, heading north. We're not following a road." Morgan was lying through his teeth. He had aborted the plan to use their safari landing strip on the Luangwa plateau because of Ol' SS's curiosity plus the difficulty in crossing the Muchinga Mountains. They were in a new location, somewhere between the mountains and Katanga's western border.

"What are you doing up there?" barked Smith-Stevens.

"Sorry, Roger, I don't understand your interest or concern. But if you must know, we are tidying up our safari camps preparing for the rainy season and stashing supplies so that we are ready for our hunting clients next year."

"I'm aloft right now. We are banking north from the Zambezi. I will find you and then we shall have a talk."

"Right," Morgan said. "See you then, Roger. Cheerio."

From across the tent, Lynch groaned. "Now what the fuck are we going to do?"

"We're going to break camp and head out," said Morgan.

"Head where?" Lynch waved his arms toward the horizon. "I've never been in this land before. Have you?"

"I've hunted around here many times with my father. I learned to shoot upland game here. Tomorrow we will enter the area called the "sponge," which encompasses hundreds of kilometers of small rivers, lakes and marshes. It's a haven for the most beautiful birds imaginable—hunters and photographer's paradise—and Smith-Stevens will not think to look for us there. We can slip into Katanga this side of Fort Rosebery. Let's get rolling."

The three Mercedes trucks carved their own road for two days. In the lead truck, Keane drove while Morgan, sitting beside him, fiddled with his binoculars, compass and maps and talked about the land surrounding them. Keane listened attentively; his fascination with the history, people and wild animals swelled as Morgan spoke.

Morgan Palmer's knowledge of Africa, especially this part of it, was astonishing, often erudite. "What we are seeing now," he said as his gaze searched the horizon, "is the bottom end of the Great Rift Valley. All that water you see out there came from as far north as Lake Albert."

"Uganda, right?"

"Yeah. And lots of people and wildlife are competing for this water and the land that it enriches." Morgan exhaled deeply and lifted his binocular. The animals will eventually lose out, that's for sure." He turned in his seat to search for the other two trucks. Lynch drove the second and one of the natives from Lusaka drove the third.

That evening, the three Rhodesians sat by the fire, the flame absorbing their thoughts, while the cackles, shrieks and grunting of wild animals hunting and rummaging in the darkness of night interrupted the prevailing peace.

Morgan's voice interrupted the silence. His mind had been on the guns. "Our mission is not only to deliver these weapons, but also to train the people who will use them. All three of us served in the Rhodesian military. We are skilled in the disciplines of a fighting force: weapons, chain of command and survival in difficult terrains. These are the things you will teach."

They had opened one crate on a remote section of the Zambezi River, to familiarize themselves with the AK-47 assault rifle. All three had fired it, dismantled it, cleaned it and then fired it again. They submerged the rifle in water, coated it in sand and then mud. They had been impressed.

Morgan continued. "This nasty rifle will become the bane of Africa. It's inaccurate but so very reliable. We are putting this rifle into unreliable hands." He turned away from the fire and looked at his compatriots. "You will attempt to make those hands reliable."

"Won't you be with us? Keane asked.

"I think I better skedaddle and cover our tracks. You keep one truck. The boys and I will drive the other two to our normal safari camps. I hope Smith-Stevens will have moved on to other interests by then. You have your radio. I will keep in touch."

On the second day they were in the "sponge," which on one hand slowed their progress, but on the other, provided a multiplicity of color, both in water flowers and birds. It was springtime below the equator causing life to burst. On one pond that stretched for a kilometer, hundreds of pink flamingos maneuvered for food. Their long legs seemed to be walking on the water while above more of them circled, flashing red and black as their wings flapped and waved, catching the sunlight like stage lights. There were ibises and spoonbills, with egrets hanging around the weedy fringe of the waterway.

There were hordes of animals as well. October vacillated on the cusp of the great rains, usually the last rasp of dry weather on the Rhodesian savanna. All species of animals congregated together near water, tolerating each other. A pride of lions, their appetites satiated from the previous night's kill, lopped near a pond interested only in the coolness of the water.

The three trucks were on the road before dawn. They carried back up gas tanks that should just take them to Katanga. Morgan was worried. He hoped there would be petrol at the border.

On the third day, their last on the "sponge" before turning south to Katanga, they stopped early to take advantage of a camp site on a bluff that overlooked the vast waterway. Lynch went hunting and soon reappeared with a pair of pheasants. They killed only what would be eaten. Morgan dug out his whisky bottle and headed to an outcrop of large rocks. "Come on over," he shouted. "Let's shake the dust out before we cook dinner."

The sun sat on the horizon, blood red, sinking fast. A stillness enveloped the valley. Morgan pulled on the bottle and then passed it to Lynch. Below him, along the pool's edge, he watched shy Sitatungas antelope move through the water. Pukus and black lechwes stretched to the horizon. This is my home, he mused. Never take me away, he beseeched the spirits.

Keane had built a hot fire under a spit to roast the pheasants. The six men, three black men and three white men, ate together with relish. Later, in their tents, they heard a hyena hooting and muttering, its voice brittle in the night.

The clear weather remained steady the following morning. They found a narrow road, probably cut by tribesmen hunting game, with poorly constructed bridges spanning the rivers. Smith-Stevens' search plane did not appear nor did the Rhodesian military stationed at Fort Rosebery. In this all-consuming vastness of land, there were scattered small villages with round huts and thatched roofs, their residents happy to exchange vegetables for trinkets.

The Luapula River marked an incidental border between Northern Rhodesia and Katanga for six hundred kilometers before abruptly cutting east to fill a lake on the Rhodesian plateau. Morgan, now driving the lead truck, turned south on a well traveled road. By late afternoon, the broad, east-west reach of the river appeared. Three very dirty trucks drove slowly down the main street of Chembe to the river and ferry terminal. The last ferry had just left for the Katanga side, so they would have to spend the night camping near the village. Lynch and Keane headed immediately to the beer stand near the terminal while Morgan organized the following day's crossing. Morgan returned to his truck, where he set up his shortwave radio and dialed in his contact in Katanga. The contact was on the frequency and responded immediately. "This is Kigali. Where are you? We are waiting."

Upemba Park, Katanga

"I can't hear any gun fire," Thomas said, his eyes peering through the mist. The dirt road sometimes disappeared from view and Thomas had to gage its center by the trees on both sides. The trees were tall and formed a canopy over the road. "Those soldiers won't come into these hills—the mist and chill would bother them." Thomas gave Samantha a tight smile. She had been silent for most of drive since the skirmish. "My home, or rather my sister's home, is not much further."

The house perched on the hillside above the point where the mist ended its ascent. The view always reminded Thomas of watching the top of a cloud bank from the window of an airplane. The house had two levels and a broad porch stretching the length of the front side. It was made entirely of wood, probably built with timber from the forest beyond. A vegetable garden occupied an open field next to the house. Parts of it were covered with mesh to keep the birds away. The earth had been tilled as the growing season would arrive soon.

Thomas embraced his sister, Kaila, and then introduced her to Samantha. She was tall, like her brother, and had the same facial bone structure that hinted of ancestors other than Congolese. Kaila's large black eyes appraised Samantha and then she smiled broadly with approval. She turned to her oldest son, "Help your uncle with the luggage. Come in Samantha. Let's have a beer while I finish preparing dinner. Do you like chicken and rice?" In the kitchen, Sam sat at a weathered wooden table. The two women began chattering like old friends.

After dinner and with the children down for the night, Thomas, Kaila and Samantha sat on the porch, heads titled toward a heaven laden with stars. Without turning away, Thomas began to tell Samantha about the game park and his childhood here. "Our father came here as a young man to work in the park as a ranger. Our mother came from a local tribe. Kaila and I were born here. We were educated by American missionaries, learned English and became Christians."

Kaila brought tea and a shawl for Samantha. They used the French language, which made the conversation more fascinating for Samantha. Thomas continued. "Much of our education was provided by our parents. Our mother understood the local plant life, which was edible, and more important, which were medicinal. The locals looked to her for cures. Our father knew everything about this tropical mountain forest. He lectured us on every animal and plant. And, we both learned to ride horseback and fire a rifle."

"And there our similarities ended," Kaila interjected. The missionaries sent Thomas away to school and I was told to find a husband." She laughed, but her voice carried a hint of disappointment.

The following morning appeared fresh and clear; the mist had retreated, pushed away by the sun's rays. Four horses were saddled and tethered to the porch railing. All had rifles slotted into a saddle pouch. "Can you shoot a rifle?" Thomas asked, while spooning his scrambled eggs. Without awaiting a reply, he continued. "I've invited two of my brother-in-law's rangers to ride with us. They know the forest better than I, and to tell you the truth, I haven't fired a rifle in years."

"Well, I'm not a practiced hunter, but I can shoot a rifle," Sam answered. "What caliber is mine?" she asked with a twinkle in her eyes. "Can we practice shooting tin cans somewhere?"

"We could, but then there wouldn't be an animal within ten kilometers. I want to introduce you to the L'Hoest's monkey. It's a crazy little creature with a white beard, found only in the rain forests around here. There's a lot to see, and I would think, for you, lots to photograph."

As they headed into the forest, Thomas explained, "These trees are over fifteen meters in height and provide an umbrella-shaped canopy over the grassland below. But the coverage is not dense which grants sunlight and allows fecundity. The miombo woodland is a rich and prodigious home for a wide variety of birds and animals. It is also vital to the tribes living here because it is their source for food, medicine, building materials and so on. Life is in balance. We must keep it this way."

"What is the threat?" Sam asked while aiming her 35mm Nikon at the two rangers riding in the lead.

"Mining," Thomas said sharply, as he turned in his saddle. "The mining companies have tremendous amounts of money and therefore tremendous influence. Tshombe plans to nationalize the mining companies. He would share the profits with the tribes living on the land."

"Are you sure of that," Samantha asked as she leaned forward to pat her horses neck.

"Yes, I'm sure. Moise is smart enough to know that if he failed to support the tribes, they would fight among themselves over ownership. Blood would flow."

They rode on in silence, heading deeper into the forest. The birds were magnificent both in color and size. Sam saw a Yellow-crested Helmet-shrike sitting complacently in a tree and snapped several photos of it. The rangers flushed out a reclusive Ruwenzori Turaco for Sam to photograph in flight.

The trail narrowed and Thomas reined in his horse so that he could follow Samantha's horse. He watched her body move in sync with her horse; confident and graceful. She seemed at ease with animals and nature and he liked that about her very much. Why are we attracted to our opposites, he pondered. The trail widened again and Thomas nudged his horse to come abreast of Sam's. "Samantha, tell me. Why did you say you couldn't speak French?" His voice had an edge to it. "You did so in Henley, when we met and again here, when we spent several days speaking English as we traveled around Katanga, a French speaking country." This deception had been bothering him since he discovered Sam's fluency when she verbally abused the mercenary in French. He didn't press and let the question float.

"I'm getting hungry, Thomas," Samantha said, avoiding Thomas's question. "We can talk about this and several other issues over lunch."

They rode without talking for another hour. The forest had become dense and a picnic spot did not present itself. But they were gradually moving higher on the mountain and eventually the terrain opened up. At noon, the rangers found a rocky bluff overlooking the vast forested area they had just traversed, tethered the horses, set up camp chairs and left Thomas and Sam to continue their conversation over coffee and sandwiches.

Thomas watched Samantha clean the camera lens and organize her photo equipment. This woman, he thought, is amazingly competent and focused, as well as very attractive. He grinned briefly and thought—in another world, maybe. "You haven't answered my question."

Sam turned toward Thomas, removed her hat and shook her tangled hair as if to sweep a thought from her mind. Then she said, softly and carefully, "As you now know, I have a bare fluency in your language. In Henley, unintentionally, I overheard parts of your conversation with those other men. I would have thought nothing of it except you were talking about smuggling weapons in Africa. I'm a journalist and journalists, photojournalists, in my case, are always looking for a good story. And, I'm particularly interested in Africa. It was deceitful, I admit, but I needed time to consider the information."

"Have you reflected on it?"

"For a long time I did nothing. My attention was on other assignments. But it nagged in the back of my mind. And then, out of the blue, you invited me to visit Katanga. I didn't know you at all but my gut told me you were sensible and perhaps involved in a scheme where you did not belong. I accepted your invitation because I wanted the Katanga story, plus, I hoped to discover the reasoning and the necessity of gunrunning and your involvement."

"Wow." Thomas rubbed his face and then scratched the top of his head vigorously.

Sam read the body language (indecision). "I know what your next question is. I discussed this with my friend, Brian Wellesley. To my knowledge, it is still a secret with him."

"He works for the UN, doesn't he?"

"Yes and his focus is Africa."

Thomas's and Samantha's conversation drifted, floating in the air, suspended without an outlet. The rangers had returned and saddled the horses. Answers would wait.

Later in the afternoon, as the fading light trickled through the arboreal canopy, the two rangers reined their horses, cautioning Thomas and Sam to hold up. Sam heard a chattering sound but saw no movement. They dismounted, leaving their horses in the rangers' care. Thomas carried his rifle, Sam her camera. As they stepped cautiously toward a grove of trees they saw the source of the noise—a frolicking troop of dark-haired, white-bearded monkeys swinging from the tree branches. Thomas whispered, "They are all females; no male, which is good. The male is very territorial. If we move slowly, perhaps we can coax some of the young ones to pose for a picture."

Thomas remained motionless while Sam circled the monkey-laden trees to gain the right angle of light. Without frightening her subjects, she crouched under the enclosure of a shorter tree, where she kneeled with her Nikon poised. Thomas watched the theatre play out, chuckling as the mothers were shrieking warnings unheeded by the younger monkeys as they moved slowly toward Samantha. A slight movement in the branches of the tree under which Samantha was kneeling caught Thomas's eye. He knew instinctively what it was, immediately realizing he needed to do something he hadn't done in years—fire a rifle. Hairy Bush Vipers are common throughout most of subequatorial Africa, feared by the local natives because antidotes don't always work and have to be administered quickly against the deadly venom. Thomas watched as the broad triangular shaped head of the snake became visible, dropping ever so slowly downward toward Samantha's head.

"Samantha, listen to me very carefully. Do not move. Do not stand up. I'm going to fire my rifle at something above you. Absolutely, do not look up!" As Thomas raised his gun all distractions evaporated from his mind. He focused only on his breathing as he aligned the rifle with the diamond shaped head. The head was very small, perhaps two inches wide and shifting slowly. He pulled the slack in on the trigger, aimed fractionally above the target, stopped breathing and squeezed the trigger. The cough of the gun interrupted the peaceful scene, frightening and scattering the monkeys. They were gone before Thomas lowered his rifle. Samantha remained kneeling, staring in astonishment at the lifeless remains of a poisonous viper.

Thomas's tension slowly ebbed and a sense of exhilaration replaced it. He watched Samantha photograph the snake. She turned and waved. She too was excited and yelled her praise of Thomas's cool marksmanship. Samantha left the shade of the umbrella tree and walked to where Thomas was standing, still holding the rifle on his shoulder. He looked down into her very blue eyes.

"I owe you, Thomas," Sam was breathless and the words tumbled out. "That was a very ugly snake. And your shot—my God, your father taught you well. Thank you."

"You owe my father, not me," he said with a broad grin. "Come on, it's getting dark. Let's head back to the barn." They mounted their horses and loped across an open meadow, exuberantly yelling and laughing to the astonishment of the rangers. The ride was a release of tension they had not acknowledged. Surviving danger enhances the immediacy of life.

The days following the snake incident were filled with exploration and adventure. Thomas introduced Samantha to the missionaries at his childhood school. They visited two villages, each the home of a different tribe. She photographed life as it had existed for hundreds of years. It was undisturbed by the turbulence occurring in the valley. As Samantha took pictures of the people and incessantly questioned every aspect of their life, a perplexing anxiety worked its way into Thomas's thoughts. He needed to discuss the gun business with Samantha. Coming back to his home in the mountains had given him a sense of peace. It was at odds with the fighting and killing in the valley. Where was Tshombe leading the country, he wondered. Would more guns stabilize the country or accelerate its decent into chaos. This uncertainty played havoc in his head.

On the evening before their set departure from the hill station, Thomas sat with his sister and Samantha on the porch. Kaila surprised him when she brought a tray with three cold beers. Not a whisk of a breeze eased the oppressive humidity. The two women chatted idly. They had become good friends. It was he who finally pushed the conversation into murky waters. "Tshombe asked me to visit Washington D.C."

"To do what?" Kaila said quickly.

"Moise wants the US to support Katanga in its independence. Moise feels I am the best equipped to present our position to the US government."

Kaila interrupted him. "Moise, Moise . . . Do you trust him, Thomas?"

"He is our best hope. I believe he is working for our new country's well-being."

"I'm going to tell you something, Thomas, something you probably didn't know. Our father, as good a friend as he was of Tshombe's, didn't trust him. Mr. Tshombe is interested in money and power, certainly not your well-being. What do you think, Samantha?"

"I don't know enough about the man to comment. My intuition tells me he is ruthless and using you for his ends, not that of the country. Especially involving you in gunrunning."

"Gunrunning," Kaila almost shouted. "What have you gotten yourself involved in? You are a science teacher."

Samantha said nothing. She sipped her beer and waited.

It was a moment of truth. Thomas had wanted to discuss the gun business with his sister and Samantha since the first day they all had been together. The revelation eased his conscience. He related how he had carried out Tshombe's instructions, opened and funded secret bank accounts, met with Belgian military officers and provided them with a shopping list of weapons. "Where the weapons come from and how they get here is not my problem." Thomas rose from his chair and began pacing the porch. "I am not pleased with what I did."

Samantha spoke first. "Who were the men you met with in Henley?"

"One was the Belgian officer Tshombe asked me to contact. I know nothing about the other man. He was to find the weapons and arrange delivery. I attended the meeting only to confirm the payment arrangements."

"He's South African. He gave me his calling card. Apparently he is in the wine business," Samantha said.

Thomas mopped his brow. "I don't know. He gave me a bank account number, nothing more."

Samantha pressed. "Where's the bank?"

"I shouldn't be telling you all of this. My God, you're a journalist. This could cause me grief. Let's leave it at this. It wasn't a South African bank."

Kaila began to talk rapidly and emotively. "Who will use these guns?" She continued, answering her own questions. "Young Katanga boys who will use the guns to kill without understanding why. We will murder our neighbors and we will kill each other. Only the white people will benefit; and of course, Tshombe and his cohorts. Our father would be so disappointed in you. You are better than this. Remove yourself from this nasty business. I'll say no more. I love you and I'm worried about you."

The following day, Thomas and Samantha returned to Elizabethville. She used the same hotel as before only now it was crowded. The bar was packed with soldiers wearing broad brimmed hats, elaborate military shirts and shorts. They were all European mercenaries, she guessed. The café emitted a cloud of cigarette smoke and loud talk in several languages. Sam took several pictures of the hired guns as they stood around the front of the hotel.

Thomas had taken her to a small restaurant before dropping her at the hotel. "Was your visit worthwhile?"

Samantha smiled. "I feel older and wiser. I'm overwhelmed. Katanga is a powder keg and is exploding as we speak. We have become such good friends, Thomas, and, like your sister, I worry about you. Be careful."

"As I promised in the car, I'm finished with the gun business. After you leave, I will find Tshombe and tell him so."

"Will you still visit the United States?"

"I have my ticket. I must do this last mission and then I'm quits." He gave a lingering look at this woman who had come into his life, so suddenly, and left a mark. "Did you get some good photographs?"

"I can't wait to develop my film in London. My best shot will be of you standing in the cloud forest."

The next morning, they cleared border control with no problem and drove, in silence, to the Ndola airport. When they had parked, Samantha turned to Thomas and said, "These days traveling with you in Katanga will have a special place in my memory. I've learned a great deal about your country and let's hope my photography reflects well on your people and their life. I've also gotten to know you, Thomas. Your are a special person, destined to lead in some way. Africa will need many such as you."

They walked together to the fence. Thomas grasped Samantha's hand in both of his and held it as he contemplated her face. She could read his thoughts and smiled. Samantha said good bye and headed quickly through the gate in the perimeter fence of the airport. Black Africans were not permitted inside.

Washington D.C.

Jay Carleton leaned on the door jamb of the State Department African Affairs conference room and watched Larry Madison, his contact at CIA, walking toward him with purpose. "You look bright-eyed this morning, Larry," Carleton said as he ushered him into the small room. A secretary followed Madison with coffee and closed the door quietly on her way out.

"I'm clear-eyed but empty-handed," Madison said as he removed his suit coat. "What news do you have on Lumumba?"

Jay was pleased they could talk in shirt sleeves. Somehow it provided an atmosphere of trust and confidence. "Lumumba has flown the coop. He was under house arrest in Leopoldville and has somehow evaporated."

The table top held no papers, just two white coffee cups. Madison drank from his before asking, "Who screwed up?

"Well, I was hoping the CIA would know. Ostensibly, Mobuto is now in charge of the DRC. Our ambassador likes him and believes he will provide stability. The army is solidly behind him." Carleton paused a moment, still evading the question to which, he suspected, Madison already had the answer. "That's the good news. We believe Lumumba is somewhere in the eastern part of the country, areas under Soviet influence. They will use him to attract support from other African nations."

Madison didn't miss a beat. "Prime-minister Lumumba needs to be sequestered and removed."

Carleton's eyes were suddenly large. "What do you mean—removed?"

"We would like to see him situated in a friendly environment—friendly to us, that is—where he is out of touch and can do no damage to our interests." Madison delivered this in a matter-of-fact voice.

Carleton's face flushed slightly. "What are your interests? Are they different than our interests here at State?"

"That's a complex subject, Jay. Our view, and this comes from the very top, is that it would be in our interests to allow Katanga to remain independent for a sufficient period to gauge Tshombe's intensions and the United Nations effectiveness."

Carleton hunched his shoulders in exasperation. "That position is at odds with ours. We have been crystal clear from the very beginning of the Congo's independence in July. The UN is in charge and we support their actions. Secretary-General Hammarskjöld would like to see Lumumba returned to his elected position of prime minister."

"The UN has military forces in the DRC and is now attempting to place troops in Katanga," Madison remarked.

"True, but the secretary-general is asking for all Belgian troops to leave Katanga immediately. His wish is for Katanga to return to the DRC.

"As we see it at the Agency, Katanga would provide a secure environment. A good place for Lumumba. They don't like him."

"I'll send this information upstairs. This tactical difference of opinion should be sorted out at a higher level." Jay Carleton stood and offered his hand. "We are not interested in black operations and I would rather not know about them."

Madison's poker-face gave a tight smile. "We won't tell you. Thanks for the coffee."

Southeast Katanga Border with Northern Rhodesia in 1960 -1961

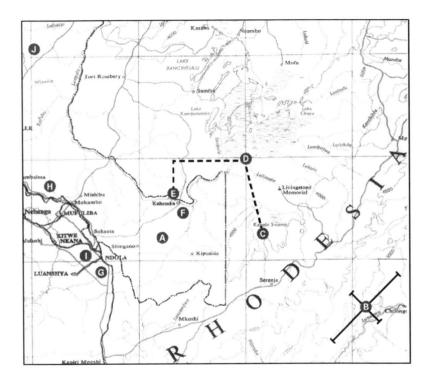

A. Katanga
B. Morgan's safari territory
C. Morgan's camp with a landing runway
D. Sponge
E. Mwenda (Weapons point of entry to Katanga)
F. Weapon training camp
G. Airport
H. Anti-aircraft gun position
I. Plane crash site.
J. Upemba National Park

NOVEMBER 1960

New York

Secretary-General Hammarskjöld's secretary ushered Brian into a large office on the top floor of the UN building in New York. The secretary-general rose from where he was sitting with two other people and walked toward Brian with a broad smile and his hand extended.

"Hello Brian. You look well. I am so glad you are here" He shook Brian's hand warmly before lead him by his arm back to the table where the two people were waiting. One, Alice Lalande, a middle-aged Canadian woman, was a close confidant of Hammarskjöld and a senior officer in the African affairs section in New York. The lanky, bearded Dutchman, standing next to her, was Cort Rynsburger, a well known UN dignitary in Geneva. They sat down without ceremony to fresh coffee and several thick position dossiers.

Brian studied the secretary-general as they settled in the sleek black leather chairs that surrounded the marble coffee table. Swedes love their coffee, he remembered. Hammarskjöld, as always, was impeccably dressed in a double breasted suit. He was average height with light brown hair and a nose too large for his face. His hooded blue eyes captured Brian's gaze. He would learn later that Hammarskjöld eyes carried his message.

The secretary-general wasted no time and explained to Brian why he had asked him to come on such short notice. "The Congo situation dominates our energy and focus. The situation is deteriorating daily and we are under incredible pressure from many sources to bring peace and stability to this area. Our problem is that "peace" is portrayed differently by these sources and their suggestions on how to achieve stability are in conflict."

Rynsburger chimed in. "Lumumba is still missing. We want him reinstated as the dually elected prime-minister. This is a test of democracy in emerging countries and of the UN's potency. We fear Mobutu will find him first and arrange for his imprisonment."

Hammarskjöld gazed at Brian intently. "I want you to spend all of your time and energy on the Congo. As of this moment, you are my personal envoy for Central African affairs. I wanted my two colleagues here to witness this appointment."

"I'm honored, Mr. Secretary-General. As you may imagine, I have a few questions."

"Why don't you and I have an early lunch together next door and leave all of these papers to these two good souls." Hammarskjöld stood, waved a departing gesture and steered Brian to a side door.

Brian could see the morning events were organized in advance as lunch was served immediately. Hammarskjöld picked at his food and preferred to talk.

"When you leave here, I will give you a thin dossier with background information on what we will discuss. The situation is grave. My reputation—my very tenure at the UN—is at stake. What I believe to be the essence of truth for all people of the world is being challenged by evil forces."

Brian couldn't taste the food. He was spell-bound. "What forces? Who are you talking about?" Brian asked.

"The colonial-Europeans who have remained in Africa with support from certain agencies of powerful countries." Hammarskjöld finally returned to his food leaving Brian with his thoughts.

Brian spoke. "The white minority in Rhodesia and in my country would like Katanga to remain independent. It would be a buffer against the wave of independence sweeping from the north. Am I right?"

"Yes, they see me as a threat to their way-of-life. But it is even deeper than that, Brian. There is a staggering wealth of minerals on the Katanga – Rhodesian border, owned and controlled by large European companies. Our intelligence knows they are funding the turmoil in Katanga and the fierce resistance in the south."

Brian nodded. "British and South African, mainly."

"I am going to ask a lot of you. You are eminently qualified for this assignment: you are strong minded, speak French, skilled in international law and familiar with all of the players. But perhaps most important, you are South African and can taste the injustice that is occurring. It will be dangerous, Brian, and I would understand if you are reluctant."

"Where should I begin?" Brian answered without hesitation.

"Study all of the intelligence reports coming out of central Africa. Rynsburger will provide them to you in Geneva. I'm sorry to ask this, but on your way home for Christmas, I'd like you to stop in Leopoldville, meet with Mobuto to persuade him to bring back Lumumba. If feasible, stop in Elizabethville, where we now have a small peace keeping force. Tshombe is employing mercenaries and skirmishes have occurred. Find a way to meet with Tshombe or one of his close advisors. I want to meet with him soon and we can rendezvous anywhere he prefers."

"I will do this at the end of this month and early December. How should I report to you? You will be in Sweden in December."

"Wait for me in Pretoria. I will arrive January 6, for a meeting with Dr. Verwoerd, your Prime Minister. We can talk then."

As Brian departed, Hammarskjöld placed his hands on Brian's shoulders. "I am so glad you are with me. Be safe."

London

Nicholas Andropolis took great pleasure in driving his Bentley. He could well afford a chauffeur—and there were occasions that demanded that he hire a temporary driver—but his commute to work in downtown London was his think time and he did his best thinking behind the wheel. His shipping business had eluded his thoughts this past weekend. The Katanga gun business monopolized his thoughts, distracting from the other pleasures available on his farm.

He cruised down Brook Street in the early Monday morning traffic. Andropolis Maritime's office occupied the first floor of a red bricked building facing Hanover Square. He preferred not to be near the other London Greeks ship owners clustered near Holborn. Nicholas parked in his reserved arrangement nearby, walked briskly one block to his office building, greeted the doorman and took the open-grilled elevator to the first floor. His nine employees looked up briefly from their desk, smiled or nodded before returning to their paperwork. All of the Andropolis employees were male and all had Greek names. Nicholas's secretary, Peter Metaxas, stood in Nicholas's private office holding a sheaf of dispatches.

"Good morning, Mr. Andropolis. I put the telexes requiring your immediate attention on top."

"Thank you very much, Peter. See if you can reach our bank in Liechtenstein."

Within ten minutes, Metaxas had Hans Steiner in Vaduz on the line. He greeted Nicholas in German. "It's snowing, Nicholas. Come over before the holiday ski crowds."

Nicholas replied smoothly in German. He and his Liechtenstein banker chatted small talk briefly before he asked, "I am expecting a sizeable deposit in our private account, somewhere in the neighborhood of one million pounds sterling. Please confirm the exact amount by telex. I will reply with instructions for disbursement. Thanks, Hans, and my regards to your family."

By noon, he had his answer. Nicholas shredded the telex and penciled the amount on a clean piece of paper. He needed to pay the Belgian general per agreement. It was a small amount considering the magnitude of the transaction.

He had no reluctance to wire the commission to their Luxembourg bank. Their services would not be required again. He now knew their customer and future business would be handled on a direct basis.

Nicholas sifted through the supplier invoices. The quantity of each item and its delivery had been verified and, in some cases, the vendor had already been paid. He authorized payment of the outstanding amounts and telexed instructions to Steiner. No one in his shipping office had a clue concerning this aspect of Nicholas business life.

One more hefty sum would be wired to a bank account in Lisbon. The rest of the money, and Nicholas smiled thinking about it, would be transferred to his numbered bank account in Antigua. This was only the beginning. There would be more business.

Nicholas had downed a whiskey at the bar before Katherine and Samantha arrived. He rose to greet his double dates, bussed each on the cheek and then lead them through the noisy main dinning room to their table in the rear of the restaurant. Once seated, he spoke to Samantha first. "It's been too long, Samantha. What have you been doing with yourself? I haven't seen you since the weekend bash on my farm." He asked the questions nonchalantly, yet his eyes inspected Samantha's response carefully.

"Work, work, work," she replied looking up from her menu. "This decade has begun with a bang. We live in a crazy world." She then dismissed the question and turned to Katherine for her suggestion on wine.

Nicholas persisted. "Have you travelled or do you accomplish your work here in the UK?"

"Actually, I'm just off a plane from Salisbury. All of Central Africa is in a turmoil. I'm developing my films now. So far, they are vivid."

"What do you mean, vivid?" Katherine questions before tasting the wine she had suggested.

"I mean, my photographs are dramatic, and probably the first to come out of Katanga."

"Katanga!" Nicholas's pulse quickened but he leaned back in his chair to appear casual in his interest. "How in the world did you arrange entering a province that is in a state of war?"

"It was a piece of luck, really. When we all were together at Henley, I met this interesting young man who lives in Katanga. I'm not sure why he was at the regatta. He found out I was a photojournalist and invited me to visit him and photograph the country. He even introduced me to President Tshombe."

Samantha talked at length about her experience. Nicholas did not press. He did not wish to appear too interested. He claimed he did not remember the Congolese man, or, for that matter, any of the men at the Henley meeting. He would have to be cautious with this woman, Samantha Norquist. She was snooping too close to his turf. Her boyfriend worked for the UN and that alone triggered caution. Tomorrow he would call Cape Town.

Katanga

The land was wet. Mud hindered travel. The rainy season had arrived right on time and tortuously hot air drifted south from the equatorial jungles. Rainstorms were announced by exciting theater: lightening streaked the sky to the west, flashing unrelentingly, exposing a dark world, always followed by the drumbeat of thunder. The storms moved in over the vast country north of the Zambezi, hovered and stayed. The rain was relentless, sometimes swirling and slashing horizontally, or more often, drizzling in a fine spray that seeped into every crevice of one's living space and, emblematically, into one's mind.

"Do you think this weather has bothered Morgan?" Keane had to yell in order for Lynch to hear because of the rain clattering on their tent.

"He probably has the same weather. Hope he is through the sponge and on firm ground," Lynch shouted back.

Keane stood in the door watching the water rush down the trench he had dug. The downpour had let up slightly allowing him a better view of the activity taking place at the end of the camp road. A truck had arrived and young men toting small duffels were pouring out of its back and rushing to large tents, which would be their barracks. He could see Kigali dressed in a broad rimed hat and poncho directing traffic. Kigali always wore his uniform. He took pride in his rank—now a captain in the Katanga army.

This was the training camp where he and Lynch would teach the Katanga recruits how to operate the AK47s. It had been raining off and on from the moment they had arrived in Mwenda five days ago. They had driven the three trucks from the river village, where they had crossed from Northern Rhodesia, to this remote bush camp. Keane calculated it was 9 km from the river. Everyday, a truck would arrive with more trainees. He wondered when he would be able to leave.

One building, near the other end of the camp, had an elevated wooden floor. It was large enough for twenty men to assemble and learn to dismantle the gun, clean it, and quickly put it back together. The firing range was still too muddy for use.

After the weapon shipment was transferred to Kigali's control and the papers were signed off, Morgan and his three natives from Lusaka headed back across the river. They had sufficient fuel and provisions for their return trip to Morgan's main safari camp in the Luangwa Valley. He needed to back track and return to his real occupation of hunter and guide.

The day before, a Land Rover had arrived in the bush camp with three white men. Keane and Lynch watched them tour the camp with Kigali. They spent a long time inspecting the rifles. The two in uniform were Belgian non-commissioned officers. The third man was an interesting spectacle. He wore high boots, high socks, short pants, a bush jacket adorned with many insignias and a bush hat with one side of the brim bent upward and fastened to the peak. Spilling out in every direction from under the hat was unkempt, long red hair. His belt carried a revolver, a knife and a club. Lynch made a snide comment about his flamboyant appearance, but not loud enough for the mercenary to hear. He seemed to be almost 2 meters tall and in excellent physical shape.

One of the soldiers approached Lynch and asked in French, "May I ask who you are and why you are here?"

Lynch understood the question but responded in English. "We're training these recruits on the use of the weapons you just looked at."

The mercenary had sidled up to the conversation. "Ah, two lads from my part of the world. Rhodesian are you?"

Lynch looked back at the Belgian. "What is your business here?"

"We will be taking charge of the camp and the training and you two can return to wherever you came from."

Keane stepped into the circle and said. "You must be mistaken. We are under contract with the Katanga government to train these men. Until we have completed our job, the rifles belong to us and this camp is under our direction. This camp is off limits and I must ask you to leave."

Kigali glowered but surprisingly said nothing.

The three men drove off. Keane knew this wouldn't be the end of it. When would this ordeal end, he asked himself.

Elizabethville

Thomas had not returned to the mountains after sending Samantha back to London. His life seemed to flounder on rocks of indecision. His home was a mile from the school where he taught; a good place, he thought, to hole up and think about his future. The guns and the killing infected him with dread. Should he trust Tshombe? Kaila and Samantha did not. He had decided conclusively to not become further implicated in gun smuggling. He would advise Tshombe of that decision immediately. His commitment to visit the US puzzled him. What could he possible accomplish since he was simply a messenger?

The old colonial golf course, now Tshombe's command center, bristled with activity. Thomas arrived near ten o'clock;

sure that Tshombe would be in the middle of the fray during the morning. He felt conspicuous, for no good reason, except for his obvious apprehension. The room's walls were clustered with maps. Telephone wiring, bare and tangled, littered the floor. There were many Europeans, some were Belgian military officers, and he noticed a new element—mercenaries. He spied Tshombe talking with Munongo on the far corner of the deck and walked toward them. Tshombe saw Thomas and beckoned.

"Hello, Thomas. Godefroid and I were just finishing up. Glad you are here as I want to talk with you. Let's head down to the pond where we can disturb the birds but not be disturbed ourselves."

Tshombe cast a spell over Thomas and he felt increasingly more relaxed as they strolled across the grounds. They wouldn't talk long—the sun baked them.

"Have the guns arrived, Moise?"

"I'm told the shipment arrived in Mwenda safely. Kigali is up there now training our soldiers. Two of the men who brought the shipment are there with him. They are ex-Rhodesian soldiers. It went well. Thank you for helping me with this business."

Thomas spoke hesitantly. "I wanted to talk with you, Moise, about this gun business."

"Nothing to discuss," Moise said quickly. "If we need more, I won't need your involvement. I can handle it now. But I do need you to make the trip to Washington, as discussed. Our situation is deteriorating. I need the Americans to put pressure on the UN to withdraw their military forces from our country. We must have American support. Come by my house this evening. I will give you the necessary documents and some funds. You should leave immediately. Kennedy has been elected. There will be new faces and new decisions. Your timing will be perfect." He mopped his brow and turned toward the club house. "Let's go inside. It's too hot out here."

DECEMBER 1960

Geneva, Switzerland

After his meeting with Hammarskjöld, Brian moved into high gear. He returned to Geneva immediately where his secretary, Gisella, had already begun to plan his schedule to visit Leopoldville and his return to Cape Town. He eliminated the prime minister from his schedule and asked Gisella to only arrange a meeting with Mobutu. He would also need to make a courtesy call on Rajeshwar Dayel, the obstreperous Indian head of the UN peacekeeping mission in the DRC. She found him a flight via Cairo leaving in three days.

Brian called Samantha in London. "Are you thinking of me?" he asked her brazenly.

"I am," she replied softly. "Where are you?"

"I'm in Geneva and I'm packing. The Secretary-General has filled my plate with the Congo. I'm to meet with Mobutu in three days."

"The Congo dominates our lives and it's dangerous. Be careful, Brian. I want you at the airport in Cape Town when

I arrive in ten days." She gave a low chuckle—then a nervous laugh. "I've lots to tell you about Katanga and Thomas. And also," she paused to collect her thoughts; "I had dinner with Katherine and Nicholas the other night. He is not all what he purports to be. We should check out the wine merchant we met who lives in Cape Town."

Brian could hear pots and pans scraping. "What are you cooking?"

"Buttersquash soup. The wine is the Swiss white you gave me." She moved the conversation to South Africa. "One day I'd love to garden at your house Brian. Can we do that soon—please?"

"We'll garden, drink wine and make love each time we complete cultivating a row of flowers."

"Could be dirty business, Sam replied laughing. "You asked for Thomas's contact. Here's his sister's phone number. His is out of order. I think flying into Elizabethville will be a problem. I had to use Ndola."

"The UN controls the airport, remember. I'll play this part of my trip by ear. Love you." He heard a kissing sound through the phone, smiled and hung up.

Leopoldville

Upon arrival, Brian learned that Colonel Mobutu wished to meet with him at his home. He now controlled both the government and the army, and wished to pull the strings from the shadows.

Mobutu received Brian on his front porch. His slight body looked trim in a uniform and he greeted Brian warmly. He seemed almost boyish, Brian thought. After all, Mobutu had not yet turned thirty. His eyes were concealed behind the ever present dark glasses, which he did not remove when they entered his home. No family members appeared, only a servant with iced drinks. Mobutu gestured to a low, round table with four upholstered chairs surrounding it. Brian waited for Mobutu to open the conversation. He, who blinks first, loses."

You are South African, I believe, Mr. Wellesley." His English had a French tone. He spoke slowly and clearly, peering directly at Brian through his dark glasses. "Your country has its problems as well."

Mobutu held the rank of colonel in the DRC army; rather humble, Brian thought, for someone with so much power. "Yes, Colonel Mobutu, that's very true. In fact, Secretary-General Hammarskjöld plans to meet with Prime Minister Verwoerd next month. The United Nations position on apartheid is very clear."

"I know that and your presence here is helpful. I am looking forward to meeting with your secretary-general in the near future. In the meantime, perhaps you can help in solving some pesky problems. Katanga, for example."

Brian liked the trend of the discussion. "The general assembly is now debating a resolution, which would demand Katanga to return to the DRC. As you know, we have peacekeeping forces in Elizabethville and we plan to send more." As an afterthought, Brian asked, "What do you think will motivate Tshombe?"

Mobutu looked away, pondering. "A great deal of blood will flow before Katanga returns to the fold. May I suggest that you put pressure on the white colonialists to the south and the erstwhile European colonial powers. They are supporting Tshombe, although he may not realize it. If they buckle, he will too."

Brian tried to lean forward but the deep chair prevented it. "We hope that Prime Minister Lumumba can be persuaded to return to his elected office. His absence is divisive. Has any attempt been made to reach him?"

Mobutu removed his dark glasses. His tight grin belied his steely eyes. "You can advise your secretary-general that Lumumba will be back with us in Leopoldville soon. I can say no more, at this time."

Mobutu guided Brain to the porch and into the tropical heat. As they shook hands, Mobutu said, "There is one other issue: your Mr. Dayel's imperiousness has become a thorn in the side of our cooperation. I'm not sure what to suggest, but Hammarskjöld should know our feeling." Again, another smile, this one enigmatic. "I trust you will have a pleasant holiday, Mr. Wellesley, and that we will meet again soon."

The United Nations Organization in the Congo's office lay on the other side of town, near where the peace keeping forces were billeted. Brian had returned to his hotel for lunch and a change of clothes. He wanted to meet with the UN's senior representative in DRC this afternoon so that he could continue his trip to Cape Town the following day. He had met Dayal before and didn't relish what loomed before him.

The equator slices across the Congo relegating seasons to irrelevance. The weather in December was no different than in June, except for the rain. Brian dressed in a tropical seersucker suit, shirt and tie and trusted the meeting room would be air-conditioned. The meeting was set for 3 p.m. in Dayal's office. The heat that greeted him when he left his hotel room was stifling. A cloying, motionless air, laden with moisture that not only drenched his clothing, it sapped any incentive before the day's work had even begun.

"Ah, Mr. Wellesley, I have very little time to spend chatting with you," Dayal muttered, his head wagging but never lifting his gaze from the papers on his desk. "You are a messenger from New York. What message do you have for me?"

"Thank you, sir, for allowing me some time. I know you are stretched. I'm here at the direct request of the secretary-general, to help organize his forthcoming visit. After a courtesy call on the President, he will wish to see you. He would like your suggestions as to which other government officials he should visit?" This was a nonsense request, Brian knew, but did Dayal?

Dayal tossed his pen angrily on the desk, rose from his chair and stalked around the desk to confront Brian. Dayal was reveling in his well-known arrogance, and he stood frowning as he looked up at Brian. "At least you are not an American. I'm sick of the Americans telling us how to run this show. They butt in yet never put their neck on the line."

"Their money is on the line."

"True, but not much has arrived so far. Mr. Kennedy wants me removed, that I know. But until my superior and friend Secretary-General Hammarskjöld asks me to leave, I will run things here as I see fit. The Americans do not support Lumumba and are now dragging their heels on our desire to bring Katanga back to this nation. My suggestion is for the secretary-general to meet with Mobutu to iron out the working relationship between our peacekeeping forces and the Congolese army. My fondest hope is that he will fly to Katanga and reason with Tshombe. In the meantime, I am moving more troops to Katanga. The situation there is dire."

Dayal's mood became calmer after his opening tirade. He suggested coffee and the two men talked for an hour. Brian prepared to depart with the satisfaction that he had overcome some status hurdles. As he turned to leave, the man in charge of all UN operations in the Congo hurtled one last request. "Why don't you visit Brussels and, as a lofty aide to the secretary-general, remind the Belgians that the world would like them to finally and completely leave the Congo."

Washington D.C.

During the slippery period between Kennedy's election in November and his oath of office in January, one man alone remained focused on the rapidly changing events in the DRC. Allen Dulles, the Director of Central Intelligence, harbored a suspicion that one Patrice Lumumba, the constantly disappearing Prime Minister of the DRC, would become a painful thorn in the Agency's side. Would it be possible for this man to disappear permanently, Dulles pondered, as he dialed Bronson Tweedy, chief of the Agency's Africa Division.

When Tweedy came on the line, Dulles asked in a soft voice, as if his mind were elsewhere, "Whom do we have on the Congo watch?"

"Good morning, Allen." Tweedy's voice carried a smooth clip, leading many to assume he was British, an inaccurate conclusion he let ride. Although Bronson Tweedy was born in England, his parents were American. He was East Coast bred, private schooling, Princeton, and now, chief of the Agency's African Division, a job that included covert operations. These clandestine and nefarious activities were implicit in the Agency's mission. The playbook for dealing with hostile foreign leaders was in Tweedy's lap. "We have an old hand on station in Leopoldville and another is arriving in Elizabethville, as we speak."

"Who is on the DRC desk here?" Dulles said, interrupting Tweedy.

"Larry Madison; smart and knowledgeable, but a rookie."

"Ask him to join us in my office in . . . say an hour. I want an update on Lumumba." Without waiting for a response, Dulles slid the receiver into its cradle and reached for his coffee.

Promptly, one hour later, Tweedy and Madison stood before Dulles's desk. Dulles came around his imposing desk, greeted both men perfunctorily and waved his hand toward three chairs. Without ceremony, he jumped to the point of their meeting.

"The State Department is equivocating on the Congo. They are supporting whoever is in power in Leopoldville. That could be Lumumba, if he returned. State also supports the UN's intervention, including their objection to the presence of Belgian troops and Katanga's secession. Hammarskjöld is supported by third-world countries and is soft on communist countries. He worries some of our strongest allies in Europe and Africa; and I'm concerned too." Dulles paused and turned to Madison. "What do we know about Katanga? Where are you getting your information?"

Larry Madison's age belied his coolness. He had been a field agent for three years and knew the score. He did not hesitate providing the director with the stark truth. "We receive reports from our station manager in Leopoldville and he has developed several sources in Katanga. We also obtain feed from Salisbury and some from Brussels."

"What is the current situation and what would our friends in Belgium and Rhodesia like to see occur?" Dulles asked.

"The white colonialists remaining in central and southern Africa support Tshombe, regret the UN's intervention and they are very concerned about Lumumba's leftist leaning."

Tweedy spoke. "At the bottom of everyone's politics is money. There is a staggering mineral fortune in the ground along the border between Katanga and the Federation of Rhodesia. Tshombe would work with the giant companies that own the deposits; the DRC would take it away."

Dulles pressed his fingers together forming a tent, while considering his options. Finally, he leaned forward and said, "Here is my suggestion. Larry, you need a well-placed source close to Tshombe. We should become cozy with him. Go to Europe, and Central Africa if necessary, and find a voice. Bronson, talk with your man in Leopoldville. We need to put Mr. Lumumba on a permanent vacation. I think Katanga would be perfect."

Cape Town

Samantha watched Brian as he drove rapidly away from the Cape Town airport. Her flight from London had been long, and her exhausted body ached. But her mind was flying. To be with Brian on vacation in Africa was surreal. She reached for his hand to ground the reality. They circled the center of the city and headed south on a good road. Light traffic allowed a smooth drive down the peninsula to Fish Hoek, a village on the shore of False Bay.

"Tell me about your home, Brian. Is it far? Is it on the ocean?"

"You will see it soon, my sweet. We will skirt the bay and take a narrow road inland for a few kilometers. I have a beautiful piece of property encompassing a hill and a forest. There is a filtered view of the Bay and an ever-present scent of the ocean."

It was the cusp of summer, warm and a fragrance of things blooming. Samantha, barefoot and in shorts, settled back in a deck chair cradling a glass of wine. Her eyes refused to settle on any one thing; she let them slide from the ocean, to the garden and finally settling on Brian where he sat watching her. There is a heaven, she thought. It is here and now.

"Tell me about your trip, Brian. Were you able to reach Thomas?"

Brian sat on a bench with his back to the garden and the sea beyond. His long strong legs stretched toward Sam and touched her. They couldn't stop touching. She sat quietly listening to his saga of Hammarskjöld in New York and Mobutu in Leopoldville. She hadn't grasped the depth of his excitement over his work until now. He was committed to the secretary-general.

"Nope, not only could I not get a phone call through to Kaila, there were no flights to Elizabethville. Luckily, Sabina Air offered a direct flight to Johannesburg."

Samantha moved on to a subject that had been bothering her. "I told you about my dinner with Nicholas Andropolis. He's involved in something shady. I saw him talking with that peculiar South African man who claims to be a wine merchant. Thomas admitted he purchased weapons from this fellow. It's time we do something with this information."

"We have almost a month together so let's not rush. Tomorrow I'll introduce you to my father. He lives on the other side of the bay that you're looking at. The following day I have an appointment with an old school friend who is now the head of Interpol here. She is already looking into our friend, Mr. van Riebeek."

"She?"

"We were in middle school together. Actually, my father knows Gillian better than I do through his law business. She was a police officer and then a city detective. My father would meet her in court. She was usually on the other side of his case. She is smart and tenacious."

"Do South Africans have Christmas trees?"

"We do. Small and scrawny, but we do. Maybe, before Christmas, we will fly into the bush to meet my brother, Jason. He's a park ranger and very anxious to meet you. But before any of this, let's have supper and go to bed."

"Let's skip supper," Sam said, as she rose and slipped into his arms.

Samantha stayed in blissful seclusion with Brian in his home on the southern outskirts of Cape Town. It was an outrageous dwelling, modern in every architectural aspect and at odds with its rustic setting. Sam enjoyed the simplicity of the house and how it dared to be so sleek and elegant amongst its rugged surroundings. The hardwood floors were soft under her bare feet, and she felt a connection with the earth below. Soaring floor to ceiling glass walls brought the sky and the nearby trees inside. The furniture, the lighting, the state-of-the-art kitchen, were all very modern, and uncluttered in graceful symmetry. It was the man who lived here who was so incongruous, for he was of the old school and steeped in tradition, so unlike his contemporary home. The garden, more than anything, reflected Brian's nature. His land stretched for five acres, much of which was wild and forested. But Sam loved the garden most and her attention focused on it from the moment she arrived. The flower beds were in disarray but beginning to exhibit new growth with spring color. The vegetable garden was a masterpiece, hallowed ground, where Brian grew unsullied food. She asked him about his passion to grow his own food.

"I got it from my mother who was a consummate gardener. She even knew the Latin names. Did you know that it was a Swede who gave names to most of the plants and flowers that we know and who published them in a book hundreds of years ago? He named the prettiest flower after himself, Linnéa. His name was Carl von Linnaeus." Sam shook her head. The things this man came up with! "As for my mother, she grew many herbs known only to the natives. Some we used to accent our cooking, others for healing. There is harmony and peace in gardening—always a sense of accomplishment, without hubris. Hands in the soil are connected with something much larger than ourselves. Gardening is, or should be at least, a part of us—it speaks of our relationship with whatever is out there that we find so difficult to comprehend." Brian said this with no embellishment, but simply as a statement of fact.

Later, much later, looking back, Sam understood Brian's affinity to the earth and what it produced. A gardener is inevitably someone with humility, who knows and accepts that the saplings he plants will outlive him—will grow to maturity long after he's gone and will be there for others to tend and enjoy. Most often gardeners are generous, with their time as well as their products, and they take pleasure in giving to others. Sam was beginning to understand that Brian was all of that and she loved him even more for it.

Washington D.C.

Precisely 12,723 kilometers to the northwest, Thomas stepped off a transatlantic flight at Dulles International Airport. His only immediate desire was eight hours of sleep in a good hotel. Tomorrow morning would be soon enough to meet with Larry Madison. In a serendipitous coincidence, just days after his meeting with Tshombe, Thomas had received a telegram from Alex McLean, his friend at the US Embassy in London, inviting him to meet with Larry Madison in Washington. Thomas remembered the CIA man from his London visit last June. No mention was made of the State Department, which seemed suspicious. The invitation fit with Tshombe's instructions and Thomas accepted immediately.

The next morning, a car arranged by Madison was waiting for him outside his hotel. Thomas's mind was fresh after a long sleep and the drive to Langley provided a few moments to gather his thoughts. Outside the car window, drifting fog revealed the slate-colored water on the Potomac

River coursing under the bridge. A lone rowing shell glided along.

Madison met Thomas in the lobby where they exchanged greetings as if they were old friends. They chatted idly about the atrocious weather and long trans-Atlantic flights as they walked the endless corridors. Madison's office was small and unpretentious, distinguished only by a large map of Africa. Thomas walked up to it, his eyes on a small hill station north of Elizabethville. He put his finger on the spot and, turning to Madison, said, "My family home is here. A beautiful place with birds, animals and unimaginable wild flowers."

Madison stepped next to him. "Where is the *Union Minière du Haut* copper mine?" he asked, moving his finger along the southern border of Katanga.

Thus began a two day education of Larry Madison. Thomas's background as a teacher instilled him with both patience and knowledge. Madison's retained the information quickly, rarely taking a note. His interest was voracious and broad. They lunched in one of Langley's cafeterias, continued at a rapid pace through the afternoon and finally, to Thomas's relief, they closed up shop, walked out into a snowy evening and Madison drove them to a country inn somewhere in Virginia.

Over dinner, Madison continued his probe and zeroed in on Tshombe. He wanted to know everything about him: background, education, family and, especially, the people he had selected to help him run the government. Thomas was tired and he decided to wait until the following morning to level the playing field.

The next morning they met again in Madison's office. It was strange, Thomas thought, he had not met another individual at the Agency. Surely everyone in the building couldn't be covert. The coffee arrived and he launched into his questions and objectives. "Larry, although I enjoyed our discussion yesterday, I didn't fly all of this way to lecture on Katanga. I came on a simple mission. President Tshombe seeks the recognition and support of the United States. Where do you recommend I start in order to achieve this goal?"

Larry was cautious in his reply. "Well, the best place would be the State Department but you will have some challenges. State is committed to the UN's position and it is they who condemn your secession. They are inserting troops into Katanga, as we speak. We cannot help you on the "recognition" element but we can supply support."

Thomas breathed deeply to hide his exasperation. "Katanga wants to be left in peace. How can you assure that?"

Madison looked at him sharply. "Nothing is assured, Thomas. But we do have powerful friends, both politically and economically, who are interested in your independence. Let us be your conduit."

Thomas was now uncomfortable. The direction of their conversation had taken a new twist. "May I ask who these "friends" are? Tshombe will want to know."

"My suspicion is President Tshombe already knows who these entities are. What I am proposing is a quiet cooperation. You need only to keep us informed of high level decisions in your government and we will supply your friends with the tools necessary for your survival."

Thomas's curiosity overrode his caution. "How would this so-called partnership work?"

"Most important, assure your president that this agency will support him. We will endeavor to influence our government's policy toward Central African affairs and do what we can to deter the UN's actions. Additionally, we have a man in place in Elizabethville who will contact you. You and I can communicate through him. We will ask you for information and you may ask us for specific support."

"This plan will not bring peace to my country." Thomas uttered this pronouncement with anguish. Madison looked away.

It snowed lightly as Madison drove Thomas back to his hotel. The coldness of the weather and of his newly acquired knowledge gnawed at his bones. He shivered. As they shook hands in front of the hotel, Madison mentioned an additional issue.

"There is a possibility that Patrice Lumumba will be looking for a new home in the near future. His presence in the north is inimical to your country's freedom. You may want to mention this possibility to President Tshombe." Madison turned and jumped into his car and headed back across the river.

Cape Town

Jillian Pienar greeted Brian with a broad smile and shining eyes. "Brian Wellesley, how wonderful to see you after so many years. You're still the best looking guy in our class. Come on in to my humble office." She pointed to a door at the end of the isle while she passed off a stack of documents to an assistant.

"You're famous, Jillian. I've watched your rapid progress through the law enforcement ranks; all deserved, I might add. You must like your work."

"It has been challenging and fascinating, Brian, but what I'm doing now is the most interesting police work I've experienced so far. I like dealing with people and problems in other countries, and that's what Interpol is about."

"My father, who sends his best wishes, by the way, told me you are married. Children?"

"Yes, two boys. What about you?"

"Still single. I work for the UN, based in Switzerland, and travel a great deal. I do have a girl friend; she's with me for the holidays."

"I'd like to meet her sometime for a drink. Now tell me, what brings you suddenly into my life?"

"Do you know anything about weapons trafficking?"

"Well, of course, it's a large part of our business. I attended a school on gun smuggling in France last spring. I'm afraid it is rampant in some parts of Africa. Why do you ask?"

Brian related the sketchy details surrounding the overheard conversation in Henley. "An acquaintance of mine from Katanga inadvertently revealed he had paid a South African man a large sum of money to bring guns and equipment to Katanga."

"Do you have the South African man's name?"

"I do, in fact I have his calling card with an address here in Cape Town and one in Stellenbosch. This man, Mr. van Riebeek, is apparently brokering the supply of AK-47s. My girlfriend overheard the discussion, which was in French. They didn't realize she understood French."

"Hmm," Jillian muttered. "How are the weapons traveling to Katanga?"

"Don't know. It wasn't discussed."

"What about your Katanga friend? He must know."

"He claims he only knows about the financing, nothing more. He was the middleman for the money exchange," Brian replied. "He now regrets his involvement. He's a school teacher and out of his depth."

Jillian remembered her French teacher's parting comment—"follow the money." She thought for a moment and then decided not to chase that angle immediately. "I think we should check out this Mr. van Riebeek. Give me a few days. I will call you and we can meet for a drink, but only if you bring along your new friend. She's the important cog in this wheel, not you." Again, Jillian flashed her broad smile and twinkly eyes.

The moment Brian walked out of her office, Jillian had jumped on the information he had provided. Thoughts ran through her mind. Smuggling weapons into South Africa was a no-no. All this country needed was an armed uprising. The long enforced policy of apartheid evoked native hatred as well as world criticism. As South Africa's Director of Interpol, she had vast world-wide resources to tap into. But Interpol held no mandate to arrest; its existence was to coordinate law enforcement agencies.

After Jillian's fingers drummed the desk for another minute, she picked up the phone and dialed the South African National Police Commissioner. Ian McQueen was the top cop in the country—a man set in his ways, impressed with his English ancestry and good at his job.

"Yes." His gravely voice rendered announcing his name as unnecessary.

"Hello, Ian. This is Jillian Pienar. Do you have a minute?"

Ian grunted and suggested, since their offices were in the same building, that she should come over and visit him.

Once seated across from Commissioner McQueen, Jillian explained the background of the case, subtly excluding Wellesley's involvement. Her office had received a tip from abroad. That was all.

Ian shuffled to his outer office and asked a subordinate to run a background check on van Riebeek. He returned, shut the door and said to Jillian, "If he has a criminal record, we will have information in this building. If not, it might take a little time. What do you think we should do first?"

Jillian was both surprised and pleased that Ian was so cooperative. "I suggest that we check with the port authority to see if there are shipments coming van Riebeek's way. If so, the cargo should be inspected. Can you surreptitiously gain entrance to the Jordaan Trading Limited's warehouse without alerting him to our interest just yet?"

"Right," Ian responded, as he stood to escort Jillian to the door. "Not much to go on, but we will look into Mr. van Riebeek's life—thoroughly. Let's talk again after New Years. Excellent to see you, Jillian."

Phillip Wellesley stood on his deck watching the sea. His thin white hair floated above his head in disarray. Summer had arrived early to the southern shoreline of South Africa. A persistent breeze carrying the pungent scent of the ocean rustled the trees surrounding his home. On this gorgeous morning shortly before Christmas, Sam followed Brian up the stairs of the house, which dangled dangerously over a cliff, and onto the sweeping deck. "Dad, here's the lady I have been telling you about. May I introduce Samantha Norquist?"

Brian's father turned unhurriedly, his gaze slipped past Brian and rested on Samantha. It was his eyes that captured her attention; they were closer to the color of sea than the sky—cobalt blue. She saw the father-son resemblance, although Brian was taller. Samantha felt instantly comfortable with this man and stepped forward quickly to greet him. "You are a beauty, Samantha, as I knew you would be," Phillip said, slipping his arm through hers and led her to the railing. "Take a gander at False Bay on a perfect morning."

Samantha surveyed the sweeping view of the bay. "Why do you call it False Bay?"

"The early seafarers mistook it for Table Bay, on which Cape Town is located, so they named it False Bay," he chuckled.

Soon Samantha sat in a chair facing the sun. She threaded her hands through her hair and gathered it into a ponytail. "I'm not moving. I may never move. This is too good. In fact, I may never leave."

"Aha," said Brian. "That suggestion is exactly what I had in mind."

Samantha lifted her dark sunglasses and peered at Brian's father. "May I call you Phil?"

"I would like that."

"Brian may have told you, we will spend a few hours with Dag Hammarskjöld the first week of January. As I recall, you were South Africa's ambassador to the United

Nations and apparently you were quite close to him. Do you mind telling me about him?"

Samantha's awareness of the sea, the delicious air and the sun evaporated as she listened to Phillip's story. He had known Dag well and they had become close friends. From different angles, they both wrestled with South Africa's apartheid policy. "I was embarrassed by it and could not justify it to the UN membership. The secretary-general was determined to influence its repeal. We both failed. After the Sharpeville massacre, I resigned. This country is a pariah in eyes of the world."

"Will Hammarskjöld's visit to Pretoria accomplish anything?" Sam asked.

Phil shrugged. "Probably not. Dag is posturing for black Africa. Verwoerd will be civil, but not cooperative."

"My last photo assignment was in Katanga," Sam said. "It was a war zone, mercenaries and soldiers everywhere. How do you think that situation will play out, Phil, and where does South Africa fit?"

"South Africa and Rhodesia are the last white colonial governments and they will do everything in their power to resist change. Katanga offers them a buffer against the flow of black independence and my guess is they will secretly support Tshombe. And then too, there is the vast mineral wealth. They will fight for that."

Sam moved to the other side of the table and again lifted her sunglasses to look Phillip in the eye. "Because of Brian's intense involvement with the UN, Hammarskjöld and Africa, I've been boning up on the secretary-general. He is tenacious in his desire to provide freedom for everyone. I admire him."

Phillip reached over and touched Sam's arm. "In my opinion, you're about to meet the greatest statesman of our time."

Two days before Christmas, Brian received a phone call from Jillian. "Hi, Brian. Sorry about our missed drink together. It's been hectic here. But I would like to bring you up to date on what we have found so far concerning Mr. van Riebeek."

"Thanks, Jillian. I was about to call you. What have you found?"

"Nothing, absolutely nothing. There's not a blemish on his record. It's like he hasn't lived. He has a small trading business, which imports wine. He bought a rundown vineyard near Stellenbosch and recently began to export his white wine to Great Britain."

"Where does he go when he leaves the country?" Brain asked.

"England, Holland and sometimes Portugal."

"Hmm. Now what?"

"I've opened a file on him. I will ask our famous Cape Town detective branch to investigate Mr. van Riebeek's early background: where was he born, schooled, etc. How do I find you, Brian?"

Jillian did not mention that the file had been open for two weeks, that the Cape Town police were quietly investigating van Riebeek and that she had already asked Interpol to look into van Riebeek's activities abroad.

JANUARY 1961

London

The BOAC flight to London lifted off smoothly from the Jan Smuts International Airport. It had a full cabin and the plane lumbered to gain altitude as it crossed the Kalahari Desert. Samantha watched from her window seat as the morning sun splashed a host of ever changing colors on the sand. Brian, who had elected to fly home via London, sipped orange juice while perusing the morning paper.

Sam turned away from the window, "Your government didn't treat Secretary-General Hammarskjöld with the dignity he deserved."

"He knew exactly what to expect. His capacity to remain calm is well known, yet he is as hard as nails. He told me that he and Verwoerd had a polite conversation. He is acutely aware that South Africa's policy of apartheid will not change from within. He will not succeed here. I am from here, I know. These white men are strong and too determined. He plans to bring change by mustering pressure from within the UN assembly. His conviction is amazing." Brian muttered this critical observation while continuing to leaf through the newspaper.

"I really appreciate you including me on your tour of the African settlements. Thank you for that." She smiled at him. "When the secretary-general asked his driver to stop so that he could mingle with the throng of black Africans gathered to greet him, I followed him and have some really striking shots. He seemed totally at ease walking through the crowd." Samantha's mind retraced her few hours with the Swedish diplomat when they had sat across from each other in the limousine. Even in the heat, there was fastidiousness about him. His tan patent-leather shoes, now dusty, matched his double-breasted tropical suit. Hammarskjöld's vivid blue eyes exuded strength. There was a Buddha-like tranquility about him.

Samantha had flown to Pretoria with Brian to join the UN delegation. When Hammarskjöld emerged from the government offices, he had spotted Brian and waved, signaling him to join him in his limousine. He greeted Samantha by name and to the astonishment of the other journalists trailing the delegation, she too boarded the limo. At the time, she had thought: how paradoxical for a man born in a country bordering the North Pole to have such empathy for oppressed people on the other side of the globe.

"What will you do now, Brian?" She touched his hand and he looked at her with soft loving eyes.

"Hammarskjöld is on his way back to New York. He wants me to concentrate on the Congo situation, to find Lumumba and reinstate him as prime minister. After that, Katanga. We're moving additional troops to Elizabethville. I'll try to visit and I will attempt to find your friend Thomas."

"Yes, please find Thomas," Samantha whispered. "I worry about him.

Katanga

1961 would be a year of turmoil for the break-away country of Katanga. January arrived toting gloomy baggage. The country bristled with combat elements, all of whom seemed to be deployed at cross purposes. The largest armed camp, the Belgian military, which was well-equipped, trained and officered, numbered more than five thousand. Their command center was at the *Union Minière du Haut*, the huge copper mine, which provided the financial incentive for them to remain in Katanga. Over two thousand soldiers guarded the perimeter of the mine, which essentially gave the Belgians control of the copper extraction. Another two thousand Belgian soldiers were camped near Katanga's northern border. The Belgian expeditionary forces received their orders from Brussels, not Elizabethville.

The Belgian army's presence further enraged the fierce war-like Baluba Tribe which dominated Katanga's northern territory. The border with the Kasai Province was blurred, with the Balubas controlling rail and road traffic in one area, while the Belgians occupied other strategic posts. The Baluba tribe imposed their laws along this border; edicts of the Katanga government didn't exist. Supporting this belligerent force were well-armed military units from Northeastern Congo, loyal to Lumumba. This small army lurked in Kasai, waiting for the Belgian army to return home. They would then join the Balubas, and strike southward.

Tshombe countered this threat by recruiting mercenaries to lead his local army, the Katangan Gendarmerie. The mercenaries were composed of many nationalities, largely French and South African, but joined by Irish, British and Rhodesian as well. They were well trained by many wars and skirmishes, and arrived ready to fight for profit. On the other hand, Katanga's army was poorly trained and ill equipped and would provide no match for UN troops or Baluba fighters.

Keane sat in his cabin contemplating his quandary while listening to the deafening clatter of the rain pounding the corrugated steal roofing sheets overhead. Thank God, Keane thought, that we constructed this shanty well above ground. In early January, he and Lynch had returned from a brief Christmas respite in Lusaka to this dismal training camp to complete their contract. Since then it had rained almost constantly, rendering the firing range a morass of mud, and the camp itself an impressive collection of rivulets separated by huts and buildings. During their absence, Kigali's rag-tag army had replaced their tents with thatched huts. Kigali's personal quarters, a large wooden building with windows on four sides, roosted near the entrance to the campgrounds, and provided him with a view in all directions. The remaining wooden building housed the weapons, ammunition and a small rudimentary kitchen. Lynch and Keane maintained their own outdoor cooking area, which, at the moment, was under water.

The two Rhodesians planned to accept the weather conditions and train the men in wet jungle fighting. The AK-47s they had hauled up the Zambezi were perfect for the environment. They would begin as soon as the bigheaded Katangan and self-appointed colonel returned. He had been absent for several days. The rumor circulating among his troops pointed to the development of a smaller camp, five or six kilometers further inland. Recalcitrant soldiers were to be jailed there. Keane made a mental note to visit this "jail" when the road became passable. He wished Morgan were still with them.

The rain diminished, allowing Keane and Lynch to launch their training program. They restricted the firing of weapons to preserve ammunition. Time was spent in the bush working on stealth and perfecting communication techniques. The young recruits were poorly educated; progress was slow. Keane noticed that the number of recruits had diminished. At first he figured they were tired of the harsh life and had returned home. Then he checked the weapons storage cabin and discovered that some of the AK-47s, including ammunition and other equipment, were gone. Strange, he thought, the missing boys wouldn't have taken the rifles home with them. He would ask Kigali about this.

One morning Keane and Lynch drove inland searching for the "other" camp. They followed their camp's dirt road for several kilometers. Lynch was the first to spot the camouflaged entrance to the side road. Curious, they removed some of the foliage and drove on to the concealed road. They drove slowly as it narrowed and scrub-tree branches slapped the side of their truck. Then they heard the gunfire. Lynch swung their truck off the road into a grove of trees bunched well away from the road. "I think we've found the camp," Lynch said in a hushed voice. "Let's skirt the perimeter. The sound is coming from the other side of this hill."

The hill top provided a clear view of the camp. Two men were sitting with their arms manacled behind them, chained to posts. A dozen men in camouflaged fatigues lounged in front of a large building, talking, eating and firing their weapons indiscriminately into the bush. "Look at the windows," Lynch whispered. "Bars. And check out the weapons leaning against the building. AK-47s. It's some kind of jail."

"Yeah," Keane answered quietly. "Now I know where our missing rifles are. Something shifty is going on. We need to watch our backsides."

Elizabethville

On January 17, late in the afternoon, during the last light of the day, an unscheduled DC-4 flight from the coastal town of Moanda landed at the Elizabethville airport. The terminal building was oddly empty. Godefroid Munongo stood alone in the shadow of the building watching the plane approach. He noticed several other groups sheltered under the roof overhang, avoiding the rain, which fell at oblique angles. He thought two were with the small UN delegation—probably Swedes. There was another westerner standing alone, smoking a cigarette—an American he guessed, by the cut of his clothes. He too, was watching the plane. Police Chief Joseph Sanimbi walked to where Munongo was standing, startling him when he spoke. "Do you wish to accompany me to the plane?" he said, as he watched the DC-4 swing around so that the passenger door faced the building.

"No, use only your squad. Take possession of the prisoners, move them quickly to your van and deliver them to Kigali. You know the plan. Afterward, make no mention of this." Munongo gave this instruction while looking straight at Sanimbi, who did not return the stare. He returned to a small group of uniformed policemen and headed toward the plane.

At that moment, the plane door opened, steps were lowered and three shackled men appeared at the door. Each was shoved down the ladder. Munongo could see clearly that the three prisoners had been roughed up and that one was definitely Patrice Lumumba. He had met Lumumba years before and remembered his tall, gaunt physique and the brief mustache and beard. His clothes were torn, and he appeared to be bleeding near his mouth. This is nasty business but necessary, he mused. Munongo turned abruptly and slipped away unnoticed. He drove directly to Tshombe's home.

Sanimbi was relieved to turn over his well-known prisoner to Kigali. The transfer took place on the outskirts of town in a field somewhat back from the road. No words were exchanged. Lumumba and the other two captives were hustled roughly into a three-quarter ton army truck and chained to a side bar. Two armed men joined the captives while Kigali climbed into the truck cab, and without saying a word to Sanimbi, headed off into the night.

Near Mwenda

The world did not learn until February what transpired on this night at Kigali's second camp. Lumumba and his two colleagues were summarily executed by a firing squad. Each prisoner had been roped to a tree and shot individually. No explanation was given; no opportunity to communicate with the outside world. After Kigali's men had shot each man, two uniformed non-commissioned officers in the Belgian military stepped into the killing circle from the darkness of the bush where they had been observing the execution. The three bodies were dumped into the back of their van and the soldiers drove away in the dark. Kigali and his men dismantled the camp — it had served its purpose.

Upemba Cloud Forest

Thomas Kimbamba was edgy. It wasn't the constant rain or the accompanying insects. As a matter of fact, he had ridden his horse this morning, following the rangers on their inspection tour of the park. Nor was the cause the children who were playing at his feet, as he sat in his rocking chair on the porch. Kaila came out to the porch with tea and cakes. The kids squealed happily and grabbed for the food. Kaila waved them away and pulled up a chair, all the while looking at Thomas to appraise his mood.

"You are brooding, my wonderful brother. What are you thinking about?"

"I'm tired of waiting for Tshombe to summon me. I may drive to the city tomorrow. So much is happening, and I feel that I need to be more involved."

Kaila poured the tea. "You were there two weeks ago and returned despondent. You seemed relieved to be free of the turmoil occurring there."

Thomas sighed. "I am disappointed with Tshombe and the direction he's taking. He's surrounded by treachery. There are soldiers everywhere. The city is bursting with plots, distrust and hate." His eyes hardened and rested on the far horizon for a moment. "I feel such great despair and such total uselessness." As he turned his head towards her, his face softened. "Our father taught us to help our neighbors, to bring progress and goodness to the land. Nature was our responsibility. As shepherds, we should protect and preserve it. He taught us life was sacred." These thoughts poured heavily from Thomas's heart, and Kaila ached for him. He was a man crying in the wilderness, a man with unrealized dreams. What could be worse?

It had been over one month since Thomas had returned from the United States. He had reported on all of his conversations; the U.S. reluctance to recognize Katanga along with the CIA's desire to have Lumumba sequestered here. Tshombe had listened to him quietly, never interrupting, just nodding his head as if the information was old news. He accepted the United States' unwillingness to become involved. It was his readiness to allow Lumumba to be exiled in Katanga that astonished Thomas. The arrangement for Lumumba's arrival in January had been assigned to Godefroid Munongo and Police Chief Joseph Sanimbi.

"I have failed you, Moise," Thomas had said with anguish at this meeting. "What can I do now to help you?"

Tshombe stood and approached Thomas, putting his hands on Thomas's shoulders. "You are a good person, Thomas. I trust you as if you were my son. I want you to stay with your sister in the hills where you should be safe. When I need you I will send a message."

Thomas had done as he was told. He returned to the hills of the Upemba Game Park where he spent his days reading and helping the rangers patrol the park. The rain remained implacable. He sat on his sister's deck watching the fine rain wash the crops along the house and the trees beyond. As the parched land darkened, the cracks opened to receive the lifesaving water. The patter of raindrops soothed his mood, and for the first time since he had returned from Washington D.C., he felt invigorated. He knew he could not remain idle, waiting for Moise's call. He saw the structure of his new country eroding with enemies, both foreign and within, all plotting Katanga's demise.

One morning, as the sun emerged, Thomas drove to Elizabethville, heading directly to the government headquarters at the old golf club. There were many new faces, especially white ones. It was like the middle ages, with courtiers vying for an audience with the king. But this day the king was absent. Thomas stood observing from a corner. The Europeans huddled at one end of the long room, enjoying each other's company, as if at a party. This is bizarre, Thomas thought, they are enemies telling each other falsehoods. The Swedes, in United Nations peacekeeping uniforms, were here to urge the removal of the Belgians, who stood next to them, in uniform, laughing and drinking coffee. Other Europeans, probably mercenaries, stood nearby in shorts and multi-pocketed shirts. Munongo appeared to be in charge, sitting behind a large table listening to many voices. Where was Tshombe?

Thomas spied the chief of police, Joseph Sanimbi, and caught his eye before weaving his way through the throng to where he was standing near the door to the deck.

"Hello, Thomas," Sanimbi said amiably. "What are you up to these days?"

Thomas shook Joseph's hand. "I'm here to see Moise. Where is he?"

"Don't know," Sanimbi muttered. "He comes and goes on his own schedule. I suspect he is handling heat from the Lumumba affair."

"What affair?" Thomas looked startled, his eyes wide. "Did Tshombe finally agree to allow Lumumba to live here?"

Sanimbi took Thomas by the arm, leading him discreetly onto the deck where few people congregated in the intense midday heat. "Thomas," Sanimbi said gravely, "much has happened since you were here last. Lumumba arrived here unobserved last week, and was taken to a remote holding spot somewhere north of here."

"Unobserved! Holding spot!" Thomas almost shouted. "What has happened to Lumumba and who knew about all of this?"

Sanimbi looked uncomfortable as he glanced back toward the club room to check if they were being observed. He found Thomas's height intimidating, causing him to rush his words of explanation. "Lumumba is our enemy. His army is on our border, as we speak. There is no way he could live here for any length of time. We did what was necessary. I must tell you in the strictest of confidence, he was executed by firing squad on the night of his arrival."

Thomas swung around to face the pond where birds gathered a short distance from the deck, placed his hands on the rail and took long, deep breaths. This was beyond his imagination. Horrific! His world was not just tumbling; it was exploding! "Who was in charge of the execution?" His voice was in an explosive whisper.

"Captain Kigali. I believe Belgian officers were present. Forget about it, Thomas. It's over . . . ." Sanimbi's sentence trailed off as he watched Thomas hurry toward the exit.

Cape Town

Good as his word, McQueen telephoned Jillian in early January to report on his investigation of van Riebeek. He had moved swiftly. "Jillian, we have developed some information. Jordaan Trading's next wine shipment will arrive in a week. We have alerted customs of our intention to check out the cargo. Also, one of our officers will drive out to van Riebeek's alleged hometown. I don't expect to find much as the town is remote and almost deserted."

"Thanks, Ian. Any feedback on illegal arms shipments?"

"Nothing. But we have only just begun to scour our records. It will take awhile."

Jillian thanked Ian and they promised to stay in close touch.

Interpol, France had responded to her earlier inquiry asking for a photograph of van Riebeek. Fingerprinting was not yet an international method of identification. In her reply, Jillian also included a photo of Adraan and suggested they open a file on him as well. Then she telephoned her counterpart in Salisbury, Rhodesia.

William Bartlett came on the line immediately. "Is that you, Jillian? Have some of our elephants wandered onto your turf?"

"Hello, Bill," Jillian said evenly. "I thought you should know that we have opened a case investigating alleged arms trafficking here. We suspect that some of the weapons might actually have crossed our border with you. Of course I'll copy you on any developments."

Bartlett's jocular amiability masked a serious and driven police officer. "Contraband weapons are chronic. They come in to the country from all directions and we're struggling to cope. Our rebel problem has shifted from isolated incidents to open confrontation. Terrorists are now working both sides of the Zambezi River. We would certainly not welcome gunrunning."

Jillian switched the phone to her other ear. "Do you have any knowledge of small arms moving into or through Rhodesia headed for Katanga?"

"Our borders are porous, Jillian. We're land-locked, so the weapons would have to pass through one of our neighbor's ports. This gives us a slight advantage over a country with a long coastline."

"True, but you have the Zambezi River running through your center."

"Odd you should mention this. Off the record, we have a nosy colonel in our military who reported some suspicious activity on the Zambezi last autumn. After a rafting trip, he reported watching a quantity of crates being offloaded from riverboats. The markings said aircraft parts, yet we have no record of the shipment ending up in our country. The colonel, Roger Smith-Stevens, actually attempted to trace—in a military aircraft—the shipment in our northern territory, but with no luck. He fingered a well-known Rhodesian hunter who runs a respected safari company. We didn't follow up and let the caper slide. I assure you that will not happen again. Let's work together on this."

"What's the white hunters name?"

"Morgan Palmer. He was a respected officer in our army. Because of that, we gave him the benefit of a doubt."

'So, you haven't talked with Palmer concerning your suspicions," Jillian asked hesitantly.

Bartlett sniggered. "Actually, we had planned to talk with Morgan. I know him personally. Quite suddenly and without explanation, the investigation was cancelled. The command to do so came from above—way above."

"Where does Palmer live?" Jillian asked.

"He lives in Lusaka. He should be there now. There are no safari treks during the rainy season."

"Bill, this gun-running business is too big. Interpol headquarters is now running the case. I would like to talk with Mr. Palmer. If I promise to be discrete, would you arrange a meeting and join me in Lusaka?"

Jillian listened to dead silence. Finally Bartlett replied. "I'll set up a meeting and call you. Be warned. If this reaches my political superiors, my neck would be on the block."

"Thank you, Bill. I'll wire a photo and background data on one individual who might be involved. Call me back—soon."

Lusaka

Morgan Palmer was worried. He suspected that the Rhodesian police were interested in his activities. Smith-Stevens had probably reported on the crates he discovered at Rapid End. The authorities could easily trace the DC-3 charter. It had been a risky plan from the beginning, unwise even though he had been compensated well. He would be able to pay his benefactor in London and, at last, be debt free. But the risk taken had been great. His world could come tumbling down. His mind methodically tabulated his options. Resolving his life came first. He needed to unburden and begin anew.

He had returned to Lusaka from his safari camp in early December. The grueling journey from the Katanga border to his main safari camp on the Luangwa Plateau was a subterfuge, a ploy to divert attention from his illicit activity. It had been a torturous drive across the savanna, battered by unrelenting rain. The two Mercedes trucks had been returned to his supplier. His pilot, Colin, had been paid, as well as his three native helpers. Lynch and Keane had left their training camp in Katanga for a fortnight at Christmas. Miraculously they had driven through Elizabethville without incident and crossed the border into Northern Rhodesia. They, too, had been paid. As a reward, Morgan had given each of them an M-14 rifle equipped with a night scope.

Morgan sat alone on his porch, brooding and vacantly listening to the rain slap the metal roof above. He missed Branca. He had briefly considered spending the Christmas holidays with her in Mozambique—some remote seaside village where they could spend their time swimming, drinking rum and making love. But the thought of Smith-Stevens sniffing around had caused him to abandon the idea.

The phone rang, shredding the silence. Morgan slowly emerged from his reverie. His own voice and his brief greeting startled him. "Hello."

"Morgan. This is Bill Bartlett calling from Salisbury. I hope I'm not interrupting anything. How are you?"

Morgan paused. He and Bartlett had been in the army together but hadn't run into each other for several years. "It's been a while, Bill. Good to hear your voice. What's up?"

"A collogue from Cape Town and I will be in Lusaka next week and we would like to visit with you. Would you be up for a chat next Tuesday, say late morning? Afterward we could have lunch."

"I'm always glad to see you, Bill. What will we talk about? Who do you work for these days?"

"I'm with Interpol. Our visit would not be official. We are working on a case and thought you might be of help. See you Tuesday." He had hung up without waiting for an answer.

"Shit. Now what do I do?" Morgan muttered, beseeching the gods.

London

Nicholas had lunched at Dabblers many times. Members of parliament favored this private club for its exclusivity and dependable food. The innocuous name masked the seriousness and diversity of discussions that had taken place in its chambers for over a hundred years.

His host, Sir Douglas Sallis-Cooper, had already arrived and was waiting for Nicholas in the lounge. "Good of you to come, Nicholas," he said in a voice too high for his burly body. "Let's go on in. I have a table away from the ruckus."

Nicholas surveyed the crowded room and then turned his attention to Sallis-Cooper. It had been over a year since their last meeting and it seemed to Nicholas that the MP had aged acutely. His thick neck had become stringy and his red hair had receded. Good living and stress—maybe. He waited for the opening salvo. Sallis-Cooper had ordered a glass of Riesling and the lunch special. Nickolas nodded his acceptance of the same.

"How's the shipping business?"

"Strong, actually," Nicholas replied. "We operate a small crude carrier but, as you know, the bulk of our business is transporting cargo and minerals. A good deal of our business is along both coasts of Africa."

"Has the political turmoil there impacted you?" Sallis-Cooper asked.

"Not really. Why do you ask?"

Sallis-Cooper dug into his shepherds' pie with relish. Finally, he looked up from his lunch and fastened his light hazel eyes on Nicholas. The eyes were opaque and revealed only intensity, nothing specific. "I am an active member of the Anglo-American Corporation. We operate in South Africa and Rhodesia, mainly, and are known for our gold and diamond mines. What is not known is that we own a sizable share of Union Minière. No need to tell you that we are concerned with the UN's attempt to take over Katanga. If they succeed, the mining properties would be nationalized and could fall into the hands of Communists."

Nicholas knew all of this. His ships carried products destined for the mines and his ore carriers transported the mined minerals to Europe and the Americas. "That would be disastrous for my company. I rather hope Tshombe will stand his ground." Where was this conversation leading, Nicholas wondered. He watched Sallis-Cooper finish his pie and signal for the waiter.

"I associate with an informal group of MPs, Tory of course, who share your concern. We are unofficially called the

Katanga Lobby. Some officers of M-16 support our activities. Our position is this, Nicholas," his eyes seemed to flair. "The prosperity of our people rests on our stake in foreign resources: Persian oil, Malayan rubber and tin and the copper on the Katanga border. As long as we realize our investment, England will do very well."

Nicholas listened intently. Did his host presume other aspects of Nicholas's life? "I agree thoroughly," was all he could offer.

"We have a favor to ask of you."

Now we have arrived at the purpose of this lunch. "How can I help you?"

"Our African friends need to import certain delicate products. They would like to ship these items on your vessels and under bogus documents."

Nicholas's mind raced. What African friends: white colonists or the Katanga government or both? "Actually, Douglas, we accept shipping documents as presented. It will be the port custom officials who might cause difficulties."

"Right. We will make arrangements."

"Rhodesia is landlocked. What port were you considering?" Nicholas asked.

"I am also on the Benguela Railroad board. It offers interesting possibilities. But let's talk no more about it now. My friends and I wanted to take you into our confidence." He dabbed his lips and pushed his chair back to offer room for his ample stomach. "I understand you are a farmer. What's your crop down there in Surrey?"

"Red wine and French food," Nicholas said with a laugh. They moved slowly between the tables, both greeting friends, before shaking hands at the door.

FEBRUARY 1961

Elizabethville

The guns and the killing and treachery clouded Thomas's mind. He was adrift.

His modest house bordered the playground of the school where he taught in Elizabethville. He loved the early mornings when he would trudge across the playing field, dodging the swarming children and the inevitable football, on his way to his classroom. He taught math and English; the latter class attracted some of the other teachers as well. Now the field lay empty and the school remained closed. It was unsafe to be out and about. Soldiers and guns were everywhere.

Thomas had returned to his home to think. He had his books, some food, his old car and, best of all, no telephone. He had become a recluse. Samantha's visit had jarred his being. She had challenged the purpose of his alliance with Tshombe and the direction of Katanga. His sister had agreed. And now, he too, was beginning to accept the reality of what was occurring in his homeland. He had formed a simple plan. He wanted to write to Samantha, to acknowledge that he had been wrong and to express his admiration for her. Then he would drive north to the gun camp and find Kigali. He would look for the truth.

Dear Samantha,

This letter carries Kaila's and my greetings and best wishes. I have been shamefully negligent in writing and only now, with the January edition of *Echo* before me, am I inspired to take pen in hand. Your photographs are being applauded everywhere in Elizabethville. The pictures are vivid. Somehow, your keen eye captured both the proud bearing of my people and the despair in their eyes. Moise Tshombe is, of course, thrilled with his portrait on your cover.

Several months have disappeared since your visit. You have been to South Africa and I hope it met your expectations. I visited Washington D.C. and returned with mixed feelings. Katanga is supported by insincere agencies, in your country and in Africa. Tshombe is being used and for no good to the people here. You were so right. The gun is the wrong key to Africa's soul.

Beginning now, I will devote my energy to work for peace. If Mr. Wellesley visits Elizabethville, he should try to find me at this address. I can help him.

I want you to know that the week we spent together here was special for me. You came into my life at a critical point and you enhanced it. Your influence was only less than my father's. Thank you.

I hope our paths cross in the near future. Please write if you have the inclination.

With warmest regards,
Thomas Kimbamba

Thomas felt released as he drove north in the direction of the cloud forest. A force, over which he had no control, was moving him to a confrontation with the man who exemplified all that was wrong in Katanga. He knew exactly where Lumumba's execution had taken place and who had arranged it. It was the insidious small camp that Kigali had secretly built near the village of Mwenda. He drove with a deliberate intensity, dangerous on rural roads shared by man and beast. Military presence was ubiquitous and check points impeded his progress. It was dark by the time Thomas turned off the main road to head for the training camp and the village by the river. His suspicions caused his stomach to churn. Kigali was training young men from the Baluba tribe and sending them north with the AK-47s to fight against Katanga. He wanted to witness the act of treason; then he would respond—forcefully.

He saw the headlights of the two trucks beaming toward him. They crowded the narrow road forcing Thomas to swing onto the shoulder. Luckily his tires found traction which allowed him to turn around and follow them. He suspected the trucks would confirm his worst suspicion. The trucks doused their headlights as they crept through the village, heading for the dock protruding into the Luapula

River. There was a large river launch waiting at the end of the dock. He saw Kigali jump from the cab of the lead truck, and soon men with weapons were pouring off the back. Thomas left his car in the middle of the village street and walked toward Kigali. Kigali saw him coming and turned to head toward the boat.

"What in the name of God are you doing, Kigali?"

"This is none of your business, Kimbamba. You are beginning to piss me off. Go back and tell your friend Moise that the Balubas will be coming to town soon, and we'll be looking for him. And, while you are at it, thank him for our equipment. One more truck run and we'll have all the men and AK-47s." Kigali spit these words with a contemptuous smile.

Thomas stepped closer. "You're nothing but trash, Kigali, and stupid. We'll come after you with a vengeance."

Kigali moved closer and confronted Thomas, poking his chest with his index finger. Thomas pushed his hand away and shoved him with such force that he fell backwards onto the dock. "Touch me again and I'll have my men blow you away," Kigali hissed before limping back past the trucks to board the boat. The empty trucks reversed direction and moved past where Thomas was standing, turned and headed slowly through the village. Thomas walked purposely to the end of the dock. The boat was already on the move, slipping into the darkness which had enveloped the river. "I will find you, Kigali," he shouted. "Do you hear me, you traitor? Your end is near."

Keane stood in his cabin's doorway watching the water navigate the tire tracks leading down through the encampment to the village road. He had opened the door hoping an evening breeze would stir the damp, stifling air inside. He was alone; Lynch had driven the truck to Elizabethville to shop for provisions and would not return for two days. A steady rain had persisted throughout the day postponing any hope of training. Keane had spent the day inside reading and cleaning the M-14 rifle Morgan had given him for Christmas. The rifle seemed almost beautiful in a perverse way; American made, 7.62x51 mm, capable of rapid fire with greater precision than the AK-47. He remembered Morgan's grin when he had opened the package containing the PVS-2 night scope, which would transform the weapon to a sniper's rifle. Yes, he could use it for hunting but the Americans had designed it for their army and armies hunt people. Keane was uncomfortable with this thought. Still, he loved the rifle.

The rain had diminished, leaving the air heavy in a black night. He heard the cough of a truck engine turning over, probably near the storage shed. There were no visible lights, but next he heard voices and the banging sounds of trucks being loaded. Strange, Keane thought. What the hell was going on? He grabbed his pistol belt and rain parka, locked the cabin door and headed down the tire tracks. The mud sucked his boots downward, making the walk difficult. He soon saw two military troop transport trucks already loaded with trainees. Kigali stood between the trucks supervising the loading of what obviously were rifles. He saw Keane approaching and moved to intercept him before he could reach the trucks.

"What's going on?" Keane shouted, noting that Kigali wore plain bush-fatigues with no rank identification.

"I didn't wish to bother you," Kigali said showing his large teeth. "Headquarters has instructed me to transfer these troops to a northern district in order to guard our border there."

"I've heard nothing about this. These men are only half trained. Who in the government issued this order?" Keane questioned.

"This has nothing to do with you," Kigali snarled. "Your job is to transport the weapons and train my men. You're slow on the training. The sooner you are out of here, the happier I'll be." Kigali turned, stalked back to the trucks and ordered his men to finish loading and move out.

Keane stepped back so that the passing trucks didn't splatter him with mud. There must be fifty men crammed into those trucks. How far could they be going cramped together like that? With an uneasy feeling in the pit of his stomach, he hurriedly returned to his cabin and retrieved the M-14, scope and ammo. He would need a flashlight and his hunting knife, as well. He climbed into his Land Rover and headed slowly out of the camp to the road leading to the near-by village, beyond which was the river and docking area. If Kigali was not heading there, Keane was out of luck. He drove using only his parking lights, his eyes fastened to the two pairs of headlights on the road ahead. Keane knew the road well. In about five kilometers, the road split, the main branch heading generally south toward Elizabethville. The other branch, a narrow road, reached north toward the river village. At that moment he saw the headlights of a car moving rapidly toward the trucks. It swerved, as if the trucks refused it passing room, before turning back to follow the trucks. Soon, they all filed directly toward the river.

When Keane reached the turn, he cut sharply to the right onto a cattle path barely wide enough for his four-wheeler. The path circled the village, ending in a thicket of trees surrounded by high weeds. The rain had stopped, allowing him to find a parking spot which would conceal his heavy vehicle without marooning it in the deep mud. He waited close to his car and remained motionless to make sure he was undetected. The villagers would surely be aware of the trucks, but he guessed they would remain inside their huts not wishing to become involved with the soldiers. Keane moved stealthily through the brush, angling toward the river, hoping to get close enough to see who was in the car. What he saw surprised him.

Thomas Kimbamba stood in the middle of the road ranting and waving his arms. He was an incongruous sight, for he was in a white dress shirt, no jacket or hat, and street shoes, which looked like loaves of bread, totally caked with mud. Kigali ignored Thomas while he watched his men leave the trucks to board a large river launch, each carrying his own rifle. The boat had two outboard engines, powerful enough to propel it upriver against the current. The two empty trucks backed around and silently headed past the village huts to the main road. Kigali walked slowly toward Thomas, who continued to remonstrate. Keane could not hear the argument clearly, but gathered that Thomas was protesting Kigali's action and threatening to expose him. Kigali grasped Thomas's shoulders, whereupon Thomas shoved Kigali so violently that he stumbled. Kigali said something in a native dialect, turned and stomped to the boat. He boarded without looking back, just as the boat began to move away from the dock. Thomas moved to the end of the pier and shouted another threat. The silence of the night, like a curtain dropping on a stage, brought an end to the drama. Keane could no longer hear the outboard engines. Thomas stood rigidly on the end of the pier, his broad shoulders bent, his arms at his side, fists clenched and his head bowed, not in resignation, but rather in anguish. Suddenly, Keane heard the engines again; the launch was returning toward the dock. The engines were cut leaving the launch to quietly slide out of the darkness. Kigali was standing on the prow holding a rifle. He raised it to his shoulder, aimed at Thomas, who stood transfixed, and fired a burst that riddled Thomas's chest. Thomas's pure soul had already risen by the time his body hit the river. The boat poised for a moment as Kigali appraised the results of his action. Simultaneously Keane shouldered his rifle, fitted the clip and focused his scope on the assassin's head. A man who respected life and had proclaimed his abhorrence of killing, held his breath before squeezing off a single round. The 7.62 mm bullet caught Kigali just below the right eye, carrying away half of his face before grazing the forehead of the man standing behind him, ultimately entering the chest of a third man. All three fell to the deck as the launch slid back into the darkness of the Katanga night.

Lusaka

When Bartlett telephoned on the following Tuesday, Morgan had suggested they meet in his office. This was not to be a social call. His office was a second floor, one-room affair facing a side street.

Palmer greeted Bartlett amiably. Jillian watched them from the office doorway. *They are comfortable with each other,* she observed. *That will make this interview easier.* Palmer was an attractive man, exuding masculinity. She found herself vaguely hoping he was not involved in smuggling. "Hello, Mr. Palmer. My name is Jillian Pienar." Bartlett had been slow on an introduction, so Jillian forged ahead. "This meeting is my doing and I appreciate your agreement to meet with us."

"Did I have a choice?" Morgan said with his charming smile. I suspect you also work for Interpol."

"I do. I am in charge of South Africa's office. As you may know, Interpol's function is to coordinate international police work. We simplify communication between police agencies in different countries. Bill and I are old friends and have worked together many times."

The inevitably of this conversation gave Morgan a sense of buoyancy. Better to face up and move on. "How can I help you?"

Jillian sat back in the rickety chair and looked Palmer in the eye. "We have a report that you were in possession of a large consignment of crates in the resort Rapid End. Apparently you had brought the consignment up the river and then transferred the crates to a DC-3. Would you mind telling us what was in the crates?" Jillian watched Palmer. He did not blink. His body language seemed relaxed.

"Most of it was supplies for my safari operation. I was laying in non-perishable goods before the raining season so that we could gain a quick start in April with our clients."

"You told Smith-Stevens is was airplane parts," Bartlett said.

"Oh, our good friend, colonel SS. I did say that. I didn't want him nosing around so I gave him an off-handed answer, hoping he would disappear. I now see he didn't."

Jillian looked at Bartlett who nodded indicating she should proceed with the questioning. She shifted her gaze back to Palmer and said evenly, "It will be easy for us to verify your claim. We can check with Mozambique customs. Lusaka Air Authority will have a flight log on the DC-3. We have already determined that no party in Rhodesia, military or civilian, received airplane parts and I do not want to travel to your Luangwa camp site in this wet weather. Why don't we level with each other? Maybe we can find a solution that will be equitable for everyone."

"What do you think was in the crates?" Morgan asked.

"AK-47s. Probably ammo and other military equipment."

Morgan stood. "With all due respect, this meeting is over. You seem to be accusing me of smuggling. I should seek legal counsel."

Bartlett and Jillian stood and headed for the door. Jillian extended her hand to Morgan. "Although that might be a good idea, this has not been an official visit and we have accused you of nothing. We are simply looking for information. With Bill's permission, I will call you next week. Perhaps, by then, you will have thought of further useful information. Thank you again for your time."

Cape Town

"Good afternoon, Jillian," a gravely voice said. "Glad I caught you. I have some tid-bits on the van Riebeek case."

"I'm all ears."

"Van Riebeek's official documents claim he was born and raised in a small farming town in the rugged country north-west of Cape Town. Our man drove up there and found less than twenty residents. The building housing the court house and police station at the time he claims he lived there burned to the ground; the only school burned also—curious, don't you think? The few old people still enduring this outpost could not remember him."

"Have you checked with Pretoria? Maybe the federal records will reveal something."

McQueen puffed. "Their records are identical. Van Riebeek is a citizen of South Africa, born here, educated here and has never been in any kind of trouble. He is a dull man who has lived a pedestrian life."

"What about the wine shipment. Did you intercept it on the docks?"

"Yep. We opened five crates. German Riesling."

"I may have some new information for you in a week, Jillian said. Interpol, France is digging into this case. I've asked them to check on van Riebeek's helper, Adraan. And also, our office in Rhodesia may have a connection. I'll call you the minute I have something."

"That's good, Jillian. I must add that we have decided to keep an eye on van Riebeek's activities, both here and at his winery. We would like to look around his warehouse. Talk with you soon." McQueen terminated the conversation.

Wisconsin

In early February, Samantha escaped London's penetrating dampness and flew home to Elmwood to spend a few quiet days with her parents. Her father, Lars, was beside himself with joy, insisting that the three of them spend time together at their lake lodge. He packed some of his best wine into the trunk of the car before they drove north ahead of an approaching winter storm. The snowstorm's arrival isolated them. Over the three days, nestled in front of a roaring fire, Samantha began to unwind. She told Lars and her mother, Elizabeth, about her visit to Katanga. Her stories of Thomas, his family in the misty hills full of animals and the snake scare in the game park, kept her mother and father captivated. Finally, she described her visit to South Africa and the man with whom she had fallen in love. Parents and daughter reconnected, quietly rekindling their mutual affection. For Samantha, it became a purge. The stress of her life needed venting. Many years would pass before she would return to the comfort and tranquility of her childhood home and hearth.

After the visit with her parents, Samantha spent a week with Meredith in New York preparing the coming year's agenda. *Echo Magazine's* January cover had splashed Moise Tshombe portrait. "We are going to be busy, sweetheart," Meredith chuckled, as she arranged a critical path chart on the wall. "The world is really screwed up. The 1960's decade promises to be painful. Let's talk about South and Central America before we take up French-Indo China. If we flew to D.C., would your uncle Arne spend a couple of hours with us?"

"I'll call him. His area of expertise is SE Asia. I have questions about Central Africa. I think Katanga is slipping into an abyss."

MARCH 1961

Cape Town

Jillian leaned into the wind as she walked from her car to police headquarters. Autumn had blustered its presence on the southern tip of Africa. Rain was in the forecast. Jillian circled the building to the rear entrance which lead to an elevator. Interpol's South African office had been assigned to the top floor rear, a non-descript but quiet location, which she liked. The bustle of activity of other police agencies did not disturb her small office. It was the first day of March. Her first interest was to fetch a cup of coffee and then she opened the van Riebeek file. It had grown thick with documents and now had smeared coffee spots here and there. After reviewing reports from Interpol and McQueen's office, she decided to concentrate on her most important lead—Palmer.

He had telephoned her last Friday. It was now Wednesday and enough time had elapsed for her to solidify the plan she had in mind. Palmer's fate was in the palm of her hand. She now needed to manipulate the Rhodesian authorities. She reached for the phone and dialed Bill Bartlett.

"Good morning, Bill. Have you got a minute?"

"For you, Jillian, an hour if you wish. I know you are calling about Morgan Palmer."

"He finally called me last week. Our conversation meandered. He equivocated about the gun running. But he did sound contrite so I dove in with penetrating questions. I think he is ready to talk but is looking for something in return."

"And what might that be?"

"Probably a reprieve for himself and his partners in crime. Do you think Rhodesia would grant that?"

Jillian could hear Bartlett wheezing at the other end of the line. Finally he asked, "What are we asking for in return?"

"I want to know who is running the illicit weapons trade in central and southern Africa. Who is the kingpin? There are many but at least Palmer may be able to point us in the direction of his organization. He can finger our suspect here and maybe others further up the ladder. What do you think?"

Jillian was surprised that Bartlett did not hesitate. "I believe it can be arranged. Palmer may have to disappear for a while. Give me a few days and I'll get back to you. Cheers for now, Jillian."

London

On a rare sunny early-spring morning, Samantha sat in the kitchen nursing a strong cup of coffee and leafing through the day's mail. She saw Thomas's letter and studied the envelope with a strange stamp. Somehow it had been mailed in Rhodesia. She slit the seal carefully. Samantha read his letter quickly and then, again, more slowly and thoughtfully. She savored his elegant prose and honesty. He had found himself. She would stay close to this man for he was destined to become a leader of his people. He would be a positive force. Samantha sat for a time remembering her visit to the cloud forest; her coffee was going cold.

She returned to the present and began to sort through the pile of mail. There was another blue envelope, spotted and worn, with a colorful stamp. The return address was the very cloud forest about which she had just been dreaming.

> *Dear Samantha,*
>   *My beloved brother and your good friend, Thomas,*
> *is dead.*

A coldness swept through Samantha's body, turning it numb. The blood seemed to rush from her head making her feel faint; she couldn't feel her lips. The letter fell to the floor; her fingers unable to grasp it. Her breathing became so labored that she couldn't get a breath, forcing her to stand and grasp the counter. Never before had she felt such an agonizing shock! A profound sadness enveloped her as her eyes spilled over with hot tears. What had happened? She picked up the letter, peering at it with glazed eyes.

> *. . . He died in February and only now am I able to gather my thoughts to write to you. Thomas not only respected you, he enjoyed your energy and thoughtfulness and he would want me to write to you. I hope you agree.*

He was murdered at night in the village where the gun shipment arrived. His body was found on the shore of the river several kilometers from the jetty. He had been shot in the chest. The villagers found his car the following morning. They told the authorities they had heard shots but were afraid to leave their homes. The training camp had been closed; the white men are gone, as are the soldiers and weapons. It is as if they evaporated.

A representative of President Tshombe brought Thomas's body to our church and gave me a letter from the President. They believe he was shot by roaming Beluga warriors looking for weapons. He said Thomas was like a son. He felt great grief over his, the country's, and my loss. The letter contained some money.

Thomas was a bright light in a dark country. He had so many dreams, which will now remain unattended. What happened to him was not right. My heart screams. He is buried near the church and his grave faces the forest he loved so much. My children and I hope you will visit our church some day.

Forgive me for unloading this long letter on you. No one here seems interested. I knew you would be. Enclosed is a picture of you and Thomas holding the snake he shot. It was on his desk.

> With love from Thomas's family in the misty hills,
> Kaila

Samantha called Brian in Geneva. She had to talk with someone. Kaila had a phone and she would try to telephone her as well. Brian was stunned. "Catch a flight to Geneva today. There's one almost every hour. We will spend the weekend together in the mountains. This must have something to do with the gun business. Come to me darling; you shouldn't be alone and we need to be together."

Salisbury

The capital of the Federation of Rhodesia and Nyasaland mirrored a complex mix of humanity and customs. The government of white men enacted laws which protected and favored the white settlers. For nine months the white population had anxiously watched events to the north, particularly the independence of the DRC and the hasty departure of the Belgians. The government secretly supported Katanga's independence, figuring Tshombe could be molded. It could become a buffer to protect the vast mining riches along the copper belt.

Morgan knew Salisbury well. He had grown up on a tobacco farm not far from the city. He had lived in the bush chasing insurgents. The city now had a decadent taste, like fruit past ripeness. Morgan was uncomfortable in Salisbury. He did not like the place.

He found a street café and settled on coffee and a barouche. He had come to Salisbury at the request of Bill Bartlett and Morgan knew it was the day of reckoning, yet his mind was blank. He stared at the street crowd hoping for an inspiration. Finally, with resignation, he walked the short block to Bartlett's office.

Bill Bartlett rose from behind his enormous desk to greet Morgan. Jillian stood by the window and she too moved toward Morgan to say hello. "This is a Rhodesian affair," she said with a smile. "I hope you don't mind my involvement?" Jillian again experienced a sentient flush for this man who conveyed an animal quality which she found attractive.

Morgan shrugged and ensconced himself in a cushioned chair with armrests. "Let's get to the meat of the matter, shall we? What do you propose we accomplish today?"

Bartlett began. "Morgan, you and I are old friends. We were in the war together. You served your country in Europe and again here in the jungle. I know your background, your family and about your sister. We can only assume that you involved yourself in this illegal activity in order to pay off your debts. Certainly it couldn't have been enjoyable." Bartlett got up and walked around his desk and sat in the chair next to Morgan. "The Rhodesian government does not wish to prosecute you but it does need to curtail the flow of arms into the country. If you would help us, we would apply a very soft retribution for your deeds."

Morgan turned to Jillian, who was still standing near the window. "What's your interest?"

"I think you already know the answer to that question." She quickly continued. "We would like the names of the people who hired you for this—let's call it an endeavor. And how did they pay you?"

Morgan studied Jillian for a moment. A cynical smile played on his lips. "I will disappoint you. I know very little about this caper. I'd like to be done with it and I am willing to exchange information once I have your assurance that you will not harass my friends."

Bartlett nodded. "You have my word."

Morgan looked past the two interrogators and began to talk. "You have it right. I needed the money. I had a huge debt and I was paying for my sister's care. This opportunity came along and, at the time, it seemed like an adventure. Now I hate what I did. I would like to expunge it from my life."

"Who paid you?" Jillian persisted.

"A South African wine merchant by the name of Karel van Riebeek. I have done a few things for him in the past in exchange for help on my loan. He is mysterious and not very nice. He simply slips in and out of my life without leaving tracks. No spoor. He always paid me well and promptly. The logistics of this arms shipment were well organized. I do not know his suppliers: weapons or money. I picked up the cargo in Mozambique and delivered it to the Katanga border, just south of Rosebery." Morgan did not mention the training aspect of his assignment.

"The money. Where did the money come from?" Jillian asked again.

"My payment was deposited to a bank in Beira. My guess is that it came from Portugal."

"Have you met with van Riebeek since you delivered the guns? Bartlett asked.

"No. He thinks I am going to take another shipment of arms to Katanga. I plan to call him and not only refuse, but also to ask him to not bother me again—ever. I had come to this decision well before you arrived on my doorstep."

"Does van Riebeek buy the weapons? Is he paid directly by someone in Katanga?"

"I have no idea," Palmer replied, shaking his head. "Now, if I may be so bold. What do you have in store for me? My life is waiting."

"We will not charge you. There will be no record of our agreement. All we ask is that you leave the country for one year. We don't care where you go so long as you do not talk about our arrangement and you do not return to Rhodesia until the year is up."

"And my friends? What about my business?"

"You can thank Jillian for the details. This is her scheme. We will not involve your friends at Rapid End. They were harmless accessories. Your pilot, Colin, will loose his flying license for six months. That will hurt a bit. We would like Lynch to commit six months as a trainer in our counter-insurgent program. We will not touch Keane and thought that maybe he could run your safari business for the year you will be absent." A smile played on Bartlett's face as he watched Morgan's reaction.

"There is another accomplice," Morgan said, his voice deep and rich.

Now it was Jillian's turn to smile. She had the next step in the ladder. Van Riebeek was her mark. "We figured you might want Miss Abreu Mello to join you on your travels."

Morgan stood. His dark eyes did not reveal his inner thoughts. He extended his hand to Bartlett. "Thank you, Bill. I didn't expect such leniency. I accept your proposal." He then stepped around the desk to where Jillian stood. "When you move against van Riebeek, please remove me from the equation. Oh yes, I will telephone Branca tomorrow and I'll be out of the country in a week. Any suggestions on where I should go?"

Jillian shook his hand. "I hear the Caribbean is a fun place."

After Palmer had left the room, Bartlett and Jillian stood quietly, harboring their own thoughts. Jillian laughed softly. "How did you arrange this? Has Rhodesia gone soft?"

"Yeah, well, I was also surprised. The powers above kicked back their decision in twenty-four hours. They would move harshly on guns coming into Rhodesia, but they are pleased that Katanga secured AK-47s. A lot of politics and our friend Palmer escaped unscathed."

"What about Smith-Stevens?"

Bartlett escorted Jillian to the door. "He was told to mind his own business. Keep me up to date on your investigation. Let's go after the next level."

Algeria

Very little escaped the notice of Adraan. His dark beady eyes were those of a raptor. He had been a sniper in Algeria, a hired gun for any element of society that could pay and remain silent. He had grown up with an instinct for survival on the streets of Oran. His roots were Berber and he actually spoke their tongue, though his mother's primary language was French.

Adraan's birth name was Battuta. He had taken his mother's family name, because his father was an Arab who lived outside of the law. His Berber mother earned little as a maid for families of French officers, and Adraan had to augment their income, which he accomplished by thievery and odd jobs. He grew up as a punk of the streets; he was not immoral, simply amoral. As a teenager, he fell in with a covert rebel group bent on removing the French. He spent a year in Morocco, in the Atlas Mountains, learning to fire weapons and build bombs. By the time he turned eighteen, he had already killed French soldiers and had been placed on the French army's most-wanted list. It was time to disappear. Adraan worked his way west to Morocco, gained passage on a freighter in Casablanca, and jumped ship in Durban, South Africa. When van Riebeek found him, he was stateless and hungry.

Stellenbosch

March was harvest time in South Africa. The grape vines were mature and voluptuous with clumps of grapes in a multitude of colors. Van Riebeek's grapes were generally yellow or green, sometimes with a light pink hue. Riesling came from white grapes, yet many white wines were produced from dark grapes; red, purple or black. The technique to produce marketable white wine required the delicate removal of the grape skin before salvaging the juice. Adraan had learned this technique well from the Dutch vintner, and when the vintner retired to Holland, Adraan replaced him. He spent his days supervising the picking and transporting of the grapes to the crushing area. The laborers worked diligently for Adraan; he frightened them.

Van Riebeek's car thundered up the drive, throwing off a dust trail. Adraan eyed the car's approach, wondering if the dust would reach his harvested grapes. He walked down the incline to where van Riebeek had emerged from his sedan.

"I understand we have a problem," van Riebeek said sternly, as he marched to the house. "Let's sit on the porch. I want the details."

Adraan sat uncomfortably on the edge of his chair, assembling his thoughts, while waiting for van Riebeek to issue instructions to his servant. He asked for a glass of wine, growling at the native servant to be quick about it. Van Riebeek turned back to Adraan, his expression unfathomable.

Adraan began his report. "I found a strange electrical device attached to our warehouse door when I was down there yesterday."

"How did you happen to find it and more important, what does it do?" Van Riebeek's face was mask.

"It's a small metal box, with two thin wires running to a metal pad. The pad is placed on the channel where the rollers of the warehouse door move when the door is opened. My guess is that it activates a signal when the roller passes over the pad, to alert someone that the warehouse is open."

"Someone? Someone who?"

Adraan gave a rare smirk. "We won't know until we open the roll-up door."

"What's in the warehouse now?" van Riebeek asked.

"About half of the wine from our last import, all scheduled to be delivered within the coming fortnight, plus four crates of small arms. They are to go by rail to Pretoria for a clandestine group of Afrikaan farmers. What they plan to do with them is anyone's guess." Adraan was speaking in French. His English still carried a slight French accent that sometimes led to unwanted questions.

Van Riebeek looked angrily over the bucolic scene spread before him. Mountains, his vineyard, a comfortable home and, most important, safety. Now this. Why? Who? He had worked patiently for this comfortable existence, and he would let nothing disrupt it. Nothing, he said to himself, as he turned back to Adraan. "Can the harvest continue if you return to Cape Town?"

"I would like to remain for two more days, after which this crew can handle all aspects of the harvest. What do you want me to do?"

"Ask Edgar to make one wine delivery run in our truck. He has done it before and it won't be suspicious. After he's left, close the warehouse, return to your car and drive it behind the row of warehouses so it cannot be seen from the street. Then find a secluded place from where you can watch the street. Let's see who responds to the signal. Also, I would like you to contact those two imbeciles who haul our shipments to the warehouse. Find out if anyone has been asking questions about our business. Get a little rough, if you have to."

Van Riebeek finished his glass of wine and headed to his office. It was his sanctuary: a windowless room lined with books and file cabinets surrounding an enormous desk. He picked up the phone and dialed his Cape Town office. Stella answered on the first ring.

"Stella," he said with no preamble. "I'm hoping you, or rather your husband, would do me a small favor. I suspect someone has been nosing around our wine shipments when they pass through the port. Maybe he could keep an ear open for information on anyone asking questions about our business. Thanks, Stella. Call me as soon as you have anything." He hung up and sat at his desk, looking at the shelf full of rare weapons and thought about Morgan Palmer.

Geneva

March in Switzerland could be brutal. Samantha arrived shaken from a turbulent flight from London. She clung to Brian in the airport, her voice a bare whisper, "Take me to a quiet place; somewhere cozy with no telephone. I want to sit in front of a roaring fire and just talk."

Snow was in the forecast, a promise of several feet, but it hadn't arrived. In anticipation skiers crowded the terminal waiting for their equipment to slide onto the luggage rack. Everyone was talking, laughing and excited. Samantha's bag arrive early allowing her and Brian to dodge through the throng and escape to his car. Brian drove resolutely around the perimeter of Geneva and headed south toward the French border. Samantha sat quietly staring at the gray featureless countryside. She could smell the snow. Reconnecting had always been a problem for her. Even when she had returned home, to Illinois, to visit her parents, there had been long periods of silence—no one quite certain how and where to begin again. Brian had not burst into her life. It had been gradual, the getting to know each other, subtle but sustaining. Now, he was a deep well and she kept discovering more qualities she loved and strengths she could draw on. When they had hugged in the airport, she had pressed her nose to his neck. He smelled clean, no cologne or soap, just him, the man. Their constant separation didn't trouble her. It was only when they were back in each other's presence that she felt exhilaration, a grateful happy fulfillment.

Not far into France, Brian swung onto a secondary road which ran beside a large lake. Its surface was dark and placid as it too awaited the storm. Sam could feel the familiar sensation of being turned on and she wished Brian would hurry. She knew they would tear each other's clothes off the minute the hotel door closed. After a few wrong turns, Brian found their lodge in a hillside forest above Saint-Jonoz. They parked and carried their luggage to the entrance just as the first snow flakes cluttered the air. A large room was waiting, with a view of Lake Annecy—a welcoming fire was lit casting the room in soft shadows. And she had been right, Brain shared her wanting.

The flames erupted from the kindling, licking at the pine logs, which caught fire quickly and the crackle of the fire added serenity to the silence of the room. Samantha sat on the floor, her back against the couch and her arm encircling Brian's leg. She stared at the blaze searching for answers. Brian massaged her shoulders and then ran is fingers through her hair and down to her neck. Their propinquity provided profound solace. They had finished supper in the inn dining room which offered a mountain chalet atmosphere and a rich dish of veal in cream that the Swiss called Zürigschnätzlets. In French, she wasn't sure. Brian ordered a second Beaujolais for the room. They had talked little at dinner and allowed the food, wine and ambiance to influence their mood.

Now, back in the room, Samantha stood by the window. A single light below illuminated the swirling snow and the purity of the landscape nearby. "Our car will be buried by morning. We'll never get out of here," she said turning back to Brian. "We may have to remain here for a week," she smiled mischievously. Sam settled on the couch next to Brian and gazed at the flickering embers.

"I want to go back," she murmured.

"Back where?" Brian said in a lazy voice.

"Katanga. What's going on there is the story of Africa. I want to do a better job of photographing the developing story and, also, I want to see Kaila. I want to know what happened to Thomas. Why he ended up . . ." her voice trailed off. "Why he ended up the way he did."

Brian turned his body so that he could face Samantha dead on. His eyes were large and serious. "You can not do that for many reasons, starting with the fact that it's a war zone. Our UN forces will soon begin an offensive. The country is bristling with foreign troops and hot-headed mercenaries. And finally, I don't think you would be allowed to cross the border."

Samantha looked back at the embers. "My editor has scheduled me to visit Lebanon. The writer, a women I have known since school days, is flying in from Egypt—in fact, she may already be in Beirut. We plan to sneak into Syria. My heart isn't in it. My mind is on Africa."

"There is an alternative—a dangerous one."

Samantha looked into Brian's eyes; they were still large and serious. "Tell me."

"What I am about to reveal is confidential. I am going to share with you the secret thoughts of a man I respect immensely, Dag Hammarskjöld." Brian moved to the fireplace to add a log or two and to organize his thoughts. He remained by the fire and continued with his thought. "Hammarskjöld knows the world is watching him. Will he and the UN have the fortitude to stabilize the Congo, in fact, all of Africa? Katanga is the linch-pin. He realizes that it isn't just Tshombe who is thwarting his efforts; it's a powerful group of Europeans and their rich and enormous companies in Central Africa. They are aligned against him and the battle will take place in Katanga."

"That's why I want to go there," Sam said in a quiet voice.

"No, you want to go next door. That's where a lot is happening. Rhodesia is where your story is brewing."

Samantha sat up, her nerves tingling. Brian had hit her quandary on the head. Rhodesia offered a photojournalist's paradise. "Yes, you are right. I'll call Meredith tomorrow. I know she'll support this opportunity."

"Wait a minute," Brian said, raising his hand. "You can't go in there alone. A young, blond, white woman! You will need a male partner who knows the ropes."

"I'll call my uncle Arne. He'll know what to do."

APRIL 1961

Cape Town

Saturday was April Fool's Day, and also the day before Easter. Autumn had slipped in quietly, providing an explosion of foliage colors, along with the soft, delicious air from the sea. The March lily appeared. Churches were filled, restaurants were busy and all of Cape Town was dressed in its best finery. Van Riebeek took no notice. He had driven to the city on Saturday to prepare for his meeting with Adraan and to investigate and respond to the strange events occurring around his warehouse. Stella's Africaner husband had snooped around the Port Authority's office and soon discovered that two city police detectives had been on the docks asking questions. An old codger, Ernie, had spilled the beans. He puffed his chest and said "he knew more about the goings on at the port than the baas." The detectives had asked about the Jordaan Trading Ltd., with particular interest in their cartage firm. Van Riebeek rubbed his tired eyes, closed them for a moment and concluded to himself that this was how they had found the storage building. He knew what they were looking for, but why now?

To exacerbate matters, he had just returned Morgan Palmer's telephone call. Palmer was reneging on his commitment to deliver the AK-47s to Katanga. Morgan justified his decision by claiming his safari business demanded attention. Van Riebeek had listened quietly, letting Palmer ramble on, offering excuses. The Zambezi flood plain was exceptionally high this year, making navigation difficult. The influx of mercenaries to Katanga was causing its neighbors to become alert to illegal activity on their turf. Van Riebeek had asked if there was anything that could be done to change his mind, but Palmer had held his ground. There was a tension in Palmer's voice that van Riebeek couldn't place. Palmer was nervous about something, but what? Perhaps all had not gone as well as he professed on the first journey.

Karel van Riebeek's life in South Africa had been tranquil. He had slipped out of Nazi Germany in 1945, just in time. He paused in Holland for two years, before taking a tramp steamer to the other end of the globe in order to disappear into South Africa undetected. He had scrupulously kept a low profile. His wine business flourished and became an occupation he enjoyed; the weapons business yielded a greater return, but he had grown to hate it. He got out of his chair slowly, his joints creaking, and sauntered to the window. He saw Adraan walking swiftly toward the office. He was too old for the gun business. It's probably time, he thought, to concentrate on his grapes. Adraan opened the door quietly, and, like a shadow, moved to a seat across the desk from van Riebeek.

Van Riebeek appraised the man before him. Adraan was like a son, totally dependent on van Riebeek. He had no interests other than van Riebeek's business activities—wine and guns. Adraan's dark eyes, set in his deeply tanned face, were passive, yet van Riebeek knew they were the eyes of a killer. Adraan would carry out van Riebeek's orders with no questions. It made no difference if the assignment was illegal. Van Riebeek had two such missions in mind.

He began to speak slowly as he watched Adraan's eyes. "What happened after our truck left the warehouse to make wine deliveries?"

"As you expected, within minutes a sedan with two occupants pulled in front, paused briefly, and then roared down the street heading for the coastal road. There is a tracking device on our truck so they could follow easily."

"How do you know that?" van Riebeek asked.

"The only people with access to our truck, besides the two of us, are the service station workers and our two cartage friends. We haven't had the truck serviced for some time, so I drove the few blocks to the cartage company's office. Emil, the blackest of the two, and generally the mouthpiece, was at his desk smoking a cigar. He was surprised to see me and seemed apprehensive. I sat at his desk and placed my hand gun on the desk with the barrel pointed in his direction. There was a small clock next to the gun. I turned it to face Emil and told him he had exactly five minutes to explain the alarm and tracking device or I would cancel his life on earth."

"Go on," van Riebeek said.

"Emil confessed that he had talked briefly with two gentlemen at the port, who claimed they were performing a government survey. He confirmed we were one of his customers. Later, he was visited by a rough talking man who gave him an envelope containing R1500 and the tracking devise. The man gave no explanation. He said he would remove the devise from our truck in a few weeks when it was out on delivery. There would be no problems for Emil if he kept his mouth shut."

"Not a lot of money for the risk. Who is this man?"

Adraan's accent assumed a French flavor, a sign that he was relaxed and enjoying himself. "I let Emil know that he was on our "watch list," an honor provided to only those who have made a grievous mistake. Another mistake and his name would be removed, permanently. I returned to the warehouse and waited for Edgar to return from his deliveries. When he did, the sedan was a block behind him. I followed the car. They drove to the city police department."

Van Riebeek drummed his fingers on the desk briefly before sinking back in his chair. "Do nothing that would alert our nosy friends to our discovery of their plot. We have one large order of munitions for delivery to Limpopo. My suspicion is it will end up in Rhodesia. If they traced it to us we would be in enormous trouble. So, let's be especially careful with this delivery. I will prepare the paperwork for delivery by railroad. It will go to Johannesburg for transfer to Tshikota. Prepare the crates as you normally would; label them "plumbing supplies." When we have the train schedule, remove the alarm from the door and the tracker from our truck, making sure they are not active, and then deliver the crates to the railway cargo office. When you return, replace both devices and re-activate them."

Adraan stood. "I'm going back to the vineyard to complete the harvest and bottling. When you are ready, I can come to Cape Town and make the delivery."

"Good. When you finish with the harvest and bottling next month, I have a job for you in Mozambique. Make sure your passport is in order."

The alleged gunrunning had captivated Jillian's imagination. She itched to move on van Riebeek for she now knew with certainty of his complicity. Interpol's headquarters in Lyon had persevered, finally tracking down some background information on him. As it turned out, he was a Dutchman. They started their trace with Holland by tapping a rarely used and notoriously incompetent branch of the Dutch law enforcement establishment—the Department of Missing Persons. Not only did they discover a record of van Riebeek living in Arnhem; Interpol surmised that the trail led even further—into Germany. Subsequently they contacted the American military, which had controlled that sector of Germany in the late 1940s.

South Africa's Department of Immigration had also found a curious coincidence when checking van Riebeek's international departures. On the first inspection of their data bank, it appeared he had not traveled abroad in 1961. They did find another "Karel," not a common name, and the investigators' curiosity compelled them to compare the personal information of that "Karel" with the man they were investigating. The similarity was extensive. The senior officer at Immigration called Jillian. "Your man has been traveling in Europe alright, but using a Dutch passport under the name of Karel von Reinhardt. He has visited Lisbon repeatedly.

Have your people start tracking there. Good day to you, Jillian."

Jillian called Ian McQueen. "I have a curious report from Interpol," Jillian said when McQueen answered. "We think van Riebeek is Dutch or maybe German. He frequently visits a Dutch border town. Interpol is exploring that lead. Also, our friend has been flying around Europe on a Dutch passport. I think we should begin asserting a little pressure on him."

"I agree—how do you suggest we proceed?"

"Let's follow the money. I venture a guess that a substantial amount is floating the wire between banks. Can you get a warrant to quietly look at his bank account?"

"And what exactly are we looking for?"

"Why the location of Mr. van Riebeek's European bank account, of course."

Guildford, Surrey

Weekend parties at Nicholas's farm fell into three categories: strictly business, small and intimate gatherings and large hullabaloo bashes. The common denominator was wine, women and abundant food. This weekend in April had been preceded by days of endless showers that had turned the farm grounds into a morass of mud. The guests were Nicholas's business acquaintances and shipping customers, plus three Tory MPs. Sir Sallis-Cooper was one of them. They had brought their wives, which restricted the indoor activities to food and talk. Conversation had eventually worn thin and Nicholas had slipped away for two hours of hunting on horseback. When he trotted Thalassic out of the woods,

Nicholas saw Sallis-Cooper standing in the horse barn. Nicholas chuckled at the PM's appearance—boots as high as his crotch and a dry-as-a-bone coat hanging open to the ground. Sallis-Cooper was a short, stocky man who belonged in chambers, not barns.

"Hello, Douglas. Had enough of the small talk?"

"I saw you sneak away. I've never worn these boots so I thought I would give them a trail run in this God-awful weather. I see your pouch has a few kills. Four or two legged?"

"Two woodcocks, only. They are tricky to shoot and a mess to clean. My cook will not be happy." Nicholas dismounted and handed off the reins to his farm superintendent.

"In truth," Sallis-Cooper said, as they walked toward the house, "I was hoping to catch you alone. I have something for you to consider."

"If you promise to remove your boots, we can chat in my office. You will be among a select few who have visited my farm office."

Sallis-Cooper stood in front of the vast gun collection displayed in cases and on the wall. He turned to Nicholas and swept his arm toward the weapons. "Ironically, it's about this that I wanted to talk with you."

"It's a hobby, Douglas. I've loved guns since I was a boy. I would rather you not mention this collection to others. Make yourself comfortable while I dig out good Bordeaux."

Sallis-Cooper began. "Over our lunch at my club, we talked about the problems in Central Africa. My friends, both here and in Africa, have been lending a helping hand to President Tshombe. Last autumn, Rhodesia looked the other way when a large shipment of weapons was transported up the Zambezi and across the plateau to Katanga. Our contact in Elizabethville, someone close to Tshombe, has asked us to assist on providing more weapons. When we investigated the first shipment, we discovered that the arms arrived in a small Mozambique port on one of your ships. It crossed my mind that you should be able to check your manifest for that shipment and find out who supplied the arms."

Nicholas fiddled with a letter opener and did not look at his guest. After consideration, he said, "I could do that for you, Douglas. Then what?"

"My friends feel that you would be able to offer suggestions on how to source and deliver the weapons. I'm not sure how you would be able to do that, and I do not want to know. You are our shipping company of choice. That's important."

"Let me think on this for a few days. Drink up, Douglas. Let's join the madding crowd up-stairs."

Nicholas Andropolis had been smuggling guns for a decade. His shipping business offered a perfect camouflage. His illicit shipments threaded the world: the Balkans, the Middle East and Africa were large markets. It had begun almost incidentally during the early 1950s when he had frequented European gun shows and exhibits. For Nicholas it was a compelling hobby. He started off with antique rifles but quickly drifted into guns that could be fired at the range. Military weapons became an obsession. He began to collect assault rifles: American, German, even Russian. Because England frowned on gun ownership, certainly military rifles, Nicholas resorted to smuggling his collection into the country. He found it easy and exciting.

It was in Frankfort, in 1955, where he saw his first AK-47. It was on exhibit only, not for sale. He struck up a conversation with a young man standing by the exhibit, who was also enamored with the Russian assault rifle and seemed to know a lot about it. The AK-47 was the rifle of choice world-wide by government forces and those opposing the government. The young man's name was Dieter Reinhardt, a Dutch citizen, and he shared Nicholas's keenness for guns. They spent the afternoon together wandering the show and agreed to meet for dinner. It was that evening that Dieter introduced Nicholas to his uncle, Karel van Riebeek. It was instant dislike on Nicholas's part. Van Riebeek was an aging and unscrupulous Nazi hiding in South Africa. He had recently established a wine importing company in Cape Town and had come to Europe to discuss with his nephew other product possibilities. Dieter understood guns. He had been trained by the Germans during the war. The embryo of an unholy alliance developed between the three radically different individuals. In less than a year, they were working together on small smuggling operations. Dieter knew how to buy the weapons. Nicholas had the transportation and financing. Van Riebeek became the broker in Central and Southern Africa.

Nicholas met other brokers, facilitators for the Balkans, the Mideast and North Africa. He ran the smuggling operation and controlled the flow of money. He loved the undercover business more than his shipping business. It kick-started his adrenaline. The financial rewards were enormous. So much so that he found it difficult to stash his profits. Antigua became the location of his main numbered bank account. He built a home in St. Kitts—on a high cliff facing the sunsets.

Nicholas could keep a secret. A select few knew about specific aspects of his business, but never the complete picture. Hans Steiner, his Lichtenstein banker, possessed the most information and he was paid well for his discretion. Nicholas communicated with Dieter and van Riebeek infrequently and masked their conversations in mundane chatter.

A parliament messenger delivered an envelope to the Andropolis Shipping Company's office in Hanover Square. Nikko Metaxas placed it on Nicholas's desk unopened. It lingered untouched for most of the day while Nicholas navigated through telexes from his worldwide shipping empire. Sallis-Cooper had telephoned the Tuesday after the Guildford weekend party to ask if Nicholas had found an opportunity to locate the weapon suppliers on the Mozambique shipment. Nicholas knew, of course, since they were his suppliers. He replied that he had located them and asked again how he could help.

"Would you handle this for us?" Sir Douglas queried. "We and your country would be in your debt."

"I will do this but I must insist that all communication come from you. This is a favor to you, Douglas, and your "friends." Send me a list of materials desired. What about the financing?"

"We expected this question," he said with a brief laugh. "I only need the total charge; a breakdown is not necessary. One of our companies, the Union Minière, will wire half of the amount to your bank immediately. The other half when you have proof of shipment."

"When do you want the products to arrive?"

"August, latest."

"What's the destination?" Nicholas had already written Katanga next to the word—August, before Sallis-Cooper confirmed it. The giant mine was located there. "Do your friends have any idea of how the goods should travel from the port to this landlocked destination?"

"Not through Rhodesia. I suggest you look at the Benguela Railroad. We could use your business." He laughed and hung up.

Cape Town

Van Riebeek felt unsettled. There were too many loose ends requiring attention. Palmer's sudden departure bothered him. How would he transport the second Katanga order? And now the police were meddling in his affairs. Stella interrupted his anxious musing by dumping a pile of papers on his desk. On top of the stack was a telex, the contents of which cleared his mind. The brief message, from a London shipping company, asked if he would be interested in meeting with the manager of a Riesling vineyard, a German client of theirs. If so, they suggested he attend a wine seminar in Athens the following week.

Van Riebeek began to plan. The telex announced the second Katanga order and he needed to prepare. He beckoned to Adraan who was sitting in the outer office. "Close the door—we need to talk. I am leaving for Europe next week. The completion of our harvest is in your hands. Make sure all of this season's growth is in barrels by mid-May. Then you should wind up your affairs. For a long time you have dreamed of returning to Algeria, to reunite with your mother and start your own vineyard. The time has arrived, Adraan, and you should prepare to leave in a month. I am too old to continue all of our activities and I've decided to spend the rest of my days in Stellenbosch. I have enough money to do that and I plan to pay you handsomely for your loyal service."

Adraan shifted in his chair but said nothing. Even for this offer, van Riebeek snickered to himself, he has nothing to say.

Always a careful man, van Riebeek booked his own air tickets. Considering recent events, he would need to slip out of the country unnoticed. He would use his Dutch passport. The given name in this passport should have been changed years ago, but now it was too late. He responded to the London shipping company, agreeing to the meeting and booked his round-trip ticket; Athens-Lisbon-Cape Town. He would arrange his connecting European travel in Lisbon.

Stella covered for him efficiently when he traveled. He would deal with the termination of his import business and the closing of his office when he returned from Europe.

London

Samantha lay sprawled on her couch, one arm dangling over the edge. Lousy weather had delayed her flight home from Beirut; her scheduled noon arrival had stretched to evening. Every bone in her body ached. She wasn't hungry, just exhausted, but she needed to make two phone calls to the states before she slipped off. She took a gulp of wine and dialed the *Echo* office in New York. Meredith took a long time to come on the line.

"Tell me about Syria. Do you have a photo for our cover?"

"Meredith, I'm bushed. Let's talk tomorrow about the mid-east. I have another opportunity cooking and would like your support. I'd like to do a story on Rhodesia next month."

"You take pictures, honey. You don't write stories," Meredith barked into the phone. "But, I'll listen. Start from the beginning."

When Samantha had finished explaining the history and potential, Meredith said simply, "I do not have a contact in Salisbury. If you can find someone who can write, I will consider this assignment. Don't forget, Syria tomorrow."

Sam looked at the phone in her hand. There was one man who would know what to do. She asked the operator to ring a number she rarely used. She called her uncle in Langley.

Arne answered immediately and listened patiently. "Sam, I don't have an answer for you off the top of my head. Give me a few days and promise me you will stay in London until we talk. Bye for now."

Quinn, Samantha's brother, blew into London unannounced the following Friday. The familiar pitch of his voice on the phone lifted her spirits.

"I'm here for the weekend. Call that man of yours and insist he join us for dinner tomorrow evening."

"How can you do this to me, Quinn?" she said breathlessly. Brian lives in Geneva and I'm not even sure he's there. Where are you? I want to see you."

"I just landed at Heathrow. I have meetings all day and I'm exhausted. Tonight I want to sleep. How about your flat tomorrow—late morning? Urge Brain to join us. I want to meet him. Gotta run, bye sis."

Samantha sensed that Brian and Quinn instantly liked each other. They were sitting in her living room nursing drinks while she perched on the corner of the sofa, silently breathing in the moment. Quinn watched Brian intently whereas Brian shifted his gaze from brother to sister, taking pleasure in the family connection. She watched them chat as old friends.

"I only assumed my post in Singapore in January and Mette has barely unpacked. Suddenly this problem with a chemical supplier in the UK cropped up and it seemed more effective if sorted it out face to face. Telexes are rather impersonal. Monday I'll visit our Hamburg office and then fly home that evening. Mette wants to know everything about you two, so I'll stop talking."

Brian explained his job with the UN and the problems he faced in Africa. Samantha detected edginess in his voice. He was so caught up in the challenges, especially the Congo, and she worried about the stress. Quinn was a seasoned interrogator. Soon the two men were dissecting the political atmosphere looking for solutions. Quinn's intuitive interest shifted from Katanga to Rhodesia. "Where do they stand, officially, on the sweep of independence flowing down Africa?"

"Ah, you've hit a sensitive cord," Brian answered. Their official posture means nothing. They resist and protest. Katanga is their firewall to protect their immense mining wealth and white sovereignty. They are a threat to my boss's grand plan for Africa."

"Dag Hammarskjöld," Quinn said. "The secretary-general's enthusiasm has infected you."

"I'm going to Rhodesia," Samantha interrupted abruptly. My magazine has signed on and we are only waiting for a journalist to join me."

Rhodesia dominated their conversation. What dangers did the assignment present? What and whom did she intend to photograph? Actually, this was not clear, even to Samantha, yet she knew there would be a story waiting for her.

She told Quinn about her visit to Katanga and about Thomas. Their conversation turned to gun smuggling and their suspicions regarding van Riebeek.

"Arms will lead to the disintegration of Africa," Quinn said firmly. "White men are fueling the fire. You need to be cautious. Leave the gunrunner to your friend, Jillian, in Cape Town. Now," he said, changing the subject, "let's map out tomorrow's program. I suggest lunch in the country and more talk of Africa."

MAY 1961

Athens, Greece

May is a good month to visit Greece: calm breezes, sunny skies and few tourists. For most, the sea remains too chilly for swimming but the air is pure and invigorating. Van Riebeek arrived the evening before his scheduled meeting, checked into the Grande Bretagne and retired immediately. An insistent knock on his door awakened him early. Through the peek hole he saw the smiling face of his nephew, Dieter. "Come in, Mr. Riesling," he said, opening the door.

"The is my first visit to Athens, Uncle. I like it. Get dressed and let's have breakfast by the pool. It's already warm."

Just before they left the room, the front desk telephoned to say they had an envelope for Mr. van Riebeek. "I'm on the way down. I will pick it up. Thanks."

Uncle and nephew sat in the shaded café patio near the swimming pool. It was early and they were alone. Van Riebeek opened the large envelope, scanned the four pages and handed them to Dieter. "Here is our new order. Can you source all of these items?" The envelope also contained a small sealed envelope with a note for van Riebeek.

> Here is a large order for the same customer. Advise the cost, your total fee and availability. Products required August. Advise Steiner in Vaduz, your bank account. Half now, half upon delivery. Confirm earliest. Will advise destination contact later.

Dieter whistled. "This is a huge order. It's the usual: AK-47 assault rifles, handguns, mortars, grenades and a large quantity of ammunition. Whoa! What's this?" he said, straightening. "Three anti-aircraft weapons!"

"What would they do with weapons like that?"

"To target aircraft, obviously," Dieter replied. "They want something small and mobile. Three would hardly be a deterrent to an invading army with an air force, so I'm not exactly sure what they have in mind. I'm not sure where to buy them."

Van Riebeek slipped on his sunglasses and looked out at the pool where a young woman carved the water doing lengths. "There is a rumor that the East Germans are working on a small missile that could be used for this purpose. You know German arms merchants, Dieter. Why not snoop around?"

"Why are we meeting in Athens? Sort of out-of-the-way, don't you think?"

"Maybe someone thinks I am being watched," van Riebeek said, still watching the swimmer.

"What are you going to do now, uncle?"

"Get some money, await your results and search for a route to Katanga. Since there is no meeting in Athens, I'm going to fly to Lisbon today. When will I hear from you?"

"This will take some time," Dieter said, folding the list into the envelope.

"Why don't you come to Arnheim when you finish your business in Lisbon? I should have some information by then."

Leopoldville

The world in 1961 presented its occupants with terrifying turmoil, unrest and chaos. Dag Hammarskjöld stood in the middle of these dire events, coolly working with all contenders, striving for equitable and humane solutions. He was a master negotiator, soft-spoken yet firm, and generally popular among his UN membership. When he replaced Trygve Lie as secretary-general, he quickly learned to prioritize and concentrate. There were too many world problems demanding his attention. Were he to address all of them, none would receive a solution. It was with this principle that Hammarskjöld developed a strategy for Brian's mission.

"Set up shop in Geneva," he had said to Brian in New York. "Don't let the politics of our people there divert you from your mission. We must put Africa on an even keel before focusing on the Soviets and the Islamic world. You are to begin your work in the Congo and South Africa. Spend time on the ground, understand the nuances of the issues, become acquainted with the government officials—in effect, grease the knowledge channel so that I can understand and deal with the situation with alacrity."

Lisbon

Van Riebeek preferred Portugal to other European wine growing countries. He had even considered moving to Oporto to live out his life on a ranch in the foothills. Even though Portugal was sympathetic to diverse politics and ancestry, he was reluctant to have the government delve into his past.

He arrived late afternoon from Athens and took a taxi directly to his favorite seaside hotel. The dining room faced the ocean and he chose to sit on the deck. He had brought a sweater, for he knew the evening sea breeze would be chilly. The waiter remembered van Riebeek and recommended a fresh fish dish with a bottle of white wine. Van Riebeek savored the tranquility, sipped the wine and allowed his mind to wander over the various transportation possibilities.

Taking the shipment through Cape Town, his normal procedure, presented too many risks. The number of crates would expose the shipment to inspection. The weight alone would announce that the crates did not contain wine. The port authority knew him too well. For Jordaan Trading to suddenly import plumbing fixtures would raise eyebrows. With certainty, he was being watched. Beyond South Africa, the Rhodesians would be watching rail shipments to the Congo. No, South Africa was not an option.

He could never duplicate Morgan's daring river exploit. He didn't know of anyone else who could navigate the river, let alone the wild land surrounding Katanga. He could possibly arrange for the shipment to be allowed through customs, a cost of doing business in Mozambique, but the logistics of shipping on the railroad through Salisbury were daunting. He had to somehow avoid Northern Rhodesia entirely.

That left two gateways; one to the East, the other in the West. The new railroad from the Tanganyika port of Dar es Salaam to Ndola would be completed in the autumn. However, the weapons shipment would need to reach Katanga no later than August. Van Riebeek wondered if there would even be a government in Katanga to receive the guns. At the moment, there was anarchy, confusion and shifting alliances. Tanganyika had celebrated its independence from Great Britain early this year, but learning the ropes of self-government would take years. Government offices would be in transition, which might present opportunities to offload the steamer and transship without custom difficulties. But, the British hadn't actually vacated their responsibilities yet, so their presence on the docks could cause problems.

Why was he in Portugal? A mysterious hand must have guided him here because, in his gut, he knew the answers to his delivery problem were in Angola. With this unsupported but comforting knowledge, Karel drained his wine glass before heading to bed. Tomorrow he would begin to research the Benguela Railway. His banker would offer a good starting point.

The following morning van Riebeek met with his long time friend and banker, Rodrigo Camargo. He was a portly man, always jolly, and smiled too often. From the beginning of their relationship, Camargo had respected the confidentualilty of their banking arrangement and, to van Riebeek's surprise, Camargo was a deep well of all types of information. The Benguela Railroad was an example.

They sat facing each other in Camargo's plush office. "So, you are suddenly interested in the Angola railroad."

"Yes," van Riebeek hedged, "I've been reading Angola history and this railroad caught my interest. What can you tell me about it?"

"The Portuguese Colonial Government built it in 1899. It stretches 1,344 kilometers from the port of Lobito on the Atlantic, roughly following the old trade route between the trading center of Benguela and the hinterlands of the Bié plateau. It took us a long time to complete because of several wars. The rail line eventually linked with the border town of Luau. Here it connected with the Belgian Congo rail system which provided access to the Rhodesian, Mozambique and South African railroad systems. It was built on resources from Portugal, but on the backs of cheap Angolan labor. Venal management, callous supervision, accidents, disease, and even wild animals impeded the railroad's construction as well."

"Who manages the railroad now?" van Riebeek asked.

"Our colonial government, but I understand the day-to-day operation is in the hands of Angolans. It still offers the main route for Central African minerals to reach a port. It sometimes carries cotton, picked by natives under forced labor, for wages too low to cover basic living. In 1960, the earliest native revolts occurred in the countryside, some near the railroad's path."

"You sound pessimistic on the future of your colony."

"It will all come tumbling down, soon." He handed van Riebeek a card. "Here is the man I suggest you meet. He lived in Angola and knows far more than I do about the railroad."

The Department of Colonial Affairs building sat back from the street; its lawn with manicured trees filtered some of the traffic noise. It appeared out of place next to the neighboring gray buildings, seeming to belong somewhere near the equator. The building's whiteness bounced the sun's glare back into the eyes of anyone bold enough to stare at the plastered concrete walls, which were separated by giant windows. Van Riebeek, dressed in a tan tropical suit, moved with the crowd of office workers. Once through the door, he was surprised that the ground floor was one great room except for a few private offices at one end. Stark, white walls were offset by ocean blue floor tiles. Ceiling fans stirred the already clammy morning air. A receptionist escorted him to a straight-backed chair near one of the private offices and promised that Señor Cunha would be free to see him shortly.

Osvaldo Rodrigues da Cunha greeted van Riebeek warmly, waving him to a chair before calling for coffee. His black hair was combed straight back, Rudolph Valentino style, and his brushy mustache of the same color rested on his upper lip. His appearance seemed to disregard the heat and moisture. "Welcome to Lisbon, Mr. van Riebeek. I understand you visit our city often, so I won't launch into a list of sightseeing attractions. Should we converse in English, or would you prefer another language?"

"English would be best for me, and you seem to be comfortable using it."

"Your banker told me you were interested in Angola." The coffee arrived accompanied with small cakes. Cunha continued, cake in hand. "Your timing is curious considering recent events occurring in our esteemed colony. You are aware that isolated armed revolts have occurred, with some loss of life?"

"I'm afraid I am not totally informed," van Riebeek said in a deferential tone. "In fact, I have never been to Angola. I'm a South African wine merchant. My travels have been, pretty much, to European wine-producing countries. I've imported Portuguese Port, hence my visits to your city. But now I have been offered a business opportunity within the Congo. I am looking at methods of shipping products there."

Cunha's eyes revealed nothing, but his broad smile invited van Riebeek to rest easily in the conversation. "Which Congo?" he asked in a tone that was almost an aside.

Van Riebeek did not wish to be drawn into a political discussion. This could be tricky, and I must trespass gently, he thought. "I'm attracted to your railroad system that stretches from an Atlantic port to the Angola eastern border. I understand you were Council General in Angola for a decade. You must possess a wealth of information on the port authority and the train system. To be candid, I need someone with this knowledge who could assist in organizing this venture."

"Ah, yes, the Benguela Railway," Cunha replied. "Not very dependable these days. Run mostly by natives," he added. "I hear the rebels have held it up on the Bié Plateau, demanding goods for safe passage. I'm afraid this is not my area of expertise. Shipping by rail in Angola has now become a dangerous activity."

Van Riebeek pressed on. "All of Africa these days offers danger. Where there is risk, there is reward. In this case, if handled wisely, the reward could be substantial." Van Riebeek watched Cunha's eyes and saw his greed. "My clients," he lied, "are currently shipping copper and other minerals on your Angola railroad. It seems to be working well. I would assume that the railroad cars are returning somewhat empty. My clients need provisions and building materials. I'd like to try a shipment, soon, to see how smoothly it would pass through your port and on to the train for delivery into Katanga."

"Yes, Katanga," Cunha wheezed.

"Is that a problem? Does your railroad go anywhere else?"

The fencing continued over another cup of coffee. Van Riebeek's mind was moving rapidly down a list of items he needed to understand. Cunha cut the silence. "The rebels worry me. I would need to contact old friends in the colony for advice on this."

"Where are the rebels in relationship to the rail line?"

Cunha stood, motioning van Riebeek to join him before a large map of Angola. He jabbed his finger at a spot slightly north of the center of the country. "The rebellion erupted here, in the hills where cotton is grown. The locals are protesting their wages, but if we dig deeper, we would find they are unhappy with the whole colonial system. I think Portugal is in for a long skirmish."

Van Riebeek asked, his German blood flowing rapidly, "Why not send in the army?"

"We have and we will continue to do so. More troops are on a ship as we speak. There are several problems. There are three known rebel groups, one now large enough to be called an army. They are ruthless. They kill our soldiers, they shoot at each other, and they murder farmers, villagers, even priests. The violence has just begun in the rural areas. When it moves into the cities, we are done for. So is the railroad."

"Where does the most significant rebel group live?"

"In the old days, when I returned to Europe on my home leave from my work as Counsel in Angola, I was asked about my life in the African country. I was always amazed at how little the Europeans knew about Africa. They wanted the riches, not the responsibility. So here is a bit of geography that will be new to you, Mr. van Riebeek. The rebels live, when not rampaging, in Cabinda, which is a small territory north of the Congo River. It belongs to Angola, but the natives there must pass through the DRC to reach Angola. The DRC is watching, but not interfering. And so, the rebels have a safe haven." Having finished for the time being, Señor Cunha extended his hand, saying, "Can you stay over for a day or two? I will make some inquiries before we talk again." He added as they walked toward the door of his office, "What currency would be used for these transactions?"

Van Riebeek headed out into the blazing late morning sun. He turned onto the main street, deciding to walk to his hotel. He knew Cunha was in his pocket. Only the details needed to be sorted out.

Luanda, Angola

Alfredo Gavarnie excused himself from the meeting and slipped into his office to accept a call from Lisbon. The connection was poor but he recognized Cunha's high pitched voice immediately. Their friendship had weakened over the years after Cunha left Angola. He had been the Counsel-General in several provinces, ending in Luanda.

Only the Governor-General for the Portuguese colony had outranked him. During the period Cunha was an important player, Gavarnie was a young, struggling and very hungry businessman. Cunha's prurient appetite exposed him to the rough-and-tumble world in which Gavarnie operated and it was there, in the bars and brothels, that the two expatriates became acquainted. They traded their desires for favors—construction contracts for women. Gavarnie's small construction company suddenly was awarded surprisingly lucrative contracts. Gavarnie bought an apartment overlooking the port yet far enough up the hill to avoid the harbor noise. He decorated it with wild colors and comfortable furniture and presented the *pied-à-terre* to his well-connected friend. Cunha took on a series of mistresses, ensconcing them in the colorful apartment. In 1954, Cunha transferred back to Lisbon to accept a secure middle-management post in the Department of Colonial Affairs. His home, Gavarnie discovered on a visit to Lisbon, didn't compare to the large country home with sweeping lawns that Cunha had maintained in Angola. By 1961, Gavarnie was wealthy and connected in the right places in both Portugal and Angola. He had stashed his profits in banks throughout Europe, and had reached the point where he planned to close his business, escape before the revolt consumed the colony, and retire to an island in the Caribbean. Cunha's telephone call caught him with his bags packed.

"Good afternoon, my good friend," Cunha chortled. "I miss you and our good times together."

"Hello, Osvaldo. Good to hear your voice after so many years. Are you coming to Angola for a visit?"

"Soon, maybe. Listen, Alfredo." Cunha then explained what he needed to satisfy van Riebeek's requirements. This included arranging for the shipment to pass unchallenged through customs, placing it on the railroad and ushering the shipment into Katanga.

"This is heavy, Osvaldo. I will need some time to think on this. Can I call you back next week?"

"You can do this, Alfredo. Your cut will be attractive. I need an answer by tomorrow, latest. Call me at my home number."

Following his conversation with Gavarnie, Cunha telephoned van Riebeek at his hotel and suggested they meet the following afternoon. By then he should have received Gavarnie's proposal and assurance that the plan could be arranged. Van Riebeek proposed his hotel's lounge, which would surely be empty midafternoon. He asked Cunha to bring a detailed map of Angola, one that would depict the details of the port area and the railroad route.

Early the following morning, Gavarnie reached Cunha at home. He explained that for certain fees, there would be no port inspection. If the arrival time of the freighter and the train was coordinated, the shipment could be carted from the ship to the railcars. The train particulars would be less sticky because Gavarnie had many friends in the railroad administration. Trains traveling inland carried passengers and goods to the villages, and by the time it reached the Katanga border, the railcars would be empty. The two old friends briefly haggled over the fee and then struck a deal. No reference was made to the political turmoil erupting in Angola. Gavarnie was pleased with his part of the arrangement. It would not be difficult to organize, plus his fee would be in US dollars deposited in a foreign bank. He would keep his bags packed.

Lisbon

Indeed, van Riebeek and Cunha were the only ones in the lounge that afternoon. Both settled on iced tea and a pastry. The refreshing ocean breeze swept into the lounge bringing a promise of relief from the heat. "Do you have a date for the arrival of the freighter?" Cunha began.

Van Riebeek pulled some papers from his valise, ran his finger down the shipping schedule, shrugged and said, "The shipment will arrive sometime between late July and mid-August. I'll give you a firm date in thirty days."

Cunha nodded. They could adjust to the timetable of the train. "We will provide eight covered railcars. Will that be sufficient?"

Van Riebeek was more interested in the presence of the Portuguese army. "Will there be troops?"

"A platoon. They'll be in a separate railcar."

Both men sat quietly after they had sifted through the details of the plan. Finally, Van Riebeek asked, still looking out to sea, what Cunha had in mind as a commission. He had elucidated the endless payments required in Angola—all excessive.

"A quarter of a million US dollars would cover everything. A nice round number," he added.

Van Riebeek had already worked the numbers and he knew with accuracy what the cost would be. "I want you to be comfortable with your commission," he said smoothly.

"Don't forget, this is a trial shipment. If it becomes too expensive, there will be no repeat orders. Dollars are particularly attractive right now." He dropped that incentive lightly into the negotiation. "Here is what I can do. It's fair, so let's not bicker. $185,000 US for everything as we have outlined. How you disperse the funds is up to you."

"I'll need most of the money up front," Cunha said, jumping at the offer.

"No, not so fast," van Riebeek replied. "If we have an agreement, within three days I will transfer into any bank account of your choice, $85,000 in cold, hard cash. The remaining $100,000 will be paid to the same account the minute my man advises me that the shipment has reached Katanga safely."

"What man?"

"I will have a representative in Lobito Bay waiting for the shipment. He will not interfere with your operation—just observe. He'll ride the train to Katanga."

"I can accept your proposal with one proviso," Cunha said firmly. "Once the shipment has crossed into Katanga, we lose control and then I would have no assurance that payment would be forthcoming. I propose the following: my associate will also ride the train to a small town called Vila Luso, which is in the hill country approaching Katanga. There is a telegraph office there. Your man can wire you confirmation that our plan is on target. Your bank can then pay me what is due. When received, I will wire my friend in Vila Luso, and the train can proceed the few kilometers to the border."

Van Riebeek inhaled deeply. "Alright," he groaned, "but the train should not pause for more than a few hours."

The deal was struck.

Cape Town

Jillian arrived in her office just after dawn. Van Riebeek had left the country and she hoped to have news of his whereabouts from Interpol Europe. She was the early bird, so she perked the coffee and headed for the communications room to check the telex machine.

Interpol Lisbon had found him and provided astonishing information. Van Riebeek had arrived from Athens. Why had he been in Athens, Jillian wondered. Interpol reported on his hotel and the name of the bank he had visited. Jillian smiled. Follow the money was her mantra. Van Riebeek had visited the Portuguese Colonial Headquarters and then, abruptly, flew off to Belgium.

Jillian dispatched two telexes. The first was to her office in Lisbon thanking them and asking for information on van Riebeek's visit to the colonial office. Whom did he see? The second went to Interpol in Benelux, asking them to find van Riebeek and set up a surveillance. She looked at her watch and wondered if McQueen would be in his office. She dialed and waited.

"Who would call me at this hour? Jillian, it must be you," McQueen's gravely voice intoned.

"Good morning, Ian. Did you gain access to van Riebeek's bank account?"

"Yes. Finally, yesterday, the stubborn bank acquiesced and gave us copies of his statements running back twelve months. Nothing out of the ordinary. No large amounts moving in or out of the country. There were a couple of small amounts deposited from up-country parties and we will check them out. Other than that, all transactions seem to relate to wine shipments. Oh, yes, one other thing. He has a bank account in Lisbon."

"Bingo." Jillian smiled and reached for her coffee mug.

Arnheim, Holland

"Your were right, Uncle," Dieter said, as he passed some papers to van Riebeek. They were sitting in the dining room of van Riebeek's favorite hotel in his childhood home town. The breakfast dishes had been cleared allowing them to spread out their notes. "We have had extraordinary luck. I found a factory in East German that is working with missiles. They can't get missiles out of their brains. You will remember, Germans were the genius behind most of the advanced weapon technology during the war. It's a laboratory working under contract with the Russian army on missile propulsion systems. They have created a small, lightweight, mobile ordinance that fires a missile capable of bringing down a plane at close range. They call it a GAM-11. The Russians were not interested in it, but the lab continued to perfect it on their own. It has not been tested."

"When will they know if it works?

"Next month. The gun is in its raw state of development."

"Will they sell it to us?"

Dieter nodded. "If it works, they will sell us one, only one, if we report back on its effectiveness. They are more interested in how it functions in adverse conditions than in the money."

"Have you completed sourcing the rest of the items?" Van Riebeek asked as he flipped through Dieters file.

"Start on page seven," Dieter said leaning forward. "Every item is priced, including the missile. Our friends in

Wiesa have agreed, for a small fee, to receive all items, to consolidate and ship to a Baltic port. They were efficient on our first delivery."

Van Riebeek sifted through the pile of papers without saying a word. Dieter waited patiently sipping his coffee. Finally, van Riebeek looked up at Dieter. "Place the orders now in the usual fashion. Have your suppliers send their invoices to our post office box in Liechtenstein, indicating the advance payment required. Its now May and the weapons are to be delivered in August. Everything must be in the Baltic port by mid-July. You have your hands full, Dieter. Better get started. I will call you in a month with shipping instructions."

They gathered their papers, paid the bill and headed out into a very wet day. "I should be home in a week," van Riebeek shouted as he ran for his car.

Salisbury, Rhodesia

"I have been commanded by the eminent Arne Norquist to escort his niece around Rhodesia. They told me it would not be an easy assignment," the plump man sitting across the table from Samantha said with a broad smile. He had introduced himself as Toby Marshall after he had sailed through the hotel coffee shop and plunked himself down at her table. His appearance was a contradiction to his nonchalance. "I spotted you from your picture in *Echo Magazine.*"

Samantha eyed him warily before suggesting that he join her for breakfast. His eyes were clear, large and blue. His thick brown hair cascaded from the dome of his head down the back and into a curl near his neck. The front half of his skull was hairless. He wore a khaki shirt, khaki shorts and khaki knee length socks. Marshall was the picture of a white Rhodesian colonialist, that is, until he opened his mouth and the Georgia accent flowed. "I hope this isn't too great an inconvenience," Samantha asked, still surveying the man before her. "I asked my uncle for a contact in Salisbury, not a guide," she added, as she extended her hand.

"Not a problem. I'm Toby. May I call you Samantha?"

"Yes, of course. How much time do you have to devote to this Norquist project?"

"I'm free most of today. Tomorrow, I'm flying up-country to check some developments along the Zambezi River and then for a brief visit to Ndola. You are invited to come along."

"I would like that very much. What is it you do at the embassy?"

"I'm the agricultural attaché, but we both know I have trouble distinguishing a chicken from a turkey. I'm an ordnance specialist. I've been seconded to the Rhodesian counter-insurgency crowd to inspect the weapons they are finding in the bush. I can discuss politics, geography and military operations, but not farming."

"Perfect," Samantha said laughing and began to feel more comfortable with both Marshall and her assignment. "I am a photographer, not a journalist. I want to take pictures of people, blacks as well as whites. Any chance of visiting some of the mines near Katanga?" Samantha asked this almost as an aside.

"Hmm," Marshall muttered with a sigh. "No mines, I'm afraid, but there's a high level government round-table gathering in an hour. We can attend and you can sneak some photos—not using a flash," he admonished.

Later in the day, Marshall drove Samantha on a tour of Salisbury and then into the countryside. Salisbury was a large town rather than a city. The center encompassed the government buildings, with broad streets separating two-story undistinguished appearing stores. Samantha thought it looked like a mid-western town: bland, prosaic and offering no sense of origin. The store owners and their customers were well-dressed Europeans. The intense heat of the day didn't intrude.

As they drove, Marshall rattled on about the history of Rhodesia and the tribes that living here, his knowledge was broad, his opinions barbed. "Before the settlers arrived, there were tribes, brutality and constant battles. The white man brought law, farming and infrastructure but didn't share their prosperity with the natives. What you listened to this morning, what you will see out here in the bush, what is going on to the north in Katanga is all about who owns this place. I'm from the South and this reminds me of another war."

They were passing farms now, cotton and tobacco mainly. Crowds of black workers, all bending in toil. "Tell me about the men running the meeting this morning," Samantha hollered over the drone of the engine.

"The burly fellow is Sir Roy Welensky, prime-minister of this British territory. He stands at the center of a group of important people here and in Great Britain who resist any form of independence for the blacks. South Africa stands with him, and this may surprise you, so do certain factions in Washington."

"Who in the states?"

"Well, hard to say, specifically," Marshall hedged. "State and Langley disagree and, of course, there are voices in congress for both sides. The huge investment in the mines along the Katanga border would be lost. Hammarskjöld is ignoring these sentiments and plowing ahead."

"And the tall fellow who said little but seemed to be the person everyone was addressing?"

"Lord Alport. He's the British High Commissioner. My guess is he's in tight with the vocal "Katanga Club," a bunch of British conservative MPs who support Rhodesia and dislike the UN."

The sound, an enraged bellowing, impaled the moment. Marshall braked while Samantha clutched her telephoto camera. At the bend in the road they came upon a herd of elephants stomping up a dust storm. The trumpeting continued from the left, now closer. Samantha saw the bull first. He was enormous; darker than the cows and was storming quickly in their direction. His large ears were flapping and wild small eyes in the huge head. She captured sequence shots until the bull's tusk filled her view finder. "Oh God, Toby," she gasped. Let's get the hell out of here before we're trampled to death! Look at him, look at him!" She was practically screaming now. Turn around, Toby, and hit the gas!"

The following morning, after a breakfast on the fly, Toby Marshall helped Samantha climb into the rear seat of a Cessna 180 Skywagon, a high-wing light aircraft that would allow for good visibility. The plane had no markings. Samantha was introduced to the pilot and blinked when she heard his nasal New England accent—but withheld comment. They flew north and then east, always hugging the ground. At the Zambezi River, the Cessna circled in seeming indecision and then banked, descending rapidly to a rough airstrip carved out of the jungle. Sam spotted several vehicles at the end of the runway. The pilot turned and barked, "I'll wait for an hour, Toby. If you are late, I will leave you to the tik-tiks."

"What's he talking about?" Samantha shouted, and then instantly had the answer when the tsetse flies began circling her body. "Good grief, Toby, they're huge and they bite! Ouch!"

"Now you know why I insisted on long pants and long sleeved shirt. Here come the Land Rovers. The flies will dissipate when we reach the river."

The guns were arrayed on a tarp near the Zambezi River's bank and not far from a submerged pod of hippos. Samantha photographed both. The terrain was different here: lush, dense and beautiful. A cacophony of sounds enveloped her: insects, birds and the rustling of fronds by an unknown creature. On the sly, she took pictures of the Rhodesian soldiers. Most were bearded and wore camouflage fatigues and floppy hats. They cradled their weapons, almost lovingly. Samantha saw in their eyes a weariness, a hardness, and acceptance of their situation. They were young men. She watched Marshall study each article on the tarp, take notes and chat with the lieutenant in charge. The listless air hung heavy with moisture and Sam could feel the sweat trickle down her spine.

Within the hour, they were airborne, pointed toward Lusaka where they would refuel. Samantha sat in front with the pilot, who entertained her with sudden banking to point out animals on the move. They circled to chase galloping giraffes, dropping to 200 feet for photographs.

In Lusaka, Marshall and Samantha stretched their legs on the tarmac during the refueling. "Toby, tell me about the weapons you just inspected back by the river."

"Same old stuff. AK-47s, of course, grenades and a plethora of pistols. The rebels have no resources; they live off of the land and return home to rest before heading back into the bush to fight again. How they acquire the weapons is beyond me. I did see one item that I haven't come across here before. It's disturbing."

"What was it?" Samantha asked.

"A landmine. A despicable weapon which kills and maims indiscriminately. If they are planted all over Central Africa, it will become a dead zone."

"Who makes landmines?"

Marshall breathed deeply, puffing his lips with a rush of air. That's what bothers me the most. The one I just inspected was manufactured in the United States."

"Where in the United States?" Samantha almost shouted.

"In Wisconsin," Toby answered tonelessly.

Ndola sat minutes south of the Katanga border in the Northern Rhodesia territory. It was a frontier town, established as a supply station for the mining operations that stretched to the west like a strand of pearls. The single runway airport received infrequent commercial aircraft and provided a military base for Rhodesia. It was here that Samantha had last seen Thomas. As the Cessna descended, she could make out the two-story terminal with the control tower centered in the middle. Her gaze drifted to the array of aircraft assembled. "Toby, look at all those airplanes. What are they?"

Marshall leaned forward and pressed his face to the window. "Looks like a couple of Vampires and that two-seater is a Fouga Magister. It sports a 7.5 mm gun. The rest belong to the Royal Rhodesian Air Force."

"Why so many fighters?"

"Dunno."

On the ground, they parked next to a DC3. Marshall explained that it belonged to the US government and was up from Pretoria. It bristled with antennas and communication wiring. Samantha wandered to the terminal while Marshall boarded the DC3 for his meeting. She tucked her blond hair into her cap hoping to not be noticed by the clutch of men standing at the bar. A food stand provided a secluded spot where she could snap pictures of the men at the bar. They were extraordinary looking: flamboyant hats, gun belts with holsters, flowing mustaches and beards. They were all European. Mercenaries, she guessed.

Later, back in the coffee shop at her hotel in Salisbury, Marshall explained. "The mercenaries are all free-lance. Some work for the mines but most are headed to Katanga to officer the native army."

"To fight whom?" Samantha's eyebrows arched.

"The United Nations military mission now in Elizabethville."

Samantha, stirring her soup and without tasting it, looked hard at Marshall. "I don't think the world knows what's going on here. What is going on, Toby?"

Marshall glanced around the near empty restaurant before replying. "We need to have a conversation, Samantha. Your uncle asked me to introduce you to Rhodesia—to the limit of appropriateness. I hope I have accomplished this. For me, it has been enjoyable. But I must ask you, no, advise you, to not disclose your sources. I must not appear in any of your pictures or articles. You did not see the DC3 communications plane, or the fighters, for that matter. The elephants would be okay."

"And the land mine?"

"Just say that you suspect they are being employed." Marshall rose and extended his hand. "I must be off now. You are headed for Moremi tomorrow. You will enjoy it. It's a magical place." He saluted and walked quickly away.

JUNE 1961

Guildford

Nicholas had driven to his farm looking for quiet time. It was midweek, summer had arrived and his superintendent had called with a list of items that required attention. He had fished at dawn and now sat at his desk thinking about guns and Katanga. Van Riebeek was confident of the sourcing and had provided a list of suppliers and the price of the items. Nicholas played with the numbers for a time before arriving at a lump sum figure he could submit to Sallis-Cooper. He decided to call the MP at his home.

"Douglas, Nicholas Andropolis here. Have I caught you at a bad time?"

"Good morning, Nicholas. I'm home alone at the moment so this is a perfect time to talk. What have you come up with so far?"

"My contacts have found sources for every item on your list, including the anti-aircraft gun. I assume you do not want to know anything about the manufacturers, correct?"

"Correct. Give me the cost and I will arrange for the first half to be transmitted to your bank next week. How do you propose to get the weapons into Katanga?"

Nicholas looked at his note pad and selected the larger of two numbers he had written. "Here is the amount my contacts require to place orders. Better write it down, Douglas, and here, also, is the number of the bank account in Liechtenstein."

"Good Lord, that's a bundle of money. When will the guns arrive?"

"That bundle of money buys a lot of weapons, pays some people to keep their mouths shut and delivers the guns to Katanga. We are looking at a late August delivery. I trust this risk on my part will result in some shipping business from your friends in Africa."

"Count on it and thank you, Nicholas." Sallis-Cooper rang off.

Katanga

"Welcome home, Moise," Munongo said respectfully, as he stepped onto Tshombe's front porch. Both men had arrived simultaneously, Tshombe from the airport, Munongo from the copper mine. Although the country club headquarters remained operative, this front porch provided the only safe place for the two old friends to talk. "I was worried you wouldn't make it back. Were you mistreated?"

"They put me in a prison—a house with some army guards. Mobutu orchestrated it. They charged me with high treason and the murder of Lumumba," Tshombe said, shaking his head in disgust. "Why I was released and who organized it is a mystery."

"You can probably thank the CIA. What did Mobutu want?"

"I did sign, under pressure, a document, which proclaimed our willingness to end our secession." Tshombe leaned forward in his chair, his face contorted as he raised his voice, "They want our minerals and they want our money." His eyes held Munongo's. "And, my old friend, they want us both dead. We will have to fight. What is the situation here?"

"Confusion and shifting alliances. The UN peacekeeping forces, mostly Indian and Swedes, are confined to the area around the airport. The Belgians are still sitting on our northern border and at the mine. Our army is not worth talking about. That villain, Kigali, disappeared with most of our weapons. All we have is a small city police force and mercenary brigades roaming the countryside. No one is in control."

Tshombe disappeared into his house and soon returned with two beers. He pressed his bottle on his forehead before taking a long pull. "Thomas Kimbamba was family. I'm guilty of overloading him with duties and exposing him to danger. His body was found full of bullet holes on a river bank. The man responsible will die a very painful and slow death."

Munongo spread his hands in a jester of despair. "Thomas's killer may already have met his end."

Tshombe thought about that for a while and then moved on. "Our second order for small arms and ammo will be shipped soon. The order includes a large quantity of AK-47s plus a larger weapon for use against aircraft. I hear Hammarskjöld is planning to come here. That must never happen." He slammed his beer bottle on the table, spilling some. "I have employed a European man, someone with actual military fighting experience, to take charge of our army. We must get ready. Our fight for survival will be this year."

Stellenbosch

Van Riebeek returned from Europe confident that his plan to supply weapons to Katanga would succeed. He sat in the seclusion of his vineyard office, carefully sifting through the tactical details. The weapons were ordered, with an expected shipment from a Baltic port sometime in July. His associate in London would arrange the shipping and pay the munitions suppliers. His responsibility was to shepherd the shipment from the port to Katanga. Part of his commission and operating funds had been deposited in his Lisbon bank account. The Cape Town bank account would be unnecessary—he would close it. He planned to tell his bank manager, a man he hardly knew, that he was retiring. This, then, would be the end of it. He made a mental note to spend the weekend at his Cape Town office, where he would cull his files for document that could tie him to this contract or to his other illegal imports to South Africa over the past decade. His winery office would yield no incriminating information if searched. He would spend the rest of his days growing grapes.

This satisfying thought had no more settled into his memory bank when the phone disturbed his reverie. "Karel, there is a problem."

Van Riebeek's nephew, Dieter, rarely telephoned. It was expensive and risky. Their conversation would be of interest to a number of South African police agencies. Van Riebeek paused for a long moment, his mind checking off options. Finally he said, "Tell me."

"The East Germans were working on the GAM-11 when it exploded, killing one of the technicians. They are unwilling to supply this item on our order."

"Ach," van Riebeek sighed. "You must find a replacement quickly."

"I have."

"Really! Tell me very briefly what you've found and then wire the specifics."

Dieter then rattled off the gun specifications. "It's a gas operated, belt fed, air cooled 51-caliber machine gun. The GDR has been making it for several years for use in troubled spots around the world. It's a Soviet design and used for many applications, especially as an anti-aircraft device."

"Does it have a name?"

"DShKM. 12.7mm. It's now in use in Vietnam. Functions like the 50-caliber Browning. Your customer will love it. And here's the best part, I paid only $6000 for it."

"Nice work." Van Riebeek set the phone in its cradle, his heart racing.

Leopoldville

I'm really bushed, Brian thought, as he watched the rain pelt the oval window of his plane. The old DC-6 descended gradually through the rainstorm aiming for Brazzaville, the capital of the Republic of the Congo. He had attended endless meetings with Hammarskjöld, usually along with other officials, each of them a zealot for some cause that required the secretary-general's attention. Hammarskjöld had involved Brian in new dramas occurring throughout Europe and Africa, all demanding research and interface with UN staff. Gisella always knew the right person for Brian to approach. The secretary-general's focus on DRC remained paramount. The Soviet's desires conflicted with what the Americans wanted. Belgium was not helping by leaving its military in place in Katanga. No one was happy with the UN's senior military officer, Rajeshwar Dayal. Hammarskjöld planned to arrive in Leopoldville in two days. Brian's assignment was to check the political pulse of DRC government officials and arrange Hammarskjöld's schedule, so that he could please everyone and come away with overall positive results.

The plane lurched causing a clatter of trays to spill in the galley. The Leopoldville airport was closed for some unexplained reason. Brian had flown to Cairo at dawn to connect three hours later with this flight to the Congo, a strangely shaped country across the river to the north of the DRC. Brazzaville suddenly appeared as Brian's flight dropped rapidly from the rain laden clouds. He would enter Leopoldville by riverboat.

Since checking luggage was a gamble, Brian carried his satchel and briefcase. He hurried across the puddle-splashed tarmac to the terminal building. The air was muggy, and even hotter inside the building. Why ever did I wear a suit, Brian pondered, and then realized the ever-dapper Hammarskjöld, always impeccably attired in a suit and tie, was influencing him. He moved swiftly through customs and headed for the taxi ramp. The rain had stopped, leaving still, humid air hanging over the city. The one traffic cop stood in a bus shelter smoking and talking with a cluster of taxi drivers. The vehicles were not moving. A cacophony of car horns and yelling peddlers greeted him as he edged along the traffic bedlam. A Renault taxi at the front of the traffic jam seemed to have an advantage, so Brian engaged this front-runner without bargaining. It was 3:30 pm. He would have ample time to find a river ferry for the Congo River crossing.

The quayside, where the taxi driver deposited Brian, looked more orderly than the airport. Lines of people led to ticket booths servicing the waiting ferries. Many shapes and types of river boats carried passengers across the two kilometers of the Congo River that separated the Congo from the DRC. Brian stood on the quay debating which boat would be best. A well-dressed dark-skinned man, standing near Brian, said with a broad friendly smile, his head waggling, "May I suggest the long launch with the blue trim on the left. It's a little more money but faster and you should be able to get a seat."

"Which queue should I use?" Brian replied.

"Come with me. I plan to use the same launch."

Brian stood in line with his new acquaintance, surveying the mass of humanity moving around the quay. There were a few Europeans, some Indians and the rest were black-skinned. No women stood in line for the crossing. The natives wore minimum clothing; many in shorts. It was a trade-off between the humidity and the mosquitoes. I must take my malaria pill when I reach the hotel, Brian thought, making a mental note.

"Are you an American?" his new friend asked.

"No, actually, I live in Switzerland," Brian responded, purposely construing his answer to be as vague as possible.

He wanted to avoid acknowledging that he was South African. "I work for the UN."

"Splendid," the man chortled. My name is Raj. I live in Bombay but I come here often to trade in gems. Have you been to the DRC before?"

"Yes, but briefly," Brian replied as he looked around the quay. "Where are the custom officials?"

"There are none. People move freely between these two countries. There is a shortage of everything in the DRC. People living there shop in Brazzaville. The Congo shopkeepers love the business and they can charge more. This border arrangement won't last much longer. Do you have any cigarettes with you, by chance?"

Brian shook his head, still watching the strange assortment of people around him. "I don't smoke."

"You will need them. Better buy a couple of packs here. The cigarettes will be your ticket for safe passage on the other side. The army rules the streets along the wharf. They will be less harsh with you if you offer them a cigarette; alas, Indians are fair game."

They boarded and found seats together in the bow. The river's current was deceiving. They were not far up-river from the mouth of the mighty Congo. The river, in its 4700 km flow from the highlands of the East African Rift, had collected many ingredients, giving it a murky green color, yet the current was swift. The launch swung its prow into the current to make headway, moving steadily toward the DRC shore. Brian could see the outline of a few buildings above the scrub trees lining the far bank. Soon the dock became visible. He could see groups of soldiers smoking and lounging near where the launch would berth. The engine throttled down to make its approach. Now Brian could make out the automatic weapons and hand guns the soldiers carried. His hands responded by clutching his travel bags.

Raj extended his hand. "Remember, do not argue with the soldiers and never let them handle your property. They probably haven't been paid and are living off what they can steal in the street. They're dangerous. Good luck to you."

The launch belched forth its passengers onto the dock. The lounging soldiers moved indolently to the metal gate, now open as an exit for the passengers. Brian watched with apprehension before edging his way into the center of the human flow. Raj had disappeared. The soldiers were scouting for a mark, someone with luggage and money, someone like Brian. He didn't look their way—didn't want eye contact. The passengers scattered in every direction. There were no cars, no public transportation. Where the hell are the taxis, he wondered. The wharf side street was wide and fronted bleak looking warehouses. A few tractors and hoists sat idle. Brian walked briskly to the end of the warehouses, and then turned onto a once-paved dirt road which, he hoped, would lead him to a taxi stand. He noticed that three of the bedraggled soldiers were following him. The street ran along derelict buildings and narrowed. At the end of the street he could see traffic moving. At that moment, two more soldiers, both carrying rifles, stepped out from an alley and held up their hands signaling for him to stop. Brian frantically looked around for help but saw only the three soldiers closing from behind. The street was deserted. Where had everyone gone? The five mutinous soldiers circled him, grinning, shifting on their feet and talking in Lingala, the official language of the

Congolese army. The tallest of the five, a rangy man wearing filthy clothes, began to talk in French.

Brian replied steadily in English. "I don't speak French. I am a diplomat. Tell me what you want and then back off."

The tall one shuffled in front of Brian, looked him up and down before growling, "You America?"

"No," Brian shot back and began to move on. One of the mutinous cohorts reached for Brian's suitcase. Brian's right arm swung out slamming the soldier hard against the building wall. Two others grabbed Brian's arms while the tall one pulled his revolver, pointing it at Brian's forehead.

"We not kill you. We want your money and suitcase."

It was getting dark. Brian quickly sorted through his options. He offered a brittle smile, reached for the cigarettes and offered them to each soldier. "I'm here to meet with Colonel Mobutu. Do you understand? He would not be happy about this."

The tall one tapped Brian's temple with the muzzle of his revolver. "I want money now. Give it or we take."

Bright lights from a headlight swept over them. The car, an open military vehicle, was moving fast but when its headlights caught the group of marauding soldiers, one holding a gun, it braked and turned so that the lights exposed the group. Three uniformed men jumped out. Brian could not see them because of the bright light. One of them barked a series of questions in Lingala. The soldier doing the talking came into Brian's view. He wore a pressed uniform with a sergeant's patch on its sleeve and an army hat. He carried a swagger stick and a revolver, which he pointed at the man in front of Brian. The five grimy soldiers moved back into the shadow of the building, attempting to melt away.

"What's happening here? Who are you?" the sergeant in charge asked Brian in a stern voice.

'My name is Wellesley, I am an officer with the UN in Switzerland and I'm here to meet with Colonel Mobutu," Brian answered evenly while tilting his passport so that the sergeant could see his picture.

"Colonel Mobutu! Really?" The soldier's eyebrows arched as he stepped closer to Brian. During this exchange, the sergeant's colleagues confiscated the weapons from the scruffy soldier-thieves and sent them on their way. "Does Colonel Mobutu know you?" the sergeant asked incredulously.

"Yes, I'm meeting with him tomorrow morning."

The sergeant walked back to his vehicle, leaned in to reach the two-way radio attached to the dashboard. He talked briefly in French and then just listened. He returned the radio to the dashboard, turned to Brian and shouted, "Get in our car. Colonel Mobuto would like to see you. For your sake, I hope he recognizes you."

Brian sat in the front seat holding his briefcase. The sergeant drove with intensity. They quickly came out of the wharf area onto a street with traffic. The cars were old and most looked damaged. Some shops were open, their fluorescent lights adding an eerie glow to the sultry night. Groups of men stood around talking and smoking. They turned to watch Brian and the three praetorians sweep past. After twenty minutes of driving through a dilapidated business section of the city, they turned into an up-scale residential neighborhood where the European-appearing homes were set back from the street. Trees and dense shrubbery concealed Mobutu's single-story home. The sergeant stopped at the guarded gate, snapped a salute, and the gate swung open. They moved slowly up a graveled circular driveway and stopped in front of a well-lit entrance. Colonel Mobutu, dressed in a flowery short-sleeve shirt, khaki slacks and strap-sandals, stood in the entrance peering out at the army car and its occupants. The three soldiers leaped out, came to attention and saluted.

"Thank you, Sergeant. Mr. Wellesley, now that I see you, I remember you. He stepped forward and shook Brian's hand. "Come in, come in," he said congenially. "Sergeant, bring in Mr. Wellesley's luggage. He will be staying with me for a while. I'll radio you when you can collect him. And, thank you."

Brian turned to the sergeant. "Thanks, Sergeant. You saved more than my skin."

Joseph Mobutu was absolutely the most powerful man in the Democratic Republic of the Congo, yet his appearance belied this fact. His stocky frame was not muscular. Close-cropped hair, clean-shaven, large dark-rimmed reading glasses with intent, curious eyes enlarged by the lens, all provided him with an appearance of a younger and docile person. He waved Brian to a chair. "Would you like a cold beer? It is one of the few things the Belgians left that we will not change."

Brian settled in his chairs and waited for Mobutu to continue.

"I'm very sorry we have caused you this inconvenience. Those derelict soldiers loitering around the docks need to be rounded up and placed in a training camp. Our problem is we have too many soldiers and no money. Anyway," Mobutu said rubbing his hands together, "I suggest you wash up and then join me for dinner. We will hold our meeting tonight, just the two of us, and tomorrow I'll arrange a surprise for you."

Brian couldn't believe his luck. He was sitting with the one man that interested Dag Hammarskjöld the most. He would tip-toe through this minefield of possible contentious dialog. To his surprise, the colonel wanted to talk about football.

"You're South African. Tell me about the teams there. Who will end up on top?"

He ignored politics and soon switched their conversation to the United States. "The US professes to be a bastion of peace and equality, all most desirable." He sipped his beer slowly while looking at Brian intently. "We, on the other hand, are accused of brutality, discrimination and class warfare. I studied history in school and it became one of my passions. Let's compare, shall we? The US is a warrior nation with troops all over the world. Now it is involved in Southeast Asia, a quagmire from which it will not extract itself unscathed. At home it subjugates women, as do we. The US mistreats its black population and here our tribes battle and kill rapaciously. We are the same, except Americans wear suits and we throw spears." Mobutu laughed out loud, stood and pointed to an oval table near the window. "Come, let's enjoy some good local cooking. It will be simple, spicy chicken on yellow rice and some local fruit. You must be hungry. Bring your beer with you."

Mobutu wanted to talk and Brian offered an outlet. "I'm a Mongo, a large tribe upriver. I was raised in Lisala, a village at the very top of the Congo River's journey through our country. The river is wide and deep at my village where it loops south for 1,500 km to its sources. The river was our life; it offered our connection to other worlds. It's the same today. Nothing has changed."

Brian devoured his dinner. A servant removed his plate and replaced it with a flat dish full of sliced fruits. "Help me understand the government hierarchy here. You seem to be in charge of more than just the military and yet you prefer to be addressed as Colonel Mobutu. My question is a bit brazen and I apologize, but who is really running the government?"

Mobutu pushed his chair back and turned to the servant lurking in the shadows. "Please clear the table and bring a pot of green tea." He turned back to Brian and said in a serious tone, "I will answer that question and in doing so, I hope you will be able to enlighten the secretary-general when he arrives the day after tomorrow. I am temporarily in charge. President Kasavubu stands before the cameras, but I make the decisions. I used to be a journalist so I'm familiar with the complexity of politics. I worked for Patrice Lumumba and admired him at the time. Regrettably he became enamored with himself and aligned with the Soviets. He became a giant headache. We asked Katanga to take him, which they did, and then they executed him. When Lumumba was Prime Minister, he appointed me Chief of Staff. The Belgians left no Congolese officer corps, so suddenly a humble sergeant was running the army. I stayed in the barracks and concentrated on training and bringing law and order to the streets. The government was like a leaf in the wind, no direction and responding readily to Western influences—especially the UN. Six months ago, some colleagues and I took charge of the government. It was not a putsch. Kasavubu is still president. My friends are bright, Western-educated young men who are attempting to quietly organize the government. When we are satisfied that the system works, they will withdraw and I will return to the army."

"So that I can properly brief the secretary–general, tell me what we can do to assist you?"

"Ah." The colonel smiled. "Now my spicy chicken dish will pay off. Three things need to happen very soon and Hammarskjöld is the only person who can do it. First, the Indian you have placed in charge of your peacekeeping forces is arrogant, uncommunicative and irritates all levels of our government and military. You have thousands of peacekeeping troops on our soil. We are trying to be polite hosts. But this man, Dayal, must go. Am I clear?"

"Completely," said Brian.

"Second. We have endured 75 years of subjugation by the Belgians. It is now almost a year since we gained our independence and they are still here. Thousands," as he waved his arms, "are in the Province of Katanga, which claims to be independent.

"Finally, that scoundrel Tshombe has been here in Leopoldville arguing his case. We actually detained him but he was released last week and returned to Katanga. I would like the UN to begin a dialog with the Tshombe government that would result in its return to our country. If this is a failure, then the UN should take military action. If these three events occur, the DRC can begin to dig its way out of the abyss." Mobutu stood and stretched. "And now, enough of this heavy conversation. You must be exhausted. I will radio the good sergeant who will take you to your hotel."

Brian thanked Colonel Mobutu for his hospitality and assured him that the secretary-general would be well-briefed before their meeting.

"Tomorrow morning I will send a car and an English-speaking guide to take you into the country. A little exposure to the real Congo will do you good. I've enjoyed our chat, Mr. Wellesley. Sleep well."

The Leopoldville airport reopened allowing Dag Hammarskjöld's plane to arrive as scheduled. Dayal met him and the two drove directly to the UN headquarters-building near the center of town. The meeting lasted 30 minutes, after which the secretary-general emerged alone and was driven to his hotel.

The following morning Hammarskjöld met with Colonel Mobutu at the colonel's home. They sat at the same table where Brian had had supper two evenings before. After pleasantries, Hammarskjöld fastened his pale blue eyes on the Congolese Chief of Staff and said pleasantly, "Mr. Wellesley has apprised me of your concerns and desires. You will be pleased to learn that, as we speak, Mr. Dayal is boarding a flight, which will return him to India. Mr. Nehru will not be happy and I shall have to deal with that in New York. Additionally, I have sent a message to the Security Council asking them to remind the Belgian member of his country's agreement to withdraw entirely from the DRC. We will issue a warning, a timetable including a penalty. Finally, and this will be the most difficult, I will communicate strongly with Moise Tshombe, through our representative in Elizabethville, that the secession is illegal and that until Katanga returns to the DRC, his state will be treated as an outlaw. I have given him until September 1 to make the appropriate arrangements. My hope is that he will contact President Kasavubu."

"Thank you, secretary-general. My chicken supper for Mr. Wellesley has, how do you say it, paid dividends. How can I help you in your mission here?"

Hammarskjöld paused for an interminable moment. His reply was measured, spoken softly and seemed not judgmental. "My fervent wish is for your country to be at peace, to prosper and to join the world community of countries. At the moment your land is lawless, tribal warfare is ubiquitous, heinous crimes are being committed, especially on women, and your people are starving. Yet, your country is one of the richest on earth. You are the man, Colonel Mobutu, to lead the DRC out of this darkness. I will help you. Let us do this together."

Cape Town

"Jillian, Ian here. We have some interesting information on your friend, van Riebeek."

"I was about to head home with a splitting headache. Good news could be my aspirin. What have you got?"

"We tapped his phone in Stellenbosch. We figured sensitive phone calls would occur there and not with his Cape Town office. We're a little behind on this covert telephone monitoring technology; the Americans are ahead of us. In fact, they sent a technician along with the equipment. This is our first try and the results are sensational. Van Riebeek is trading in arms, but we knew that. He has a large shipment scheduled to leave the GDR next month. We should assume it's headed for Africa."

"Where, specifically?"

"It was a short conversation. The call emanated in the Netherlands and they never mention the destination. Curiously, their discussion centered on a 51 mm automatic rifle. We looked it up. It's an anti-aircraft gun. Who would want to shoot at aircraft?"

"Did you obtain court authority?"

"Regrettably we did not. We needed to move fast and our courts are unfamiliar with wire tapping—the request would shuffle for days between bureaucrats."

"There are several possibilities. Let me chew on it. Great work, Ian. Thank you." Jillian's headache was gone and her mind raced. Palmer had mentioned a second shipment for Katanga and this was probably it. The first shipment came up the Zambezi River; they wouldn't dare try that again, she mused. If we bring van Riebeek in for interrogation, we'll never find the people running and financing the gun trade, but we're close. She could feel it—soon he will make his fateful mistake.

JULY 1961

Maputo, Mozambique

Adraan's journey from South Africa to Katanga was circuitous and carefully planned. He traveled under his own name on a commercial flight to Maputo, Mozambique, entering on a valid South African passport. Then, he disappeared. He camouflaged his trail by working his way slowly up the coast, spending a day or two in small lodges and changing buses frequently, until he finally arrived in the port city of Beira nine days later. When asked for identity verification, he used his Mozambique passport. The next day he was on the daily passenger train to Salisbury, traveling in the second-class compartment where the Rhodesian customs officials only made cursory inspections. In Salisbury, he missed his connection to Lusaka, which worried him because terrorist incidents frequently flared up in the cities and police were constantly asking for identification papers. Adraan found a hotel near the railroad station, where he remained secluded until just before his train departed at dawn.

Van Riebeek had provided Adraan with a Portuguese passport, easily secured from his well-paid contacts in Lisbon. Adraan justified his poor pronunciation of Portuguese by explaining how his family had migrated from Algeria to escape the conflict and had later moved to Mozambique. His French and complexion supported his story. He instinctively moved in the shadows. He had learned very early in life how to blend in with his surroundings and not attract attention. He rarely looked anyone in the eye. He dressed conservatively, usually in black, always with long-sleeved shirts. If this was out-of-place, he would alter his clothing. He lived an intentionally unnoticeable life.

If asked, his purpose for travel was wine. Even in the sun-drenched center of Africa, Europeans demanded wine and lots of it, especially Spanish and French wines, which were imported through Mozambique. His story line was a good one; it held up under a cursory inquiry.

Lusaka presented few problems for a wine merchant from Mozambique. He splurged, finding a comfortable hotel with a swimming pool, where he could hole up for three days. He bought a small duffel bag with shoulder straps. Finding appropriate bush clothing was not difficult. He discovered a well-equipped camera shop where he purchased expensive lightweight German 8x42 binoculars. The handgun presented some difficulties. Ultimately he found a Colt .38 with the serial number removed, sold to him by a hotel employee. Refreshed and equipped, Adraan booked a seat on a train to Ndola, where he would be met by someone from Katanga and taken into the country. He had adhered to van Riebeek's timetable. It was now late July. The weapons would already be on the high seas, arriving in Angola the second week of August. Adraan would be there to receive them.

Cape Town

The telex from Interpol headquarters in Lyon, France told the story. They had traced Adraan's background to Algeria. It had been tough going because of the French officers' April putsch in Algeria that had left the government and police offices in disarray. Finally a rap sheet on Adraan arrived in Lyon. Jillian read it with interest.

Adraan is believed to have killed three French Legionnaires and an unknown number of Algerian citizens in the early 1950s before disappearing. His family name is Batuta, which is Berber. The report indicated that the suspect has a large red birthmark on this left forearm. Jillian whistled. Things were finally coming together. Time to pick this creep up, she decided as she dialed McQueen.

"How odd, I was just about to call you," McQueen said. "As you know, we have had an on-and-off surveillance of both van Riebeek and Adraan. It has not been easy when they retreat into the vineyard in Stellenbosch. We have three men up there. They called in yesterday to report that they haven't seen Adraan for several days. His car is on the grounds. Van Riebeek, on the other hand, is there."

Jillian held the disconnected phone in the air. That little shit has skipped town, she thought. After an angry minute, she dialed passport control. "This is Jillian Pienar at Interpol. We would appreciate any information you could give us on a South African citizen, Adraan Batuta, who may have left the country within the last two days. Start with the air terminal. We need the information today." She hung up.

Within the hour, passport control called back. "He left last night on IAA flight 231 for Maputo. We checked with our friends there. They confirmed that Mr. Batuta passed through passport control on a South African passport and indicated that he would be in Maputo for several days on business. He gave a local hotel as his contact point."

Jillian sent a wire to Interpol in Maputo asking them to check the hotel and to put out an all-points alert for the whereabouts of Mr. Batuta.

She then sat motionless at her desk, taking in deep breaths. Her mind searched for connections. Adraan is an illegal immigrant, wanted for murder in Algeria and now has disappeared into Central Africa. He works for van Riebeek who, we know for sure, is complicit in shipping weapons into Central Africa. If we don't find evidence confirming this soon, we'll have to bring Palmer back as a witness and I don't want to do that. If I can trace the money, I can implicate van Riebeek. We know there is another shipment of weapons going to Katanga, but where is it? Jillian moved aimlessly around her office. I want the people who are behind this gun running business. Van Riebeek is only a small fry, she was sure.

Luanda, Angola

Two men sat facing each other in a booth near the back of the Piquance Restaurant. No one in the capital of Angola could remember the origin of this popular dining spot. It was thought that a Frenchman had opened it, not a

Portuguese. The food was literally breathtaking. Unless the order was tempered, the spices would lift the scalp from one's skull. Cold beer accompanied each dish and it was beer that Osvaldo Cunha and his friend Alfredo Gavarnie were drinking this early July evening. Cunha had arrived from Lisbon midafternoon. Alfredo had collected him at the airport and deposited him at his hotel for an hour before the two walked the main street to the Piquance.

"You've been away from Angola for a while, my friend," Gavarnie said as he held his beer glass up for a toast. "Do you think your senses will tolerate a typical Piquance dinner?"

Cunha laughed. "I will order cautiously. This restaurant is part of my fond memories of Luanda. I was vice-counsel here for three years, you know. Good days. Now times have become difficult, as I understand."

Gavarnie responded, "The natives are seething under the Portuguese yolk. Violence in the country is a daily occurrence. It's time for us to leave." Gavarnie let his gaze sweep the restaurant. He knew most of the patrons, but he saw no one of interest. It was still early. He looked back at his visitor from Lisbon. "This scheme you are suggesting, it will enhance our departure from this infernal country, right?"

The ex-vice-counsel leaned forward so that he could speak softly. "Our shipment will arrive on August 15, a Tuesday." He extracted some papers from his coat pocket and placed one sheet in front of Alfredo. "Here is all the information you will need. As you can see, it's a small tramp freighter that can easily berth in Lobito Bay. And here's a copy of the manifest."

"What about the train with the ore from Katanga?"

"It will arrive a day or two before the ship. Unload the ore on the dock and have the train ready for departure when our cargo arrives. The freighter is heading south. An ore-boat will be coming up the coast the following week."

Gavarnie studied the paperwork before returning to the conversation. "Here's what I have organized, Osvaldo. If you approve, I will need funds immediately."

"Tell me, my friend, what have you planned?"

"The railroad—the Benguela—is in poor shape. The track has been maintained but the steam engines are derelict and of old technology. They still burn wood," Gavarnie said, rolling he eyes. "The train will include the empty copper ore cars, to which we will add eight box cars. Of course there will be a caboose for the conductor and switchman. In the middle of the train we have included two passenger cars, one for passengers and the other to carry a platoon of soldiers. Recently, insurgents have stopped trains at gunpoint looking for provisions and arms. My understanding is this shipment ostensibly covers supplies for mining companies, which is exactly what the rebels are looking for."

"One added feature," Cunha said cautiously in a hushed voice. "The train will arrive with a representative from the supplier of this shipment. He is to monitor your transfer of the crates to the train and then he will accompany the shipment back to Katanga. He will present no problems for you.

"Our arrangement was altered, after much haggling," Cunha continued, "thanks to your suggestion. We will be paid in full when the train reaches Vila Luso. Have the train pause there for several hours to give you time to contact me in Lisbon. The man traveling with you can also verify the arrival with his superior. When our payment is deposited to my bank account, I will call or wire you and the train can continue its journey. But until I contact you, the train doesn't move further. You will need to arrange your return to the coast from Vila Luso."

"I need some money now," Gavarnie's voice was higher and clipped. "Nothing will happen unless we grease some palms up front. We have to pay the stevedores, the railroad, and most important, the customs officials."

De Cunha pulled at his mustache, a habit when he was unsure. "Tomorrow, when I am back in Lisbon, I will deposit to your Lisbon bank the funds you require for immediate payments. Keep the operation simple. Take care of the customs officers and move the train out promptly. Very few people locally need to know about this arrangement. Be cautious. Execute flawlessly. Ah, I see our dinner coming; we'll need extra napkins I'm sure."

The next day Gavarnie sat in his Luanda office contemplating two secrets, both of which were constantly on his mind. Gavarnie's life in Angola had always been solid and praiseworthy. He enjoyed spending time with his family; he loved them very much. He never worked on Sunday; to be in church with his wife brought him a sense of tranquility. Soon everyday would be Sunday. No one could accuse him of being a profligate person. Gavarnie treated his employees with fairness; his civic generosity was well-known. He had achieved much and was respected among his friends and business associates. Yet his two secrets clouded this cherished image.

While on a motor vacation with his family in Europe, Gavarnie had precipitately established a numbered bank account in Monte Carlo. He did not tell his wife; it would be a surprise later. He opened it in US dollars, a difficult currency for him to possess, so the bank kept the balance requirement modest. The account gave him a warm feeling in his belly, plus the thought of having an asset in glamorous Monte Carlo sent Alfredo's pulse racing.

He had three bank accounts. The one in Luanda was modest, a joint account with his wife. It was so transparent that the branch manager would casually comment on the balance when they met at the golf course. A large amount of funds flowing through this account would not be judicious. He had instructed Cunha to deposit the advance to his bank in Lisbon. There was nothing shady about this Portuguese checking account. He would use it to transfer dollars to Monte Carlo and escudos to Angola.

His second secret was more delicate. It happened so casually, thinking back, he had difficulty putting his finger on the exact instant he had crossed the line of illegality. Most of his company's building projects were government sponsored and spread throughout the country. He remembered one particular job well—a small hospital in a picturesque village in the hill country. It was on a river so beautiful that he would drive with his family to the construction site and spend a weekend on a ranch along the river. As usual, he made it a point to know his employees. The laborers were local. He treated them well and paid the same rate as he would have in a coastal city. One young man caught his attention. His skin was dark but his hair texture appeared European, which implied he might have mixed blood. Roberto Lobo was handsome, outgoing and clearly a leader. One evening he invited Gavarnie to his home to share a dinner with his family. It was especially enjoyable because everyone spoke excellent Portuguese. After dinner, Lobo suggested that they take their smokes outside, and soon they were immersed in a wide range of topics, always dealing with Angola. Lobo spoke persuasively about the inequities in the country. He had become a dissident; his rhetoric was iconoclastic. In spite of his leftist leaning, Gavarnie hired him to work permanently for his company, promoting him to foreman over other building projects in the neighborhood. He figured out later that this exposure had provided the "Wolf Man", as Lobo was called, with sources for his army of insurgents.

Gavarnie became involved, enticed subtly by his excitement of the purpose and, in the end, by the money. In the beginning, Lobo needed supplies, nothing dangerous like weapons, usually just general supplies and medicine. Gavarnie realized he was financing many of the purchases. Within a year, "Wolf Man" ran afoul of the Angolan military. There had been a gun battle, several combatants on each side died and a price was placed on Lobo's head. He had surfaced as an outlaw.

By association, Gavarnie becomes an outlaw as well. He wore his fifty years well but he yearned for an easier life. His two sons aspired for European schooling and his wife was constantly haranguing him about the heat, insects and the mediocrity that surrounded them. The day Lobo slipped into Luanda and presented Gavarnie with a bag full of escudos was the moment he committed to the rebellion. In his heart he felt Portugal should go home and return the land to its people, and this rationalization sustained his unlawful activities, which accelerated over time. Lobo robbed banks and Gavarnie deposited a share of the funds to his nest egg in Monte Carlo.

In late July, Gavarnie decided to make a quick business trip to the hill country. The Wolf Man would be interested in this mystery shipment scheduled to ride the rails to Katanga. It wasn't a mystery, really; Gavarnie knew damn well it was weapons. The trick was to receive his final payment and then share some of the guns with Lobo.

Cape Town

The antiaircraft gun heading for Katanga troubled Jillian. Knowledge of its existence had been gained illegally and made the information too sensitive to share outside of police channels. Yet her instincts told her to advise Brian Wellesley. She knew his position with the UN required him to frequently visit the Congo. UN troops were stationed in Katanga. Finally, good judgment took hold and she placed a call to Brian's office in Geneva.

Moremi Game Reserve, Botswana

Winter arrived in the Okavango Delta in June and by July, the water in the floodplains had reached its high point. Game-viewing would be extraordinary. Samantha peered out the plane window studying the land below. It looked wild and desolate, but earlier she had noticed a vast waterway and wondered if it was the Okavango Delta that Brian had talked about so much. She would soon see it. The drone of the engines slackened and the plane's nose dipped to begin a slow descent toward the Bechuanaland Protectorate and the frontier town of Maun, where Brian would be waiting. She felt her blood rush at the thought.

The 30°C heat embraced her as she stepped from the plane onto the metal stairway. She stood stunned for a moment before the disembarking passengers nudged her forward toward the waiting bus. When the bus disgorged the passengers at the entrance to a small terminal building, a woman with a clip-board touched her elbow and asked, "Samantha Norquist? Please follow me. Brian is waiting for you." She spoke Brian's name with the familiarity of a sister. "We'll dispense with the customs formalities. Did you check a bag?"

"I did."

They were now at the far side of the terminal where small planes were parked. She saw Brian leaning on the wing of a Cessna, talking with a man in overalls who seemed to be fiddling with a wing flap.

Brian turned when he heard her shout his name. He slapped the mechanic on the shoulder and smiled broadly as he walked with long steps to meet her. They met mid-way across the tarmac and hugged, laughed, kissed and laughed some more. The customs lady finally interrupted them. "Brian, better get a move on. They're waiting for you in Moremi."

Sam handed over her luggage and then climbed into the Cessna's copilot's seat and watched Brian fine-tune the controls. He wore large bent sunglasses, which were pushed up against his forehead. Suddenly the propeller turned, the mechanic slapped the fuselage with a "good-to-go" wave, and the Cessna purred, bounced and twisted to the end of the runway.

They were airborne quickly, banking to the north away from Maun. The high-wing single-engine aircraft granted them extraordinary vistas in three directions. Brian flew like a fighter pilot, leveling off at a low altitude so that he could point out landmarks. The terrain was bleak, void of life, except sparse, scrub vegetation. Small villages appeared with huts made from the earth. A desperate existence, Samantha thought, as she watched scantily clothed natives move about. Suddenly she noticed a large bird trailed by several dozen chicks. "Oh Brian look! What's that bird?"

Brian saw it too and dipped the plane down for a closer look at an ostrich family.

He banked the Cessna toward the west so that Sam could see the desert. "You're looking at the Kalahari, which stretches to the Atlantic Ocean. It's the ancestral home of the San people, whose roots reach back to the beginning of time. Their history is fascinating. They speak by clicking their tongue. My brother, Jason, will bend your ear for hours about the San, the desert and the animals there."

The plane pointed north again allowing them to view the beginning of a vast water delta. "Is that the Okavango?" she asked, stretching to gain a better view.

"Yup, sure is. You are seeing it during flood. We'll visit it in a few days to take dugout canoes into the vast reed channels. We'll see some animals and lots of birds. The water has an interesting story and Jason can give you a more complete background. The Okavango River begins in Angola, where it's called the Cubango. The rains began in that country in November and continue for six months, causing the river to swell and dump precious water onto the Kalahari Desert. It's a river that grew tired of looking for the sea, giving up in the Okavango Delta. It takes months for the water to travel the thousand kilometers from Angola, causing the delta to reach its widest flood expansion in June. In the winter months, when the flood has reached its high point, animals from many kilometers around come here, creating one of Africa's greatest concentrations of wildlife."

Gradually the land changed. There were rivers now, and trees and dense shrubs by the water. Brian noticed the animals first, banking for a better view. Samantha shrieked. "Giraffes! Lots of them. Look, we are frightening them—they're running. Look at those spindly legs!" She was breathless with excitement. Soon zebras and antelope joined the giraffes. It seemed to Samantha that the entire veldt was moving. They were over the Moremi Game Park now, where, soon, she would see these wild animals close-up.

Brian flew in low, buzzing the four men gathered at the end of the landing strip, then banked sharply to check if there were animals on the runway. After a bumpy landing, they taxied toward the men waiting to greet them. Samantha climbed out first, grabbing the wing strut and dropping smoothly to the ground. When she turned, she saw Brian standing before her holding a silver tray with tall glasses. She looked back to the cockpit where Brian still sat. There were two Brians! The one before her was a shade thinner, slightly shorter and just as good-looking.

"Hello, Samantha. I'm Jason. Why don't you ditch my brother and come with me." He handed Sam a glass, the bubbles frothing at the top. "Some champagne? For fortitude, of course."

Sam was overcome with delight. She beamed at Jason as she accepted the glass and took a careful sip. Over her head, the brothers smiled at each other.

The three Rhodesian men were introduced, the Cessna secured with straps, and the champagne consumed before they headed off in two Land Rovers down a rutted road toward their camp.

The two open four-wheelers passed through a land that had been occupied by man and beast since the beginning of life on the planet. It looked used, tired, and waning in the heat of the day. The dry elephant grass stood listless in the hot afternoon sun. It was a flat land, checkered with groves of knob thorn and mopane trees, and occasionally an isolated large feverberry. Jason pointed out a giant sausage tree, with five trunks, melded together at the base, leading to branches splayed outward holding their heavy fruit. The loose sandy soil reflected spoor, most leading to the surrounding bush-willow. Sam began to see animals, some quite close. They seemed relaxed, paying no attention to the two vehicles moving unhurriedly past. In the distance, on one grassy field, stood twenty or more impalas. Near them, in their own corner, a zeal of zebras grazed unconcerned, while a pack of hyenas watched both, their huge, strong jaws agape.

The road passed through a forest, which bordered a grassy plain. Jason drove the lead Land Rover with Samantha perched next to him. He suddenly slowed, pulling the car to the side of the road while holding up his hand, signaling silence. She heard a sound that made her skin crawl and sent shivers up her spine: it was a deep, throaty, guttural snarl—not really a growl. Jason pointed, whispering to her. "Look at the grass about 200 meters to your right. There, see him? Can you see his head?"

"My God, it's a lion!" Sam mouthed without making a sound. "It's huge!"

'We might be in for a show. Look in the distance over near that large mopane tree. There's a lioness and I bet she's in heat."

What followed was rough foreplay. The lion circled the lioness, attempting to get close, only to receive paw cuffs. She moved away to lie down, paying no attention to her suitor. The deep growls continued as the male strutted around the tree preparing to make another foray. Everyone watched this theatre in rapt awe. The men in the second vehicle quietly cheered when the lioness acquiesced and was mounted. The copulation took less than ten seconds.

"That's it?" Samantha questioned, raising both hands in the air palms up, while still watching the pair who were now on the ground resting.

Jason laughed. "If we want to wait around for twenty minutes, they'll be at it again. If they're not interrupted by other lions, that is. This great romance will continue for several days."

Their camp site stretched from a grove of trees to a shallow pool. The large sleeping tents formed a semi-circle facing the pool. Each had a canopy sheltering two deck chairs. An enormous stone fire pit occupied the center ground, with a long dining table nearby. The white linen and silverware were already in place. Beyond this was the kitchen, servants' tents, several showers and toilets. The sun had slipped away, unacknowledged. It had been a long, hot day but now a coolness touched the evening. Six humans sat by a roaring fire, their gazes transfixed by the glow, their thoughts meandering. No one spoke, allowing the cacophony from the bush to invade. There were grunts and chortling and even a passionate roar in the distance. This land belonged to the sound-makers. The visitors sipped their drinks. They were the guests.

Dining by lamplight with five charming men, somewhere on the Mopane Tongue, that part of the Moremi that jutted into the Okavango Delta, would be a moment that Samantha would savor for the rest of her life. The Rhodesians had just formed a company called "Africa Under Canvas," and this camp would be the featured attraction in their brochure. Tomorrow Samantha would return all favors by photographing the camp, plus their safari forays into the bush. It would all start at dawn when the animals were on the move.

The bush dinner rivaled Les Ambassadeurs in London. It was exquisitely prepared and presented. After dinner, back by the fire, they all sat swirling French liqueurs while watching the Southern Star emerge in a velvet sky. Their talk centered on local politics, both in the Bechuanaland and in Rhodesia. The Rhodesians thought that a new independent country would soon be formed here. It would include a large part of the Kalahari Desert and the Moremi Delta area. Jason hoped for this and he became animated explaining how the Moremi would be a protected wildlife park, which he, of course, would manage.

The fire's glow ebbed. The sky remained clear, the stars multitudinous and crisp. Brian led Samantha to their tent, his arm gripping her shoulder lightly. They stood briefly by the tent opening, looking at the pool bathed in starlight. "When we arrived," Sam murmured in a soft voice roiled by wine, "I noticed a large log by the pool and I think I saw it move."

"Impossible. It must be the wine," Brian whispered as he buried his face in her hair and began to spread kisses along her neck. "Would you like to step inside to view my etchings?" he murmured, now kissing her brow and nose. She chuckled, took his face in her hands, pulled it down so that she could kiss his mouth. Their hips closed; Samantha pressed her loins hard against his arousal. They moved awkwardly through the tent opening, stumbling on the flap lip, laughing as they undressed.

Samantha stood, weaving slightly in the center of the tent, eyeing the two rather narrow cots on either side. Her slacks now lay in a heap on the floor. She leaned back into his arms and reached one arm over her head to grasp his neck while he caressed her breasts. "I want to make mad love right now," she groaned, "but those cots"—she didn't finish the sentence.

Brian gently grasped her hips, guiding her to her knees. Then he was inside her, moving slowly, thrusting deeply. She let her head tip toward the floor, her hair falling to one side of her neck as she thrust her buttocks upward, feeling sheer ecstasy. "We are not so different than those lions," she murmured. "If you come in ten seconds, I'll run naked and shrieking through the camp."

Twenty minutes later they lay wrapped in each others arms on one of the cots. "And now, my lion," Samantha said, with a coy smile, as she lay back on the cot, "I want you this way so that I can watch your eyes flutter when you come again."

For five days Jason toured Brian and Samantha through remote areas of the Moremi and into the Okavango Delta. They saw no humans, but balancing this was a superfluity of birds and animals. Some lived here year around, others were near the delta in anticipation of the flood water. The elephants, lions and wildebeests gathered together near the water, too thirsty to bother with each other. "The best way to see the Delta is in a *mokoro*," Jason said, pointing to a narrow canoe with two folding seats. "Climb in carefully and I will show you a stupendously lush masterpiece of a wild and untouched land, surrounded by the clearest, softest water you have ever seen or touched." He launched the *mokoro* into the reed-fringed channel and stood in the stern with a long pole to propel the canoe.

The sublimity of the days swelled Samantha's heart. She was deeply in love and she relished their growing togetherness and silent understanding of each other. One morning, while they tracked an elusive spotted leopard into a grove of trees, her mind skated to an image of the evening before them, sitting with Brian around the fire under a galaxy of stars, sensing the wine relaxing and heightening the anticipation of them coming together. That night, when they sat together with the others by the great fire, Samantha's eyes rested on Brian, and soon she led the way to their tent. Their insatiable sexual appetite for each other expunged any desire to discuss the past or plan the future. They lived wondrously in the moment.

AUGUST 1961

Katanga

Elizabethville bristled with activity. From his hotel window, Adraan watched loaded troop-carriers drive through the city streets, his inquisitive mind calculating their identity. Most prevalent were UN peacekeeping forces, but he also observed men carrying weapons who were probably mercenaries. At night he could hear gunfire in the distance. On the first day of his arrival, he called Stella.

"I'm here," he said in English.

Stella reacted smoothly. She recognized his voice and had expected Adraan to report in upon his arrival in Katanga. "August fifteenth. Call when you arrive." She hung up.

The date gave him a start. The ship would arrive in the Angolan port earlier than expected. Fifteen days to arrival; he needed transportation to the copper mine—quickly. "I hope the train is loaded and ready to roll," he muttered to himself.

Joseph Sanimbi wiggled a finger, signaling Godefroid Munongo to join him on the deck. August arrived bearing dire implications for Katanga. One was unfolding in the war room at the old golf club, which was packed with representatives from every faction of the combustible, young country. Sanimbi spoke softly as the two men distractedly watched the aerial activity on the pond.

"Our shipment of guns will arrive at the end of the month."

"Good," Munongo nodded. "Our troops desperately need weapons. Moise suspects we'll be attacked within the month. How are the guns getting here?"

"Through Angola."

"Oh, the Benguela. Who is organizing it?"

"That's why we needed to talk. The South African man is here in Elizabethville. He will meet the ship and bring the weapons to us. He's leaving for the mine today. The train must depart soon to make the connection. Please contact the mine manager, Bordeaux, and instruct him to release the train—if it's not completely loaded, too bad."

"I'll do it today. What a clever scheme to use the Benguela Railroad. Mobutu will never guess."

Four days later, the ore train chugged slowly away from the copper mine. It cautiously circled the enormous pit until the narrow gauge leveled, allowing the train to accelerate. It headed west toward the Angola border, passing through an uninteresting land of parched earth and scrub bushes. The terrain rolled with hills, periodically providing a shallow lake or a thirsty river. This country longed for the rainy season. Adraan was ensconced in the caboose with only a brakeman who spoke almost no French. Adraan was pleased; he preferred the silence. The train passed through Dilolo in the black of the night and headed into Angola.

ANGOLA 1961 - ROUTE OF THE BENGUELA RAILROAD

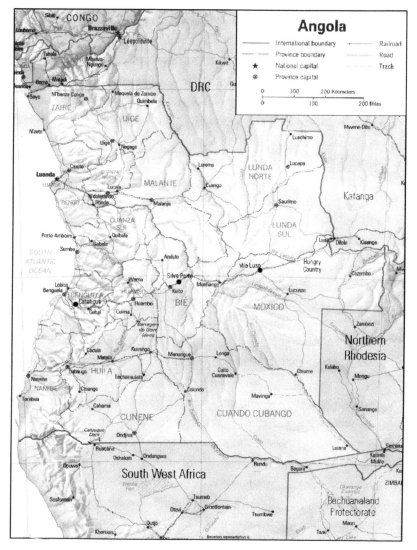

Angola

The sea had frolicked and roiled for a week but now lay beguilingly calm, its surface a deep blue, sparkling in the early morning sun. Lobito Bay's Harbormaster sat in his elevated office at the end of a sand spit, searching the horizon with his binoculars. He saw the black smudge almost immediately, resting inertly where the slate gray of the ocean met the gainsboro gray of the sky. With his eyes still plied on the far object, he reached for his phone to call the harbor pilot.

"Claudio, our visitor is now on the horizon. The ship will be off the outer banks in an hour. I suggest you alert your pilot's launch, and hustle to it."

Lobito Bay, midway down the Angola coast, was arguably the finest natural harbor in all of Africa. It offered both deep water and a safe anchorage. Like a great hook, a sand spit sheltered the anchorage from the sea, allowing large ships to moor within one hundred meters of the docks. The 200-meter-wide spit also provided an idyllic location for not only the port authority office, but also homes for the harbor and railway employees. Quite close to the shore stood a white church with a tall, sleek steeple. The nearby school was also white in keeping with the monochromes of the seaside town. Children could be seen trudging across the sand to school. They would be pleased with the pleasant day and the prospects of swimming after class.

The Benguela Railroad ended its trek across the center of Angola on the Lobito Bay quay. The railhead rested between one-story storage sheds and large pits for dumping minerals on one side and the pier on the other. Like spokes, four rail spurs branched out from the main line to allow switching. The three cranes along the docks could off-load from small vessels and lighters and then swing their cargo directly to the train. On this perfect day in August, a train was positioned to be loaded.

The harbor and the town to the south were shaded from the early morning sun by a hill studded with homes and small shops. Alfredo Gavarnie scrutinized the harbor's activities from the deck of a seafood restaurant pinched into the side of the hill. He carefully inspected each activity. He could see the freighter steaming toward the port. The harbor pilot's launch cut slowly along the sandy spit shoreline and began to circle the lighthouse on the tip. All seemed to be in order but his stomach still churned with anxiety. He knew the customs office was closed. They had been paid royally to remain at home until this ship was unloaded and the train had departed.

His gaze ran down the length of the train as he counted the cars. Between the engine and the wood carrier in the front and the open mineral rolling stock at the opposite end, there were two passenger cars and eight freight cars. The ore cars would return to Katanga empty. A few passengers in Benguela returning to the hill villages would occupy the first car. The other passenger car was reserved for the platoon of federal soldiers that he had requested and sponsored. He knew the soldiers were not necessary but it was all part of his arrangement with Cunha.

The number of cars had been kept to a minimum because the trip back to Katanga would be uphill most of the way. The wood-fired steam engine belonged to a different age. Diesel engines were pulling trains in America and

Europe. This relic would need to be replaced soon, Gavarnie thought, but he wondered if that would happen with the growing threat of insurgency. Probably not, he concluded. Probably the railroad will cease to operate and the country's economy will be ruined, which is why I must move my family away from here. The little engine was beautiful, in a quaint way, with an enormous searchlight perched atop the front. Below it, skirting the track was the grated cowcatcher. Townspeople could smell the train coming well before it came into view. The fuel burned was eucalyptus, which wafted a unique aroma within the billowing smoke. Angola possessed coal and oil deposits, but they languished from lack of attention. Fast growing eucalyptus seedlings had been imported from Australia and planted for fuel on thousands of acres on the plateau near the rail track.

Sighing, Gavarnie turned away from the harbor activity to order more coffee, and noticed a short thin man studying him from the entrance. The man stood out because he was the only one in the restaurant wearing long sleeves. They eyed each other for a moment before the man came forward, "Señor Gavarnie?"

"That's right. You must be Adraan. I've been wondering where you were. Sit down. Have you had breakfast?"

Adraan's expression offered no insight into his mood or thoughts. His black hair had been cropped tight to his scalp. Green eyes looked out from a pale face. "I had several days to kill before the ship was due to arrive, and it appeared that Benguela offered the better place to linger." He looked beyond the deck railing to the harbor and offered a hint of a smile when he spotted the train. Nodding in its direction, he said, "That little engine will never make it up the mountain, even with empty ore cars."

"Apparently you didn't notice the Garratt engines in the Benguela rail yard. We have two of these steam locomotives. The engine is divided into three parts; the boiler is in the center frame with two steam engines on either side. The design gives it twice the power of the little guy you are looking at, as well as an ability to negotiate tight curves. And to further your education, this unique railroad employs track using the Lamella rack between Benguela and Catengue."

"I noticed that," Adraan replied with interest. "How does it work?"

"It's a rack-and-pinion railway. Running between the two rails is a third toothed-rack rail. The trains are fitted with cog wheels that mesh with this rack rail and are thus able to operate on steep gradients. It was quite an achievement to build. Catengue's altitude is 550 meters, so coming from sea level through the Lengue Gorge, the train must power up that steep incline. We have always considered it a blessing that the railroad hauled the copper down the mountain, not up."

Adraan finished his breakfast and poured himself more coffee. "My instructions are to supervise the transfer of our cargo from the steamer to the train and to accompany the train back to Katanga. As I understand it, we will pause at a village on the plateau, where each of us will confirm to our employer that all is well and that the train is close to the border. Is that correct?"

"Yes, that's right. Whom do you work for, by the way?" Gavarnie asked, shifting gears slightly.

Adraan didn't want to enter an information exchange but he thought a quick, factual answer might head it off. "I am here to make sure all of the consignment is shipped correctly. My employer is simply an agent who organizes complex orders and their delivery. Actually, I don't know the suppliers or the customers."

Gavarnie handed Adraan a map of the rail system. He pointed to Benguela on the coast, and then moved his finger up the mountain range at Cubal. He tapped on Silva Porto, and said, "Here they will replace the Garrett engines with the standard steam engine you see below you. From here the trip is quite comfortable, slowly ascending through the middle of a vast and fertile plain. You will see many crops, especially cotton. I will drive up and meet you in Vila Luso. We'll make our wire communications from there, wait for an answer and then part ways. The Katanga border is only a few hundred kilometers up the track. There will be a small armed guard travelling with you although it is unlikely that problems will occur." Gavarnie pushed his chair back and said, "If you're finished with your coffee, why don't we drive down to the harbor; I see the vessel is in the anchorage and beginning to off-load your cargo."

Adraan stood well away from the loading activity watching Gavarnie chat with the individuals who were supervising the unloading and loading. No one appeared curious about the wooden crates and no wonder, as they were similar in size to the others, with markings that were a jumble of numbers and letters including the ultimate addressee. Adraan had memorized the nomenclature. He knew which crates contained the AK-47s, where to find the ammo and grenades, and most important, the location of the 51-caliber machine gun. The stevedores struggled with the heavy crates and stacked them only three high in the railway cars. At noon, on the dot, the loading was complete and the workers began to straggle out of the harbor area. Gavarnie appeared by Adraan's side to say goodbye.

"You will have two passenger cars to yourself this afternoon," he said to Adraan with a broad smile. "The train will lay over in Benguela for the night, departing for the interior tomorrow morning. I suggest you find a hotel room near the terminal."

"Will the rail cars be secure?" Adraan inquired.

"No need to worry," Gavarnie replied quickly. "The railroad yard has security. Anyway, the Garrett engines will be coupled during the night so there will be plenty of people around."

"I want each car locked," Adraan said matter-of-factly. It was an order, not a suggestion.

Gavarnie groaned. He now knew for sure the crates contained weapons. "I will instruct the rail foreman in Benguela to have sixteen padlocks for you upon arrival. I'd like them back when we meet in Vila Luso. Enjoy the trip." He spun around and hurried to his car.

Later that afternoon in Benguela, Adraan visited each railcar to make notes of crate locations and to padlock the sliding doors. By nature, Adraan was suspicious, an attribute that compelled him to be extremely careful.

When he felt confident that the shipment was secure and of no interest to the men working in the railroad yard, Adraan sauntered into the small coastal town of Benguela.

He found a hotel called the "Lookout" with a view of the waves crashing on the rocks below the cliff. He decided to take dinner on the deck to enjoy the sunset. He sat alone, in the corner enjoying the sea air and the solitude. Adraan was comfortable with himself and preferred to be alone. He allowed his mind to drift over events in his life, their impact and his planned resolution. He would be home soon. He had been paid well to deliver the guns to Katanga. His mind dwelled on each aspect of the train trip looking for a weakness. Gavarnie was the weak spot, he thought. He would be careful of him.

In the morning, uniformed soldiers, each carrying a rifle, boarded one of the passenger cars just as Gavarnie had said. Adraan did not see an officer, only a sergeant, who sat by himself. The soldiers looked to be reservists, not regular army, and their insouciant demeanor suggested they were on an outing. Meanwhile, Adraan's car filled with locals, all of whom seemed to be carrying something alive. Oh well, he thought as he secured an empty bench seat at the end of the car, this will soon be over and I can begin a new life.

At six in the morning, the locomotive's horn gave a long and low hoot. The giant Garrett engine, billowing fragrant smoke, began to move slowly along the old rusted rails. The train turned inland almost immediately after leaving Benguela and soon ambled up the Lengue Gorge. Progress was slow once the rack-and-pinion cogged wheel had been engaged. The enervating seacoast humidity vanished. A few passengers threw open the car windows to gorge on the pure, silky mountain air. It took all day to scale the mountains. The train stopped briefly at numerous villages along the way and by the time they arrived at Catengue, only Adraan and a few others passengers remained, along with the car full of soldiers. Adraan had brought food and water in preparation for the long night. The train steadily circled the mountain slopes, until, at an altitude of 1800 meters, it finally crossed the range to the plateau beyond. A little before dawn, they reached Silva Porto, where the giant Garrett engine was replaced by a standard steam engine. The fuel car was replenished with eucalyptus logs, all split into meter-long lengths. Adraan took count of the crew; the engineer or hostler and a fireman were riding the cab while the switchman joined the conductor in the caboose. During the morning, the conductor would detrain, since no passengers would board along this stretch. Adraan thought about moving to the caboose, but decided he should stay close to his cargo. He had replenished his food and water at the station and was now set to survive the long pull up the valley.

This segment of the trip was interesting. Corn mills, sawmills, tile works, lime quarries and agricultural settlements punctuated the train route. He saw forests and farms; the land looked fertile. Stretching out to the horizon were fields of maize, cotton and coffee, with vast spreads for cattle. It was obvious that this railroad was the lifeline for Angola's interior.

At a stop where the train picked up water and firewood, Adraan slipped out of the passenger car, walked along four of the railcars, unlocked the padlock on the fifth and climbed inside. He had brought with him a small crowbar, but hefty enough to open a crate. Adraan opened two, removed the lids and sifted through the packing. He found what he was looking for and began to assemble an AK-47. It was new, clean, oiled and ready. In the second crate, he located a large quantity of ammunition for the automatic rifle. He then put the assembled AK-47 along with the ammo on top of the packing in the first crate and returned the lid but did not fasten it. It would be an hour before they reached the next stop. He slid the car door open completely so that he could sit on the edge, feet dangling outward, to watch the countryside slide past. He could not stop dreaming of the future.

The village of Vila Luso lay on the eastern edge of this cultivated fertile valley. It provided the last outpost of civilization: food, tools, petroleum, even a basic medical clinic. There was a restaurant and a telegraph office. Security came from a contingent of six soldiers stationed near the north end of town. To the east there was nothing except a lonely track of rail leading to the Katanga border, 400 kilometers away. Adraan had heard that this land was called the "Hungry Country" because it was nothing but sand and bush that produced no food and held no water. The train track followed the old trade route taken by the Arab slave dealers, who knew that they and their slaves would die from hunger and exhaustion if they misgauged their food and water supply. Today, there were no animals out there, only periodic bands of robbers.

Adraan's gunrunning train pulled into Vila Luso as the first light broke over the valley. A small gathering of villagers greeted the train, anxious to learn what goods were scheduled for their village. Adraan and the last of the passengers disembarked. The soldiers also clambered off the other car, unkempt after three days of travel, carrying their duffels and weapons. Adraan surveyed the scene as he stood on the dirt embankment. Would this be the end of the military protection, he wondered. He got his answer as he watched a military truck swoop into the station area and the soldiers piled into the back. The train crew all seemed to be headed into town—he hoped for some breakfast. He grabbed his duffel and followed them.

Gavarnie, accompanied by a young Angolan, found Adraan in the restaurant. "Mr. Adraan, I'd like you to meet a friend of mine who lives in these parts, Ricardo Lobo. He has been my construction foreman for many years." They chatted in a mixture of Portuguese and Spanish. Then they walked to the telegraph office and waited for it to open. The telegraph service was for the railroad; the local businesses rarely used it. The room was small with a single telephone on a desk in the corner. A telegraph clerk worked behind a counter, with a grille extending to the ceiling protecting him from unknown threats. Adraan had anticipated this inconvenience. He handed the clerk a short message in Portuguese addressed to van Riebeek's Lisbon banker stating that he and the consignment had arrived, without incident, in Vila Luso. The banker's instructions were implicit. The remaining amount of commission that van Riebeek owed Osvaldo Cunha would be transferred within minutes to his Lisbon bank account. Adraan did not expect a reply, merely a confirmation that his message had reached its destination. It came through in less than an hour.

During the wait, Gavarnie telephoned Cunha in Lisbon. They chatted about trivialities which was their signal that the mission had been completed. Once Cunha received his full payment, he would move funds to Gavarnie's Lisbon bank account. Cunha asked for the phone number at the telegraph station with the promise that he would call back before noon. This would require Gavarnie to linger in the office whereas Adraan excused himself and headed back to the train. He had noticed that Ricardo Lobo seemed to be traveling with a group of men. Their cars and trucks were parked around the corner on a side street. One was a crazy lemon color.

Adraan found the hostler on his knees mending the brake system of his steam engine. He looked up when Adraan approach and smiled. "Have you enjoyed your trip so far?" he said in English. He caught Adraan's surprise and continued. "I spent a year in England training for this job. My English is limited but I do enjoy using it when I am able."

They chatted amiably for a while before Adraan turned the conversation to his real intention. "What speed will you reach crossing the Hungry Country?"

"No more than forty or forty-five kilometers per hour. Why?"

"I hear there are bands of thieves out there," Adraan offered with a tight smile.

"There are probably only very few left; besides, I wouldn't stop for them." The engineer laughed.

"What if they shot at you? Your cabin is very open."

"The sides are steel. I would shove the throttle forward and kneel behind the steel plates."

Adraan listened intently to this response. He carefully reached into his jacket pocket and withdrew a wad of bills and handed 5000 escudos to the engineer. "If we are ambushed, I want you keep the train moving. Push the throttle forward and protect yourself. If you do this successfully, I will pay you another 5000 when we arrive in Katanga."

"What will you be doing if we are ambushed?" the engineer asked.

"I'll be persuading them to leave us alone," Adraan replied dryly.

Gavarnie and Lobo found Adraan waiting for them in the passenger car. Alfredo looked ebullient; Adraan worried that he would embrace him. "I have received a reply from my people and all is well. Our arrangement has been completed satisfactorily. And so, I wish you a good trip to the finish line. I, in turn, will drive back to the coast. I'd like to get a start on the journey this afternoon. "Gavarnie started toward his car before turning back to Adraan. "Oh yes, would you please return the padlocks to Ricardo. You won't have security problems between here and the border."

There are few places on earth more desolate than the Hungry Country. The train's whistle cut the invasive silence, disturbing nothing. Each car swayed to the rhythm of the engine, the clicking of the wheels echoing the sounds of a tap dancer. The track cut straight across the bush land, disappearing into a wall of darkness gathering in the east; the land leveled to allow greater speed. Adraan sat on a crate with the AK-47 in his hand and gazed out both open doors at the countryside flying past.

The Wolf Pack struck about an hour out from the protection of Vila Luso. They had driven out to intercept the train in two four-wheel-drive open cars and an old, lemon jalopy that looked like an abandoned taxi. They looked threatening with rifles protruding from the open windows. Earlier, Adraan had seen their dust trail and knew they were coming for his guns. What he couldn't view from his angle was the pile of trash placed on the track. There were no trees to offer logs and the bandits didn't want to risk using one of their vehicles. The 5000-escudo bonus went to work as the locomotive increased its speed and easily plowed through the barrier, as if nothing had been there. Now the three vehicles were racing alongside the engine—Adraan could easily see them—and a man in the lead car stood and began to fire his rifle at the engine. They resembled the American cowboys he'd seen in the movies; they were laughing, shouting and waving their guns. Adraan pushed the lever forward that limited the AK to single shots, rested his elbow on the crate and began to synchronize his aim with the sway of the railcar. After he caught the rhythm, he fired and the standing cowboy reeled sideways, slumped, and finally collapsed and fell over the side of the open car. The cars kept speeding alongside with rifles visible but there was no shouting, just faces with looks of astonishment. Finally it sank in that they had been shot at from the train, that there was someone on the train with a weapon. They turned and fled, leaving the body along the track. The train hostler never missed a beat, easily guiding the locomotive on ahead.

Adraan had both sliding doors open and could follow action on either side. He knew that the thieves would return with a vengeance once they regrouped. In a short while, they did. Their second attempt came from the rear; one car on the right and the other two cars speeding up on Adraan's left. They were looking for the railcar where the gun shots had come from and soon spied it in the middle of the string of freight cars. Adraan lay flat, pressed into the floor, concealed behind siding, as he watched them approach. They would begin firing at any moment. He knew that they thought they were after a single-shot rifleman. The lemon jalopy came abreast first, guns blazing from the windows. Adraan's AK-47 was set to fire automatically. He poked the nose of the rifle around the edge of the door and let loose a lethal dose of automatic fire, destroying the windows and the dented hood of the old vehicle and, surely, annihilating anything alive inside. The driver's foot remained on the accelerator causing the now nearly-topless lemon sedan to bump its way out across the endless bush. The car on the opposite side of the train could not see the disaster that had befallen its compatriots and continued to pursue the train, firing at the open door. Adraan saw Lobo sitting in the front seat, waving a pistol. These people are too dumb to die, he thought grimly. A blast of rapid AK fire flew over their heads. They reacted quickly, spinning off in the opposite direction. He was sure they would not return. There would be hell to pay for Gavarnie. Adraan would now be *persona non grata* in Angola, an amusing thought, because he never planned to return to this part of the world again. He heard the low wail of the locomotive whistle and knew the hostler was celebrating his train's escape and his personal reward to come.

Elizabethville

Tshombe walked slowly through his garden, occasionally bending to pick up fallen flowers and branches. Munongo followed him totting a sheaf of papers, which seemed incongruous considering the fading light and Tshombe's preoccupation with the garden. "Look at my lobelia, Godefroid. Have you seen vivid blue like this?"

"I remember the Katanga sky of my youth, a perfect, beguiling blue. Now it is perpetually gray. Maybe the heaven senses our predicament."

Tshombe smiled, tilted his head toward his second-in-command and spoke, his cadence showing no urgency. "We have been a country for one year, my friend. Have you forgotten? What a terrible year it has been. We are threatened on all sides."

"From within, as well," Munongo added. The UN troops are pushing toward the center of the city. Our Belgian friends are reluctant to confront them."

"Who will, then?" Tshombe frowned.

"It will have to be our own men, led by foreign soldiers."

"Mercenaries," Tshombe groaned. "They are everywhere. How long must we tolerate them? Will we ever have our own officers?"

"Not soon, I'm afraid," Munongo replied. "Our status is fragile. We must accept the support we are receiving from ambiguous sources and you know who they are. These diverse factions want us to remain independent. They are apprehensive of the UN. They loath Hammarskjöld. We cannot allow the UN to make further inroads."

Tshombe considered Munongo's observations. "If we are to use our troops and mercenaries, we will need more weapons. Do we not have a shipment arriving soon?"

"It arrived this afternoon. The boxcars are on a siding at our terminal. Apparently Angolan insurgents attacked the train near our border—someone must have tipped them off. The South African fellow riding with the shipment fought them off with one of our AK-47s. The rumor is he killed several."

"Will this be a problem?" Tshombe questioned.

"I doubt it. He was doing a favor for the Portuguese army. I know what to do with the weapons and ammo with the exception of the 51-caliber machine gun. It's large and we have no one who knows how to fire it."

"What about the South African?"

Munongo shrugged his shoulders. "He's packing and will leave tomorrow."

The President of Katanga sat quietly looking out at his garden. "Then, here's what we need to do," Tshombe said impassively. "Pay this man—say $1000—to remain here for another month. Ask him to take the machine gun into the jungle and train two squads on its use and maintenance. We will be attacked any day now. The UN will attempt to land troops at our airport. If we could shoot down a plane, it would cause a worldwide ruckus, but then our enemies would not be so anxious to threaten us." He paused a moment and then looked squarely at Munongo, "Remember, I don't want to know anything about this, just in case I'm asked someday."

Cape Town

Where had the winter gone, Jillian wondered. I started chasing van Riebeek six months ago, and here we are in the last week of August. The gunrunning file lay open on her desk, highlighted, clipped, and spotted with coffee drops. The paper on top was the local bank summary of van Riebeek's deposit account. This was an outrageous invasion of privacy, she thought, as she scrutinized the contents. No large movement of funds appeared on the ledger. Most could be pinpointed to wine shipments, both in and out of the country. There were a few small deposits from unknown sources in the far north of South Africa, which would need to be run down, but nothing from Katanga. The only notations that interested her were a few sizeable deposits from a bank in Lisbon. Strange, she thought. Why did he have an account there?

Interpol Lisbon had joined the hunt and they were good at their job. They identified the arrivals and departures of a Mr. van Riebeek, who sometimes traveled under the name of Reinhardt, a Dutch citizen. His visits were easily traced to a four-star hotel facing the ocean. A record of his phone messages led them to a prestigious private bank. When asked, the bank manager politely explained that his bank did not offer numbered accounts; there was nothing secret about the bank's operation. He had confirmed that he had known Mr. Reinhardt for many years and that they usually met during his visits to Lisbon. The manager admitted that the account received recently several significant deposits but regulations did not permit him to discuss the details. At this juncture the investigation had stopped and the Interpol office in Lisbon asked Jillian for instruction.

Jillian reflected on the facts she knew. Adraan had vanished. He had certainly connected with the shipment of weapons destined for Katanga. But which port of entry and how would it travel to the interior? She made a decision and wrote a telex message for Interpol, Lisbon.

POSSIBLE LARGE ARMS SHIPMENT PASSING
THROUGH LOBITO BAY. DESTINATION
KATANGA. URGENT YOU INVESTIGATE
RECENT VESSEL ARRIVALS AND TRANS-
SHIPMENTS ON BENGUELA RAILROAD.

She felt certain the guns had traveled along the Benguela
rail line, but she needed more—and soon. Time was running
out.

The aircraft gun discovery tugged at her thought
process. It didn't fit with the other weapons. She had left a
message for Brian with his Geneva office, alerting him to the
antiaircraft gun. Had he receive her warning?

SEPTEMBER 1961

Katanga

Adraan sat pensively in the army troop carrier cab as Joseph Sanimbi drove slowly over the rutted, seldom-used, dirt road. His mind was on Algeria, vineyards and his mother. The money he would earn for this extra month of work would buy more acreage for his vineyard.

In the back were ten Elizabethville policemen and two large wooden crates. The dust settled like fine powder on Sanimbi's pressed police superintendents uniform. He should have worn fatigues, Adraan thought, as he watched the rugged and wet terrain slide past. The road shadowed the Katanga—Rhodesian border snaking eastward into a remote and dense forest. There were no villages here, which provided a safe and remote place to practice firing the great machine gun. Adraan would teach Sanimbi's men how to assemble and take apart the weapon, how to clean it and, most important, how to fire it with accuracy.

After several hours of driving, they found a clearing in the forest. Here, no one would hear the rat-a-tat-tat of the gun. The policemen unloaded the crates, removed the lids and placed the parts on a tarpaulin spread on the ground. Adraan went to work, explaining in French the operation of the gun. The components fit together easily. The muzzle was heavy with fins for air circulation and it took two men to screw it into the housing. Adraan mounted the gun on the tripod, placing the wheel assembly aside. The second crate contained the ammunition. The gun was gas operated and belt fed. The cartridges were ten cm long, quite heavy, with a round nose protruding from the casing.

"The DshKM can be used as a heavy infantry field gun as well as an anti-aircraft weapon," Adraan explained. "We are going to practice shooting at planes." The men practiced by decimating the tops of a few tall trees on the edge of the clearing. At first they were apprehensive but the experience of actually firing the large weapon was exciting. Soon they were vying with each other for a chance to work with the machine gun.

Later that day, after returning to Elizabethville, Adraan and Sanimbi met with Munongo to discuss the employment and logistics of the weapon. Logically it should be placed near the Elizabethville airport where the enemy would attempt to land, but the area was overrun with UN peacekeeping forces. Fighting between the UN forces and pro-Katanga elements had begun. As UN forces spread throughout the city, key Katanga officers were forced to flee to secret hideouts.

"Our airport is closed to all traffic," Munongo announced. "Our information is that the UN is planning to fly additional troops here to disarm ours and expel our Belgian forces. Secretary-General Hammarskjöld is on his way to Leopoldville now to work out a strategy with Mobutu. Tshombe has warned Mobutu that he will shoot down any plane attempting to land in Katanga."

"If a plane cannot land here, where would it go?" Adraan asked.

"A troop transport coming from the north would approach our airport from the northwest," Sanimbi observed. "If it was not allowed to land and did not have enough fuel to return home, it would most likely maintain its altitude and glide just across our border to the Ndola airport. Let's find a location for our great gun along the border about half way between the two airports."

Munongo slapped his knee and smiled broadly. "We have a plan. I will explain our strategy to Tshombe. He feels that if we shoot down just one plane, our enemies will back off. Joseph, find the right spot and set up our small camp. Station your men there and provide them with food and communication equipment."

"And what are my instructions?" Adraan asked in a quiet voice, looking to Munongo for his answer.

"Per our arrangement, you will work for us until the end of this month. In the beginning, I think you should be the one to operate the weapon."

"You're asking me to shoot down a foreign airplane?" Adraan's voice was low and steady. "For that I will need to be paid a lot more and I need to know exactly how I will leave Katanga—unnoticed."

Leopoldville

On the evening of September 17, Secretary-General Dag Hammarskjöld attended a welcoming banquet in the villa of the officer-in-charge of the UN operation in the DRC. Mobutu attended along with most of the Leopoldville diplomatic corps. Hammarskjöld was ebullient, exhibited no fatigue and attempted to talk with everyone in the room. The conversation focused on the outbreak of hostilities in Katanga. Dag announced that he would fly to Elizabethville the following day, Sunday, to reason with Moise Tshombe. Brian was apprehensive about the plan. He had remained on the fringe of the cocktail crowd talking with Dag's two exhausted Swedish pilots. One engine on the chartered UN DC-6 was a problem and they were worried because the DRC mechanics were unfamiliar with the equipment.

Brian awakened early Sunday morning, September 17, with a headache. He had been awake most of the night thinking about the mission to Katanga. His first instinct was to call Samantha to vent some of his worries and concerns.

The secretary-general and his delegation marked time for most of Sunday, finally arriving at the airport late in the afternoon. The repaired faulty engine had been reinstalled on the DC-6. Hammarskjöld was in a hurry and would not allow the pilots time to test-fly the repaired engine. It had been decided to fly at night to avoid Katanga's French-built Fouga Magister fighter planes. The UN entourage boarded the old DC-6 after darkness had descended and two tired pilots and a very old airplane droned into the night, heading first east to the Congo border before banking south to avoid Katanga air space. Everyone on board worked for the UN; some were security guards and heavily armed. Brian sat near the front of the plane, too tired to either study the papers in his briefcase or to doze. He had telephoned Samantha from his hotel. Her voice was edgy with concern and instead of voicing his private concerns Brian had attempted to sooth her mood with trivial banter about a trip they were planning to visit her family in Illinois. He had promised to call her from Ndola, their likely destination. With this thought he settled back, closed his eyes and listened to the drone of the engines as the plane lumbered across the cloudy skies.

At 11:30, Brian felt a hand on his shoulder. "Brian, come and sit with me. We have about an hour before landing." It was Dag Hammarskjold, still in his suit and tie. They settled in next to each other while the rest of the plane's passengers slept. Dag had been writing poems, not studying briefing papers. He wanted Brian to read one, handing over his creation sheepishly and sat quietly waiting for Brian's critique. The poem described in perfect cadence the life of a small boy growing up in rural Sweden. The boy had an umbilical connection with the dark forest, the silver bark birch trees and the clear lakes. It was a happy story, but it did not end well. It was so pure, so perfect, and so full of an essential peace that prevailed before the small boy died.

Brian turned to Dag. "You have allowed me to intrude on something very personal. It's beautiful poetry. I now understand with greater insight why you are so effective in bringing people together." He chose not to acknowledge the sad ending.

The plane bounced in sudden turbulence as it began its descent. One of the pilots emerged from the cockpit looking for the secretary-general. He leaned down next to Brian and quietly explained their flight plan. "The Elizabethville airport has been closed. A Katanga radio wave-length has ordered us to turn around or be shot down. The UN force's radio reported that the city was under siege and suggested that we land in Ndola. We knew Ndola would probably be our destination, but I just wanted to make sure that this is acceptable to you, sir?" the pilot asked.

"Yes, Ndola will be fine," Dag replied. "When you contact the airport, ask them to relay to the UN officials our plan and our need for accommodations. Thank you, Captain."

As the plane descended rapidly, Dag turned the conversation to Brian's father, a man he admired and how important Phillip had become in Dag's life. He was overjoyed with the hope that Phillip would indeed move to New York and spend time with him. He then began speaking quietly about his plans for Africa and the peace process there.

Suddenly the plane banked sharply. Strange, Brian thought, for they were flying at a low altitude. Why would the pilot want to head north again and into Katanga airspace? After a few moments the plane swung back on a southerly course—probably on final approach, Brian guessed. Hammarskjöld turned to Brian to continue his monologue on peace in Africa. Without warning they lurched violently and the left wing dropping radically. To his horror Brian realized that the engine was on fire. He could see through the window how the flames were streaming out from behind it. He looked over at Dag Hammarskjöld who locked eyes with him. His piercing blue irises were almost obliterated by their dark pupils. The plane was shaking; passengers were screaming. Brian felt an excruciating pain in his right shoulder. In shock he clasped it and he saw it was covered with blood, but he could not reason why he was bleeding. Bullets were riddling the fuselage, delivering death and destruction. The plane was now in a steep dive, with the entire wing aflame. The crack of gunshots pierced the darkness; then there was nothing but the sound of crunched metal and the crackle of flames. Brian didn't hear the explosion as it tore through the fuselage, scattering metal and body parts several hundred yards from the crash site. He and Dag Hammarskjöld had already succumbed to the barrage of bullets from the ground.

London

Her sleep had been erratic, interrupted by dark, meaningless dreams, and mostly contorted memories of her childhood in Wisconsin. She had drifted in and out of wakefulness and now, in the dawn's early light, Samantha felt as if she had not slept at all. She lay there, on a bed in disarray, trying to assemble her thoughts from the evening before. She remembered them now; her mind had been on Brian and his visit to the DRC. He had telephoned from Leopoldville yesterday afternoon confirming he would fly to Katanga that evening. She had been anxious, for no good reason, and now this unfounded concern drifted back, shrouding her in an ominous cloud. Somewhere a telephone jangled. She tried to dismiss it but the ringing was persistent. Slowly Samantha emerged from the tangled sheets, crossed the bedroom and answered. "Hello."

"Samantha, this is Kathryn. What are you doing?"

"Nothing. I'm not awake yet. Why?"

"There's news coming out of Africa. Turn on your telly. I'm coming over—unlatch your front door."

Samantha stood dazed still holding the telephone receiver. Africa, she thought. What has happened, her mind began to scream.

Samantha rarely watched television. She fiddled with the knobs and finally the black and white screen flickered and focused on a dark object, burning in a field. There were firemen moving along the perimeter, flushing the object with their hoses. The realization of what she was watching hit her just as the announcer began to describe the sketchy events surrounding the mysterious crash of Secretary-General Hammarskjöld's aircraft somewhere in Northern Rhodesia.

She knew in that instant that Brian was gone. Time stopped. Her life stopped. A coldness captured her body. Samantha shrieked in agony and despair yet no sound came from her throat. Her heart burst, but there was no blood. Her unseeing eyes stared at the television screen, grasping nothing. Her knees refused to hold her upright and she sank to the floor, her face in her hands. All thoughts drained away, her mind was empty, her body numb. In one instant her life ceased to have any meaning. Nothingness consumed her. She pushed the world away and thought about dying. Her head pounded, her heart jerked, her breathing became shallow but she did not cry. Samantha's head hung down and she bowed to the sudden, life-altering anguish that was beginning to consume her very soul. She was alone. Then her scream pierced the silence of the morning.

Cape Town

Jillian Pienar stared at the headlines in stunned silence. "What happened, what happened?" she kept saying to herself in an anguished whisper. "Brian was on that plane," she gasped. "My God—how awful." She stood for a long moment, her mind unable to settle anywhere. Then her eyes rested on the gunrunning file still sitting on her desk. Was there a connection? She sat down, reached for the file and began thumbing through the contents. She already had her sights on Adraan; Interpol was looking for him throughout Africa and Europe. He would be captured eventually, but she had uncovered nothing that would implicate van Riebeek. The money trail had evaporated in Portugal, although wild reports were beginning to arrive with tales of trains, gun fights and a shipment of unknown goods traveling across Angola. This file, she muttered, will remain on my desk until we catch up with this fellow van Riebeek.

London

Bad news travels swiftly. On September 18, the world awakened to horrifying reports of a plane crash somewhere in Central Africa and that Dag Hammarskjöld was on board and had perished. The Rhodesian officials in Ndola, where the crash occurred, had provided sketchy information to the UN Headquarters, the Swedish government and the press.

Nicholas had spent a quiet weekend in Guildford and on this gray Monday morning reluctantly packed his valise and prepared to return to London. In his rush, he had neglected the morning news broadcast. His awareness of the disaster came from a phone call from Sir Douglas Sallis-Cooper.

With no preamble, Sallis-Cooper said, "What's your take on the news?"

"What news?"

With astonishment, Sallis-Cooper related the known details of the plane crash. "Nicholas, the entire world is focused on this. Questions are flying. I am fearful that the aircraft gun will be traced to us."

"Not possible." Nicholas felt his heart pound.

Sallis-Cooper growled, "I know nothing about your business, Nicholas, but I have it on impeccable authority, that the South African who shepherded the weapons into Katanga was the one who pulled the trigger."

"Trigger? What are you talking about?"

"Good Lord. Are you still asleep? First reports out of Rhodesia indicate the UN plane was shot down by anti-aircraft fire. You need to eliminate any connection between that gun and us. Do you follow me?"

Sallis-Cooper hung-up leaving Nicholas stunned. His mind was tearing through options, all new to him and dangerous. He knew with certainty that van Riebeek must disappear.

Algeria

Like a shadow, Adraan slipped out of Katanga unnoticed in a truck driven by Joseph Sanimbi on one of the numerous unmarked roads neglected by the security forces. In Ndola he caught a bus to Lusaka. He had already destroyed his South African passport and suspected his Mozambique passport was, by now, flagged in Rhodesia. Sanimbi had given him an address in Lusaka of an Indian who forged identification papers; passports were his specialty. How ironic, Adraan thought, that the police chief of Elizabethville leads me to a criminal. He found a low profile hotel catering to non-white foreigners that was conveniently located near the airport. He showered, changed his clothes and set out to find the passport man.

The address was on the second floor of a three-story office block on a busy side street. Adraan sauntered around the building before climbing the stairway to the second floor. The businesses on the ground floor tended toward retail trade, whereas the names on the doors of the second floor offices were ambiguous. An insurance office's double doors had a brass plate announcing its name. The sign on the next door proclaimed "Antique Pistols". At the far end of the shabby hallway, he found the address he had been given. The door plaque announced simply "Numismatist". Knocking on the door seemed appropriate, but instead, Adraan turned the door handle and stepped into a well-lit office. A man sitting behind the counter looked up. He flipped up the attachment over his thick eyeglasses that allowed him to inspect coins more closely. Inside the counter were displays of many coins, mostly foreign and some quite old. The short, heavy-set proprietor rose from his stool and greeted Adraan in English, his accent disclosing his Indian origin.

"Good afternoon, sir. You are very welcome to see my many coins. If you are looking for rare African coins, you are in the right place. I have customers from all over Europe." His smile was infectious. He moved to the back of a display counter walking with a cane. Adraan noticed that he dragged his left leg.

"Joseph Sanimbi gave me your name and suggested that you might be able to help me with a small passport problem." Adraan's request was matter-of-fact; his eyes were steady.

"Oh yes, Joseph," the Indian sighed as he moved slowly around the counter to the door, which he proceeded to lock with a bolt. "How is Joseph? A nice man, but I believe he has big problems now." He returned to his stool and pointed to the other stool. "Please sit down and tell me how I can help you."

"I want to fly out of Lusaka with no security problems. My valid Mozambique passport would be, shall we say, inconvenient at best."

"Where are you headed?" the Indian asked. He sat motionless on his stool with his hands folded on the desk in front of him.

"North Africa."

"You are not European, I gather. What languages do you speak?"

Adraan replied quickly. "English, as you know, French, Arabic and some Spanish."

"And what is your mother tongue?"

"Berber, actually." Just admitting to his origin gave Adraan a tingling sensation in the back of his neck. He was going home, finally: home to find his beloved mother, home where he could sit by the shore and smell the ocean, where he would eat figs and dates and feel the warmth of the Mediterranean sun. "Yes, I'm a Berber and I'm headed for Algeria. What nationality would be most acceptable to the authorities here and in Algeria?"

The Indian dwelled on this question for some time, all the while letting his liquid gaze rest on Adraan. "You should leave here as a European," he said without hesitation. "A Spaniard would be preferable to a Frenchman. Since you are going to Algeria, which has its own troubles right now, you would be better off with a second passport from a neighboring country. Why don't you become a Moroccan? You're a Berber; you can use your real name."

Adraan nodded, thoughtfully. "Yes, that makes sense. Can you do it?"

"Of course I can do it," he scoffed, "but can you afford it?" The Indian flashed a big smile. "Half up front; it will then take me three days after you return with photographs."

Adraan paid the requested amount gladly and left the office light-hearted. Once he had his new Spanish name he would book a ticket to Casablanca.

The Rhodesian passport-control officer inspected Adraan's Spanish documents perfunctorily. To Adraan's surprise, the officer spoke to him in Spanish without looking up from his papers. "I see from your stamps that you've been all over this part of the world. What is your interest in Rhodesia?"

"I am a student of archaeology and hope to write a paper proposing an excavation around the headwaters of the Zambezi."

The passport officer slapped the exit stamp on Adraan's passport, looked at Adraan and said, "Have a good trip."

Adraan's flight to freedom took him to Morocco via Ghana. He arrived in Casablanca in the early morning hours, which gave him the rest of the day to reach Tangier by land. His Spanish identity had served him well, but was of no further use. He would take his time, stopping in Tangier before catching a coastal ship to Oran. Everything was coming together as planned, he thought. I have more money than I ever dreamed of, stashed in a Swiss bank. I am finished with the gun business. He thought briefly of van Riebeek and the past business, but decided he was done with that as he looked out over the rooftops toward his bright future.

There were few passengers on the old coastal steamer. It called at several ports before reaching Oran, the first Algerian port-of-call on its schedule. Adraan waited in line for the light to turn green over the passport control cubicle. Finally it was his turn and he walked quickly to the window and slid his Moroccan passport through the slot. The official had taken his time with each passenger as he was now doing with Adraan. He turned to a desk behind him and appeared to be leafing through a log book. Finally he returned to the window and spoke to Adraan in a low voice. "Please step around the gate and follow me." Adraan followed him to a small gray office with two chairs and a desk. "Wait here for a moment." The officer left and closed the door.

Three men entered the little office where Adraan was standing apprehensively. Two were uniformed police officers, the third, a civilian, was first to speak. He asked Adraan a few questions about his home in Morocco and his travels in Africa. Finally he closed the file on the desk and faced Adraan with a limpid expression. "Welcome home, Mr. Battuta. We have been waiting for you for a very long time. It is my pleasure to inform you that you will now be our guest for the rest of your . . . I hope, miserable life." He turned and left. Adraan felt the cold of the metal as the handcuffs clamped over his wrists. He could feel his heart stop for a split second before starting again and racing crazily inside his chest. He suddenly felt freezing cold.

Johannesburg

Rory McCray was a familiar patron of Diggers's Pub. The end stool at the turn of the long, polished bar belonged to him—exclusively. If someone mistakenly occupied the stool when McCray arrived, he would be asked politely to vacate it. If he resisted, McCray's enormous fits would help the intruder down. Diggers attracted adventurous men: some rough in bearing, large and slight men of all ages, yet the eyes of each man standing at the bar reflected the same intensity—mischievous and sinister. They were loners and came to Diggers for a pint or two and to share stories of their exploits with other men of the same bent. They came from Africa and Europe: Rhodesians, French, Irish, Belgians, one German and even an Israeli. Frequently a familiar face would suddenly disappear. The absent man would be in the field, on assignment, and would return full of hair-raising stories and flush with money. Only the bartender and a few others in the run-down neighborhood knew that Diggers was the unofficial hang-out for mercenaries. All had been trained by another country's army. All loved their business and the rewards.

McCray's appearance distinguished him from his mates. A red walrus mustache hung from his upper lip and bright-red, lank hair protruded from under the broad-brimmed bush hat that never left his head. He was a big man, a broad shouldered Scot, who had seen action as a young man in India and later, after leaving the Highland Regiment Black Watch, had fought as a mercenary in various turbulent areas of Africa. In late September, just days after the UN plane crash, he had left the employment of Union

Minière in the Congo and returned to South Africa for some time off. Before departing, a mine officer had casually inquired if he would be willing to take on a singular task in Cape Town for a good deal of money.

"What's the job?" McCray asked, his eye's narrowing.

"I don't know. But if you are willing to listen, someone will contact you in Johannesburg."

McCray found a comfortable boarding house in a neighborhood where a new resident would not stir up curiosity. He had no more unpacked when the landlady knocked on his door. "You have a telephone call. The phone is on the wall in the reception area."

"Yes?" he muttered into the receiver.

"McCray, I have a message for you. Here is my telephone number. You many call me anytime this afternoon from a public phone." The phone went dead.

It had begun to rain and McCray borrowed an umbrella. It was a small woman's umbrella. He chuckled to himself. I look ridiculous, but the call is intriguing. He stood in the shelter of the phone booth, dialed the number and said to the voice that answered, "This is McCray."

A high pitched voice, almost feminine, began to speak. "Listen to me carefully. I will only repeat this once. I am simply a messenger. Someone important would like you to permanently eliminate an individual who lives near Cape Town. He lives alone and access to his home is easy. He is not well-known and his death would be a footnote in the papers. If you agree to do this, 3000 Rand will be deposited to your local checking account. An envelope containing all the information you will require will be left with your bank manager. If you complete your mission successfully, another

7000 Rand will be deposited to your bank account. Think about this opportunity. You have the rest of today to call back with your bank account number. Goodbye."

McCray was a careful man who confronted danger with forethought. He disguised his true nature not only with his rogue appearance but with a nonchalant, insouciant demeanor. He had accepted within an hour. 3000 Rand to take a look—why not?

Within two days, the money and the envelope had been delivered. McCray sat in a coffee shop and perused the two pages of instructions. His target was an old man living on a remote vineyard near Stellenbosch. There was a map of the grounds showing an access to the property near the rear of the home. The target would not be expecting an intruder, does not have a guard and would not be armed. The note carried a brief statement, thrown in to assuage any reluctance on McCray's part, which explained that the man he was to assassinate had caused pain and death to many innocent people and that his activities were illicit and deleterious to the stability of countries in Central and Southern Africa. McCray smiled as he read the last line—you have only one week to accomplish this assignment. He cradled his coffee cup while watching the passing parade of people. McCray began to formulate a strategy. He would do this job, collect his fee, then find a woman and head for the beaches in Mozambique.

Three days later, a well-dressed, rather good-looking, middle-aged man, carrying only a small traveling bag, boarded the first class section of the Blue Train, which would carry him across the center of the country and in nine hours, deposit him in Cape Town. His mustache was gone, his red hair trimmed tight to his scalp and he wore the conservative but casual dress of a tourist. A camera dangled from his shoulder to clinch the impression. The boys at Diggers would not have known him. Resting on the bottom of his traveling bag was a 9 mm Luger 438.

Singapore

On September 18, Quinn headed for his usual lunch at the Mong Hing Restaurant near the US Embassy. His group of friends always gathered on Monday around the enormous circular dining table in a private room overlooking a small garden. They were young diplomats or business men and most spoke a dialect of Chinese, and in Quinn's case, Malay as well. It was at this beginning of the week lunch that information changed hands with alacrity.

The news of the crash came through embassy channels first. Peter Wythe, the political officer at the US Embassy, spotted Quinn and moved to intercept him with the news. Peter had heard Quinn talk about his sister and her friend who covered Africa for the UN and knew that Quinn would not be arriving for lunch if he was aware of the tragedy.

"Quinn, I have shocking news. Dag Hammarskjöld's plane has crashed in Northern Rhodesia and all have perished. If you like, you're welcome to use my office at the embassy to call your sister."

Quinn stood stock still. It took him a long time to respond. "I'm stunned, Peter. My sister's friend always traveled with Hammarskjöld when he visited Africa. Can we go to your office now? I must call Samantha in London."

On Wednesday evening of the following week, Quinn packed his bag for his trip to Cape Town. Mette sat in their Ridley Park home bedroom watching her husband methodically sort through his preparation. "I talked with Samantha again this morning. She will fly to Cape Town tomorrow as well. Brian's funeral is set for Sunday, October first and I should be going with you," her voice was almost a whisper.

"Better you visit Sam later in London. She would appreciate that more. And anyway, I have several items of business requiring attention on this trip. I'll be gone less than a week."

Quinn had talked with his sister several times since the horrible plane crash that claimed Brian's young and vital life. At first, Samantha had been unnaturally quiet—withdrawn. He had called her yesterday to confirm that he would be with her for the memorial service. She had said something that disturbed him.

"I know who is responsible for Brian's death. One of them lives in Cape Town and he should be punished."

Quinn suspected this person was the wine merchant. He worried that Samantha would attempt retribution—to take the law into her own hands. All the more reason for him to be with her in Cape Town. If necessary, he could do this deed. It went against his Zen training and the teaching that all life is precious. He would think on this, but he had taken the precaution of asking Peter Wythe to advise his counterpart in South Africa, that he may need a weapon. Wythe had not questioned the request, but merely said, "I'll arrange it."

Cardiff, Wales

"Operator, I would like to place a call to Maputo." The voice was deep and mellifluous. "Yes, it's in Mozambique. Here's the number. I'll hold on while you try." Palmer sat in his apartment near the university campus and hummed a Welsh tune as he held the telephone receiver. Suddenly the voice that had been in his ears for six months answered.

"Branca, its Morgan."

"Oh my god, Morgan, is it really you? Where are you?"

"Hold on, my pet. I'm in Wales, but I'm leaving soon. I've a little business to attend to in Cape Town. Why don't you put your jewelry business on hold and join me there. Then I'll take you on the vacation we have always talked about."

"Yes, Morgan, yes. I'll start packing now. Where are we going?

"I have a small bungalow in St. Bart's. It's next to the sea and the sand is as pure and white as the flour in your kitchen. I will be registered at the Sea View Inn in Cape Town. Meet me in three days. Bye for now."

Stellenbosch, South Africa

It was now the end of September and the world was still recoiling from the horror of the plane crash and Dag Hammarskjöld's death. Van Riebeek had been thinking of nothing else—he was frightened of the implications. On this evening, he was working late, frantically cleansing his files. As he dug through the files, he dreamed of retirement, growing grapes and living a quiet life. The scratch of the door latch snapped him from his reverie. The old man stood frozen behind his desk. He glimpsed the outline of a person standing in the darkness near the door. He did not recognize the intruder but his small hooded eyes betrayed no alarm, only astonishment. He had not noticed the gun—yet. "Who are you?" he asked in a level voice.

"We have never met," said a voice in the shadow. The 9mm Luger 438 was pointed at the old man's head. The hands holding it were steady.

"What do you want?" The old man detected the gun; his eyes were now riveted on it.

"I've come to settle your account." The voice was smooth, his reply cold.

The old man peered at the intruder, shrouded in darkness and mystery. "I am an old man and have nothing to hide. Take what you want and leave. I won't chase you," he croaked as he fell back into his chair.

"I am a messenger from an anguished world. The suffering you have caused cannot be forgiven. Many hopeful human beings have perished because of your evil deeds. Soon, the police will be coming for you. Your purpose in this life is over. I will save you from anguish and pain. Instead of rotting on Robin Island, I will usher you across the great river."

The report from the Luger seemed loud in the small room, the inevitable scent of cordite especially thick. The bullet entered the old man's cranium above his left eye and removed a large section of the back of his head. He died instantly. Another bullet entered his heart, more of a celebratory act than a coup de grâce.

The assassin opened the office door and slipped quietly into the night.

OCTOBER 1961

Cape Town

On a tree fringed hillside over looking a mellow sea, Brian's family and friends gathered to remember him and to say goodbye. His brother Jason had brought Brian's ashes back from the charred forest in Northern Rhodesia. A low, rough-hewn table, holding flowers and a picture of Brian, sat between the gathering and their view of False Bay.

Samantha sat in front between Brian's father, Phillip, and Quinn. She stole a quick glance at the picture on the table and her heart bound rapidly. She closed her eyes and allowed her mind to caress the two short years she and Brian had known each other. He had brought into her life calmness, a tranquility she had never known and it balanced and broadened her being. Their life together had been large: full of music and art, travel and sports, long discussions of books and theatre and, above all, their expectations. She had loved him more than life itself. For this to be truncated so brutally was still beyond her comprehension.

She listened to his friends speak of a man that she new better than any. Her thoughts drifted to her own life and what should come next. As the ocean breeze rustled the leaves in the trees, her thoughts transfixed on the man she held responsible for the wreckage of her hopes and dreams. At that moment she watched Jillian Pienar move to the table and, with emotion, recount her school years with Brian and the great admiration she felt for a life of so many accomplishments. She spoke of how justice might somehow help cleanse the tragedy.

Quinn would return to Singapore the following morning. He and Samantha had spent the afternoon after the memorial with Brian's family and then excused themselves and returned to their hotel. Brother and sister talked about the past and the future well into the night. Finally, Quinn stretched and said, "My flight home leaves early, I think I'll head for the sack. Will you be ok? When do you return to London?"

"I'm going to visit Brian's home. I know it's silly but I want to spend some time in his garden, cultivating the flower beds. Then I will call Jillian Pienar, Brian's friend who is heading up the investigation of van Riebeek. I won't rest until he's brought to justice."

"Will you visit Elmwood soon? Mom and Dad are concerned about you."

"No, not for a while. I have several assignments waiting for me. One is in South America. I'd like to visit Southeast Asia too and spend some time with Mette again. I love her as I love you, Quinn. Thank you for coming all this way to be with me." She hugged him long and hard.

The following morning, Samantha drove south from Cape Town toward the peninsula. The West Hook was sparsely populated with few arterial roads and traffic was light. She used the coastal road along False Bay and drove slowly until she reached Brian's house nestled so beautifully among the rolling hills. The acreage spread over the top of a wooded hill affording a filtered view of the Bay and the ever present scent of the ocean. Sam remembered the entrance and turned onto the gravel drive leading to the house. When she emerged from her car, she stood transfixed, finally letting the flood-gate of emotions open. Now, for the first time since losing Brian, she could see him in her mind's eye: his tall, sinewy body, his unruly hair and his soft smile when he looked at her. She could feel his presence, and her longing to feel his arms around her threatened to consume her. Her tears, so long held in check, finally flowed freely. Had she been there a minute or an hour? Sam didn't know, but she slowly managed to collect herself. She was with him at his home, alone, and it was acceptable to cry.

She found a small spade and a trowel in the tool shed near the house and began to cultivate the dirt at one end of the garden. The tips of Brian's vegetables were protruding from the earth and some of the flowers had bloomed—for it was early spring. She could smell the earth and the sea as she began to dig along the rows of plants. The touch of the earth on her fingers and the knowledge that she was tilling where Brian had devotedly gardened caused the ineluctable catharsis she had been seeking. She wept uncontrollably, allowing her anguish to well up and dissipate. What started as a moan became the roar of her grief as she screamed her sorrow to the wind. She slumped down on her knees and buried her wet face in her hands and wept in loud gulps.

It took less than an hour to tend the garden. She uncoiled a hose in order to water. The irrigation system would do its job, she noticed, but it gave her pleasure to water Brian's plants by hand. Who would care for his garden, she wondered sadly as she looked around? Finally, at the far end of the garden, where it ended near the trees, she began to dig. The ground was soft from the spring rains and gave way easily to Sam's spade. When the hole reached about 50 centimeters in depth, Samantha tugged her ponytail around to her shoulder and cut off a large lock of hair. She placed in carefully at the bottom of the hole, filled it half way up and then collected a Peony she had dug up earlier and planted it on top. "Something lovely will grow out of this place, Brian," she said softly. "And remember that peonies are called an old woman's plant because they often take a long time to become established. But once they are growing, well, they last a lifetime."

She resisted the wish to linger on Brian's land. To simply stay there, to lie down on the ground and just disappear with him forever. But the house stood in composed silence watching tolerantly the ceremony transpiring in the garden and she knew it was not her time or her place. She washed the garden tools, brushed off her muddy clothes, gathered her things and drove away without looking back.

Jillian hesitated before answering the phone. Her mind lingered on yesterday's memorial service and the passing of Brian Wellesley. "Jillian speaking."

Ian McQueen's gravel voice cut through the receiver. "He's dead, Jillian. Someone shot him in the temple, execution style."

"What! How could this happen? You have a team of watchers at the vineyard."

"Yes, true. Three men. But when the lights go out in the vineyard, they too retire. Someone got in there last night and shot van Riebeek. His cook found him this morning. I'll have more for you later in the day."

"Ian, van Riebeek was on the middle rung of this gun smuggling ring. Let's search his files thoroughly. I wanted the person at the top of the ladder. We should move swiftly or we may never know."

Time moved quickly now. Samantha had slept until late morning and awoke still tired. After calling Phillip to say goodbye and to promise she would return soon, Sam packed her bag, checked out from her hotel and headed to the airport. Her late afternoon flight would take her to Nairobi, where she would connect with a BOAC flight to London. By late afternoon, the weather had cleared and the plane's lift-off was smooth as it headed north-east toward Rhodesia and Katanga, two names etched in her mind. Her port-side window seat provided a view of the sun heading to the rim of Africa. Below her lay a continent already shrouded in darkness.

The feeling of complete emptiness followed her. She rested her head on the seatback and wallowed in the sensation of this utter aloneness. She would have to pick up the tools of living and begin again, she supposed, but she didn't know how or where. She was not even sure where she wanted to settle; South America perhaps—she used to have a yen for Argentina and Chile. Her thoughts drifted back to her childhood in Elmwood, to her father's dominant influence, but in this moment, something her mother had told her came into focus. Elisabeth often talked about her love of the liturgical music of her church—she laughingly called it plainsong—and how it applied to life itself. She and Samantha had been sitting in front of the fire in the family room at their lake house. Her mother's eyes had drifted out the window to the falling snow over Emerald Lake.

"I feel that the plainsong represents our lives. It is an unadorned chant—simple, humble and methodical. It seems to say that ultimately, at the end of our time, we are left with only ourselves. When the cymbals and drumbeat of the counterpoints in our life diminish, there is only our plainsong. It is loud at times, then a whisper, but always in our voice—the music of our soul. It's too bad we don't hear our plainsong until we reach the end of our time. Her mother had turned back to her and in her eyes Samantha had seen the sadness and longing that had also been part of her mother's life.

Samantha peered through the plane window and watched a blood-red, malevolent, half sun descend on the horizon. It had sunk rapidly, its warmth and light for this day—finished.

AUTHOR'S NOTE

*F*ocus is a work of fiction. Most of the names, characters and incidents in this novel are the product of the author's imagination. Dialogue between portrayed authentic historical people and fictitious characters never occurred. Their conversations were created to accommodate the unfolding story.

My historical references came from books, library research and the web, and the latter's accuracy is, at times, suspicious. Given that this book's story is pure fiction, even though it occasionally incorporates actual historical incidents, it should not be considered, even in part, a work of history.

Both Moise Tshombe and Mobutu Sese Seko played significant roles in the early years of the DRC history. Both ruthlessly ruled the country, bilked its assets for personal gain, provided little improvement to the social and economic structure and certainly abbetted murderous struggles, both between tribes and with neighbors.

Tshombe can be implicated with the imprisonment and execution of Lumumba in January 1961. Villagers certainly did not kill Lumumba, as Tshombe would have liked the world to believe. Most likely, military personnel, both Katangese and Belgian, executed him.

In 1963, UN forces finally succeeded in capturing Katanga, driving Tshombe into exile, first to Northern Rhodesia and then to Spain. In a twist of history, he was recalled to Leopoldville in 1964 to become prime minister in a coalition government. This government lasted less than a year and resulted in Tshombe fleeing again to Spain. His story does not end there. In 1967, the jet aircraft on which he was traveling was hijacked to Algeria where he was imprisoned. Tshombe died in prison in 1969, allegedly of a heart attack.

I dwelled on the activities of Colonel Mobutu, rather than on any of the other host of political players in the early years of the DRC because he was the main power broker and historically the most durable. As a young man, he soldiered for the Belgians in the Force Publique. After leaving the military, Mobutu spent several years as a journalist, and it was because of his writing skills that Patrice Lumumba employed him as his secretary. In June 1960 Lumumba became the DRC's first prime minister. He immediately elevated Mobutu to the rank a colonel and appointed him Chief of Staff of the Congolese Army. Mobuto soon became disenchanted with the Prime Minister and orchestrated his imprisonment and ultimate exile to Katanga. In the autumn of 1960, Mobutu led a putsch and placed the "College of Commissioners" in charge of the country. He then focused on his real enemy—Tshombe.

My story leaves Mobutu in this position. For the next twenty-five years this corrupt figure would lead, loot and dismantle the Congo to a point equal to how it was when the Belgians left. He changed the country's name to Zaire, expelled foreigners and nationalized major mining interests, while failing to prevent the genocide in Rwanda from spilling across the border. The world remembers him in his signature leopard skin toque and large round glasses. He too fled for his life, first to Togo and finally to Morocco where he died in 1994.

From the Congo's independence in 1960 to the present day, who knows how many humans have died from tribal warfare, village feuds, disease, government persecution, malnutrition and starvation or outright murder? The data is not clear on this gruesome subject, but surely four or five million Congolese have been lost—more than the population of Norway. The sad truth is that the world isn't counting, nor does it seem to care.

Dag Hammarskjöld died in a mysterious plane crash near the Northern Rhodesian town of Ndola in the early hours of September 18, 1961. Witnesses reported a bright flash in the sky. Search and rescue teams were unnecessarily delayed before reaching the crash site five kilometers from the Ndola airport. Of the sixteen passengers, two had been thrown from the burning fuselage; one was found alive and the other, Secretary-General Hammarskjöld, was dead.

Theories of the cause of the crash and persistent speculation of an assassination abound and even today new studies are emerging. Some are curious, such as the one reported by the first official UN officer to see Dag's body, a Norwegian Major General. He observed that Hammarskjöld had a hole in his forehead which was subsequently airbrushed from photos taken of the body. Hammarskjöld's bodyguards carried handguns and ammunition pouches and it was suggested that some of the bullets had exploded due to the heat. Later British tests proved that the bullets could not have penetrated a human body.

Archbishop Desmond Tutu claimed to have written evidence found in South Africa implicating British M15 and the American CIA, which involved a bomb placed in the wheel bay of the plane set to detonate when the wheels were lowered.

Recently, new compelling evidence has been discovered purporting that the DC-6 was shot down by another plane. The best book I have read on the events leading up to and following the crash is *Who Killed Hammarskjold?*, by Susan Williams. Her exhaustive research and conclusions are astonishing.

Any of these plots could have received support from either Great Britain or Belgium for they both coveted the copper mining operation in Katanga.

The most logical explanation involves the two pilots who gave up sleep to help in the repair of the faulty engine, and became exhausted. This is factual information. Additional convincing evidence leading to human error was the discovery of the wrong airport landing charts, charred but readable, on the deck of what remained of the cockpit. They were for another Ndola airport located in the Republic of Congo. The difference in altitude of the two airports is considerable.

The only cause of the crash that can be conclusively eliminated is ground based machine gun fire.

Numerous in-depth studies of the crash as well as biographies of Hammarskjöld, Mobutu and Tshombe are available. The books on Dag's life reflect on a quiet, humble, thoughtful man who was impassioned with the desire to improve the condition of mankind.

> *"We are not permitted to choose the frame of our destiny. But what we put into it is ours. He who wills adventure will experience it—according to the measure of his courage. He who wills sacrifice will be sacrificed— according to the measure of his purity of heart."*

> *"Then a tree becomes a mystery,*
> *A cloud a revelation,*
> *Each man a cosmos of whose riches*
> *We can only catch glimpses."*

> *"Slutet,*
> *Du skall bära det –"*
> The end,
> You shall endure it

Dag Hammarskjöld
From his book, *Markings* (*Vägmärken*),
more accurately translated from the Swedish
as *road signs*.

ACKNOWLEDGMENTS

I am indebted to several people for their support during the writing of *Focus*. My brother, Henry, provided both encouragement and wise counsel throughout the writing of this story and I am most appreciative of his dedication. Three resolute friends, Robert Leland, Penney Thomas and Marty Noll read the original manuscript and offered both valuable critiques and grammar improvements. Each provided a unique talent or insight to improve and clarify the text. The graphic arts for the cover and maps were provided by Loc Tran. My editor, Katie Morris, (Noise Reduction), provided the most penetrating influence, which resulted in a rewritten manuscript. Throughout the writing of this novel, my wife, Marianne, patiently polished the manuscript and shored my confidence, for which I am deeply grateful.

—

Focus encompasses, in Book Three, Samantha's story. Books One and Two can be found in an earlier novel, *Counterpoint,* and describe segments of the lives of Samantha's father,

Lars, and her brother, Quinn. The term "trilogy" will be considered only when a third volume has been completed with the stories of Samantha's other two brothers, Erik and Kyle.

—

The author, Steve Pearsall, and his wife Marianne live in Crystal Bay, NV, on the north shore of Lake Tahoe where they rejoice in nature's beauty and their growing brood of grandchildren.